THE
STAFF
OF
IRA

CARL SHEFFIELD

Brilliant Books Literary
137 Forest Park Lane Thomasville
North Carolina 27360 USA

PROLOGUE

My existence came to be, growing up on a planet called Boldlygo. I am called Ira. I was born on the planet of Boldlygo, a Galaxy unknown to the outside world. Through the years to come it would be proven that we were the most intelligent beings in all the universes. We had uncanny abilities. Had powers beyond our own minds, that made us superior in every way.

I never knew my mother, for reasons unknown I was told I was created in a lab. Well, I'm getting ahead of myself. In the beginning the Busies and the Unicorns ruled all Boldygo. The Busies were super intelligent, the Unicorns are magical. In pure harmony, they lived in a beautiful world for thousands of years.

The Pegasus flew with great pride, the Unicorns walked freely on the planet. The suns of our planet, one was of yellow, the other with a purple haze. This gave our world a perfect climate. All living things were as one. The Busies were a species that shared the planet with the Pegasus, and Unicorns. They've built the city of Domain. In years to come it would be talked about through many generations.

The Busies brought the stone from the planet's core. Under no condition did they ever tire. My father would tell us of the Busies doing this. However, I have no way of knowing. The writing was placed in the archives. That's all we had, plus our learnings.

My father was Tudo. A very understanding being. He lived in the palace that was provided for the Royal Blood, the leaders of council, for the planet. The palace was so divine built by the Busies and the Unicorns. My grandfather would tell his tales also of the Pegasus. Stories of all in the past.

My father would tell his stories how the Pegasus with the wisp of the wind would fly through the air. How marvelous they must have looked in the glow of our moons. Ject, as we called him, was my grandfather. He would walk the streets of Ratio with my brother Ren and myself by his side. My father Tudo was a wandering man. Tudo would fly through the galaxies of Space. When he was home, he told the stories of the Busies and the Unicorns as if they were still here.

"Father" I would ask. "Where are they now?" My son, he would say, "They live beyond the Marder-To-go's, beyond the Falls. They live in the ancient city that no one can see. The city is where we go when we ascend."

I would ask, "What is ascend?"

He would always tell me, "When it is time to go my son, you will know."

As I have said, "The stones the city was built from, were carved with great precision and placed by the Unicorn and the Pegasus." Grandfather said.

These words rang in my ears for many years. Much would happen before I could fulfill my destiny.

CHAPTER 1

THE STAFF OF IRA

In the beginning a species called Busies, from a planet so far in space were on the verge of extinction. The great Busie Maoke called a grand council. I am Maoke he said, "Only the Unicorn is greater than I. The Unicorn has given to me the power to write the legend of the great city to come." I have called this meeting, for I have looked into the portal. I have seen our future, thousands of years from now. Please come forth we must make a great discussion of this. Several days we spent in council at the Great Wall, with the ancient city behind us.

Standing by the portal I waved my hand in a great circle, a mirror image appeared. Only vast lands did everyone see, with the mountains to the east. The rivers and falls were the colors of greatness did everyone see. In this greatness was a large city with people. (HUMANS)

"We must devise a way to populate the city" I said to everyone.

Looking around the great portal only Busies and furry animals did everyone see. The Unicorn and the Pegasus of the air, stood with silence.

I was questioned about this, "The city, where is it?" The people, where are they?"

"Did you not hear a word," I said. I answered with a voice of thunder.

Therefore, I am here listen to me. "We the Busies and Unicorns will never be able to live with the creation that we are going to create."

In a thousand years, the Busies will be extinct, unless we act now. Our planet is hidden from the outside world. Many travelers have passed us by. "It will happen, we will make a loving peaceful race of beings. This alone will be our scientist's whole creation. Taking the DNA from us, the Unicorn and the Pegasus to make an entire race of beings."

I said to everyone, "While this is being done, we will go forth to the place I have selected." We will build a great city. The only city on the planet besides here."

"Why can't we all live here?" one questioned.

Sadly, as I lowered my head to say, "I also must make other things happen to balance the good." When the city is built, I will write in the history for all. Someday one will come and change it. Then and only then can we live in harmony with man.

"The crowd of Unicorns and Busies whispered amongst themselves." Who is man? Where is man? What is man?

"All your questions will be answered" I said. "In time, you will see that I am right. I will close the city with a shield. A gate here so no one can find it from the air or by land."

This discussion made all the Busies wonder. "We have always been free to go wherever we like"…Why change?

"I am truly sorry for our species to live on the planet, it must be done this way." I said

There weren't a lot of Busies now in our world. So, create this race we will. I looked through the portal every day with great sadness.

"Come walk with me," I said to the Unicorn.

The Unicorn and I walked for days looking for the place I saw in the portal.

"It's here I tell you." I said to the Unicorn.

In my thoughts, I went into great meditation.

Opening my eyes, I said to the Unicorn, "Beyond the mountains, I knew it was here."

The rivers and Falls of colors. In our words that means, beauty that falls from the mountains. "From this day forward, the Marder-To-go's, will be written in our words and the word of man." I said.

The Unicorn looked at Maoke, "What is man?"

"I am not sure," I said, "I know only we will be the reason for bringing him to our paradise. He will be strong with power. You will see my friend. Man, will save us. We must go, I shall reach the place before the moons come."

I led the Unicorn deeper into the forest. The Pegasus had never been here. Little furry animals were everywhere.

Along the river of the path the Unicorn asked, "If no one has ever been here why is there a path?"

"May be from the animals," I replied.

"Look at the Sweet Grass," The Unicorn said. He marveled at the size, dropping his head to feast.

"Maoke, look how big it grows!"

"Wait! My friend" I said, "It will be prohibited to eat here. The Sweet Grass is old. This will also be written. Dont let your eyes or stomach control what is ahead."

Along the path the Unicorn said to Maoke, "I understand what you mean." Great one.

"Always remember, something must always stay the same, while others change. It is very close Uny." "There on the hillside." I said. Overlooking the valley, we walk to the top of the hill.

The Unicorn said to Maoke, "Never in my mind have I seen such beauty."

The valleys to the far west. The mountains formed high, and to the sky.

Beyond the mountains is the city. This is where we will build the Great Wall. We will surround it with a marsh so no one can walk. The sides of the mountain so steep no one can climb. To each being we create, we will place in their minds a small dot in their DNA, this to be passed along to their children so they won't look for the ancient city."

A great shield will be placed from the mountain top. If someone looks, it will appear that a great mist lies on the ground. Here where we stand now, the palace will be built for the council and the Royal Blood.

"You will see the City of Ratio will be built, It will be a vast city. This will let our descendants see the valley known as the Valley of the Unicorn. For that's what we saw, a great Valley of Unicorns. Fruit trees grew everywhere. Sweet Grass, the wild root that will come to be called bread, this will be in the minds of all our creation."

"I think it's nice. It will take forever to build" The Unicorn said.

"It will take as long as it takes" I said.

The Unicorn and I walked for hours then settled for Sweet Grass and wild Simons. They were not quite ripe, yet were still tasty.

The small fruit we call Bibs, Gotches, we at the time didn't know they would be destroyed in the building of the city. It was the only place on the planet they grew. Sadly, to say it is now too late to change the history.

I will write in the words about them, how the fruit made the sacrifice for the way of life for our people. My mind raced fast to see the things I could do for his race. Sadly, I could not be a part of their lives to come, for their time I see is forever.

"We will build this city," The Unicorn said to Maoke.

Then Maoke, "The Pegasus and Unicorn will go to the back of the valley of the ancient city." To live until.

The Unicorn reared on his hind legs. The Unicorns in the valley gathered around as Maoke told his tale. Single file they walked to the river, then to the city of the ancients, never to roam the valley, until....... With the wisp of the wind we were gone.

CHAPTER 2

The building of the Great Wall began. The Busies, and the Unicorn, and the Pegasus pulled the stones from the core. They knew my plan. They had the Busies, and the great scientists directing them. Week after week.... Month after month.... The Great Wall was going up.

Several months had passed. One day a small animal stood on its hind legs

The head scientist Bota asked me, "What is it he thinks?" Great one

"Why are we building a Great Wall? There is nothing out there" Maoke replied. I watched the animal, as it went on its way.

Time comes and goes. Several years had passed. I called everyone together. "We have done good," I said. "Today we rest." I went to the portal. I Made a motion with my hands, the portal opened.

A mighty ship passed by, I could read their thought, they wondered of our planet. The big ship scanned the planet, to find no lifeform except animals. They have no use for that. They're vegetarians like us. I thought of the big ship. Where were they from, who are they. The big ship roared as it went to the darkness of space. I thought of it again. This I will write of, when I return to the city.

I told everyone. We will continue our work tomorrow, rest today. I will leave the portal open if you wish to view the future of our race. You will see why we must do as we are doing.

Evening was coming as the suns set behind the Marders. Leaving everyone I returned to the ancient city to my archives. Night had come to our world once again.

The morning brought another beautiful day on Boldlygo. Everyone stood and chatted with each other.

I said to all." I will return to the city, much writing must be done, as well as drawing of the city of Ratio." Maoke said.

The plan for the palace must be made, as I've seen it through the portal. We will have a king and queen to rule all Boldlygo. They too will be powerful. The minds of the Busie and the blood of the Unicorn, if they stay on the planet, they can never die.

Our race, and their descendants will venture into strange worlds, it is already written, in the archives in the ancient city where only I'm allowed to go. I am not deceitful, but cautious. That's the way it should be. There's always the need for someone to be in power, a leader, a King, a Queen. I will carry this into history for our descendants to carry on.

I worked hard writing and considering the future of our people. The Great Wall was progressing as planned. Nothing could stop the Busies, they were all powerful. Looking across the mountains darkness would come again to the planet.

The morning came early, I came from the city to close the portal. No one found the future as interesting as me. Looking one last time with all my power, I saw exactly what I wanted. The place where I was to build the city of Ratio, and the palace. The plan, the placement of each stone, every walk way. Unto, the future of our people, our creation, the natives of the planet of Boldlygo. Men, woman and children, not like us, but of man.

Suddenly it came to me, "Who is man?" "How do they come?" I must look harder. The city of Ratio, it will be written, the natives will take the city of Ratio. Living in harmony with man.

It took many years to build the Great Wall, one hundred miles long, forty miles wide. In the middle of the valley, too steep for anyone to penetrate, I will create the dome. Then the ancient city will be hidden. It will be finished.

The Unicorn and the Pegasus carried the stones to the Busies. placing each stone with great care, with writing on each stone. After the six hundredth year, it was done.

Everyone gathered around, as I spoke. "It will never be cold or hot, this will be a paradise for everyone."

There were strange plants began to grow on the north slope of the range. Sweet Grass grew in abundance so did the Simons and the bread root. A wild fruit, this we never named. The fruit was sweet with a fragrance from the bloom that could be smelled forever.

I went back to the portal opened it again. A ship went by, I thought someday someone will discover this planet. Especially when the city of Ratio appears. There must be a way to hide us, together with the other Busies, we could control our minds, create a shield so that we cannot be detected from a ship. If the planet was scanned, it would show inhabitable. I thought this may be passed on through DNA from our descendants. I thought it would be helpful.

In the seven hundredth year of building we rested. The Unicorn and the Pegasus, along with the Busies never tired. Yet no one objected to rest. Everyone knew me, I was the oldest, I was their leader. Everyone looked to me for guidance.

It was time for me to build the gates of the city. I built one to the South, One to the North. For a reason, I will keep this for myself. The Unicorn and Pegasus had water and grass to last for eternity. No one would thirst or go hungry.

Stones were brought from the core. Each cut to fit with precision in each joint. With years and years of cutting and fitting, we took another break.

I called everyone together, "You may leave the city, go as you please." I will ask you to appear here in four moons rising. For that day is the day we shall start building the city of Ratio. The only city to be seen by the native people of our world until man comes."

"The only thing I'm still afraid of, are passer byes." "

"One Busie," said to me.

"Maoke, move the planets"

I said to him. "I was not sure this could be done."

Send the Pegasus one said. "look for a place where travel is not."

I wonder, "Yes maybe this could be, calling them to our aid."

The Pegasus came to me two days later. The big black stallion asks? Yes Maoke, "What may I do for you?"

Kneeling before me. I said to him," Leave the city I said, fly to the highest point. Watch for travel, watch for whom may pass in the day and in the night. Leave no direction unturned. Return to me in four cycles of the moons, with your report."

"It will be done, as you wish Great one" The mighty Pegasus left the herd with the power of a sky vessel.

I wondered about that also. Why we, the greatest minds, the most powerful Busie, Unicorn and the Pegasus, why we did not have a flying ship? Of course, we never needed one. Where would we go if we had one? To another planet maybe. This I must meditate on.

Everyone left the ancient city, I was left alone. It was time for me to leave the wall and go to my archive. I must see and study them. They were left for a reason, yet by who. I went into my chambers to study. I took out the plans for the city of Ratio, and the palace. As I made a sketch on the parchment that occupied me.

In my chair, I touched my face with my hand. I feel that this will not be large enough. I must write with the chambers here looking to the Valley of the Unicorns. This will be next to the living quarters. The Great hall with a room there. A room to the west and a council room with twelve chairs. The table should be in the shape of a half moon. There should be ten chair, and a stand here. Let it be written when you need to be heard you must stand.

I continued to write most of the day. In the late afternoon, I made fresh tea. I cut a Simon and reached for a piece of fresh bread. I was looking at something I've never seen before. How did I over see this? It was written in our words. Only the Keeper of the staff has the power to move it. With a wisp of the wind it can be moved. I saw on the parchment new stars and new moon and new sun.

Am I really reading this? We already have moons and suns. This was in another galaxy, yes! Who is the Keeper of the staff? What is the staff? Better yet, where is the staff?

I begin to look through the old relics of time. I'm not sure how old it is, here my first time today to see any of this. Maybe it was not meant to be seen until now.

I sat back, had my tea and breadroot. There was so much I still did not know of my people, my world or my race. Did we just come into existence? Years has taken its toll on all of us. We are here to make a better world for our children. Our chief scientists came to me:

"Maoke, you must come," the scientist said.

I left the archives to join him. He explained to me what has happened.

We did as you instructed great one. "With the DNA from the Unicorn, the Pegasus and the Busie. We have created a small life form. I'm not sure if it is what you want." Bota showed the way to his lab.

I was excited looking down into a small bay tray. There was a small being.

"What would this being look like," I asked Bota? "What image will it possess?"

"We're not sure how it will change. Maybe your portal can show us the way." Bota replied.

"Non-since!" "You are too intelligent for that...You created it, you should know." Maoke remarked.

Bota said, "Maoke, no one has been born here for over a thousand years. Were, not sure how we got here. Your word has been the only thing that has guided us."

"Bota you alone have served well. Tell me in your own words" I said.

"We need a female subject to seed a life," Bota said. "Conceive in her wound. With her DNA and ours we can do this."

I wondered with my hand on my face, rubbing my jaw," Yes, a female."

Maoke asked, "Where can we find this female?"

"We will need to go to another world for this," Bota said.

"How do we do that?" I asked?

"In a flying ship," Bota replied, I propose to build one, I can you know. The liquid metal that runs through the core. Come to my building Maoke, I will show you something you won't believe."

I followed Bota to his lab, in the back of Botas building, was a small ship.

"Very nice Bota I said, If you build it, who will fly it?"

"Learn as we go Maoke, learn as we go" I said

"Then build your ship," I said. "Let your apprentice work on the creations of our race."

"As you wish Maoke" Bota said

I walked to the portal. With the wave of my hand a mirror appeared. I saw my world as it was. I thought to myself, what is in the future for us? Will we finish what we start? Will someone come and destroy it? Will we be as we are forever? I think not, I won't let it be. Our race needs to live; the months went by. I stayed away from the lab, and the Great Wall. In my reading and writing of the laws of the archives when the city is built, I will place these in the halls so all people can read. The words must remain the same or taught by someone in all the years to come. Deep inside my thoughts of meditation, I flew through the sky. I looked down on a wonderful creation. Made not only by me. Made also by the Unicorn, The Pegasus and the Busie as they were.

Bota, as intelligent as he is, has yet to finish his flying machine. His apprentice has also failed to create a species. I returned to the archives. Looked through the many things that are here. The long ago relics I never knew existed. Yet were there, the entire time. I would look for hours through things then return to my parchment. I sipped my tea and thought that someone had placed these things here long before me. I saw again only the Keeper of the staff has the power to move it. "Move what" I said "What was this staff? I saw again, the stars, the sun, and the moon. I must find this staff. I went to Bota. Inside his lab, he had constructed a pattern of a flying machine. In the short three months, I had been away. I marveled, it was magnificent.

Maoke, "In one year it will fly," Bota said, looking at me without expression.

"Fly where?" I ask. "Which way do you go? What do you do when you are there?"

"I only told you I could build it I did not say anything different."

"Why are you here Maoke?"

"In our life, have you ever heard of a staff?" I asked?

"A staff no Maoke, never" Bota answered.

"Hearing a voice behind me I turned," It was the Pegasus.

"I have heard of a staff," Replied the Pegasus. "It's called the staff of Ira."

I looked at the Pegasus, "How is it you have heard of this and I have not?"

"I cannot answer your question" replied the Pegasus "Ive only heard of it many years past. I cannot say how long it has been. Long ago is all I can say."

Bota the Pegasus ask, "Why are you constructing a flying machine.

Bota said, "To go to other worlds?"

The Pegasus said, "I dont know why you are doing it. This could prove to be dangerous to all of us."

I waved my hand "I will never let that happen, I promise."

The Pegasus said to Maoke, "I have done as you have asked Maoke? I've found a place where there is no travel from the sky machine. All we need is to move there."

Replying, "When everyone returns at the end of the month, our minds together we will move us." I was scared for our race; I was always trying new things. After all, I was the most powerful Busie here.

I said goodbye, went back to my archives. I look through the boxes and papers. Day after day, on the morning of the fourth moon, when everyone was to return, I found it. In a box in the back of the archives. Months of looking, reading and writing, there it lay. A long box seven foot long, I opened it. It was all dusty, I took it from its resting place.

Through the relics of time it was there. Who put it there? Was it powerful? If so why did it not have a guardian? I took the staff and wiped it off with my robe. Seven feet of wood I have never seen. I rolled it in a cloth and took it to my chambers, waiting for the day to test the staff. I would let everyone take their turn with it to see if they had the power to rule the staff of Ira. I'm not sure why it is called this. It doesn't matter I have found it. I thought it would only be right to let everyone have their turn with the staff. I walked from the city to the edge of the shield. I noticed the Unicorn was walking with me.

"Maoke, "Where is your journey?" The Unicorn ask.

"I will go to where the new city is to be built" my friend.

"Care for some company?" The Unicorn, ask.

"Please come walk with me," I said.

The Unicorn asked, as we walked "Do you think it is wise to build the city?"

"It is the only way to save our race," I said. "Even your race and the race of the Pegasus. We need each other to survive." I said "Dont ever forget that. We will build this city for the ones to come. That is all I will say about it."

The Unicorn asked, about Bota "What does he plan to do with the flying machine he builds?"

"I did not reply at the time." I kept walking.

Walking on we stopped by the falls at the Madre-To-go's. We stood in the water in silence. Watched the color of the water then on to the site of the city. I told the Unicorn about the staff of Ira.

"The Unicorn replied "There is a staff Maoke, but I never believed it. The Pegasus told me many years ago, one would come, take the staff of Ira and do great things for the race of the Busies."

"Do you know or have you heard his name?" I asked.

"No Maoke, I haven't." The Unicorn replied.

I visit here often, I told the Unicorn.

He looked at me with those dark eyes.

"Yes, Maoke I know, I have watched you from the shadow of the trees." The Unicorn said, "This has been a dream of yours. Do you think it will come to pass?"

I told him, I believe it will as sure as Bota, and his flying machine will fly. Even if I must, build it myself!

The Unicorn said, "Maoke, I'll help you build this city, I cannot speak for the others.

I'll take the stones from the core where, Bota gets his metal. Piece by piece, stone by stone, it will be built. "We may live there for a while ourselves. Rest assure my friend this city will be built."

The Unicorn said, "I want to see what it will take to do this."

I will tell you now, "I have in the relics of time, in the ground level in the city of ancients. I have found the staff of Ira.

I have wrapped it in cloth. Everyone will have their turn with it, to see who has the power to control it. "

"Why do you think its powerful?" The Unicorn ask.

"It must be powerful," I said. "The writing of the archives says only the Keeper of the staff can move it. With wisp of the wind it can be moved. New stars, one moon, one sun. A different part of a distant galaxy."

Uny said to me, "I think you have dwelled on this matter so long you are possessed by the factor of the staff." As I have said Maoke, "I myself will help you build this city, I cannot say for the others. I owe you this much. After, I will find solitude in the corner of your valley to live whatever days I have left. Is that understood?"

"You cannot die my friend, not on this planet" I said.

"When Bota builds his machine, I will go to another planet." The Unicorn said, as he walked away.

Thoughts ran through my mind, We must start construction soon. We must. I thought hard of what the young Unicorn had said. Would he go to another world? If so would he die? It was hard for me to think of this. For thousands of years we have walked side by side, we were as one. There were times we could read each other's thoughts. I won't let that enter my mind again. Still the thoughts are there.

I must go to the portal, I must find a way to go further. If only there was someone to speak to about this.

Returning to the city, I told the Unicorn of the gates, I told no other. Once we come here to live, then and only then will the gates close. The valley will give us all we need.

The Busie, the Pegasus, and the Unicorn came back from there rest, I was greeted by all. The rest did us good, they all agreed.

I told them we would start construction on the city of Ratio soon.

CHAPTER 3

The great door to the lab was open. Everyone marveled at the machine Bota had constructed.

"What is it?" One said. "Why is it that you would build such a thing?"

Bota stood from his work. "My friend, it is called a flying machine. It will carry us forever through the space of time to another world. Maoke, needs a female, we have tried to create and failed. The power of the Unicorn, and the Pegasus is not enough. This ship will be ready soon, then I will leave for another world." The Unicorn came forth.

Bota, "I will travel with you. I must complete the city of Ratio. I have given my word. Us alone with the Pegasus have carried the stones we have carved to place at Maokes request. I must finish this task. He can build the palace for himself."

"Days went by, the Unicorns and the Pegasus carried stones to the city. Finally, a foundation formed. The city was being built. Stone after stone, building after building, room after room, shop after shop. Several years had passed since the last rest break.

I asked everyone, "Do we need a rest, all agreed?" Walking to the top of the hill where the palace is to be built, I looked over the grandest city on the planet. The city to be seen by the eyes of our descendants."

Bota had his flying machine completed. He had gotten good at flying. Sometimes he would lift off and stay gone for hours. Then land, adjust and off again. I sent all away one more time.

Bota called to me, "I have supplies for months aboard. When the sun rises across the Madre-To-go's I will leave. The Unicorn will come with me. You have given them four moons again. We will be back before then."

"Maoke, Sweet Grass, and hay was loaded aboard with breadroot and tea." Bota said. The shields were lifted so they could leave.

The Unicorn asked Bota, "Where do we go?"

"I'm not sure my friend Bota said, maybe we will spot a ship and follow them." Moving into the atmosphere I said, "My friend hold on here we go."

"Were moving real fast" Uny.

"Yes, Bota I see"

Bota said "Faster than the Pegasus can fly. We can go faster"

The Unicorn looked at me "Just how fast?"

"We are flying at the pace of a meteor flying through an open sky" Bota said.

For one week, the Unicorn and I flew through space, we saw know ships. I tried to keep track of where we were, how far we had gone. Then I realized we were lost. Lost with no idea of how to go home. One and a half cycles of the moon. From a far I saw a light in the distance.

"Uny I said, "a light"

"Yes Bota, I see it. It is a ship." Uny said.

I followed the ship for several hours it seemed. Then it started a decent to a planet. A beautiful planet, it was. Just different in color from our world. Landing, I emerged from the ship to see some strange beings. He tried to speak the words. It was not the words of my world.

A being came to us. Took his hand and touched his head, I did the same. Their words were as one. "Greetings from Boldlygo." I said

"Greeting from Plano" The Palatonians said to us. "We have never seen your race before." He said.

"We are called Busies" I said. "From a planet in the spores galaxy, we are lost. Although we are an intelligent being, I am ashamed of my ignorance. This is our first ship, and we know nothing of space travel."

"Are you alone?" The Palatonian asked?

"I have a companion," I said, "He also will be strange to you"

I waited, and listen as the Palatonian told Bota to have me come forth. Bota called, I came from the ship. A silence was upon the crowd.

"What is it?' One asked?

"It is called a Unicorn, he is very powerful" Bota answered. "Like me, he is new to space travel."

"I am called Kao, the captain of this ship." The Palatonian said. "If you are intelligent as you say you can learn from our map studies. We have mapped the universe, solar system and galaxies."

Walking in a building, the beings showed us on a big board with lights of many different colors. These are maps to us. All planets, there to the far side of the galaxy was a lone planet.

I knew this was our world "Here," I said. I showed him. "This is our planet. With two moons and two suns."

"No one lives there." Kao said.

"That is Boldlygo, our world." Bota said.

"Tell me" Kao asked "What is it your called".

"I am Bota, this is Uny. No other names do we have"

"We've come to your planet we have detected no signs of life." Kao told Bota.

"I cannot answer that" Bota said "We are trying to build a great city"

"Do you have weapons?" Kao asked?

"Weapons? What is weapons?" Bota ask"

"They cause war on others." Kao said.

I ask, "Why would someone do that?" It is so barbaric. No, We have no weapons. We look for means to repopulate our world. We need something we dont have. You see, nothing has been born on our planet except males in over one thousand years."

"How many of you are there?" Kao asked?

"Maybe a few hundered, sad to say. We wish no harm to anyone. We are a peaceful race". "Kao, if it pleases your council, we dearly would like to learn more about the system. Maybe we could find a planet with females on it. "

"Females" Kao said.

"Yes, someone we could transfer our DNA and alter it some so it doesn't look so much like us" Bota explained

I see Kao said, "We have females. Our travels to other planets showed very profitable. Maybe we will trade."

"Trade?" Bota asked? "I'm not familiar with the terms." Looking at the Unicorn.

Uny said to Bota, "It's like this…. I have hay…you have Sweet Grass…you want hay. We trade"

"Oh," Bota said, "What is it you would like to trade?"

"I will give you five females for the Unicorn" Kao said

"I cannot do that, he is not mine to trade." Bota replied "Besides what will you do with the Unicorn?"

"I have always heard they are powerful. Drink the blood of the Unicorn and live forever." Kao said.

"That is not true" Bota answered.

The Platonians made his move, then stopped. "I cannot do this" Kao said.

Bota told him, "If he tried he would destroy him."

"I thought you were a peaceful race" Kao said.

Yes, "Until we are threatened. Then we will not be defeated so easily" Bota said.

The Platonians all laughed. "You have nerve Bota, that I say."

"May we study your star charts?" Bota asked "I hope to go far away some day."

"Really" Kao said "How long would you like to be gone?"

"I dont know" Bota replied "I'm the only being on my world that can fly"

"Go home Busie, In two moons I will come to you" Kao said "I will take you to a planet far away. Maybe you will see the galaxy and universe that lay before you."

Bota, and the Unicorn said their goodbyes. Walked up the ramp with five females.

Kao told his first mate "This will be something to see in years to come."

After twelve hours in flight Bota landed his craft in the hangar. He had gotten so used to flying it that it came natural. Maoke greeted Bota and Unicorn. They told their stories. Everyone was in Awe.

"We must finish the landing pad at the palace" Maoke said.

After arriving, Maoke could not believe what he had heard. There was life out there. Bota showed everyone his prize. Five females, walking to them the females ran into a huddle.

"I'm truly sorry" Maoke said "I will not hurt you"

In a language of words, he had never heard, one woman came over to him. The woman took Maokes hand and touched her head so they could have the same words. Each Busie did the same. For several minutes, everyone touched each other.

"What species are you?" Maoke asked?

Bota told Maoke, The Palatonians have star charts and maps to guide them through space and time.

Bota, ask the females, "Come to his lab?" Bota ask, "Maoke to join him?"

"Why are we here?' One asked?

"We wish to give you our DNA so we can populate our world. Our race is dying" Bota said

"We are to mate with you?" The female asked? She walked to Bota and touched him. "It can't be done."

"How do you do this on Earth?" Bota asked?

"A man and a woman gets together. See this as she pulled up her clothes. Where is yours?"

Bota looked down he saw nothing. His apprentice told him "There are other ways to do this, I will show you"

Bota's apprentice took the DNA from each Busie, but not Maoke. He transferred the DNA to impregnate the females. Several hours later he gave his report to Maoke. "It is done"

"How long will it take?" Maoke asked?

"I do not know" the apprentice replied. "There should be great success"

CHAPTER 4

I stood and watched the Unicorn and Pegasus. Everyone started moving the stones to the place Maoke had chosen for the city.

Bota called to me. Maoke

Yes, Bota, "How may I help you?"

Bota said, "Have them place everything on the ship. "We can move every stone within a month or less." It will take several months to do this, I can move it in two moves."

"Then move the stone" I said.

Bota did as he said. "I sealed the valley as I left for the city. I had the plans in my hands to start the construction of the city."

For two months, we worked hard to bring the city into view. Slowly from the ground to midway to the height that it still stands.

Bota moved his ship to the place I showed him, The ship set down to the ground I myself thought it would take several places for all the ships. The brush and trees were moved, pads were laid for the ships. It was a tiring day as we all gathered for the meal.

Bota said "It was great." We will begin the palace in three days." On the third day into the construction a strange ship landed. It was the Palatonians, graceful people almost as the females we have. They looked almost the same, they were human.

Bota brought them to me.

"I am Maoke, leader of all Busies." I said.

The captain said, "For many years we have flown by with no scan of life."

I said, "We are not humans we're humanoids, we have no human DNA. We would appear on your scan as an animal."

The Palatonians stayed two days with us. Talking and Gathering all the supplies they could place on the ship. The ship lifted skyward on the second day.

Bota told me he would be gone for a long time.

Thought ran through my mind as Bota and the Unicorn departed. Bota left the planet of Boldlygo, him and the Unicorn.

There was no rest everyone continued building the palace. Weeks had passed into months. Stone after stone, slate after slate, on the last day I was sent for. Walking into what would become the chamber of council. I was handed a stone.

"What is this?" I ask.

The Unicorn, and the Busie said, "It was the last stone great one.

"Why have you given it to me?" I asked.

The Busie replied. "It is the last stone! It is up to you to put it in place."

I placed the stone then said "It was done."

"The palace was a grand building of all." The Busie told me."

There was one building left to complete by your wishes. There must be writings, this I will place on the building.

"I looked through the portal for the city of Ratio," It was breath taking.

"The apprentice said to me. To the back of the palace", I would want my lab".

I asked. "Why there?"

The apprentice said, "It close to the palace. To the right of the lab an area a building so grand to place the ships, a landing area to the west, one to the east."

I rubbed my chin "hmmmm. "I gave him permission." The work began again. It took several years and it was done.

Kia came to me. Kia was the only female Busie, the others had fled. She was now infertile she no longer could reproduce.

I asked," Kia, what is your bid?"

"Kia looked long at me, "I wish to take charge of the females."

I said to Kia "I have been gone from the city I almost forgot the were here."

Kia gave her report, "They are with child, what they may bring is not up to me they will be in labor, four more moons.

"Good I said. I gave her permission, "Go do as you will with them." I left the palace for the ancient city to my archives again.

I studied the words that the females used. I found the words that the humans spoke, were much easier than the words we used.

I called to the others, asking the others, they all agreed. "So, it will be written the words of the humans will be spoke. Taught to the young in both languages."

I read further into his archives reading again only the Keeper of the staff can move it.

I have let Bota leave, without taking the trials of the staff. I must test the others.

The Pegasus and the Unicorn had gone to the far side of the ancient city to live forever, to do as they will. Everything that I have foreseen has been done. One building left to complete.

The human women were taken to the city of Ratio to live. I walked with them on the path. Outside the city with a wave of my hand. "This is for you this is what we have done." the females looked at me.

"Maoke they said. "Will we ever be permitted to leave here"?

I asked, "Why would you want to, this is a paradise." You and your children will be taught our ways.

"A female replied "I understand what you have done, my mate and children are on Earth.

"I asked," You were taken from them?"

She replied," Yes, it was not the right thing to do." The Palatonians took us, made slaves of us. There was no reasoning. It was doing as they say or die! When we saw the lights in the sky we didn't know, we thought it was a star shooting through the sky. We were very frightened when we saw a machine as it is called. Never in my life have I ever, or anyone else seen such. I really want to go home."

I am sorry." There are five of you all with child, all will be female babies. There will be five more until you can't bear children."

"Then what," she asked.

"You must see Kia she will explain everything."

Walking to the palace past the falls. Stopping to overlook the Valley of the Unicorn, the palace was built here for this reason. This area was built, known as the staging area. The lab was almost complete it had been a long time, a working progress, our planet now had a promise the females were having babies now it was the wait.

I went to Kia. "How long after they're born can we transfer the next DNA to them?"

Kia said "I'm not sure maybe they will know." The females that stand above the others I'll ask her. She has children on Earth, she will know.

Kia went to the city where the females were standing in the shadows, she heard them say.

"They tell me we are to live our lives here, have their children, we have no choice.

Kia entered the building, "I have heard what you've said, have five babies each. I'll see you go back to Earth, I will give you my word. It will start our world."

"First I need your names" Kia said.

The one that stood above spoke, "I am Kesha, Lora, Nannie, Nichole, Lea."

"You know who I am, In five of your Earth years Bota will return." Kia said. "The child you are having now will be five, there should be four more from each of you when he returns." Lea asked Kia, "Tell us what our children will look like."

Kia replied, "I don't know this I cannot say," not even Maoke knows. He told us he saw this through the portal into the future."

"I want to see this portal he talks about." Kesha said.

Kia said, "I will ask Maoke, the only thing it is in the ancient city." It is forbidden to take you there.

Kesha asked Kia? "Will you take me to the palace I will ask him myself."

Maoke greeted them. "Kia why are you here."

Maoke "Kesha wishes to speak to you." Maoke pushed back the parchment "speak"

Kesha said "This city if I understand you built it for your dependents, is that correct?

"Yes, I said. "The palace for the Royal Blood." This is true.

Kesha ask, "Are your Royal Blood?"

Maoke looked at her "I am the most powerful being on this planet," so yes I am Royal Blood."

"When my baby is born, it takes two cycles of your moon." Eight weeks to heal before we can conceive.

Maoke ask, "So what is it you ask Kesha?"

"I will only do this again if the DNA, as you say comes from you. Maoke not only for me the others also."

Maoke said "I will give you my DNA, but not the others."

"One more thing Maoke" Kesha said.

Maoke looked up from his parchment, "Yes Kesha what"

I wish to go to this ancient city. "I wish to see this portal. "

Maoke said, "It is forbidden, I cannot".

Kesha ask, "Then tell me what am I having. Will it be a human or monster, what will the child look as?

Maoke stood, with a voice of thunder. "ENOUGH" "Go back to your city, leave me know"

The humans ran from the palace.

Maoke called to Kia, "We'll talk later. I find the humans disrespectful. After all the hard work, years of building this human orders me. Humans maybe this was a mistake.

Days, weeks, months had passed. It was time for Kesha's baby. Within five hours there were five others being on the planet. Maoke looked with great ah! The babies were perfect humanoids. Looking almost as a human. just different in the eyes, they were bigger. the body was slimmer, arms were longer. Maoke marveled at the little ones.

Kia told Maoke. "Remember what Kesha said, it will be your DNA?"

It wasn't long the new babies took on a different form. This also pleased Maoke.

I ask Kia? "Why have they changed?"

Kia replied. "I have no idea. Maoke took to one of the children. He took to Kesha.

"Maoke, had ask Kesha to come to the chambers." Kia has told me of your request.

"Kesha ask, "What was that Maoke?"

Kesha. "It will be written you will return to Earth after your fifth child. I'll give you my word as leader of all Boldlygo."

CHAPTER 5

Bota was flying through space at speed he never knew could exist. The Unicorn was handling the trip very well Bota told Uny, "We have been seven months my friend. We still have a way to go."

Uny replied, "I understand Bota."

The Palatonians were on board to teach. Bota had learned from them. All the planets stars of chartered space.

One of the crew told Bota. When we pass the great planet with the rings around it, we will be within three day of the blue planet called Earth.

I tried to write it all down in my journal. I would need it for future reference.

There are other planets Cam said, that have life. "Some as the humans Kao give you, some evil. Earth is one, I have been there several times. Earth gets its name from the water. The planet is seventy fine percent water.

Let me tell you Bota, "Earth will not accept you." I have been there several times. Maybe the Unicorn I'm not sure. They are very primitive very protective of their people. People of Earth will kill what they dont understand.

Cam said your race Bota, "Is superior in every way," I have noticed you. Bota you may be behind in your space travel your intelligence is far more.

Cam told Bota, "look you built this ship," all that is on it. Cam ask, "Bota maybe you could build for our planet."

Bota said "I can only ask Maoke?" Please dont speak of this to your people.

"Cam told Bota, "Not to worry."

It was good I had Cam as a teacher. Yet I knew Maoke would never build a ship for the outside. The Palatonian ship ahead of us called for a stop. I ask cam, "I am not sure Bota, unscheduled stop."

"Kao came aboard, tell me Bota how is your trip.

"I told Kao it was good."

We're stopping for supplies, "You can come along, the Uny can come also, Do you have means of payment.

I open a small bag it was full of stones.

Kao said, "You will do well with the stone." Kao ask "May I see one." Bota showed Kao a big red one.

"You may keep it if you wish Kao. I have plenty of them"

Kao ask, "Where do you find stones as theses."

"Their everywhere on my world", Bota replied.

We entered the Milky Way as Kao said, thousands of stars' millions of systems. A small planet just to the west of the galaxy. The Unicorn looked at me with those big eyes. Our ship went to the floor of the planet.

Coming from the ship Cam said for me to wait.

On the floor of the planet Kao was talking to this being, all were looking at us.

I told Cam "I did not like these being." Several started toward us.

Kao, walked toward me. "They dont like you native."

Well I thought the feeling was mutual.

Cam, come from behind me with the Unicorn. "Suddenly everyone stopped."

What is that, One said, "I never have seen anything like it." Cam stood between us.

"Kao what is the meaning of this?" Cam said. "You have betrayed my trust." There is nothing worse than this.

Cam said, "you will not hurt Bota or the Unicorn". "If you try they will turn their powers on you."

Kao said again "I want those stones".

Cam replied, "You cannot have them Kao".

Then I will take them. Slowly Kao walk closer.

The Unicorn reared, gave a bray. The sound was so mind piercing it shook buildings.

Bota said to me. "Cam this is not right."

Cam said, "When I return I will speak to my king of this."

Bota, "I cannot speak for the others on the ship. I will stay with you on your journey to Earth."

"The crew said to me the same. I did give my thank to them."

Cam ordered the supplies they were sent to the ship. I paid with two green stones, they agreed it was enough.

We left the floor Cam took us to the darkness of space.

"Cam told me to mark that planet off."

I replied," Already have." I did ask Cam, the name? He told me it was called Van Worth. There was so much to learn to pass on to ones that follows.

My mind went to home. First time I've thought of the planet since I left. I left Maoke with it all. I am sure he has done his best. In the time, we have been in flight to this planet called Earth, I wonder if it exists. All I know for sure is the word of Cam. He said he has been there before. I know only one thing, we kept going. I would sleep while Palatonians took control. Cam, awakened me just as we came by the great planet called Saturn.

"How did they get their names?" I asked.

Cam said, "There has been space travel long before my time." Long before you, and Maoke.

"Who are they?" I ask."Where do they come from?"

Cam said, "Some come from so far they carry their families with them because they would be old before they return home."

"Bota you will age if you stay gone from home long. This I tell only you, stay gone for thirty years then you will age fast. This must be pasted on to the ones that follow."

I told Cam, I will write it down. I ask Cam, "What is there for me to do if they will not except me on this planet?

Cam said" I will look for the females, when we get them we will leave,"

I said to Cam "Somehow I do not believe it will be so easy".

Cam said, "I have a country in mind, you will see they know me there". I told you I have been there several times. Most of the planet is undiscovered and in some of the places there are paintings on the wall of ships. I have seen them myself. For two months, I lived with them, they are human. They also have others names. The ones I speak of are called Indians.

I told Cam, That is where we will go. We must have a large place to land.

"I know Bota, on top of the grand Mountain you will see. When we land, they will come."

Cam, you once said "They will kill me."

"They really will not understand." Bota.

Cam said "I will go first."

The rings of the planet were so beautiful. I have never seen such things before. The universe itself was an experience.

I ask Cam, "If there were other planets before Earth?"

Cam replied, "There is three."

My people will learn from the thing Cam teaches me. The things I enter in my journal. I believe they will improve space travel, yet sometimes I feel I have been in space before just not here. In all my life, I thought, how long have I been alive two thousand years I could not say. I only know Maoke had been around forever. I thought sometimes I did miss home, yet the feeling was not as Cams.

The Unicorn came to me. Bota he said, "I will not make the journey back. On this blue planet, I will spend my last days, then I will ascend.

I cannot leave you my friend. "Maoke would never forgive me."

Bota it is in Maoke's writing. "A native a Unicorn will take a journey only one returns".

"That is a day I wish not to see my friend." Bota said.

"What will you do?" I ask.

The Unicorn said, "live, I want to walk the field. I want to see the streams, taste the grass. Bota we will meet again I promise."

Speeding through space. It was hard to understand thing. We were intelligents it was still hard to understand the simple things. In my own words, I will write of my travels with the Unicorn. My time with Cam, his crew would I ever have a crew. Cam told me he was a captain in the Plano command. He had fought in several wars. Always victorious.

I was writing in my journal when Cam came to my room. "Bota come quick."

My heart beat fast. I was not thinking of seeing what I saw, I thought another ship. One that would mean us harm. Instead I was looking at a small blue dot, I looked at Cam. "I thought it would be bigger It's not as big as Boldlygo."

My friend Cam said "Were still millions of miles away". By the end of the day you will see how beautiful it really is.

Cam, had one of his men at the controls. We left what was called the bridge. Sitting at a table Cam said to me. Bota "Your engineering of this craft is magnificent." When we return to your world I will speak to you Maoke.

I looked at Cam. "What will you ask him Cam?"

I would ask, "Maoke, to let you construct a ship for me and my men? Of course, we would help."

Cam, I'm not sure he will do that. Yet feel free to ask.

Cam and I had become good friend. I told him he was in charge. The end of the day had come.

Several hours later a sentry of Cams called, "Bota it is time".

Replying, "time for what," I said?

Come Bota "Cam said feast your eyes on something you will hunger for."

Walking to the bridge I saw a big blue ball, sitting in space. In my life, I've never seen such beauty as this planet that lay before me. It just kept getting bigger. Cam give the order to come from hyperspace to impulse. Before me was the blue planet called Earth. This was the end of our journey. The reason we left home. What seemed a life time ago? I was tired, I wanted to move around.

Cam said "We will enter the Earth atmosphere go above the clouds stay until dark." We will descend to the mountain. I'll go first tell the Indians of you. I'll tell them of the Unicorn also. Then you can come off the ship, let them see you. Offer them a gift, I have found Indians like this. It will give then the chance to see you Bota.

"I agreed with Cam."

The ship landed Cam stood on the ramp, one hour later Cam said," they're here."

Cam took a container off the ship. "Bota wait for me to call."

The humans were as the female that Kao give to me, the first time we met. They were half dressed long black hair dark eyes, dark skin. I could hear Cam speaking.

Cam walked to the ship. "Bota come off the ship."

I went first, the Indians backed up fast starting talking in their native tough, then pointed to me.

"Great spirit.", the Indian said.

Cam said "Uny come of the ship."

The leader came forth pointed to the Unicorn. Touching my arm, said to me, "come."

Cam said, "let's go."

"Cam, where are we going"

Cam said, "I'm not sure Bota where were going".

The Indians lead us down the path alone side to a cave. The leader took a pole put fire to it, it flamed up. later I found it was called a torch. This I must write in my journal. The torch showed shadows on the cave wall. There were painting of all shapes. Painting of thing they have seen. There was a painting of an alien could have been me. I knew this was impossible. On the wall behind what could have been me. There was no mistaking, It was a Unicorn.

Cam I said "How can this be." Boldlygo is the only planet where Unicorns live.

Cam told me, I wasn't seeing the whole picture. It was written before you.

How Cam, "How can this be?"

"You must write of this Bota. Talk to Maoke when you return."

The Indian were showing dots and more dots. Then a bigger dot small dots for stars, dot for the moon, a bigger one for the sun. Below the sun was a ship, with some type of being looking through the portals.

I ask Uny "What do you say."

Uny said, "Bota I cannot answer your question. For thousands of years I have lived on the planet. The only word was from Maoke."

Cam ask, the Indian, "Does the animals lived on their world."

The leader said no, "They were heavenly sprits. In the clear night skies, you could see them fly leaving their signs.

The leader I found later was the chief. A big black stud charged the Unicorn.

Uny said to me, "Bota I do not wish to engage this animal in combat."

The chief reached for the stallion.

I told Cam, He is trying to protect his domain. We watched as the chief took control of the stallion. Soon after the calm or the horse. The chief invited us to his dwelling.

I must say, never have I seen a living place as this. It was a place to live, sleep, cook. Several people were inside. The chief had meat cooking.

I told Cam, Tell them I only eat vegetables. The great sprit would be very angry if I eat meat. Beside the fire, I saw what looked like bread I pointed to whatever it was, I'll have that.

A very young girl pointed. The chief nodded the girl give me the bread.

"The chief said, "It was made from corn."

I had no idea what corn was, I just nodded my head, It was good.

The day ended as Cam led the way back to the ship for rest. Cam and I sat long into the warm night air talking of things to come.

Cam said, "Morning is coming Bota"

Being a Busie I don't have emotions. I dont know beauty or how to describe such. The woman I looked upon was just that. She was beautiful.

"Cam inquired of the girl."

The chief told Cam, "Her mother and father were of a tribe they were at war with."

"Cam said, "The chief killed them took the girl raised her as his."

She had the bluest eyes. Topaz the stones on Boldlygo were not that blue. She was strong willed you could tell by the way she talked to the others.

The chief said "She had strong sprit."

This I could see.

On the ship, Cam said, "We would stay for two days."

Uny said to me," I will stay here Bota," after all I am expected.

The morning passed, this girl with the blue eyes, I could no erase from my thought.

I ask Cam, "Maybe she could help us finding the females."

Late afternoon the chief sent for us. The chief told Cam The stud that challenged the Unicorn, had settled down. I suppose they came to an agreement.

The chief told Cam, He gave strick orders, not to rope the Unicorn. He was to roam free. He said to all, "protect the animal."

Late afternoon Cam and I let the Indians board the ship, they were amazed of all the lights. They ask several times, "What makes them work?"

I noticed the girl with the blue eyes lingered. She spoke to me.

"I know you are from the stars. I have seen this at night in my village before."

I explained as briefly as I could, why we were here.

She looked at me, "really," she said. "You need female."

"Yes," I replied.

The girl said to me, "There are female in my old village. Maybe they will come here for you. If you will take me with you."

"The chief what about him?" I ask.

The girl said, "You could ask him if I could go? Tell him we will return someday," she replied. "Yet I dont want to return. When I was taken from my village my mother killed my father killed. I wanted to run, wanted to keep running until I reach the far side of the Earth. I did not know which way to run. Now I know it's with you, I will call to my sisters. Take us to your world, we will give you children, boys if you wish.

"We want females" I said to her.

Then she asks, "Why only female?" She just looked at me.

I told her, Find your sisters we will leave when you return.

I told Cam, What I did he looked at me them smiled.

Yes, my friend, "That just what we will do when they return".

The warm yellow sun had gone down. Leaving a red hot glow in the western sky. The glow reminded me of the liquid metal from the core of the planet I made the ship from. I remember taking months' years to take the liquid, making the sheet of metal.

Maoke would say." Bota you are wasting your time." I proved him wrong. The construction of the ship was simple. Electrical was ok. The shields were the hard part. They had to be mixed with two kind of minerals so the ship could enter and leave the planet's atmosphere.

Sitting on top of the mountain, gave me time to align the sensors for the flight back to space.

Cam said to me, "Bota the girls should return soon. He said it would be a good idea to leave."

Cam Sipped his tea. "Bota do you want to go to other places. Theres several places I have in mind.

I told him, I agree. I told Cam We needed several female.

Cam said Russia. "Theres a village, I know people who lives there. We will also need supplies. The more people we take the more supplies we'll need.

I told him, I understand. The next morning the girls returned. There was five, four females one male. I saw them at the edge of the mountain. Running into the ship the girls were looking around.

"I ask, the one with the blue eyes? Is someone you know coming?" she said know. I knew she was looking for the chief. The girl introduced the male, his name was Weston. The girls name was Madison, Shell, Gore,

I ask, "What is your name? "she replied.

"I am called Tomeka," She said.

The girls looked at me strangely.

I said to them. "Please dont be afraid, I'll never hurt you."

We're not afraid of you. "You're a spirit. Tomeka said only sprits go to the stars. We want to go with you. Tomeka said we were to have children."

I told them we would talk of this when we go to the stars. I walked around looking for Cam. Where had he gone. We need to leave before the chief show up. Tomeka was very beautiful, I dont think he will give her up so easy.

Walking down the ramp I saw Cam appear from the woods. The chief was with him.

I told the girls to stay on the ship. The chief come forward. Reached out his hand.

"You good to me sprit."

He bowed then took his band of Indians down the mountain.

Cam went to the bridge. I closed the ramp as Cam took us higher into the darkness of space. The girls were the color of the clouds. They could not believe what they were seeing. One more stop.

Cam said, "Then we were going home."

CHAPTER 6

L ooking across the Valley of the Unicorn. I sat in deep thought what a beautiful view. Time comes time goes it waits on no one. It had been over two years since the children had been born. It was a wonderful thing to see them running around doing thing children do. I've seen this thousands of years ago, My thoughts went to Kia. Hundreds of years ago, when she was a young child. Running into the ancient city.

I said to myself, "It was time for me to go to Kesha."

"Kesha, are you ready to have the DNA. You have three children you need two more before Bota returns. I give you my word, have five babies you could return. I understand your sisters have four babies. You must have five, or stay here until you do." Kesha walked to where I was.

"Maoke it's too bad I can't mate with you" Kesha took my hand rubbed her vagina.

I said. "It's useless Kesha I feel nothing, nothing. It's impossible to mate with you. I have let you move into the palace, your children I love them being here. Yet I have no feeling it's not that I dont care for you I just dont know what else you want."

Kesha looked at me. "You tell me you care."

"I do Kesha", I said.

Kesha said, "Then take me to this ancient city. Show me this portal, ive heard you talk about."

"I cannot it is forbidden Kesha."

Kesha pointed to the child laying on the floor. The child was lying in the sun. Despite the native look the child was beautiful.

Maoke, Kesha raised her voice. "This is your creation this child your DNA, Royal Blood. That's what this place is for, isn't that correct."

"Yes, Kesha it is."

Take me Maoke, "Falling into my arm."

Kesha said to me, "Take me to your bed make love to me please," Maoke.

Kia came into the room.

Kia said "The lab is ready for the transfer." Kesha picked the child up from the floor. Turning then walk away.

"Kia ask, for a name?"

Call her Oma, "Her name is Oma." Kesha replied.

"The others were waiting for you Maoke." Kia said.

I said "let them all take my DNA."

The transfer went well. The female went back to the palace.

"Kia ask, Maoke about the city?" Maoke replied.

"No outsiders Kia you know this. Some rules are not to be broken."

I spent hours writing, placing thing in the archives. Writing on the parchment I stopped. Why has she gotten to me, could it be possible for me to care for this human female.

Kesha took the children went to the city for a visit. I went to the lab to see Cha.

I ask Cha a question? I told Cha "No one needs to know?

Cha replied, "I'm sorry Maoke, as advance as we are we dont have that technology. Maoke what you ask for will happen someday. Just not today."

I told Cha Kesha wants me to take her to the Ancient City. "What do you say of this?"

"Maoke even you should not break the law of the planet. We are the leaders of the world. We must set example for the young ones."

Cha asks me, "What do you plan to do with the staff of Ira?"

"That will wait," I said. "I must go to the ancient city." I thought, if I can't take her to the city I will bring the portal to her. I rubbed my face as I thought-I can't do that. She does not need to see what the future holds. Kesha will be gone when Bota returns. Closer to the ancient city I walked. My mind was running wild on what to do. I must close my mind to all thing around me. I must think.

When I arrive at the city I must open the portal, look further than I have ever looked before. I must see the future of our people not only the city of Ratio. I must see not only the present, I must go beyond. I must see thousands of years. I can I'm powerful, I have seen the future before. I need to look father than ever.

Stopping at the falls that fell from the Madre-to-go's mountains. Sitting watching the water fall from the mountains seeing the vibrate color. How beautiful it appeared. Several times I thought I heard sounds behind me. Standing-walking on- I hid in the shadows of a tree. The sweet grass grew thick. It was large. I was completely hidden. Someone was following me; it was Kesha. Stepping from the shadows.

Kesha, "How dare you follow me! You have broken a sacred law of our people! The falls is the line. It is not permitted to go beyond. "A Busie appeared followed by a Unicorn. Maoke, "What it the meaning of this?"

"I am truly sorry she followed me." I said to him.

Maoke the Busie said, "You were leading her to the ancient city."

"She followed me." I replied.

Kesha started to speak.

Carl Sheffield

The Busie spoke. "Silence female."
The Busie said, "laws are not to be broken."
I replied, "I know the laws, I wrote the laws."
"Maoke I know you are the creator of this planet. Yet I believe you should be exiled."
Kesha said "He did not bring me. I followed him".
Maoke, "Take this female back to your palace. Never come here again female."
Kesha said to me, "I thought you were leader here."
"I am Kesha. Even I should not break the laws. It will be written this I promise."
I was shocked everyone was telling him what to do. I thought to myself, I'm leader here, leader of Boldlygo.
Standing-looking across the Valley of the Unicorn, the palace the great city of Ratio. Everything here is because I desired it. My creation made for the humans, then the disrespect they give. Not all of them were bad, just Kesha. I sat day after day considering the future of the humans. How dare them to tell me what to do. I deserve allegiance.
The day was coming to an end. The suns went down over the Madre-to-go's. When a light appeared in the western sky a ship appeared. Who was it? Better yet where did they come from? Maybe a few thousand feet. I suppose they scanned us then left. The morning came to our world once again. That brought Kia to the palace. "Maoke where is Kesha? I can't find her."
"Where would she go?" I ask. Maoke replies, "I saw her on the path to the falls." I said to Kia, "I will go look for her." The other girls were scared for Kesha. Lori told me Kesha has gone to look for the ancient city. I told her I already knew. Walking to the falls I find that Kesha was not there. A noise from the bush, "Kesha!" I called. A figure stood. "It is not Kesha Maoke, its Cha. Maoke Carry her she will be asleep several days." It was as Cha said. Two days later Kesha woke up. "Maoke she has awakened," Kia said.

"I told Kia I would be there. I must put my writing away."
Walking to the lab, I see that Kesha was laying on the table.
When I entered the room, Kesha sat up. "You really dont want
me to see that city Maoke?" Kesha asked, "Why can't I go there?"

"Kesha it's our rule, is our laws are no outsiders. Forget it
before I do something I'll regret. Believe me Kesha, I will lock
you up." I told Cha, "A council comes tonight after the suns set".
Much to talk about. Kia said she would pass the word. I sent
word to the city. Watching the suns set over the mountains the
natives started to appear. Walking through the courtyard several
carried packs full of fruits. Some carried Sweet Grass others
carried vegetables of what grew here. Everyone gathered around
the table. "There are some of you that has tried to tell me what to
do. It would appear I have misjudged the humans. The humans
are hard core people. Some of them seems to do as they wish."

Cha stood there. "Maoke only one of them has a problem.
Why is that Maoke? The humans that live in the city never cause
a problem. They work at their homes and take care of their
children. Only Kesha causes a problem. Since Kesha lives at the
palace we here think she is your responsibility. She has on two
accounts tried to go to the ancient city. Maoke she knew it was
prohibited."

"Maoke you are the leader of our race. You have always been
there for us," Cha said. I looked at all that was there. I said, "I am
the reason for all that is here." Cha said," Maoke if she continues
to look for the ancient city I will place another sleep on her." This
time she will not awake until Bota returns. I'll see Bota returns
her to Earth or where ever she comes from before she wakes up."
I did not like this. Telling me how I should rule the people.

Cha spoke again, "Maoke we made the chambers, so we
could vote on matters at hand."

"Speak our thoughts!" Kia came into the room. Turning
towards Kia I asked, "Where is she now?" Kia replied, "Maoke
she has gone to the city." Maoke said, "see if you can locate her."

Kia replied, "As you wish Maoke." Kia went out the door as Kesha was crossing the staging area. Kia ask, "Kesha where have you've been?"

Kesha said, "I do not need to answer to you!"

Kia said, "You must watch the children."

Kesha replied to Kia, "I was told I had to have children. I was never told I had to take care of the children. You watched them Kia." Besides who will take care of them when I leave. Kesha walked around the court yard. I can't wait to leave this place." Time comes, time goes. Kesha sisters had five children. I did promise them they could return to earth. It was almost time for Bota to return. I sat talking to Kia, I told her to bring Kesha before me.

Kia said, "If I can find her Maoke. Maoke I think sometimes she tries to find ways to upset me. Not only me you also Maoke."

Kia found Kesha told her to come to the chambers. "Maoke wishes to speak to you."

Maoke looked up from his parchment as Kesha entered the chambers. Pouring a cup of tea placing it beside her.

I ask her, "Kesha what about the fifth child? You only have four."

Kesha was walking in a circle. "I will not have five children Maoke. I suppose I will need to stay longer."

Know Kesha, "Maoke said, weather you have the fifth child or not, you are going back to Earth. This I promise."

Twenty-seven days later a ship roared across the sky. Bota had returned. Landing on the pad, Bota came to the palace. Bota said, "Maoke you have done good I see."

I give a nod. "How was your journey?" I ask.

I told Maoke. There are thousands of things I have learned. I have written all in the journal. You would not believe this planet called Earth. Maoke sadly to report the Unicorn did not return.

"I foresee that long ago Bota."

"Maoke someone foreseen that also." Bota said.

"I dont understand what you mean Bota." I said

"On Earth on the walls, cave painting of me and the Unicorn. A ship just as the one I constructed. Maoke it all was painted on the wall. I dont know how, it was as one of our people had been there before us. It was my belief that Boldlygo was the only place where the Unicorn existed."

"I cannot answer that Bota, please sit." I told Bota all the women have five children. Kesha had only four.

"Come with me Maoke," Bota said. "I have something for you, a gift. A gift just for you Maoke. Maoke she has blue eyes. Her eyes are more blue then the sky." Maoke got real excited.

Yes, "Bota show her to me."

Walking to the staging area, Bota told me he had ten females five male.

"Good Bota good."

Walking to the ship, Bota called to the ones on the ship. Tomeka was the first to come down the ramp. Maoke looked upon her beauty.

Now Busies don't have emotions as humans, Maoke thought this human was beautiful

Kesha spoke, "let me tell you about the race of males on this planet."

I said to Bota. "We must send you back to this Earth as soon as possible. Take Kesha, and the other that want to go. I give my word five children I would send them back, Especially Kesha. Bota she is trouble."

Bota said he understood. "Maoke I will ask Cam if he wants to go home. I believe he will go back with me."

"Of course, Bota, bring them to the chambers."

"As you wish Maoke".

Everyone gathered at the chambers. Kesha entered the chambers with Gore. Kesha looked upset. The time I've spent with her I knew there was trouble coming.

Kesha started talking, she would not stop. time after time I would speak.

Kia, Cha spoke, Kesha would not stop.

Tomeka stood so did Madison, walking to Kesha. Tomeka slap her across the face.

Tomeka said to Kesha. "I have heard enough from you; do you ever stop."

"You dont know what you have got yourself into." Kesha said.

Tomeka told Kesha. "I know exactly what I've got myself, my sisters, my brother into. This will be my home my family my life. You will leave as soon as Bota is ready. You will also leave this council."

This seem to please Maoke as he looked upon what was happening.

Kia whispered to me, "She is strong this one."

Tomeka walked to Maoke bowed. "Sir if you will let me my sisters stay I will take this--this woman's place. I also will take care of her children."

Maoke give a nod, "Yes so be it."

Bota did leave with Kesha, Lori, lea. Nannie decided to stay. Her request to Maoke was to have only one more child.

Nannie told Maoke "She would stay to watch her children grow help with their schooling. I promise you I will give you no trouble. When my unborn child is born, I will go back to Earth."

I said. "Then you will die."

"Humans die Maoke." Nannie said

The ten women Bota brought with him took the DNA. Only Tomeka was given mine.

Tomeka said to me, "If it pleases you I will move to Kesha room. I'll be close to the children."

"I give my approval." To Kesha.

Time past Kesha children grew, they were very intelligent. Tomeka has had two children. Two girls, the sound in the palace was the best. Never can I remember in my life hearing such. The

Busies never, when the children were young. Of course, these were half human.

Cha called to me, "Cha said there is a different in the way Tomeka is caring this child."

I ask, "What is the different cha?"

Cha said, "I can't say just different."

"Something more Cha," I ask.

Cha said" "I wanted to give you a progress report. I sat Weston down, Maoke he is not very intelligent. I'm sorry ive tried to train him, he can't comprehend. Maoke I would like to do is extract his DNA. Maybe transfer it to a native female."

"Do the transfer I told Cha, which daughter of Kesha's is the oldness."

"The females Maoke, they are of your DNA is this ok with you."

I told Cha, "You have my permission, go ahead."

Cha said. "Something on your mind Maoke."

"Cha I wish there was a way for me to be with Tomeka. She has come to my bed, she takes care of the children makes my bed takes care of the palace. Yet I cannot feel a thing for her."

"I'm sorry Maoke, Cha said, however I am still working on the process with great care. Someday Maoke just not today."

I told Cha, "I must take leave go to the ancient city. I will be gone for several days. I will tell Tomeka."

Tomeka was sitting in the great room. Several females were there. Tomeka stood walked to me as she turned the wind caught the silk scarf around her neck. The long black hair, those topaz eyes. She was breath taking even in my body she was beautiful. On another world, she would have been a queen. Here she would always be a woman having a baby. I told her this several times. She would touch my face. Look at me with those topaz eyes.

"Only for your eyes Maoke." Tomeka would say. I know you can't feel my love. Yet Maoke in the time I have been here I have found, I have fallen in love with you.

Tomeka, "I must go to the ancient city, it is forbidden for you to go."

She said, "I understand Maoke".

Maoke said to her, "Please dont follow me."

Tomeka smiled. Something Busies never do. "She told me she was too close to giving birth."

I turned to walk away when Tomeka spoke.

"He will be strong with our people, he will be most powerful. The child will change thing."

Walking from the room I stopped suddenly. "What do you mean he?"

Your son Maoke. "I'm caring a male child."

Maoke said "No Tomeka you are mistaking, it will be a girl"

Walking to me she took my hand placed it on her stomach. The baby moved.

I tell you Maoke "I will give you a son to carry on your work."

Kia heard this, "She is right Maoke, she is with a male child."

I must talk to Cha of this. I walked to the lab. Entering Cha's lab, I called to him.

Tomeka is with a male child. That's why you said it was different.

Cha said," Maoke there's no way. I split the chromosomes."

Turning to leave, remembering the writing, the Keeper of the staff has the power to move it. Will he be my son, he will be most powerful! I must go to the city if Tomeka has the child before I return, send for me.

Yes, "Maoke as you wish."

"Cha it is written I wrote the law. One day one will come change what is." I walked on to the falls, sat several hours. Lost in deep meditation. Then went on to the city.

CHAPTER 7

I walked the path to the gate. Entering the gate, I was greeted by two Busies.

"Maoke good to see you." By the Great Wall where the portal is, everyone shared the morning with tea. Sweet Grass was severed also. I must say it was great, I give the report of the palace.

Everyone, ask of the humans.

I told them of the accomplishment we have done in the time they have been here.

Tar I ask, "Where is the staff of Ira?"

Tar replied, "Where you left it Maoke."

I ask, Tar to bring it to me. "Do not touch it Tar leave it wrap?"

Yes, "Maoke as you wish."

When you return, I will have our people gather around. There were a few Busies left in the ancient city now, all had not fled. The staff was placed in a cradle on a table. In the warm morning sun, each one picked up the staff. Then it was my turn.

I could feel the power rush through the staff. The power was there, yet I was not the Keeper of the staff. Neither was the others that was here.

Each one said nothing happen.

One busie ask. "Maoke what was supposed to happen?"

I told him If you were the keeper you would have known. I wrapped the staff in its cloth, I told them he has not come yet.

Walking to the portal, waved my hand. I looked further in to the future than I ever had. There were ships of many. There were people both man and native. I did what I said, I looked deep into the future.

What is this Tomeka, leaving. There were several others. Wait! What is this, hmmm. I must talk to her. Closing the portal, I left the city, back to the palace.

I told Tar as I was leaving for them to come to the palace. You can start your own blood line It will be possible.

Tar said, "Maoke I am satisfied being a time keeper."

The other Busies said they were content being in the city.

You should come see the palace. The city of Ratio. I walked away Tar said to me.

"Maoke I do wish to leave the city. I would if possible to go on one of Botas flying machines. However, Maoke I will stay here until he returns. Maoke what about the Unicorn."

I told him, The Unicorn Desitny was not on this planet. It was of Earth someone there knew he was coming. There were images of him painted on the walls of a cave.

Tar ask, "How did they know he would come?"

"I can't answer you. Maybe they have a portal also." I turned walked away.

Reaching the palace, the suns had started to sat behind the Marder-to -go's. I took the time to examine the staff. Covering it with the wrap I went to the chambers, then to my sleeping room. Tomeka was sitting on the side of the sleeping bed.

"Maoke it is time for your son. I'm glad you're here."

Taking her in my arms, I walked to the lab. Kia was playing with children,

Kia told, the children to go to the home of Madison. Kia told me to wait outside.

Cha did what he had to do. Moments later a cry was heard, Tomeka cried only once. Then a whimper. Kia come to the door with a blue eyed baby boy.

Cha said "Maoke I do not understand."

I looked at Cha. "Cha he is the first of many male children to come of Royal Blood."

Cha ask, "Kia would have a child. I can take Weston's DNA if you want."

Kia said," It is true I would like a child, it would take several years to have the child." I must decline. Cha ask Maoke, "Would you want Tomeka to have another child."

I told him know, She wanted to give me a son she, could do know better. She has asked to stay until he is grown. Then return to Earth, I gave her my word. I will send her back if she wishes, with any other human that wants to go. I must return to my son."

Kia ask.? "What name did you give him?"

Looking down upon my son I told her, "He will be called Ject."

Kia ask. "Where did you come up with that name?"

The first of the females that Bota brought here from the Palatonians they no longer give birth. Bota would leave, stay gone for years. Sometime he would bring other, sometime he would return without. Bota should be here soon. Once on one of his crusades, he told me they were planets everywhere. There were human on most, as well as other being. A small planet outside the Earth atmosphere called Alpha Centauri he wanted to see, just never took the time. This I will write in my archives, maybe someday I will go to this blue planet called Earth.

Cam is still with Bota so is his crew. They have been very loyal to Bota. When Bota returns, he will take his place here. He must teach the ones here and the ones to come. Bota helped in saving our race the humans, the Busies, yet we are all as one.

Over the years, we have increased over two hundered. I see this as good. Cha told me he was still working on the day, we could mate with the humans. Yet my belief it wants be in my life time, or his.

My son was with his mother, sitting on the stoop. Tomeka was still as lovely as ever. I tell her all the time. Even with no emotions I somehow felt the love. I will hate to see her go. It has been several years since Ject was born. Today my son is seventeen. His older sister twenty-five. The girls will remain here on Boldlygo. Bota said the humans on earth would kill them. Especially the one with the native look. I have asked Cha about that.

Cha said, "Maoke I'm still working on that also. Maoke there is so much to do Cha said, with each generation the children will be more intelligent, look more human.

My son spent several hours a day in the chambers with me. I had him take up the staff. There was nothing. Chan's DNA produce a male. He also was given the staff. So was Bota on his return. There was nothing. Cha's son Lon, was very intelligent. The child worked by his father every day watching, I believe he was more intelligent than me. Ject worked alone side of Lon. The boys spent most of their time together. Ject was smart, not as Lon.

One morning my son come to me.

Father "I would like for you to take me to this ancient city, I hear you talk about. Lon and I both want to go."

I looked at my son, placed my cup of tea on the table. "It is forbidden to go there, am I an outsider father."

Tomeka, said to Ject. "It is our law my son. We will never go there."

Ject said, "Then another request."

I said yes, "I'm listening."

Ject said, "I want Bota to train me as a pilot. Lon wants to carry on in his father place. My sisters are too busy having babies"

I told my son the stories again.

"Yes, father I know the stories. I still want to be a pilot."

I said to my son. "If this is what you wish Ject, someday you will lead your people. You will take my place."

Father until then, "I want to learn to fly as Bota. My mother, Ject said it is my understanding you are leaving."

"I am going back to my world my son." Tomeka said.

"Mother, father said you will surely die."

"Ject every one dies in my world."

"Then you must stay here mother."

"I cannot my son," Tomeka said, "When Bota leaves I will go with him."

Father, Ject pleaded, "please tell her."

"I have already talk to her my son." I have explained

Ject said, "I dont understand humans. Good son you are half human."

Yes, mother I am, "I have a better outlook on life than you."

Father "Bota is constructing a new ship. Bigger, faster this ship will be so much more."

"My son come walk with your mother and me?" Maoke ask.

Father, Ject said, "I have seen all that can be seen here. I will walk with you. Just spending time with my mother is enough."

"Father when you built this place you did a good thing. The place you decided to build even better. The city, the palace, lab, staging areas. I see all good. How did you decide to build here?"

I looked at Ject. "I looked into the future through a portal in the ancient city"

Ject said, "A place I'm forbidden to go."

Tomeka took her sons hand. She took Maoke hand. Tomeka spoke to them.

"My son, I came here to do what I have done. One hundred thirty-four years I have been here. Maoke I have been very happy here. You have given me life, I give you a son. In my life to come I will always love you. In my world, I could have never loved one, as much as I love you."

"My son I love you as much, as I do my daughters. I will tell the stories of the stars and the people who lives here. No doubt they will think I'm crazy, yet I'll tell the stories anyway."

It took almost a year, Bota took his new ship out of the hanger. Pulling the ship to the staging area. Lon come to see the ship. "That is the biggest of all."

Lon spoke to Maoke. "Ject will go with Bota to Earth.

I will ask my father, "If I may go also." I can continue my studies on board. Maoke Ject and I need the time for our minds to run wild and free. Someday Ject will be leader of our people as I will be head scientist."

"I see Lon what you mean. Then you have my permission. Lon, go to your father tell him what I have said."

Lon said, "As you wish Maoke."

The big ship looked great flying around. I had my doubt if he was going to get the thing off the ground. Yet this was Bota we were talking about.

I did marvel at Botas work. When he returned placed the ship in the hanger. Bota walked over to me. "Maoke what do you think?"

"You have done good Bota. I am proud to say you are one of the best of our race."

Maoke said. "look what Cha and you have done."

Tomeka laughed out loud. "What they have done, it was the females that did something."

I thought. "How long before the keeper comes." The white haired girl, who will their mother and father be. Will they be Royal Blood?

Bota's crew eagerly supplied the ship, waiting to depart on the second day. Botas crew pulled the ship from the hanger, Bota walked past the old ship. "I'll let you set this one out, touching the ship." Then went on to the big ship. Tomeka, Cha several from the city shown up.

Everyone waited for Bota's word to board the ship. Bota was taking them back to Earth.

Bota said his goodbyes they were gone. The ship went gracefully into space. This was the biggest ship Bota ever built. It would not be his last ship, there would be other ships in the future of our world. There would never be another one as this one. Sometimes I wonder how Bota even knew how to do this, yet Bota was a super intelligent being. As the ship went into the darkness of space, I thought someday I'll go to this blue planet called Earth.

Walking back to the palace I called for Tomeka. Then realized she was gone. In my mind, I knew I'd never see her again. I would like to think, while she was here she was happy. I dont understand human affection. I wish I could. It shows in the humans of Ratio. Mothers, fathers alike holding their children loving then. The natives, the Busies we never do.

If all females on Earth were as Tomeka, I'm sure the blue planet would be a wonderful place to live. Tomeka told me more than once, she loved me. One day she told me what it meant, I replied, "I do feel that way. I just dont have the emotions Tomeka, or how to show it." I told Tomeka, I've tried so hard to understand your ways." She would say I love you anyway. When she reaches Earth Tomeka will age very quickly. Soon after she will die. I truly hope my son is with his mother.

CHAPTER 8

Ject thought, flying through space was nothing new for Bota. I must say he was a legend with his crew. Bota's crew was well seasoned.

I stayed closed to my mother. Spent as much time with her as possible. She would tell me how someday I would stand in my father's place. So, will your son their son and so on.

My mother said to me, "Ject when you return to our world, take care of your father the best you can."

"My son you are part human," she said. "On Earth the humans will not accept you. In fact, they will try to kill you. Human are like that if they can't change it they will kill it."

"My people may accept you. They would never show you to another tribe. It would cause great panic. My son try to live your life to the fullest. Study hard, learns from the Busies. They are very intelligent, learn what they will teach, build your life to the fullest. Then take your fathers place when time comes. Lead your people never let anything come between you and family. Everyone has a destiny mine is on Earth, you're is a different path. When two streams run together then splits, then you walk alone. When we reach Earth, our streams will have spilt mine will be on Earth. Yours will be in the heavens above. If there is life in me, every night I will look into the heavens. I'll know your there somewhere.

My son spent most of his time on the ship with me. Ject knew he would never see me again. I know this disturbed him, it disturbed me. I told him, one night all about life with a woman. Ject told me he had never been with a woman. I told my son," When you return go to Gore. She will have a daughter that will be of age take her to your bed."

Ject said, "I didn't think we could mate."

"I told my Son not with humans. Gores daughter is as you, a native. She will be your mate. Mate for life. My son you will be a traveler, I can see this. When you're around the ship the look on your face when you want to go. If you mate with her my son, remember her, your children, give her love, she will give you love."

I told Ject, "Time grows close. You can see the color of my hair change. My face has started to wrinkle."

I looked upon her. "Mother I can see. You still have the bluest eyes ive ever seen. My father eyes are blue. My eyes are blue. Know eyes could ever be as blue as your mother. That's what I need mother a blue eyed female. There is none on Boldlygo. Only the royal blood.

"Maybe your sister," Ject looked at me.

"Mother my sisters all have dark eyes."

My mother said, "I know my son, your sister that grow inside of me. Ject it will be your duty to take her back to your father. She will be called Mya! She will be a surprise for your father. Tell these words to him. I've wrote them down on a parchment."

My love,

I have loved you always. Give you the love you so desired. I took care of Kesha's children as if they were my own. I give to you from my body three daughters. I give you a son you love more than life.

Now my love, your son will bring to you another daughter. Maoke I give her the name of Mya, from my people. She will be strong with our people. She will do great things while she is there. As I write this down, I can feel the power flow through me. Our daughter Maoke, she will be strong with power.

Your son does not know it yet; his mind is becoming more powerful than he knows. I love you Maoke. I love, my children. Sorry to say I want be there for Mya.

I Wish I could see through your portal to see them safe on their journey home. I will always cherish the times we had. The love I had for you.

Now I must leave you in body, never in spirit, this you will see my love. As I have told you many times I could not have loved a human on Earth, as much as I loved you on Boldlygo. Remember me always Maoke.

With all my love,
TOMEKA.

I was dying. I need my child born first. We were several months from Earth. Sitting on the bed I felt my child that grows inside of me move. Time goes on as we fly through space.

A voice called to me, a voice I've never heard before. "Tomeka it is time for your child." Do not fear Tomeka. Maoke you will see again.

"Ject call to Lon, the baby comes." Twenty minutes later she was born. She was a native child. Yet had more human than native. The child smiled as she opens her eyes.

Mother I said, "She has eyes as you." Mya smiled closed her eyes went to sleep. Lon handed the child to Bota. Taking a cloth Bota washed the child give her to me. I place my new born to my breast. Pulling, nudging she had her fill. Mya slept.

In the month left on our journey, I would talk to her told her all I could. She would look at me with those alien eyes. They were the color of mine. They had her father's shape. I tried to tell her all, as young as she was, I doubt she will remember.

Ject was with her always. "Talking to her she would look at him, make sounds as if she was talking to him." I suppose in ways she was. I was holding her, when Bota knocked on the door. I had Ject send him to me.

Bota ask, "How can I help you Tomeka?"

I told him of the voice I heard just before Mya was born.

Bota told me, I cannot answer your question? There is no other on the planet. Maoke is our leader he has always been there for us.

I told Bota, It was not Maoke this I know. I have never heard the voice, yet it was male.

Racing on through space Mya grew fast. Her strength grew, her power grew also. I thought as we traveled on how over the years I was on the planet how strong with powers these being were. The daughters I left behind the son by my side, the daughter I'll send back to Maoke.

Time went on Bota sent for Ject. Bota told Ject we had entered the solar system of Earth." I walked with my son as he stood by Bota. Ject marveled at the planets as we past them.

Mya was growing fast, faster than 'ive ever seen a child grow. I wondered what would it be in a thousand years. I wondered would Maoke be alive, if so would he think of me. I'm not sure how long

I will live when we reach Earth. My thought went to Maoke, how I have miss him.

Bota said to me. "Tomeka you are a part of our history."

Cam said to me, "You were the first female of Boldlygo to have a child in space. I promise you as I stand here Tomeka, your name will live in our hearts, our lives. In our archives of history. I myself will write of you. In my journal of my travel to Earth. I will tell of the time I found you on Earth. How I brought you to our world. Our children will read of you through the thousands of years to come. You will never be forgotten."

I ask Bota, "How long will I live when we reach Earth."

Bota replied. "Tomeka you have been gone a very long time, you have started to age now. When we enter the Earth's atmosphere you will age very fast." You will die within a week. You were a very young woman when you left. There will be no one there you will know. In our time that will be over a hundered years on earth. Our time is different."

I ask "Bota to mark my grave. Tell my son, this way into the future he may stop, see where his mother lays."

Bota said, "I promise."

I ask my son? "Come Ject walk with me to the sleeping room." My son spent several hours talking before I went to sleep.

I stayed, held my mother's hand. "Mother I think sometimes my human side shows. My father said that sometimes, that could be a problem. This I must talk to him about when I return." I left my mother went to Bota on the bridge.

Bota ask me, "Is she was resting."

I told him she was.

Bota told me my body was taking on a different feature. Your body is getting stronger.

I told Bota, I'm growing up. This trip will be sad for me, yet very educational.

Bota told me of my mother request.

Bota I wish that also. Someday when I return I will stop and see her."

Bota told me he would make a stone with writing on it, it will say. TOMEKA WOMAN OF THE STARS

I said to Bota, "That would be enough."

Lon said to me, "We are not supposed to have emotions. Somewhere inside I feel something. I do not want to feel this way again. Tomeka was like a mother to me also. Ject Lon said, several times I called her mother." I embraced Lon my friend forever.

Lon told Ject, Tomeka will be missed by all on our world.

Standing on the open vast prairie, Bota did as he promises. He marked my mother's grave. My mother died in my arms holding Mya. I will never know why she wanted to return to Earth. Mya was growing fast. I in my thought, I believe Mya will remember.

Leaving the floor of Earth to another place. Bota waited until dark. Then placed eight people on the floor to start a new life.

Bota said, "We would take people from other places. Bota said he would like to do this very soon." When we return to our world, I will make a smaller ship. One that would fit inside the big ship. It would be easier to move around without being seen.

Bota said, "This would be a must."

Flying low over the water Bota called it an ocean. I have read of this in his journal. Bota told us someday this would be a vast country, with millions of people. These humans will evolve to a mighty race. Bota said to me. "Ject when this happens there will be wars of wars." Humans will try and conquer country. Even Maoke knew this.

Bota said to us. "Watch this, he slowed the ship hit the water." We were moving under water to depth unknown.

Bota I said to him, "Wait I must show this to Mya."

I told him I've never seen so many creatures.

I ask, "Bota what are these things called. He said, the Indians called them fish. Each one had its own name."

Lon pointed to one.

"Bota said, "It was called a shark."

Cam got our attention, here look. "Some kind of creature with legs. Cam said it is called an octopus. Indians said the legs were very tasty."

Bota said, "Indians were like sharks. They would eat anything."

I could not believe how beautiful it was. Mya just stared at all. There was so much life under the ocean. We surface went higher into the Earth atmosphere. Bota said we must wait until nightfall.

I ask, "Bota why we come so high. He told me in space you are weightless. We would fall unless we used our engines. Bota said I have wrote all in his journal. You need to read this. If your plan to be a great pilot."

"Someday I will be a great pilot as you Bota." I ask, "Bota, when you're out here Bota do you ever see other ships.

Bota said, "I've only encountered one ship. It was the Palatonians. There still with me today. Cam has been with me for many years. He would like to return to his planet soon. I need to ask your father a special request for Cams loyal service. If he may have the old ship. I will ask on my return."

Bota dismissed me. I went back to Mya I swear every time I leave her she grows. My powers are getting stronger also. I find meditating help me when I clear my thought I swear I can see tomorrow. Sitting on the mat, I no theres no way this can be. I open my eyes nothing. Closing them again relaxing my body there it was again. Mya spoke to me. "I can hear you Mya. Mya ask, "Where is my mother,"

I said to Mya, "She is gone Mya."

Mya said with her mind thought, "She never said goodbye."

I open my eyes, Mya was sitting on the mat. She was crying something I've never seen, she held me my mother. Mya was only nine months old. I felt a feeling I've never felt before. My mother said these feeling was from my human side. Trust them my son she would say. they could keep you from making hasty decisions.

Bota found what he was looking for. From a country called Russia he took twelve females, three males. From a country called England he took thirty females, eight males. From Spain, he took ten.

Climbing to space Bota said. "It was time to go home," I agreed." Bota called Lon.

Bota ask, "Lon to talk to the humans. They're probably scared to death." He told me to go with Lon… Ject, Bota said. "Look for a female, one that will serve as a mother for Mya."

As you wish Bota. "Walking to the galley all the humans were waiting." "May I have your attention."

One of the male stood. He was a big Russian, spoke with a very thick Russian accent.

I am Nicolai "I am not afraid of you."

Lon said to them, "I dont want you to be afraid of us. Please listen to me I could see there was mates in the crowd. They didn't want to be separated. If you have no mate over here. There were four mates.

Nicolai ask, "What Is it you want?"

"I must first ask you if you are sick." Some could not understand me. I showed them something it want hurt. I took their hand placed over my throat. They did the same, when this was done I explained.

"Long ago our people spoke a different language. For hundreds of years we learned to speak your words. I speak many different words."

"Why have you taken us, one said? Why have you brought us here?" Why did you want to know if we were sick?" The girl said to me, come here I said. Placing my hand on her stomach,

"Oh you are a lucky woman. Your child will be the first human child born in space of our world."

"Your world," she said.

I told her I'm sure there has been others. Yet not from my world.

"What are you?" She, ask.

"I am called Lon, this is Ject. Ject what are we called." Lon started to speak when Bota walked into the galley.

Bota said, "They are called natives. I am a Busie. We are from a planet call Boldlygo. It will take two years to go there." I ask, "What is your name."

Looking strange, "She said it was Angie."

Bota ask, "Do you have a mate."

Angie replied. "He was killed in a mine, I'm alone."

I ask Angie, "Since you are having a child, Would you like a job,"

Angie replied, "What kind of job."

I said, "Taking care of my little sister."

Angie ask, "Does she look as you do."

I told Angie, She has more of a human look, she is beautiful. I'll be with her most of the time. I will need someone to watch her when I'm at work. The girl smiled. I ask her to look at me. She lifted her head.

Lon said to me. "Ject she has blue eyes as your mother."

"Yes, Lon I do see that."

I listen to Lon, tell them of our home. How beautiful it was. The reason why they were here, the woman could not believe what she heard.

"So, you want us to have children, that look like you." "Why can't you have them yourself?" She asks?

"I explained to her we dont have females. The ones that are there takes too long to produce off springs. To save our race me must do what we must. You have five children you stay with them until they are sixteen you can return to Earth. This I promise. Even if I must take you myself."

"We have built you a beautiful place where you will live with the children. All you want will be given to you. There is no crime no sickness. We have no killing of anything. We eat no meat. If you break any of things the laws I have said to you. You will be sent back to earth."

"When we reach our home, there is another race. Like Bota there called Busie. One of them is my father. He looks nothing like me. I myself come from DNA, I know you dont understand. We are very intelligent species."

I ask Angie, "Come walk with me." I ask, Angie when her baby was to come."

Angie replied, "Two months."

Opening the door, she stepped in. Angie saw Mya lying on the mat. Mya stood walked straight to Angie looking at her.

Angie ask, "How old is she."

I told her, By her standards, she is nine months old.

Mya ask, "Ject is this my new mother."

I told father of her eyes Ject.

Angie ask, "Mya where is your father."

"He is at home Angie."

"Mya what do you mean?" Ject ask.

Mya said, "Father knows I'm coming home. Oh Ject, Mya looked at Angie, "Boys they think there so smart."

From that day, Mya was always with Angie. I guess you could say Mya felt the motherly love Angie had.

"Bota said she was doing good."

Angie kept getting bigger. I left them went to the bridge. When I return, Angie was sitting on the bed with tears in her eyes.

"What is wrong." Mya just looked at her. Then she showed me the letter. "You said I was the first woman to have a baby in space."

Angie what I said was, "you were the first to have a human baby in space."

Angie said, "I found your mother letter, was she human."

Yes, "DNA from the Busie, my father made me. My mother carried me give me birth. My father is Maoke."

"Who is Maoke," Angie ask.

"Wait you can read words." I ask.

Yes, Ject, "Angie said I'm not stupid. My father was a teacher. Ject your mother stayed with your father all these years. Then she went back to earth. Why did she do that? Ject you also said your father doesn't look as you do."

"I said to her that's right. He or, our race can't mate like you do on earth. My species he has created, we can mate with our own kind, we cannot mate with humans. Well not yet anyways. Lon is working on that."

"Ject am I to take your mothers place."

"I suppose that's up to you Angie."

Angie ask? "You said we have a city."

I told her yes, The Royal Blood lives in the palace. The child I'm carrying would live there also.

"My father would care for the child also. They would be my brother or sister. We would teach them our ways."

"What is the name of the city?" Angie ask.

I told her it was called Ratio. It's a beautiful city Angie. Built by my father, Bota the Unicorn, Pegasus. Angie if you decide to do this with my father his appearance my scare you."

Angie ask, "Did it scare your mother."

I told her know, she was great with my father. They spent a lot of time together. There was one other. Her name was Kesha, she was pure evil. My father wrote her out of the archives. Her name can only be found only in a few places. Kesha's children didn't like her.

"My mother adored my father, he can't feel human affection. He knows how he feel, he just can't show it. That's what was wrong with Kesha."

"She always followed him to the ancient city. She wanted to know where the city was. Each time she was caught. Cha, Lon's father came to my father."

Cha told my father, "Maoke I'm going to cause a great sleep to fall on her, lock her in a room."

I told Angie she was mean. Bota got her from the Palatonians. They still serve with Bota, there on this ship.

Angie said, "I think I would like being his mate. I'll take care of Mya, my children also."

Mya said," Well it's about time. I'm growing so fast don't you think.

"Yes, you are," Angie said.

"I must return to the bridge. Angie, we have been on the ship a lone time. Leave the ship room go to the others talk to them." Angie played games with Mya, she had taught her. Mya like the game where you would hide your face in your hands.

"Mya would say you can't see me."

"Angie said, "She never smiles."

I told Angie She dont have feeling as you do.

Ject Angie said, "You mean the children dont have the humor."

Maybe someday Angie, "Cha said the reason was because of our intelligent."

Angie ask, "What does this Cha work on?"

I told Angie everything. His son is here, you met Lon. He also studies science. Lon will take us father than Cha. Just as I will lead our people, as my son will someday. First, I must full fill my destiny.

Angie ask, "What would that be?"

My mother said, "I would be a traveler, it's in my blood."
I want a ship of my own, my own crew. I must work hard to
achieve this. I will help Bota build a ship for me. I will fly to
other galaxies find other being, talk to them learn as I go."

Angie said, "Ject it would appear you have your life planned
out."

Angie, "I hope you stay forever, one thing I didn't tell you.
Time here is different than on Earth. If you stay here for thirty
years if you return to Earth you will die, as my mother did. I
don't understand humans they dont want to die, yet they run to
death every day." Botas ship enter the universe of Bova."

Bota said, "We would stop on the Moon of Corning. Take
on some supplies tomorrow."

The Moon of Corning was as Bota said, it was small. There
was a small band of being lived there. Bota went with Cam, as
they walked out on the surface they appeared.

I was surprised to see they spoke our language, all are
welcome one said. I took him to be the leader.

"We do not get many passer byes," He said.

Bota said to them, "We have no weapons. We were a
peaceful race."

One that appeared to be a leader ask, "Why are you here?"

Bota told him of our mission to Earth. He told him of the
humans on board,

Bota said to him. "We need supplies. We can trade stones
for what we need. We have people from Earth. They need to walk
around."

The man said to Bota, "Have your people to come from the
ship. Please tell them not to eat the berries. They are sacred to us.
Please tell them to stay together."

Bota told them what he said. They agreed, not to eat the
berries. The leader introduced himself as Quad. We have lived
here over five hundred years. Sometime ships will stop.

Bota said to Quad." We could start stopping on our way to and from earth. That would be good, Quad said. What kind of trade do you have to offer? Fruits, vegetable, Sweet Grass.

Quad ask, "What is Sweet Grass?"

"Very good food I said." "It grows all over our world. The area around the Marder-to-go's."

Bota said, "In some places the Sweet Grass is sacred to us, as your berries."

"Lon brought bread to share."

Quad took a small piece of the bread. "He said it was very good." Quad ask, "Your city do they have trade, with other colonies?"   Quad said, "This was the only settlement. They do take the stones we trade for."

Bota showed Quad the stones." Taking them from a small bag. Bota pour a hand full."

Quad said. "That one will supply us for a long time. Quad said, "I'll trade with you."

Bota said, "I'll pay you with stones."

Quad replied, "That will do." Angie come from the ship.

Angie said, "It's nice here." She asks me, "Is Boldlygo was this nice."

Angie I said, "It is much more than this." I was standing next to Angie.

Mya said "Put me down Ject, I want to walk."

"If I put you down, you will hold my hand. Mya didn't like that either".

Angie ask, "Mya walk with me? Let's go back to the ship, Angie said to Mya, baby is coming." I knew I needed to go to the ship," Mya please." Mya knew Angie needed help. Mya was too small to help. Mya called to Ject through mind thought, "Ject help."

I heard her as if she was standing beside me. I started running Cam reach for Angie as she stumbles.

Mya caught her lifted her up as you would fly. Laid her down inside the ship. On the floor of the ship, a son a daughter was born.

I spoke to Bota I said. "Never have I seen two before. My father will greet you well."

Mya said, "Me to ject."

"I picked her up yes, little one he sure will." Thought ran through my mind. how powerful is Mya. Seeing what she did with Angie.

The next day our supplies were loaded. Bota give quad two stones.

He looked at Bota. "You said you would pay me one stone."

Bota said. "Quad two stones show good faith."

Quad bowed to me. "It will be good to see you again."

Bota told Quad, It might be awhile. I'm going to build another ship, It will be for Ject. We said our goodbyes. Cam took the ship higher into the darkness of space.

Hold on Mya said," Hyperspace hear we come."

The babies were doing good as we split through the aero of space. The crew was content. We still had always to go.

CHAPTER 9

Maoke cut a Simon. It's has been seventeen month Bota should be home soon. Funny I keep having this dream. A dream of this female child calling to me. Kesha's children have left the palace. Tomeka's daughters has also left the palace, I was alone.

Kia said, "It's just a dream Maoke."

It's a dream. one I don't understand. That's the thing, I'm very intelligent. I should know these things. After my morning meal, I went to the path to the Marder-to-go's. I past several natives along the path. Some would stop ask questions. The falls were a regular meeting place for mating ritual. It was an event that happen here. Children everywhere would ask, "Sir, how are you? Good to see you." I could tell our world was becoming to be a wonderful place to live.

Maoke was going to the falls. Each would say, "I would say it's good day for a walk." The falls were not forbidden to the people. Just the Sweet Grass, do not eat there. I wrote this long ago. In the ancient city, the Sweet grass grew in abundance on the hill side. The Busies' that lived there were content to stay. They could live their lives without any one causing them trouble. I managed to ease my way through the gate. Opening the gate, closing it behind me. Tar met with me.

Maoke, "What brings you to the city?"

Tar I said, "I wish to look through the portal."

"Something on your mind Maoke?"

"Dreams I'm having."

Tar rubbed his face, "Dreams Maoke?"

"Well Maoke let's see." Tar said, "Maybe I can help you. After all I am a time keeper. Tell me before you look into the the portal."

Old friend, "A child calling me father. I have no children. A female with two babies. I'm told of this dream."

Tar said, "Try to reach out with your feelings, meditate. It may not be a dream. Reach out and feel what you see. Then maybe you will be able to see your dream. It's almost like Tomeka is calling out to me."

"Maoke, humans dont ascend as we do," Tar said.

"Do they not Tar?" I ask.

I walked to the great wall and waved my hand. The portal opened to let me see what I could see. Considering the portal, a voice in my ear as plain as if she stood beside me, a faint whisper. I could not see her, yet she was there. My love, "I have sent to you by our son. A woman, alone with our daughter. I've named her Mya. I named her after my people. Maoke, this woman will serve you as I did. I'll always be around when a warm breeze falls on your face, a cool wind through your window. Maoke it will be me. Someday we will see each other again. Live in the ancient city, you hid from me, until then my love."

I turned to look, there was no one there, what did she mean? We will see each other and live in the ancient city. Falling on my knees, I've faced my trials. A child coming to me, It will be good to see the child. Have someone in the palace again. This woman if Tomeka is ok with her, then I must wait to see. A daughter I didn't know. I looked deep into the portal. I still look for the Keeper of the staff of Ira, there was nothing I could see.

I felt so sure at the time it was me and then my son. Now I'm not sure what to expect. It is written, one will come with the power to move it. He will be the Keeper of the staff. Wait, what does this I see? A female with white hair. She will come from Royal Blood, she will be Queen. A child from a native. When will this happen? Strange, I cannot see who this white haired girl be. All humans here have dark eyes or green. Wait her eyes are blue yes, blue Royal Blood. The eyes of my off spring this is good.

Leaving the portal, I went back to Tar. I have once again seen our future, the future of our people. It was strange Tar it was strange. Tar and I talked several hours of the progress we have made. Leaving Tar, I went back to the palace.

When Bota returns, I'll talk to him of staying home. Maybe he will start teaching some of the people living here. We need more people trained natives as well as humans.

Cha called for me to join him. Maoke, Cha said, "How was your trip to the city."

I told Cha all I had seen. Your son Cha, will be a great scientist. His son also.

Cha said, "Look what we have become. What we are, Maoke look where Bota has gone. How did he know how to build a ship? I have meditated on this forever it seems."

I said, "It has taken over five thousand years to do this."

I told Cha of the dream. The child Ject is coming with. The woman that has two children, born in space. Human babies one boy and one girl.

Cha ask, "This child Maoke, does she have the eyes of blue?"

"In my dream, always. We will see, Bota will be here soon."

Cha worked hard every minute. He tried to find a way to mate with the humans, it was useless.

Cha told me, I will give up Maoke. Maybe it was not meant to be. We were lucky to go as far as we have, I was happy.

I walk down the path to the city of Ratio.

Everyone said, "Morning Maoke." Some natives nodded. I got smiles from the humans. It was a great thing to see. I marveled at the city, the building, and the streets. Bota once told me people on earth lived in skin houses. Made from the animals they would kill. They would kill the animals for food, use the skin to make a lodge. I thought it was barbaric. He told me they had to lite a torch to see in the night. We do burn a torch in the palace, yet we get our power from the wheel that turn from the water. All in all, we were thousands of years ahead of the earth humans.

As I'm turning the corner a human came to me, he bowed.

Maoke, "I wish to return to Earth on the next ship. I'm very happy here I left my wife's children. I need to go return to them."

"How long have you been here?" I ask him.

He said he's have been here for several years. I told him I was not sure how long it would be. Tomorrow I will leave for the city again. Walking back to the palace taking a Simon, I looked across the valley of the Unicorn. As I'm eating the fruit many thoughts raced through my mind. We have done good. The city was growing with humans. Our numbers of natives have grown and our race will continue to grow. Soon we will have centries to carry massages soon everything we need we will have. I went to my sleeping room. The room I shared with Tomeka for so many years. I do not understand why I have these feeling. Maybe because I miss her being here. Lying in bed I went into deep thought.

The suns went down the moons come up. Some where I feel asleep. I found myself floating through the air. Something touch me on the arm. Turning to face the touch. There was someone beside me. Holding tighter I open my eyes, it was Tomeka. She looked at me, simply said. Soon my love soon.

I come awake with a start. Heart was racing what did she mean. I don't understand I'm leader of these people these beings. This is not normal, lying back on the bed I found myself in a simple place. It was the ancient city, the archives. I open my eyes, standing in front of me was Tomeka. Someone was with her.

"Come to me, come to me Maoke." She said. Holding my hand, she reached for this being.

She spoke again. "My love I've waited for you. Soon my love." She called this being me, it wasn't me, awake I was, it was another dream.

On the morning, I went to Cha.

I told Cha of the dream.

Cha I said, "It was me, changed into a different being. How could this be."

Cha said to me. "Go talk to Kia talk to Tar." Go Maoke, go to the far side of the valley. Talk to the Unicorn, the Pegasus. Ask them for their feeling on this. Something is there, I'm not sure why Tomeka is lying on your mind. Go Maoke they still have their powers."

I told Cha, "I'll be gone one week." I'll find Kia, maybe she can answer me.

"As you wish Maoke, just go."

I was gone longer than I expected. I was in the city for two months. I found nothing in the archives. There was no help from Kia, no help from the others.

I said to everyone, "I must leave. It was time for my son to return. I must be there to welcome my new family he has brought me." In the palace, it was as if I had been gone forever. Standing on the stoop I cut a Simon. Looking to the west the ship appeared, far in the distance of the sun. Flying over the city with a roar, circling around brought a few from the city. Running to see the new people. Flying over the city again then settling down on the staging area. I must say, it was a magnificent ship. It was as large as the palace.

The ramp went down. First to show them self was Bota, Cam then my son. The girl with the three children a small female native. Now there was something different about her. It was as the dream said. It was my daughter, it was Mya. I could see here mother in her. The likeness was great. The blue eyes. I was waiting on the pad. Ject held her hand, dropping her hand she ran to me.

"Father Mya called.' Running to me.

I picked her up. "How did you know I was the one?"

"Mya said, a girl knows her father."

I held her closed to me.

"Now put me down," She said.

Ject walked to me, "Father this is Angie, her two children."

I said." Angie, you are welcome." Mya was pulling my hand.

Father may I have a Simon." Ject has told me so much about them."

"Ject take her," I said.

I did a half way bow. Angie I said. "You are a beautiful human." I'm sure Ject has told you of the Busies. We do not have emotions as humans. I said please excuse me I must see to the others. Ject show Angie to her quarters.

Angie said to me. "My quarters will be as your sir."

"As you wish Angie, I was not sure."

Maoke, Angie said, "Ject has chosen me to be with you. I agreed long before I got here."

I said to Angie. "I was not sure you would want to be with me. In a dream Tomeka come to me told me you were coming. She also told me of my daughter Mya. I must see of the others. I bowed to her walked to the staging area." Cam was working with Bota to place the newly arrivals on the floor.

Lon ask me, "Maoke where is my father?"

"Lon where he always is I said? "In the lab".

"Lon I said. "You sure have grown." Lon left went to the lab. Cha said to his son.

"Your trip Cha ask?"

"Good father, it was long. Father there is a human you must meet. She shows great promise."

"I'm sure she does my son." Cha said. Yet there is great work that must be done. Lon I will meet her at another time." Lon worked by my side for three weeks. Lon always talking of the female human.

I told my son, "Bring the female before me." Lon left the lab looking for the human he had met on the ship from earth.

I was walking through the city. Angie was beside me, the children she gives birth to were growing fast. My daughter Mya was to.

Father, Mya said, "I love the city its beautiful." I walked here the other day.

Angie ask, "Mya, you were alone?"

Mya replied, "I go to several places I'm always alone unless Pep comes alone." I'm growing fast.

I said to my daughter, "You surely are."

Mya saw the native child she called Pep, running to him.

Father this is Pep. "He is a true native of Boldygo not like me, Pep is my friend. Father can he come to the palace, maybe stay a while."

I looked at Angie, she gave her approval.

I said to Mya. "That would be fine" We continued to walk through the city. The natives would come to us ask all kind of question.

One native said to me, "Maoke she looks as Tomeka, except for the hair."

Thoughts, solid flashes of her went through my mind. Then it all come back, after all these years. MEMORIES!

Tomeka hair was black, Myas was dark drown. There was much talk from everyone in the city. Angie and I walked most of the day, then decided to go back to the palace. Pep had return to the palace with us. He was more to Mya than she let on. Mya would soon be eleven.

"I said as much to Angie." Mya was showing as on Earth what was called a teenager.

The children were sitting on the stoop having a Simon, Angie told Mya it was time for bed." I was waiting by the stoop.

Mya replied. "Yes, mother I'll be there."

Mya said her goodbye to Pep. Angie stopped in her tracks. It was the first time Mya had called her mother.

I ask Angie, "Did I hear right." Angie turned to me she had tears in her eyes."

I ask, "Why the tears?"

Angie said to me Maoke, "It makes me happy to hear her call me mother. I dont think Tomeka will mind. She is the one that left."

Humans I thought, their emotions I dont understand them.

The morning came early I thought. Pep came in followed by Mya.

"Morning father," Mya said.

Mya I ask, "Did you have a sleep over?"

Mya replied, "Know father Pep is like me, he likes to rise early. Were, going to look around the city. We're going to places we've never been.

I said to Mya "Oh you are."

Father, "We're also going to the lab to see Cha. Father we will be gone all day. Tell mother I'll be home later."

"As you wish My daughter." There was no need to worry of the children. Each native or human in the city of ratio watched after all children

Mya said, "Oh father you're so wonderful."

Mya and Pep walked off, "I see my daughter has grown up at the age of eleven, with the mind of twenty year old." Mya was very intelligent. I thought if her mother could see her.

A voice from behind me "I can see her Maoke." It was Angie.

Angie said, "We must go see Cha today".

I ask Angie" "Why do we need to see Cha?"

Angie replied, "The time is right to conceive a child. I will take the DNA."

"I ask her if she was sure."

Angie said, "Maoke if I wasn't sure I would not have asked?"

Angie and I entered the lab. Lon was with the human female he had taken to. She was a very beautiful girl. I have noticed females from Earth are just that, beautiful.

I told Angie, Ject is not interested in a woman. Ject can only talk about space. Always asking Bota of leaving. Bota told me he will make a great pilot. Walking to Cha, I could tell something was on his mind.

Cha I said, "Something on your mind."

Cha said to me. "Maoke my son Lon wants to mate with this human."

I ask Cha, "is this wrong Cha?" I thought that's why there here.

Cha said to me, "They want to take the mating ritual. Maoke, he knows he can't mate with her. The child will come from DNA. He needs to take a native girl. Yet this one is above intelligent of the other." "Let it happen Cha. I'm with Angie."

Cha said "I've never took a mate, always working."

I said to Cha, "Yet you have a son from DNA."

"I see what you mean Maoke."

I said "Beside Cha, you're a Busie." I told Cha, Why we were here at the lab." Cha took Angie laid her on one table. In minutes, it was over Angie could see something was on my mind.

Angie said, I'm going to see Ject."

Ject was at Gores, she was over, well very old. I'm told Gore looks the same as she did when she arrived here. Gore was sister to Tomeka. They were the only ones that remains. They ask to stay they didn't want to have children? Maoke granted their request Madison had ten, Gore had nine. They were one of the first, they were family.

Gore and Madison had active parts in the city. I've met them over the past several years, each time I go to the city. On several occasions, both women ask my options. I was welcome to her home as any being was. Boldlygo was a beautiful place to bring up children.

My mind went to Earth, all the people on Earth how they fought between them self. I was thankful we were a peaceful race. Gore told me, even the race of Indians was always fighting.

I told Gore, "I come to see Ject."

Gore said, "Ject was out back with her daughter." I walked around the house, called to him.

Ject said to me, "Yes Angie."

We must talk, "Come to the palace tonight, much needs to be discussed."

"Gore said goodbye."

Walking back to the palace back I could see the children sitting on the stoop. "Pep was eating bread cake; Mya was eating a Simon." Juice was running down her face from the Simon.

Mother Mya said "We've had a busy day."

I ask Mya, "What have you done today?"

Pep looked at me. "She is full of energy. I can't hardly keep up with her."

Mya touched Pep on the nose with her finger.

"I'll take it easy on you tomorrow." Pep said his goodbye.

Mya embraced him whispered in his ear. "See you later honey."

I was sitting at the chambers when Ject called my name.

"Angie"

I said to him, "Come in." I ask Ject if he was to become a pilot."

Looking at me. "Angie, you as my father, would love to see me mate with Gores daughter. I say why can't I do both."

I said to ject, "Then you must let her know your feeling ject. See if she wants the same. Sometimes it will get lonely for her. Mating here on Boldlygo is for life. You must think of the children."

Ject said, "Look at Bota he has known one. "I truly want to be a pilot."

"Ject what I'm saying, sometimes you will be gone for years. Someday you may never return. Do you think that would be fair for her?"

Ject said, "I see what you're saying Angie."

Remember Ject, "I give you a refresher course, your mother has already give you long ago."

Tomeka said, She sees you a traveler. "Go, fly your ship, go to unknown places. You have all the time in this world."

Ject said, "She may not wait for me."

Son I said "There will always be another, this I promise you."

Ject said to me, "I suppose your right." We talked several minutes. Walking to the stoop to leave, Ject said, "The twins sure are growing."

I said to Ject with a smile. "They want to follow Mya and Pep around all the time. I told Ject to see Bota. Help him build your ship. I have a captain for you. Gores grandson, his name is Oso. He will be very loyal to you. Ject, see Gores daughter first, if she agrees to let you do this. See Oso take him to the lab, Bota will train him. I know when you get your ship built, when you leave he will learn much.

"As you wish Angie," I said. "I'll see her tomorrow." I said, "Thanks for the talk Angie.

Ject left for his sleeping room, I went to find Maoke.

From the stoop, I heard every word. "Angie had no idea I was there." I was Happy for my family, the new woman in my life. Most of all for my son. I walked to the table where a bowl of Simons was. I cut a Simon taste the wonderful taste it gives, watched the suns over the Marders. Lights come on as the city come alive.

I did thank of what Angie said to Ject. If not Gores daughter, there would be others. Just as I know someday there will be a way for humans and natives to mate, I feel it. Going to my sleeping room I found the day's events helpful. Somewhere in the night I fell asleep.

Angie, ask me the next morning, "Maoke, would be possible to talk to the humans that lived in the city?"

"I ask, "For what reason."

Angie said, "To train them the ways of the planet, the ways of Earth."

Maoke said to me, "Take them train them." Let them learn our technology. Let some go back to Earth, let then start a city.

Angie, "Are you forgetting why there here".

Angie said. "I know why we're here, even me Maoke. Someday there will be more than the city can hold, then what will you do. You say only the young can go."

I knew Angie was smart. More intelligent than the others, even more than Tomeka.

You see Maoke, Angie said. "The natives were having children, true slower than the humans. Yet with each native child born there is ten humans being born."

I told Angie. "I never thought of that, maybe we should keep it simple. Maybe we should not bring any one back for a while. I told Angie it's time for bed."

I went to sleep, with Angie lying beside me. Only to wake flying through space. Something touched my hand. I turned to see Tomeka.

My love, "The woman in your bed, she is strong. Let her have her way. Give her what she asks for."

I said to her. "I'm not sure I can." I said, "The humans are here for a reason."

Yes, they are, what about in years to come."

"Maoke, let her take them, train them. It's just one more step closer to being with you. Tomorrow go to the city write all you can of things to come, Maoke dont forget to place me in the archives."

Suddenly I was awake my heart was beating very fast, Angie jumped.

"What is wrong Maoke?" She asks?

Lying beside her I said, "It was a dream."

Angie ask me, Tomeka again? "Maoke go to the city write of her." Maoke looked at me.

"What do you mean?" I ask

Angie said, "You have forgot to do this. She will come to you one more time.

I ask Angie "You would know this how?"

Trust me Maoke, "Then and only then will she come again."

I thought to himself. I've never been afraid of anything. There never was a reason to be. Now I have a woman haunting my dreams, another one wanting me to dream. I must bow to their wishes. Angie slept through the night. When morning came, she looked through the window. The two moons were going down the suns were raising from the east. I sit on the side of the bed. "Angie, I must go to the city. I'm not sure how long I'll be gone,"

Angie looked at me, "It will take if it takes, takes my love."

CHAPTER 10

I have always wondered of time. The thing about time it waits on no one. It comes it goes not only for us for everyone. I was gone for several months. When I returned Bota ask for council. Kia, Cha, Ject, Lon, Angie, Bota, was waiting with Cam.

Sitting behind the council. I ask, "Bota what the council was for."

Bota stood explained about Cams years of loyal service to the crown.

"Bota, I have watched this for a while. Cam, has proved himself more than once. Bota, what is it you ask?"

Bota said, "Maoke I have completed a new ship. Another one almost complete. Maoke what I am asking is payment to us? The old ship my first, I with your permission give the ship to Cam. He has agreed never to tell of the ship or its origin. Cam has been with me for many hundreds of years."

Bota, "Bring Cam to me." Cam entered the council, I said "Cam come forward." Cam, dropped to one knee, rise Cam. "This council has asked to give you Botas first ship? What would you do with the ship."

Cam said, "Maoke I would continue to explore the frontier of space. Go to the thousands of planets that I know that are out there."

"What about your home planet, I ask?"

Maoke, "I have been gone so long if I did go there, theres know one that would know me. I have no desire to go their sir."

Cam I said, "It's not you I worry about, it's the ship. I do not want others to come here with their ships."

Cam said, Maoke I understood.

Cam ask "Sir I do have one request. I would from time to time, like to come back. This place has been my home for many of years.

Maoke granted Cam his request. The council broke.

Cam his crew pulled the ship out of the hanger went aboard then left. The ship went higher in to the abyss of space. Bota watched his ship leave my first creation, hard to watch it go.

Why! Bota Angie said. "Your acting like a human, didn't know you had feeling."

Bota replied. "Everything has feeling Angie, Just know emotions."

Angie said, "Kind of the same thing on Earth."

I ask Bota. "Have you have trained a crew?"

"Maoke the ship is ready to go. I've give it to Ject. The crew is six humans ten natives. They will be leaving when the suns rise."

I said at Angie. "Go to the city see if your humans want to go to Earth.

"Tell them my son leave tomorrow. Tell them to take only what they need."

Bota said, "I will tell Ject to drop them somewhere."

"I told Bota to give them the coin. Have them to pass it on to their children someday someone will come. Take the children home, that's the way it must be. Only the young ones."

My son or Bota never said how long he would be gone. Ject never made a comment of leaving. I think he was in a hurry to leave. Ject was a wandering being.

Angie ask, "Something on your mind Maoke?"

I said, "Angie you are stronger than Kesha, stronger than Tomeka. Ive never seen a human with a strong will or mind".

Angie replied. "Maybe it the part of the world I'm from. Maoke we're a little more advance than the Indians. I'm not saying bad thing of them."

"I understand Angie, I said. Yet I can see it in you."

"My brother, myself our father taught us well, he was a teacher. Even my mate on Earth. He was in the mine when it caved in. That's why I had a hard time when Ject went into the cave to retrieve the metal. It really upset me."

I told Angie. "The cave as you call it is as safe as this room were in."

Angie ask, "Maybe Bota, can teach the humans how to make them safe on Earth?"

"Then Angie let's ask him?" I said.

Bota was very busy building his craft. Angie and I went to the lab. Holding to my arm the baby was in a cradle as Angie called it.

"Cha walked to us, morning" Maoke, Angie.

"Maoke Lon will be in charge before long" Cha said.

Maoke Bota said. "how can I help you."

I said, "Angie will speak to you."

Bota replied. "Maoke I'm really busy."

"Listen to her Bota." I said.

Bota give a short blow with his breath very well. "How can I help you Angie."

Angie said to Bota. "Let the humans be a part of your work. Mostly teach them Let them learn how to make the caves safe. So, they can extract the minerals from the ground.

Bota said, "They only have to come Angie. I've notice most of them just sit around doing nothing. Let them come, they will be welcome. I want let them work on my ship, I will train them to work in the ship. Ject left with his crew, each one trained by me from lift off to land. I told Maoke I will pick ten natives for sentry duty.

"Good Bota we will need them. Very well Bota do as you need to."

I left for the city of Ratio with Angie. Walking through the city streets something caught my attention. Stopping I stood by a shop. I told Angie to come "look!" Angie looked inside the shop. Pep, Mya the twins. There were several native children.

I ask, "What are they doing?"

"Angie said, "It appears Mya has found a class room."

"I dont understand I said."

Angie replied, "You know Maoke for someone who is as intelligent as you are, I surely wonder sometimes."

"Explain that Angie."

"Maoke she is teaching school."

"I'm not sure why. If it please you I'll ask my daughter, when she comes, if she comes home."

Maoke ask me, "What do you mean?"

Angie said, "For the last three nights, she hasn't come home."

Maoke ask, "Does this up sets you. I told him no, I think our daughter has her own place.

I said, "She must live in the palace. That's why I built it.

Maoke, "She may not want to do that." I said.

Angie walked over to where a family of humans were. Sitting on the stoop, Angie approach them. She told them what Bota had said. "The men said yes, please. We'll do anything were going crazy. We can't fish, hunt."

Angie, told them to go to the hanger in the morning. Most humans really dont like to sit around. The Indian were always doing something on Earth, or that's what Bota, told me.

Maoke, ask, "Hunt, fish what does that mean?"

Angie said, "Go to the forest kill an animal skin it eats the meat. Take the skin make cloths. Fish, you take a stick place a line on it place bait on it drop it in the water wait for the fish to bite".

I ask Angie, "What's wrong with fruits bread vegetables?"

Angie said, as she walked away. "Why do I even bother trying to explain. I'm going to the palace, there is something I would like to see.

"I'll join you later" I said.

Walking through the city I went to the wall where the writing was. I stood looking at the writing. I was still trying to understand what it meant. Most of all, how it got there. I study the writing, it was cut in the stone, I never did this how did it get there. I'll ask Tar.

Tar said, "Maoke I never did this, it will remain a mystery." A faint breeze across my face, there was no wind. Suddenly a voice I heard.

Maoke, "The writing on the wall let it not concern you. It is for the future race a child will come with the staff of Ira. He will move our world. You must not tell anyone. Someday in the ancient city after your ascension you will meet the child. He will grow into a man. The child will be your fourth generation grandson. Ject will have a son, his son will have two sons. One will have a son, it's all wrote in your archives.

Maoke ask, "Why have I never seen it."

The voice said, "Maoke if you read every day you will never read it all, as we stand here it is being written."

"How, I said."

"I'm a time keeper Maoke. There are other some you know, with a wisp of the wind the voice faded. Soon my love soon. Tomeka!

As Angie said, "Too intelligent to understand." Walking to the palace, I know now, four more generation of our people, our race will be saved. I went to the table, cut a Simon Mya come in.

Morning Mya I said. "What have you been doing? I haven't seen you in days.

"I have a job father" Mya said.

A job Mya.

"Father, I'm teaching the children in the city. I have several humans, and native. I also have the twins. Father, the humans, there not as smart as us. Only the twins are different."

"I ask, "My daughter what she means.""

Mya said. "The twins are well like Ject and me. Ject can talk across the galaxy to me. I can do the same. The twins can talk to each other the same way."

"I ask Mya, "How she knows this.""

Father, "I hear them talking all the time. That's how I knew you were at my class today, with mother."

"They spoke to each other. Look theres mother and father."

"I saw you from the window."

"Well we must not let that go. "I said

"I was thinking the same thing father." Angie was listening to me as I talked to my father.

Angie ask, "Are your sure Mya."

"Oh, mother I'm very sure. My father had never heard the twins call him father, it made you happy."

In the court yard, it was a day as others, the first sentry come to the palace. He was undecided on coming in. The palace was for the Royal Blood. He had a message, he must go in. Walking to the great room. Looking at walls the way the stones were placed.

I saw the sentry enter the chambers.

Bowing to Maoke. "Sir, theres a council at the lab. Bota wishes you presents."

I ask. "Who are you."

"I am the first sentry sir. Should I carry a message sir? That's what we do carry messages."

I said to the sentry. "Tell Bota, I will join him shortly."

I thought, this will be good. "I told Angie I was going to the lab. Bota had sent for me." Entering the lab, I ask Bota, what can I do for you?

"Bota said, Walk with me Maoke." Inside the hanger Maoke looked at a fabulous ship.

I ask Bota, "Are you going to take it up Bota."

Bota replied, "Yes Maoke. You want to come with me."

"Maoke replied I think I will."

I knew what I was doing. I knew Maoke wanted to fly.

I said to Maoke, "Come aboard." It was exciting for the first time in his life Maoke left the surface of Boldlygo. Maoke looked through the portal window. As the ship went higher in to the sky. Maoke saw his world getting smaller. He knew this was good. He also told me he could see why it was my life.

Bota, told me as we were flying through space." Maoke, it will take another year, to finish the other ship."

Bota I said, "I thought long ago the ship you built after the first would be your last."

Bota said. "I will make one more ship Maoke." I want one more run at Earth. When I return, I'll start your teaching, I will build ship in my spare time."

Cha was on the ship.

Maoke he asks? "There is something I must ask you? I would like to take the DNA from the prominent ones. The DNA it took to create our race, store it in our data bank. Just the ones that will be powerful to our people someday. I have found a way to store DNA. My son Lon discovered it. Maoke Mya will be the first one. Mya is great with power, Angies twins also. I must say Maoke, to be completely human I can't say why they have the power they have. Maoke I think the boy, and Mya would be a good match." Maoke looked at me. "She is ready know Maoke. My son has found a way for the child to look more human."

I ask, "Are you sure Cha?"

"Yes, I'm sure Maoke."

I must talk to Angie of this. I told Cha we will talk more later. The ship landed on the staging area. I said to Bota, "Maybe someday you can take me to Earth. Bota find me two sentrys for the palace." Bota said, "As you wish Maoke." Angie was laying on the bed talking to the baby.

"Good evening my love," She said. It was the first time she had ever said that.

I replied to her, "It is a good evening Angie. Angie when you hear what I must say, I'm not so sure the evening will be."

Angie ask, "Maoke what is troubling you?"

"Cha and Lon both have found a way to take DNA and store it. Cha wants to give it to a native girl."

Angie said, "Isn't that what it's all about Maoke? Unless you are talking about something else."

"Your son Joey Angie, Cha wants to give joeys DNA to Mya." Angie looked hard at me. "Cha said it will be more human, than native."

"Maoke, I would be honored not sure Mya, will. I suppose you want me to ask Mya if she is ready to have a child?"

I stood looking at her. "I would like that Angie, I dont think I can."

"If that is what you want Maoke, I'll see to it." I laid on the bed with Angie. Somewhere in the cool night I fell asleep. Mornings I have found on this planet was beautiful. I left the palace to talk to Mya. Mya said to me, "Mother I'm with Pep. Why can't I have a child with him? Pep wants a child we can mate together."

I told Mya of the DNA. I told her the child would be almost human. "Talk to Pep, see if he would have a problem with it. If not, we will proceed."

CHAPTER 11

Time comes and goes. It had been almost two years since my son has left. Today was Mya's birthday. Mya would be thirteen. I sent the sentry to Mya. Have her come to the palace. I was sitting on the stoop looking over the Valley of the Unicorn.

Coming into the palace Mya walked to me.

"Afternoon father, how can I help you?"

"Mya, you said once you could call your brother across space."

"Yes, father I remember. I talk to him all the time. I lay in bed last evening, talking to him several hours. He is doing good. Ject told me his ship would go faster than before."

"Where was he Mya?" I ask.

"He was passing the Earth's moon father. He would be going to the surface today. Is that all you wanted father."

Know Mya, "I will ask you of the transfer."

"Father I ask Pep of this? He said it was up to me." Pep said, "Angie had children when she come here. You had no problem with it, Pep will be fine. The transfer can take place any time father. I have one request."

I ask Mya, "What is the request."

Father, "Write of me in the archives."

Yes, Mya, "You will be in the archives, beside your mother."

Mya took the transfer, she carried the child nine month later. Something went wrong, it was no different than the others. My daughter was never the same. Bota left for Earth three weeks later. "Mya, said nothing to me of leaving."

Mya walk up took my hand. "I will never see you again father, not in this life."

Mya, went aboard the ship, Pep beside her. Angies son was marked also.

Joey said to me, "I have called you father since I arrived here as a small child. You said we could not die if we were on the planet.

I explain to him. "With DNA, it was different." Our lives here started to change, I could see it in Angie.

Bota told me when he returned from Earth. "Mya went to her mother's grave laid down died. Maoke, Pep also did not return." Bota said, "Pep stayed on the Moon of Corning." For some reason, I think this with Mya bothered Bota.

Bota said to me, "Maoke I did not encounter Ject while I was gone. I'm scared for him Maoke, It has been eight years."

Bota open the class teaching the humans. The natives all would be together as crew members. I decided after Mya's life, the breeding to all would stop. The loss of a child, not only the child the ones left behind. Angie was never the same.

In the warm morning sun, as it was each morning here on our world. Sitting having my morning Simon my tea. Angie come to me with a request.

Maoke Angie said, "I wish to return to Earth. I've served you as I thought you deserved. You have been very good to me, my children. I could not have asked for anything more.

Angie I said, "If you return to Earth you surely will die."

Angie looked at me with those big blue eyes. "I know Maoke. "That's what humans do on Earth."

"I ask her if she had talk to her children?"

"I have Maoke. They wish to stay here."

I stood as she came to me, I'll ask Bota, The next morning I spoke to Bota.

Bota said. "I'm glad you're here The ship is done." I ask Bota, "When are you leaving for Earth.'

"Tomorrow Maoke, "I was coming to see you."

"Bota, Angie wants to return to Earth."

"Then Maoke I'll take back to where I found her." Three weeks later, sitting on the stoop I looked to the west a ship.

The sky roared, my son had returned. I greeted him on the west staging area. Ject come from the ship, something told me he had heard of Mya.

Farther, Ject said. "I stopped on the Moon of Corning. Pep was there he told me of Mya. I feel at a lost. I wondered why she had stopped coming to me. I'm sorry I wasn't here."

I told my son. "Dont let the human in you cloud you thinking. That was the way of your mother. You must forget the human in you. You're a Busie, be strong. Walk with me Ject, tell me of your quest."

Father, "There is thousands of planets, mostly all are populated. One hundred fourteen of them have humans, some have another species. There much more advance than Earth. I'm not sure how they got there."

I told my son, "I needed him to stay here for a while. Someone need to be in the palace. I'm going to Earth, with Angie. "

"Father she will surely die, with in one Earth day. You really want to witness that."

I told my son, "Someday the aging process will be found by one of the scientist. It's there Ject, they have not found it yet, I feel it is there. I will not bring humans here for a while. Our race is alive, that's what we set out to do, was save us. Even if it was through the body of a human."

Ject and I entered the lad. "I told Cha and Lon to stop the DNA for a while. I told them we will leave for Earth soon. There was so much to do, so little time. I must go to the city I must write of my daughter. I must write of Angie the city of Ratio. We the being of Boldlygo must never forget them. Never can we forget the part each one played in the birth of this planet."

Walking alone to the ancient city I met Tar.

"Maoke nice to see you." Tar said.

I told Tar, "It had been too long. Yet I'm afraid it will be longer my friend. I'm going to Earth I must look in to the portal. I must write of Mya."

Maoke Tar said, "I understand, it was a tragedy of her, time goes on Maoke."

"I give Tar a strange look." Then walked on. "How dare him, talk to me like that. She was my daughter." In the city, I went to the great wall. I open the portal looked hard. Only darkness could I see. What did that mean.

Walking to the archives I wrote several hours of my daughter. I walked around for a while. Returning to the parchment I wrote of Angie. Several hours of her, maybe they would ascend to a higher plain. I only had writing of this. I could not be sure. Kia had left the city of Ratio for the ancient city. There she would stay always.

Several hours of my time writing I met with Tar. I Told Tar, "Place all my writing in a place in the city of Ratio. Make a new archive for our people. I told him to place someone there to be the keeper."

I embraced my friend. "I told Tar I may never return." Then I left for the palace. Everyone was waiting when I returned.

Bota said, "We were ready to leave."

I said to Bota, "Just a few more minutes." I walk to the stoop that over looked the Valley of the Unicorn. What a beautiful view

I thought. Look where we were, thousands of years ago, to what it has become. I looked around at everything we built.

Father, Ject ask, "You ok.? I took my son give him an embrace. "Been around humans to long." I said.

Ject said yes father, "They do get to you after a while."

I told my son, "The palace was his."

I must leave the place I've loved for thousands of years. I turned, walked on the ship I never looked back. Bota took the craft higher into the darkness of space. I tried to spend time with Angie, one morning she asks me.

"Maoke why did you come with me."

I told her, "My ascension has come. On this blue planet Bota calls Earth I will ascend. Angie, I will not make the trip back to Boldlygo."

The next morning everyone was eager to be going to Earth. Bota sent for me, walking to the bridge as one says.

Bota said to me, "Maoke we would be stopping on the Moon of Corning. Maoke someone there you should meet. The moon is a regular stop. We'll drop off things for Quad. We also will bring supplies on."

"Very well Bota do as you must." Bota sat the ship down on the pad. Pep was the first one I saw. Pep walked to me bowed.

Maoke, "It's good to see you." I told Pep we were going to Earth. Pep told me he had decides to live on the moon for his life.

I said to Pep. "I've come to say goodbye." Several hours later Bota closed the ramp. Bota took us higher into the darkness of space.

The closer we got to this blue planet, the tighter Angie held on to me. Her hair had turn gray. The skin had started to wrinkle.

"Maoke my love," Angie said. "I never could take Tomeka's place. I did love you. I know you dont have the emotion as we do. Bota tells me tomorrow we will be on Earth. Never to see each other again."

I did not need to be a human to see she was dying. I felt this, It was a feeling I did not like, one I did not understand. I sat with her passing the Earth's moon. Bota help place Angie on the floor of the planet.

Angie died on Earth beside Mya, and Tomeka. I was lost a feeling I've never had.

Bota said, "I wish I could have taken her back to the country I found her."

"I saw Maoke, stand from the grave when it happens. How I was seeing this I was not sure. Tomeka was standing in front of me, with Mya. Their hands were stretched out. Maoke took their hands, they moved through the air as a leaf on the wind. Looking down, Maoke's body lay over Tomeka's grave.

I buried my long life friend of so many thousands of years. I placed him between Mya and Tomeka. I marked the grave with a marker that read. Maoke, father of the stars so all could see.

My crew ask, "Bota where to now?"

Leaving the plains of Mexico, I went higher into the night, I decided to go to Venice. I was doing what I wanted to do. That was to go out there. I must say the loss of Maoke, still lingered in my thoughts.

After several years traveling through space. Talking to the crew we decided to go home. The crew was happy. I wrote in my journal of my travels. Venice was not a planet you could live on. Landing on the staging area, Ject greeted me.

"Bota it's been a while."

"I said to the young captain, looks as nothing has changed."

"Ject, Told me of all the things that had happen."

"I told him of his father. I told Ject, of what I witness.

Ject said to me. "You know Bota my father was always destin to be with Tomeka."

Ject and I were sitting on the stoop. Cha had sent a sentry.

Bota, "Cha ask, for you to come to the lab."

Cha called from Behind the lab. A new staging area was built. On the pad four new ships were sitting.

"Well I said, that makes six. You and you son have done good."

Cha and I were the only Busies left.

I told Cha, "I would talk a walk to the city." Walking the streets of Ratio, I saw many beings. I knew all I looked upon were all DNA transfer. We have done what my long life friend wanted to do so many thousands of years ago, Save our race, they will continue to grow, we will survive. Even if it is through DNA and the body of humans."

Returning to the lab Cha was having evening tea. Cha called to me, "Join me Bota."

"I told Cha, where I had been. I said everything is as Maoke, had seem."

Bota told Cha. "Look from the time we were in the ancient city, to where we are now."

Bota ask. "Do we do as Maoke, should we die? Do we just walk to the city?"

"Bota Maoke is missed. I cannot answer your question." Cha said.

Ject is in charge now. He is thinking of a mate. So is Lon.

Bota said, "Tonight my friend, I will return to the ancient city. Live until I'm needed again continue my work. Cha walked to me giving me an embraced."

I told Bota I must stay a while longer. There are things I must write. Then I'll leave the lab to my son. I can work on things in the lab of the ancient city.

I told Cha, Until I see you, and Ject again."

Bota did leave, Left his work, the ship he had constructed. The one that is on parchment to be constructed by someone that comes after us. I myself have looked at the parchment, it won't work. Bota said it would, Bota was so intelligent. From the core, Bota took the metal, formed the ships. From the ground, up.

Learned to fly them. Bota was the best of the best. He was the greatest pilot ever. In years to come, that comment would prove me wrong.

I was thinking of my father as I eat a Simon. How Maoke left it all to me. I wish I could have went longer. Lon and I work long to learn about DNA. Still hard to understand how you take particle from bodies to create a being. I knew Cha would be leaving soon. Lon would carry on in his father's place as I have carried on in my fathers. As good of a pilot I had become I never flew the big ships again. Earth I still see when I closed my eyes.

CHAPTER 12

Our suns peaked the eastern mountains. The morning would be a beautiful as every morning. Sitting on the morning stoop having tea, my mind went into deep thought. I thought back of the time I was a pilot, had my own ship. The different planets I visited. The different climates they had. Earth was the one I never understood, yet intrigued me the most. There were four seasons as the Indians would say.

I was one of the few being to ever seen what is called snow. I've seen the violet storms of the southern territories. In my years of live here, there has never been a storm, no rain no snow. It is always a beautiful day. My father saw to this. It is written in our archives. I spent hours there after my father's ascension. Over twenty years now. My father's request all his writing be placed with a keeper. A library for all to see.

Years has passed I think of him, my mother, my beloved sister Mya. The bond we had with each other. I have other sisters, none as close as Mya. I sometimes think I feel her reaching out to me. It's as the wind blowing I can hear her calling to me. The cruel thing that happen with the child, Mya was never the same. Yet I still feel her close to me.

Through the years, time comes time goes. It was always the same. Watching the suns come up over the horizon, I bathe myself. I had a breakfast of Simon with the Sweet Grass that grew here. I was going back to the archives today. I wasn't going to read. I was going to see Beth. Beth was a human, was a beautiful person. I've told her on several trips that I enjoyed spending time with her. Beth told me she enjoyed my present. Today I would ask Beth something. I have thought of this for several weeks. The passing of Mya, Angie, Maoke, my mother. Cha thought we should not have children for a while, at the time I agreed. Thinking back that was a while ago.

Lon was in charged now. Knowing what was wrote in the archives, Lon started the DNA again. Several children had been born, each one a little more human DNA. This give them more human look. I pass the lab spoke to Lon. He knew where I was going. Walking the path to Ratio I looked at the water of the stream, that ran alone the path to the fall, then to the city. The stones were everywhere, there was always someone here by the water. The humans called it a park, well that was ok with me.

Walking into the library, I saw Beth smiling.

Looking, into my eyes Beth said. "Ject I've never notice before, you have blue eyes."

I said, "Yes, I do."

"I told Beth at one time there were only four people that had blue eyes. Now I'm the only one."

"There were four of you," Beth ask. I told her my mother and father-dropping my head. I said, "My sister Mya."

"You know Ject, I was reading of her this morning. It was written Mya was strong with power." Beth said, "Ject you are here also. It reads of your mother. What was she like? Why did she return to earth?"

I told Beth my mother was a wonderful human. She took another woman's children, raised them when she arrived. My father cared for her, and her for him. You would have loved them Beth. I still don't know why she went back to earth." I said to Beth, "You must understand my father was a Busie. Busies did not look like we do, they were the first of us. As you dont look like me."

Beth said, "Ject I still would like to be your mate."

"Beth, would you not be better satisfied with a human? We cannot have children as humans do. I believe you call it sex."

"Ject could we still have a child."

"Yes, we could. Lon would take my DNA transfer it to you. You would carry the child then you have the child.

Beth said "Let's do it."

I ask Beth. "You would give up your library of the archives?"

Beth replied, "For you Ject, yes I would."

To Beth I said, "It gets lonely in the palace. I come here today to ask you something." She smiled as all humans do. I ask her of the smile. Beth said, "It's an expression when people are happy." We spent several days in the archives reading of my people. One morning Beth was reading.

"Ject what is the staff of Ira, Where is it?"

"I told her it was at the palace. I'll show it to you when you move in."

Every child I said, "Take their turn to pick it up when they reach the age, whoever picks it up the globe glows will be it keeper. My father wrote that."

Beth said, "Ject listen to this. One will come from the city of the ancient and claim the Staff. The keeper would rule the world. A female of royal blood the keeper will come from a family of power. Ject who is this, who are they talking about."

"I told Beth I had known idea."

"She come to me in a baby voice."

"Please tell me Ject? Beth said.

"Honestly Beth I have no idea. My father saw them in the portal of the ancient city only he could not see the person only they will come."

Beth ask. "What of the white hair girl. The one to be Queen."

"I can't answer your question. Beth it's not that I dont want to answer you, I dont know who any of them are."

Beth kissed me on the face. "I've never had a kiss, I said to her. How did you know of them?""

"My mother told me Ject. She was told by her mother from Earth." She said they do it all the time on Earth. It was a way to show affection."

I ask Beth, "What did I do to get a kiss."

She smiled, looked at me replied, "Just being here."

We read the archives most of the day.

Beth ask, "Ject when do you want me to move into the palace."

I said to her, "You can move in today if you like."

Leaving Beth, I went to the lad. I told Lon the news. Beth showed up with her thing. We sat talked late to Lon. Beth lay her head on my shoulder, our suns went down the two moons come up.

"Beth said, "The purple was so beautiful." Our first night we slept together, holding her while she was sleeping was something I found I enjoyed. Beth's long dark hair lying on my arm, I can't explain. My, father said to let that side of me go. I didn't want to, I liked what I felt.

The morning come early, too early. Beth looked a little different than she did when we went to sleep. I ask, "You feeling ok?"

Beth ask, "Ject will you do something for me." Placing her leg over me.

I said to her, "anything Beth. You are living in royalty now? What is it you ask?"

"Take your hand and rub my private area." Beth said.

Well I was totally confused of this human behavior.

"Ject touch my breast please." Beth was moving vigorously as the wind blows the grass. Moving the way, she was, moaning then the yell. Then stop, stop.

Beth lay still for what seam minutes. I ask, "Are you ok?"

She turned to me, "kiss me. Ject tell me you love me." Well I felt something it was my human side. Once again, I remember my mother's talks. I suppose this was one I should remember.

I looked at Beth, "I love you," I said.

"Ject I know we can't mate like my race does. Ject if you do as you did now. It will be enough, I promise."

I laid back on the bed. Beth lying in my arms. I'm not saying I know about humans. Beth had a nice body, I did like touching it. Her breast was full. I mean, well they were as the mountain peaks. When I touched them, she was ready again? I tell you I think I enjoyed this too. I got up to bathe, Beth was asleep when I left for the lab. In the lab, I told Lon about all that happen. Lon just looked at me. I also told him about the DNA. Lon replied, "As soon as she is ready."

I knew what he meant. "I talked to Beth about the DNA transfer."

Beth said, "A certain time of month she would let me know." Beth placed her arms around me.

"Kiss me ject. Touch me and caress my breast. Again, Ject I'm almost there."

Her body would shake as she would moan. Then she wanted to take a nap. Females and humans, I'll never understand them. Beth told me she loved living in the palace. She told me it was almost her time for the DNA. Beth would tell me all the time she loved me. I would tell her the same. I tried to understand the word love. Humans had a way to use words. Maybe it was something they could hold on to. I did care for her, it was always as my mother said.

Beth and I had taken several years of DNA. She told me the last time she had given up. She told me early morning lying on my arm, "Ject I have failed you. I have failed you as a woman and a mate." I could tell she was not pleased.

"All I wanted was to give you a son."

Water fell from her eyes. It was not my first time to see this. I asked Beth of this. Ject, she said, "They were called tears. Sometimes humans do this when they're not happy, sometimes when they are sad."

Well I was confused again. Humans I think they should be exterminated, all of them.

"Silly boy, then you would die too. You're half human" Beth said.

Yes, I am, "With a Boldlygo attitude dont you forget that."

Beth told me, "Ject I will leave the palace. Then someone can give you a child."

I told Beth, "I will talk to Lon. He would find a surrogate female."

I told Lon, "I dont want to know her name." I went to the palace to tell Beth.

She looked at me. "Ject this I will not do."

Beth left the castle, she went back to her library. Sometimes I would stop in to say hi. She would always tell me she loved me. I still believe her, Beth just could not have a child, something she wanted. She wanted to give me a son. One day I dropped in.

"Ject I can't stand to be here."

"Can I go away? "She asks?

Beth I said, "We dont go anywhere."

One week later Cam flew in. Landing on the staging area, "Cam said he was going to Earth." When Cam left, he took eight people Beth was one of them. I was alone again.

I told Lon to take the DNA, transfer it to the female. Lon, she must understand.

"When the child is born, the baby is mine."

Lon said, "The child was for a family that wanted a baby. She knows she is only a surrogate."

I sat thinking of Beth today. Just a short few weeks since she left. Before Beth left, she told me to read the archives. I would go to the archives two to four hours a day. I read the same thing. I read about Maoke, Tomeka, Mya, Bota. The ones that has come here and several to come. I read of the writing on the wall, the staff of Ira. I read of the white hair girl. The most I look for was the Keeper of the staff, the female with power. Who is she, when will she be here. I stand here now, the only one with blue eyes.

I contained to go to the archives each day. I read everything that was pertaining to me at the time. Late one afternoon I took writing in hand. I started what my father did in the beginning. I could not see into the future as he could, I have no portal. Yes, it's true I knew about it my father had no secrets I was the leader of our world. I could only write what was happing day by day. I went back to the palace. To the place where Maoke placed the staff of Ira. Still I wonder why it was called that. Maybe someday someone will come with that name, maybe that's why Maoke called it that. Yet I remember reading of the staff long before Maoke found it.

I took the staff from its case. The long rod felt heavy in my hands. Whatever it was, I could feel the power flow through it, it made me tingle. I was not sure what power it had. Yet I knew it would be most powerful in the hands of the keeper, whoever he was. Walking through the palace I tried with all my strength to bring forth the power of the staff. As hard as I tried the less power I could feel. I wondered who he would be. Still I wondered again of the white hair girl that would rise to be queen, who is she. Who will her father be. It will be a mystery until then.

I went back to the cradle where Maoke placed the staff long ago, I placed the staff on the cradle where it will stay until someone comes to claim it. The trail of the keeper is held once a year. Everyone is given the chance to see if they're the keeper. Humans, natives, male's females.

I cut a Simon walked to the stoop, looking across the Valley of the Unicorn, a light appeared in the west. I thought for a moment it was Cam. A strange ship landing on the staging area.

I started walking to the ship. The ramp open then I knew it was Palatonian, a ship from Plano. The captain come forth.

"Greeting from Plano."

I replied, "Greeting from Boldlygo."

The captain introduced himself as Kao. I'm am captain of the Palatonian air guard.

"I know who you are captain. Why are you here?"

Kao said to me, "I'm looking for a lost friend, the last time I saw the man was on a ship from this planet.

"Oh, captain I know the story. You turned on your friends. Tried to rob Bota. You tried to take from him, what was not yours." The captains sentrys stared to come forth. "Captain tell your men not to embark. You sir will not be staying."

Kao held up his hand. "Go back to the ship Kao told them.

Kao ask, "tell me young one what is it your called."

I told him, "I am called Ject, son of Maoke."

Kao looked at me, "Maoke, Where is your father?"

I told him, "My father has ascended on Earth. He has gone to be with my mother, Tomeka."

Yes, Kao said, "I do remember the woman, very lovely."

"Yes, She was I said. "Captain once again, what do you want here."

Kao said, "He looked for Cam."

I told him, "Cam is not here. My father before he died, for Cams loyal service, give Cam the first ship Bota made. Bota ask, for Maoke approval. Maoke granted it. Cam left several years ago, I have no clue where you could find him."

"There is something I wish to talk to your leader about." Kao said.

"What would that be Kao?" I ask.

Kao said, "I'll take that up with your leader, then talk for I am the leader."

Kao said, "My government would be very interested in your people to make ships for us. Several of them." He went on to say.

A thought in my mind, Kao knew, we could build a ship at a faster pace. "Captain how do you pay for a ship?"

"Oh, Ject no we want them all, all you can build. We want to be masters of the universe."

Then it hit me just as I thought. They wanted to conquer the galaxy, not just ours. All that really disturbed me.

I ask Kao, "How would you pay for this?"

Kao replied, "Trade, pay with stones."

I told him, "We have all that."

Kao gave me this strange look. "Well we could over run you, take what and we want."

"Well you could try."

"Kao, what I would suggest you to do is go back aboard your ship leave." I would be interested in staying allies we only have four ships. We will build no more. The ships all fly the Boldlygo crown. We will take no more metal from our core. There is nothing here for you." Kao went aboard his ship.

"Someday I will return," Kao said.

I said, "So be it." I returned to the palace. The thought of the keeper come to mind. I wish he would come. I walked the streets of Ratio every day. I could see humans as well as natives, doing their daily needs. Some would speak, some bowed. I looked upon what the elders did all those thousands of years ago, how long was it? I can't remember? The writing in the archives read, it took several hundred years to build the Great Wall. The old ones with the help of the Unicorn, the Pegasus, come from the ancient city to build the city of Raito. The completion of the city, most returned to the ancient city, other went later. The Unicorn, the Pegasus now all gone.

I did read in the archives of one traveling to Earth with Bota. That was Botas first journey. I do remember, the Unicorn stayed with the Indians, the Indians thought he was a great spirit. I guess in some ways the Unicorn was a spirit. The chief said he was not to be roped or corralled, he was to run free. I wonder at the time; how many humans saw the Unicorn?

Bota wrote in his journal of the Indians, they had pictures of the visit painted on the cave walls, when they arrived. The Indians told them they were expected. Bota was showed the painting Bota said he could not believe what he saw. On the cave walls, pictures had been painted everywhere. The chief told Bota the place where they lived was called Mexico.

Bota wrote several entries of earth. As his journal reads, it was a primitive country beautiful as it was. There was water everywhere, it was not Boldlygo. I sometimes read Bota's journal. I wrote in the archives about it. I also wrote all children must be educated, humans and natives. This I would write of also. People should be trained in the art of star charts. It's a road to Earth through space.

The planets that are out there, the galaxies, the universe all should be taught. Some places you must enter a portal to go there. It's a weird feeling to go through a portal. There were so many other places. I think Bota went to all of them. I was with him once, we traveled to a place not that far from here. There were people that looked human. Yet had pointed ears, their skin looked a little different. It was written, they were called Claxton's. I must say I do miss Bota.

I missed the travel someday I will do it again. I'll walk to the hanger, take my ship out my crew. Someday maybe my son by my side. We will fly through the sky; endure all the greatness the universe must offer. Maybe stop see Pep, Quad on the Moon of Corning.

Being alone I had too much time to think. I think of Mya, my mother. I wrote of them in the archives, however my father wrote of them before. The great thing she did when she was here. Mya will never be forgotten, through the many thousands of years to come Mya's name will still be called. I feel some day her name will have special meaning, more than now. Bota made several entries of her. I must enter them also.

After my walk in the city I went to the lab. Lon greeted me.

Ject Lon said, "I have something for you Ject. Another breakthrough in DNA."

I just looked at him.

Lon said, "I'm sorry for my father's mistake with your sister."

"Lon that was a bad one," I said. It was a long time ago.

"I'm not sure you should be messing with the DNA," I said.

"This time I'm sure I can take the DNA by altering here in this strand determines male or female. I took my DNA and transferred it to a female. She is with child, a son." Lon talked long of the thing he had discovered. The day just lingered on. I told Lon I was going to the palace.

Ject Lon said, "Something I must show you. In a room behind the lab there were vales of blood everywhere."

I ask, "What is this place Lon?"

Lon said to me, "It was a DNA storage area Ject." "Everyone that has been here in the past, I have worked hard to place them here. Mya, your mother. Ject I can place their DNA into other female's way into the future."

I ask Lon, "Have you found a female for me?"

"I have Ject, She has had the transfer. She is doing well. Ject you will be called when the child is born. You will take the child, she will return to the city. I tell you now Ject, you will be very satisfied."

I told Ject, "The humans outnumbered the natives. We need to slow down the transfer. Ject we need to send the young back to Earth. Our race is surviving that's what it is all about. Since Maoke started this. We need to go to Earth."

I told Lon, "I could not leave the planet. The Palatonians could not be trusted."

Lon said to me, "Ever think what would happen if they would attack."

I told Lon, "I think of it all the time, were a peaceful race. If they did attack, well let me say it scares me to think of it." I ask Lon, "How hard would it be to create weapons, just for security." Lon just looked at me.

I said to Lon, "I'm going to the palace." Stopping by the table to have a Simon, I took several with a stalk of Sweet Grass. Walking to my room I took a bath looked out the window.

The night come slowly. I watched the suns go the moons rise. lying in bed a million thought were racing through my mind, somewhere I fell asleep. Just to be awaken, I was floating through space. My father I saw at the pool of water. Beneath the falls of the Marder-to-go's.

Father I called to him, reaching for me. I went to my knees. Father, "How can this be, you have ascended."

MY father said to me. "Come my son, walk with me."

Walking beside the stream the sound of the water smooths my thought.

I told my son a secret. "Touching his head a portal open to the ancient city.

Ject he said, "Son come with me."

Stepping through the portal I went to my knee. Standing before me was my mother. She as my father was in human form. How I was not certain.

My son much to talk about. I ask my mother, "How are you here." She looked at my father. My mother said, "Ject your questions will be answered."

I said, "Yeah when." "I told my father the Palatonians, are trying to come to our world."

"Ject, when or if the time comes my son. You will have the power to save the city." If you need the staff, the power will be given. It's our promise to you and the humans."

"Ject you're not the keeper, my mother said. He is still to come."

The humans, "There is a problem with the numbers father."

I said, "Lon suggest a trip back to Earth. Only take the young ones."

I ask, "Mother where is Mya. She is in the city Ject."

I started toward the bridge. My mother called to me. "I'm truly sorry my son the city is not for you. You cannot go beyond the bridge. Ject speak to her with your thought."

"My father took me to a Great Wall, the one I've read about in the archives." On the Great Wall was an image of a mirror of the city."

"Look, into the portal Ject."

I did as my father ask.

"He said to me." See Ject, "We watch you as we see everything your mother watches you always. Remember this we will always watch. My son when you need the staff the power will be granted to you."

I ask, "Father how do you know this."

Suddenly I woke up. My heart was racing. I jumped up from my bed, walk to the window. It was a dream. A warm breeze blew across my face. mother!

The suns had come up over the eastern mountains. I dressed had my Simon went to the lad. I told Lon of the dream.

Lon said, "You saw your mother, your father."

Lon "I'm telling you this to see if you can tell me what it means."

Lon replied Ject, "It's a dream that could become reality."

I said, "It was only a dream."

I told Lon, "Look I know you're working on DNA. I need a ship built."

Lon looked at me, "You Ject, why we stopped going anywhere."

I said to Lon, "A small ship, one that will store inside the big ship. One we can go to the surface leave the big ship in space."

Lon just looked at me.

I ask him, "How long do you think it will take to build."

"One year ject," Lon said.

I told him to build the ship. "Have it to carry twenty-five people." Once it is constructed, we will go to earth. I will find humans, as well as natives I'll train them." I'll train them myself.

"Will you be going Ject?" Lon ask.

"I said to him "I only wish, yet I cannot." I belong here with our people.

Lon talk to me several hours, he said, modifications will need to take place on the old ships. The decks were not designed to carry a craft.

I told him, "do what he must."

I said to Ject "On the ships, I build in the future I'll design them to hold a craft."

I said, "I have several apprentices that could start right away. I told Ject, "Give me one year. I'll give you a ship you want believe."

I told Ject, "I've built a new engine I'll place it on the ship. The power will come from matter. The power is something you want believe. I'll make the ship capable of carrying several people." I ask, what will we call the ship?"

I told Lon, "We will call it a shuttle. Make it for short range. Actually, "Lon make it also for inter galactic travel. Make several of them Lon. I'll start the training."

Lon called me to the lab early. "It had been eight months since I ask him to build the craft. I never went to him to ask on progress. Lon was very capable of doing anything. He was very intelligent.

Ject come in, "Let's walk to the hanger." Lon show me something I could not believe.

I looked upon a ship so elegant he had gone beyond my thought. "Is it ready I ask."

I said to Ject, "Yes it was ready."

I took two ships from the hanger. "I called the two captains I had trained." Taking both captains aboard I told them this is your final instruction, captain take your ships take your crew. I myself have assigned the people. Ive trained each of you. You have a complete team, take the ship go into space return tomorrow. I'll brief you on your mission.

Ject, "Is the mission to Earth?"

I said to Lon, "It is."

"Ject is the captain to bring back humans."

I told Lon, "It would be brief. After we place the ones we carry to Earth, we will not bring any one back. I will tell the captains before they leave."

I told Lon, "I wish I was taking it." I also told him if he ever built another ship, it must be as this one, he agreed.

Walking away from the lab to the corner of the stoop, looking across the valley, many thought ran through my mind. Why dont we just leave thing alone. Just go back to the way it was. Even as I thought, I knew I could never let that happen. Taking my bath lying on the bed somewhere in the late evening I fell asleep.

Another beautiful morning had come to our world. Yet every morning, every day was the same. I thought of the seasons of earth. I ask old Bota once. What made this planet lay so heavy on our minds?

Bota said to me, "Ject it's the thrill I suppose, just going there."

I today still believe this. I was waiting by the lab when the first ship returned. This ship would be the first to leave on the journey to earth. The humans that was returning to earth was eager to leave. This was something I could never understand about humans. A paradise they have here, just to return to uncertainty. The crew worked late into the night. Supplies were loaded on the ship, all said their goodbyes then were gone. Lon and I told the captain not to bring anyone back.

I told the captain, "the other ship will follow behind you." I told him after the humans have been placed. Explore the planet if you wish. You must remember you being human if you stay long you will start to age. Captain I know you have questions. Do as I trained you I promise you will have no problems. Now go to your ship. Have a safe journey.

Captain I said, "let me tell you now." When you see, this planet called earth you will never be the same. Watching the ship leave the staging area, then into space. I ask Lon if the humans were given coins.

Lon replied they were Ject, "they know what to do with them." Someday their children or their children come back to the planet to the far end of space known as Boldlygo.

CHAPTER 13

Lon finished the ship in a few short months. The shuttle was great, it would hold forty people including the captain.

I told Lon, I was going to the city. Walking the path along the stream several children were at the park. Seeing them brought back memories of Mya. I remember we sit near the bank let our feet dangle in the water. Mya would let the water creatures bite on her feet. She would tell me it felt funny I miss Her after all these years, even in my dreams i miss her. Mya was a lovely being. I walk into the city left word at several places.

I said to all humans, "The ship will be leaving soon. If anyone wanted to go come to the hanger by the time the suns come up." I stopped by my tea shop. I had a cup of tea with a bread cake. Walked back to the palace. I was on the stoop looking across the valley, thought what a beautiful view, as the day had ended. I changed into my sleeping attire went to bed. The moons had come up. Lying in bed watching the moons rise high in the evening sky somewhere in the night I fell asleep. Ject, a voice call me, wake up. Sitting up in bed, a voice I've never heard before, who is there. "Ject come to the Moon of Spores. I said, "I cannot."

"Ject your father said come."

I woke up my heart was beating fast. My father said, I must never leave here. Why was I being called to the Moon of Spores, WHY!

I got up went to the great room. I took a Simon, from the bowl cut it in half. Walking to the Moon of Spores giving off the purple haze. My father told me once that Bota went there with Cam. There was a being there. Bota said, they welcome them. My father said, they spoke our words how I'm not sure. I wanted to know who called to me. I must call a council on this.

Looking through the window I could see it was early morning. There was no need to go back to bed. I made tea watched the moons set behind the Marder-to-go's, it was beautiful. I went to my room changed into my attire. People was gathering at the hanger deck.

Lon brought out the ship. He looked at me,

Ject he said. "This is a masterpiece."

I agree," I said "You have gone beyond this time." Lon waved to the captain.

Ject, Lon said, "Watch this,"

Lon waved again. The bottom of the ship open, clamps from the inside reached down.

I could not believe my eyes. The clamps picked up the shuttle retracted back inside the ship, as the doors closed. How wonderful it was. No more taking the ship to the planet floor.

Lon said, "When you're in space, the doors can be open from the shuttle. When the shuttle is clear, the doors will shut automatically. What a wonderful world we lived in.

I thought the technology we had was beyond that of others. We are superior being at least Lon was. We are a peaceful race, wondered how long that would last. In years to come it would prove not to be that far away. I fear now the Palatonians could easily over run us. I in my dream, my mother and father told me they would watch over us. Was it a dream or was it real, I have no way of knowing until it happens.

I've told no one of my dream of the moon. I find myself every night, wanting to go. I took leave after the ship left. Walking to the falls took of my pack, had a bread cake. I lay on the soft grass under a small bush that never seemed to grow. I have been here in this same place several times. I brought Beth here once. I wonder of her sometimes, she went to Earth with Cam, she is dead now. I am two hundered thirty eight years old the bush has never grown. In the afternoon sun, I fell asleep. A voice brought my eyes open. "Ject come to the Moon of Spores." I sit up looked around, nothing I could see.

A warm breeze blew in my face. I saw her my mother, she reached for me.

My son, "You are troubled."

Mother I ask, "Where is my father?"

My mother said to me, "Maoke is with Tar. They must rewrite something."

"Mother I need his council."

My, mother ask, "Ject, tell me what it is that brothers you. Your father can not come."

Mother father said. "I was the leader of all the human, as well as the natives."

"Yes, you are my son."

"Mother am I dreaming, or is it real."

"Do you want it to be a dream Ject?"

"Know mother, a dream can't become reality."

"Can it not my son."

"Mother I am concerned of my people." I said to her.

My mother said. "Ject the staff will work for you if you ever need it. You must remember you're not the keeper, he is to come."

"Who is he?" I ask.

I cannot say ject, "When he does come he will do great thing for our people. He will be most powerful."

Your father said, "You will meet him in the ancient city someday."

She told me he would be human with native DNA.

Mother I ask, "How can this be?"

"My son, all you need to do is believe."

With a wisp of the wind she was gone. I stayed on the bank of the pool. The falling water smooth my thought. My mother said, "Believe."

I believe I'll take a trip to the Moon of Spores. See who is calling me, find what mystery awaits there. Would I find my destiny I think not, it is here, leading my people?

Still the voices call to me. Ject come to the Moon of Spores.

Walking the path to the palace, I marveled at the size of the Sweet Grass. I remember my father wrote in the archives, not to eat here. All the vegetation that grew here was different.

I have been to several planets, It was different here than on Earth, or under the sea of earth. The life under the sea was something to see. It was unbelievable how foliage could grow under water. Bota took me there once, Just to show me the creation of another world. That is what it was another world. There were all kind of species of what is called fish. Some had other names, some I didn't know. We do have fish here, they're protected as the giant Sweet Grass. On the blue planet people eat the fish. I still dont no why. The local natives of Earth eat meat, hundreds of pounds of meat. Humans of Earth eat more meat than anything. Maybe that's why they dont live as us. The climates, is different. I'm sure that play a big part in their existence. I sat having my evening tea, alone I was. Watching the moons rise, the purple haze was strong tonight. Suddenly a faint whisper, Ject come to the Moon of Spores.

The next morning the sun come shining through the window. I went to Lon, I begin to tell him all about the voices.

Lon looked at me as he does with that look. Ject Lon ask, "What other thing can you see, or here?" "What do you plan to do about it?"

I told him, "I was not sure. I needed to tell you. Lon I can't leave here leave here."

Lon said, "Find you someone to train as a captain."

I thought of Oso. Angie ask me of him once. That was several years, ago. I needed a captain for the shuttle, a personal captain. Walking to the city I went to Gores. Gore was sitting on the stoop.

I called to her, "Morning Gore."

"Gore replied the same."

I said, "I look for Oso."

Gore explained, "Ject Oso left on the ship to Earth, he went as a crewman. You must find someone young to train." I ask Gore, "How did she know i wanted to train him?"

Sometimes Gore said," I can see thing." I turned to leave.

Gore said, "You could talk to my grandson. He is very intelligent I've never told anyone. He can talk to the sprits of the Moon of Spores. Before I come here, when I was on Earth, my people could talk to the sprits. The holy man would do this for hours. I remember this as a child."

I told Gore, "There is voices calling from the moon. I want to go my duties are here."

Gore said to me, "Ject, your destiny is here. Your duties are whatever it takes to lead your people. If you need to go, go. I'm sure we will be fine. Gore said to me, go talk to Maoke.

"Ject, he will hear you. He will give you a sign. Ject go before you are a father."

I ask Gore? "What did you say?"

Gore told me, "Ject you soon will be a father. I have seen this now go talk to Maoke.

My father said he watched us. I thought of this as I made my way back to the palace. Sitting on the stoop, father hear me.

What must I do of these voices. Walking to the lab, Lon called to me. I've never seen Lon so excited, except when he went to Earth.

"Ject come here I have news. Lon lead me into another room. On a table were two babies. Lying side by side two male babies.

Lon said, "There two weeks old one for you one for me.

I walked to the edge of the table. I saw something Lon didn't see. One of babies had blue eyes. I picked him up. I told Lon, "I would take this one, picking up the child. I will name him, Tudo."

"A forceful name," Lon said. "I will name mine Cra." "In the old words, it means man of intelligents."

Time comes time goes. It's kind of ironic how time waits on nothing or no one.

I took Gores grandson, I trained him as a pilot. Kohl was as she said very intelligent. I trained him for several months.

On the fifth month, I told Lon I was taking out the shuttle. Lon ask me, "Where was my journey?"

I simply said to him. "The moon of spores." "I told him again, of the voices that call to me from the moon.

Lon ask, "Who do you think is calling?"

I give a nod with my head, as I walk to the shuttle. "I dont know Lon they keep calling."

Kohl ask, "Would you like to take the controls."

I replied! "You are the captain." Kohl took the shuttle into the darkness of space that I so dearly loved. I wish sometimes I could have went forever, Cam did. I think of him sometimes. Bota also went for a long while. One day he gave it up. It was the love of space he endured. Bota was the first of our space age, he constructed the first ship, learned to fly it himself. Bota was the king of space, he loved every moment of it. Kohl speaking to me brought me back to my own thought.

Kohl ask, "Where are we going?"

"Set a course to the Moon the Spores." I told him. Flying around the moon thought how beautiful it was from space. I thought, it almost looks as earth.

I said to Kohl, "Look there's a village they have a landing pad."

Kohl sit the craft down on the pad. We were greeted by a group of people, they were humans. I couldn't believe it, humans here in our own yard. Fifty thousand miles away. We spend two years traveling looking for humans. Unbelievable!

Kohl ask, "How did they get here?"

Opening the hatch a voice said. "Come ashore."

In my native body, I thought they would be afraid of me. Kohl and I, were welcome.

The human said, "I called Garf. I am the leader here. We don't have many visitors here."

I told Garf, "It was just me my pilot."

"Which of you are the prisoner?" He, ask.

"We are not prisoners. Why, would you ask that?"

"That's what we are. Garf said. Everyone here are prisoners of the Moon of Spores. I myself have two life sentences."

"We saw children on our approach."

"They were born here." Garf ask, "If you are not a prisoner who are you."

I am called "ject." A quite look come on his face. "I am leader of Boldlygo." They backed up a few steps.

Garf said "Ject."

I told Garf, "The voice called to me here."

Kohl spoke. "I myself have spoken to the sprits from here."

Garf ask, "You're the son of a Busie."

I ask him, "How would you know this. How long, have you been here."

Garf replied, "Over fifty years." Most of us were placed here by the Palatonians. They took us from Earth carried us to their planet. They used our women then placed us here. The

Palatonians that brought us here said the planet we could see. The ruler was from a Busie. He called you by name. Maybe the sprits called to you. Come, let me show you around."

Garf took me to a clearing behind the village. There were mounds of dirt piled high. "This is where we bury our dead. Why do you think they call to me?"

Garf said, "For help."

"Garf how can i help you."

Garf said, "The moons, belong to the Spores galaxy."

"I told him that would be correct." Ject Garf said, "We need supplies, living condition could be better."

I took the humans hand. "I will help you, from this day, you will not be prisoners any longer."

Garf I said, "You can build a city here, a great city. I will send you supplies. I also send help send help. On my world, we have no prisons., No crime if you have that here. I suggest you build a prison to hold them. You can expel them from the city. This you must do if you want my help. We, my people will not allow someone to destroy what we have built. Later we will build an outpost here. Place some of our people here to live with you."

Garf said to me. "That would be great, if you can do this." Kohl, took the shuttle to the darkness of space. I told Kohl, "I trained you to be a captain. Your duty will be to bring supplies to the moon. We'll gather some natives, as well as humans. Ones that want to work. I told Kohl, "When you're out here, always watch the sky. You can't trust the Palatonians. You never know when they will come.

I need to have council with Bota. Maybe he will come to the falls. Several months Kohl carried supplies to the moon every day. The last six month Garf had worked hard to build the moon to what it was. It showed great progress.

Garf told me on my visit yesterday, "Ject, I'm very pleased of the progress."

I told him, "I would see him soon."

I told Kohl "Ready the ship."

"Ject I need you to return in two month" Garf said, there will be something he wanted to show me."

I told him "It would be an honor."

Arriving on the west staging area, I left the shuttle Crossing the walk to the palace, a sentry came to me. Sir you're needed in the lab.

Ject Lon ask, "What is your outlook on the shuttle."

He asks, "Are you going to keep them in bay."

I knew what he wanted to do.

"Lon, "You want to go to Earth."

Lon replied, "The last time, the captain was not there long."

Lon, I said, "I can't go I'm needed here."

Lon said, "If you have no an objection, I would go. Take DNA maybe transfer to some of the female there. Leave someone there to watch them. look Ject my work is done; my apprentice can take care of whatever."

I told Lon "We have enough trouble. The humans on the moon, the Palatonian, I need to go to Plano. I have already planned it. Lon, I can't keep you from going. You have as much right to go as any one. I ask Lon, "About his son."

"I have that taken care of that. Karin your servant said she will take care of him. Your son my son will grow together."

"Then go Lon, take what you need."

"When do you expect to leave?" I ask.

Lon said, "Maybe in a month."

Very well I said, "That will give me time to go to Plano." I ask Lon, "If some of the humans on the moon wanted to go, will you take them."

Lon replied, "Yes Ject, of course."

I went to checked on my son, he sure was growing. I picked him up, walk to the stoop. I showed him the Valley of the Unicorn, the Marder-to-go's. I explain to him of all things. His big blue eyes looked upon all with concern. From the palace to the city of

Ratio to the mountains, even into space. Tudo even at a young age considered the far reaches of space. I knew some day he would go. Who would his captain be. Where would he go. It would be as Bota or myself. It didn't matter, if he was going. I knew someday he will stand here with his son. I'm sure he will do the same. Thinking our race will live on this paradise we call Boldlygo, as on Earth.

I had no clue what Lon had In mind. I assure you whatever it was, it would be great. The Moon of Spores had come up. I was ready for bed, lying back I closed my eyes. I found Mya running through the palace. Mya was so beautiful. I looked down at my body lying on the bed. I was flying again a voice called to me.

My young captain, "I have watched you. You have learned good." I turn to see Bota.

Bota ask, "You wanted to see me?"

I ask Bota, "What part of the quadrant is Plano?"

Bota, "I have read your journals, it's not there."

"You are right," Bota said.

I also told him, "It wasn't in the archives."

Bota said, "Yo u are right again, Ject"

Bota told me, "Leave the planet to space set a course to the north west. Set the speed of your shuttle, it will be a twelve hour trip."

The shuttles, "I replied."

"Ject we see you through the portal. That's how I knew you wanted to see me."

I ask Bota, "Did you know there are humans on the Moon of Spores. They said the Palatonian landed there one day let them off."

"I knew there were some being there." Bota said, "He went there once with Cam several hundred years ago,"

"I'm going to Plano to stop it," I said to Bota. "The moons belong to us. I'll go to the moon on my way back.

I told Bota, "Lon is planning a trip to Earth. I'll see if anyone wants to return to Earth."

Bota looked at me, "You can't quit can you."

I told Bota, "I do wish it was me going. Lon has picked his crew. He is taking DNA with him from his storage bank he calls it. Bota I must stay here, I do miss it."

Suddenly I was awake. I sometimes wonder as intelligent as were are, why it takes so long to understand things. I lay in bed looking out the window. A ship passing passing in the night, too far off to see who the ship might be. Looks as a star moving yet I saw it.

I thought of what Bota said in my dream. He was right, I couldn't stop. I loved the travel, I was as my mother said once. I was a wandering being, was I to ever go out again. I think I was doomed to stay here forever.

I knew as I said it I would fly outside our system, only once more. I must lead my people, stay with my son until it was his turn to lead. I hope Lon will have success on his journey.

Tudo called for me early. I could hear him talking to Karin.

Tudo said, "Karin where is my father must tell me. I would like for him to cut me a Simon."

I'm here son."

Tudo said, "It's about time I'm hungry."

Then Tudo, "You should have let Karin cut the Simon. Well I could have father, that's your job."

I looked at Karin. "He is growing fast" she said."

Ject, Karin said, "He is so intelligent."

"I know Karin," I said. "I can see it.

"I can't keep up with both children, she said. We must have someone to come help."

I told her to go to the city, the choice she brought back, I must say I was well pleased. "She brought back gore."

"Now, I could go to Plano."

Sitting Tudo down, I gave Gore an embrace. I thought this will work.

Gore said, "Tomeka told her of the palace. She said, "She had never been here. In all the years, she had been on the planet."

I looked at her. "Gore that's been a long time. I'm two hundred years old."

"Gore ask me, If I went back to Earth, would I die?"

I said to her, "By the time you set foot on Earth you will die."

I ask her, "Why would you want to go back. The world you once knew is gone. Over three hundered years, your Earth has changed."

"Someday I would like to go, I'm used up."

"I never told her of my mother being in the ancient city. I'm not sure what Maoke did. He always said humans did not ascend." This I knew nothing about.

I went to Kohl, "Told him to ready the ship. We will leave on the suns." Kohl ask, "Where are we going."

I told him, "Plano."

He asks, "Is that wise Ject?"

I told him have the ship ready, "Kohl, if you wish I will go alone."

"It will be ready, as you wish Ject." Kohl said.

I left Kohl, walk to the lab, I told him "we were leaving with the suns."

In the lab, Lon said to me, "Ject have a pleasant journey." I sat long into the night talking to the girls. They talked of the children mostly.

"They're to intelligent Ject." Gore said, "I have never seen children so smart. Ject Its as their brain never stops working."

I told them, "I can't answer their question." I said, "Lon could answer us, walk with me."

Entering the lab Lon was still at work. Looking up as we entered.

"Over here Ject Lon called. How can I help you?"

"Lon the girls said our boys, it was as if their brain never stops working."

Lon said to us. "I have already given them test," your right. "They're very intelligent. Ject my son will go beyond me in DNA. This I promise you, before I leave for Earth. I will with your permission test all the children."

"I ask Lon, "What he hopes to find."

"Ject there's, all kinds of work here. There's no need to waste a good mind."

I told him to do it. "I told Lon, he'll need someone to write for the archives."

I think of Beth each time I think of the archives, I must replace her.

Lon said, "I'll find someone test them."

"Lon let me know," I said, Lon did say our sons would be important in years to come. Our off springs will be with each generation even more intelligent.

I wondered of what Lon said. How could they be more than they are now.

Someday Ject it will happen. "We will mate with humans. You will see I am right."

I thought, as I left the lab, I know it will never be in my life time, yet someday. I slept peaceful that night. In the early morning, I went to the stoop, cut a Simon watched the morning sky. I went to the hanger, Kohl had the ship ready.

Ject, he said, "Take care."

I told Lon, "We would be back by night fall. With the rising of the sun Kohl lifted off into the darkness of space."

In short time Kohl, had been with me, he had become a remarkable pilot, "I told him so."

He smiled, "Had a good teacher."

We flew through space in silence for a few moments. I left my seat went to look at the star charts. Bota always told me to watch for things. Star charts were a big part of space travel. My mother told me stories of her people, how they would gather their things, living quarters move it all for days before they would build it back up. Moving only thirty to forty miles. In less than an hour we have moved thousands of miles. I often wonder if Earth will ever amount to anything.

I was all over Earth, took people from several places. Some were a little more intelligent than others. Kohl called to me.

Ject he said "There's a ship coming up on the left side."

"It's Palatonian," I said to him. "If I'm right they will come around we will follow them in."

"Kohl said see a good teacher."

I looked at him, "Experience Kohl." Following the ship as it made its descent. Kohl landed the shuttle beside the Palatonian ship, lowered the ramp. We were met by a captain.

"Greeting from Plano," he said.

"Greeting from Boldlygo," I replied.

"We, were ask, "Why we were in Plano air space?"

I told the captain, "I must have council with the King, or the title of government."

"Come this way," the captain said to us. "It might take a while."

"I can wait," I said to the captain. "Should I have my man stay with the shuttle"

He said, "It will be fine."

I told Kohl, "Close the ship." The hands held device Lon made work fine. A push of the button the ramp went up, the door closed.

The captains said, "That was impressive. Does all your ships do that."

I replied, "know."

He said," I have been told that you were master builders."

Your people, your planet all has reach the writers of our archives.

Captain I said. "Your people also have reached our archives. As we spoke to one another, I could feel the tension build. I stopped, captain I said. "There is no reason for you to feel of us as you do." I can feel the desire you must hate us I'm not sure why. Maybe it's the human in you."

"There's no human in me." He replied.

"Captain your more human than you think. You would like to destroy us, take my ships."

"We're a peaceful race. You have weapons? You try to conquer whatever. If you can't then you destroy it. You have weapons on your ships. I dont understand humans destroy, or kill what they dont understand."

He turned very fast, made a fist with his hand. "I could crush you, just like that," The captain said.

"You just prove my point sir. Destroy or kill what you dont understand."

A voice spoke.

"I am Cot." leader of Plano.

Cot and I, "Walk up the steps of a remarkable building." I told Cot so, he was pleased. Cot ask his captain to leave.

Sir, "With respect could he stay."

Cot said, "Well I usually dont let my people sat in on council."

"I need him to learn."

Cot smiled, "Yes I see he smiled again. Something we never do, why I'm not sure."

I could see the captain was disturbed. I could feel the hate build. This man wanted to kill me. Standing next to me I could feel his tension build. It gave me an uneasy feeling. Thinking someone could feel this way of me. I suppose in time some of our people will feel this way. Especially the humans. Cot showed us where to set. The captains sat to my left.

Cot said to me, "How can I help you."

I'm am Ject, "leader of Boldlygo. In the past, we befriended the Palatonian. One of your people lived with hundreds of years. His name was Cam also my friend. We give him a ship, by my father's request. It was the first ship Bota constructed."

Cam stayed with Bota many hundered years, flying through space. We give him the ship for his loyal service. It was on the first trip the Palatonian, tried to rob Bota. Cam stood with Bota. It was over a bag of stones.

Cot held up his hand. "Ive never heard of this, nor was I aware of the account."

"I'm sure you weren't sir. I was there when we give Cam the ship. Cam has returned several times. The last time it's been over thirty years. I was not there when the captain tried to rob him."

"This is a lie," the captain said.

Captain you said, "You have heard of our ships, have you heard of your captain Kao." He went silence.

I have heard of him, "he was my father. If you say my father did this, I'll kill you here."

I jumped up, "Then kill me Palatonian, for your father tried to rob Bota and Cam."

Cot said, "Stop, stop this now."

I told Cot, "I apologized, I did not come here to complain of the captain."

Cot ask, "Why are you here Ject?"

"I come to address a pressing situation."

Cot ask, "What would that be."

"The Moon of Spores."

Cot said, "I know of the moon. I've never been there."

"The moons sir, belongs to us," I told Cot. "Your ships have carried humans there, placed them with no supplies. They have called to me. I went to them after the Palatonians used them up. Then took them to the moon discarded them. That will stop, there is a prison being built. To house a prisoner, it must be paid in full, with one clear stone.

"Cot, and I talked for hours."

Cot told me, "Ject there would be no more people carried to the moon. I will also send them a ship load of supplies."

We took each other's hands. Kohl and I went back to our ship.

The captains said, "You may have won him over. The next time I see you I will crush you." I said, "Captain close your eyes, now open them again. Now you have seen me again."

"Leave here native do not return. OH, captain I'll be back. I have an open invitation."

I told Kohl, "Take us up, swing wide. We're going to the moon." Kohl pushed the shuttle, coming from hyperspace just short of the Moon of Spores. Garf was waiting.

"Greeting Ject."

I looked around, "My you have been busy." Ject, "I would like to think you for the supplies. The prison is built, or at least the first stage."

"The first stage Garf." I said. He told me later he wanted it bigger. I ask Garf, "Do you have a guest?"

He replied, "No, there is hope."

"Garf we're here to bring a message. I told him Lon was going to Earth. If some of your young would like to go, I'll send a shuttle."

"Something keeps us from aging Ject, must be the water." Garf laughed loud. I thought, humans with their humor.

I told Garf, "we will return tomorrow. I'll take those that want to go."

"Until then," Garf said.

Flying through space Kohl ask,

Ject, "Who is going to captain the ship to Earth?"

I looked at him, "Why you are Kohl."

Kohl replied. "I'm not ready for that."

I said to Kohl, "If you do the way I trained you, you will do fine." I could see the disbelief in his eyes. I told Kohl, "When we land, go to your grandmother. Tell her what it is you are doing. The word has already been given, to any one that wants to go." I left Kohl went to the palace to my son.

Morning come quickly. Kohl was in front of the hanger. Standing with him was twenty five humans bound for earth. I told Kohl I sent the shuttle to the moon to receive the other. I said to him captain ready your ship. When the shuttle returns, you can board at your will. It took three hours to go to the moon and return. On the fourth hour, the ship lifted off, higher into the darkness of space. It would be a four year voyage to Earth and back.

Lon's apprentice asks, "Ject should I carry on as usual?"

I told him yes. "Just as if Lon was here."

"I went to the palace. "Gore was with Tudo and Cra." I told Gore I was taking the boys to the city. I'll watch them today. You may come back tonight ready them for bed. I took the boys to their favorite tea house. Each one had tea with a bread cake. I was content with tea. The boys carried on as if they were grown. The conversation was, well not something a five year old should be talking about.

Tudo ask, "Father may I someday be a pilot, Cra ask the same?" I'm sure you both would be great pilots. Your destiny is not a pilot my son.

"Then what my father."

Tudo someday you will be leader of our planet. Cra you will take your fathers place as head scientist.

Cra said, "My father is that."

He is I said. "You will take his place in the lab, as Tudo will take mine."

Tudo ask, "Father may we go to the falls."

I said to my son "I'd love to." The boys sat playing in the water as I sat on the stoop.

Watching the boys play my mind drifted to space. Maoke should have let me wonder a little longer. I will let my son go until he tires. Then he will be ready to take my place. Only then I will ascend. The afternoon lingered, it was almost dark when we returned. I told the boys to head for the palace. Up the street they ran. Gore ready the boys for bed. Several minutes later she come to the stoop. "They went fast to sleep" Gore said.

I was watching the stars come into the heavens as darkness come.

Gore ask, "If she could sit with me?" Ject, when you consider the the sky what do you see."

I replied, "Darkness, freedom, peace, loneliness. I suppose anything that waits for me. Maoke should have let me run."

"Your destiny is here Ject," Gore said.

"Gore, all I ever wanted was to be a pilot," go forever.

Gore said, "Goodnight," then stopped, she turned around. "My grandson said the same thing Ject." When he returns Gore, the ship will be his, I will give it to him.

Gore said, "I'll see you tomorrow ject."

"Good night Gore." I said.

I sat for what seemed for hours. Looking toward the sky. A light appeared moving slowly across the heavens. The night was so clear it's from the wrong direction to be Palatonias. What was east in space the Moon of Spores. I watched them go until the ship was out of sight. I wondered who they were, where did they come from. I should take a shuttle go after them, I dare not. I feel empty without lo. If Lon had he been here I would have been gone. I must find another captain for myself. I'll go to the city tomorrow.

In the eastern sky the morning was full of color. Dressing myself I went to my sons room. Tudo I called Cra was in the other bed. Boys lets go the city. It didn't take long the boys were up ready to go. It was a wonderful life we lived. Watching the boys run, they knew we were different from the humans. It made no difference to them. We all lived as one, the humans children would come out when the boys were around.

Father, "Tudo would ask, May we go play?"

The thing about humans children they took to us as we did them. They never met a stranger, there were none. The boys were growing so fast. I sometimes wondered what their son would be. Why did I say that? Maybe that's the way it supposed to be. Maoke didn't say. Was it to be the royal blood was to have male children. I think not, my mother had females. Four of them. I never see them. None could compare to Mya, none had powers.

It is written the white hair girl that is to come. Her mother her father who are they. A human female to be queen. She will have native DNA. I should go to the archives today. If I went every day I could never read it all. Some of the things I have read has happen, some to come. The white hair girl when will she come. The Keeper of the staff when will he come. Little did I know that would not take place for almost one thousand years into the future. I still wonder who they are, when they will come. I can't say, all I know, they will be royal blood.

Sometimes I think of all that is to come. Everything in the archives speak of it. Is the keeper to be of my sons blood or his son. The white hair girl I think of this often. My father knew this I believe, yet he spoke not a word.

I was in the city today looking for a captain. Someone too train I made it known to all my mission here. Let all come to the lab tomorrow to try for the captains seat. I lingered most of the day in the city. The boys were hard at the games. They were in no way ready to go. The tea shop where I spent most of my time when I was in the city. I was having tea the boys said they would like a bread cake. I told them after they eat we must head back to the palace. We started for the lab when, a young human stopped me.

Sir he bowed.

"I held my hand up, "You do not need to bow to me."

"Sir you are the son of the Great one. It is custom to bow."

"What can I do for you?" I ask.

"I here, you look for a captain."

I told him, "I was."

He asks, "Can humans come?"

I said, "Everyone is welcome. I must tell you some will not make it."

He said to me, "I will be there."

I could tell the young human carried himself well. I ask, What is your given.

Replying, "My name is Comp, grandson of Madison, she was Tomeka sister."

"That makes us blood I told him."

"I am Ject, "Son of Tomeka, son of Maoke."

I knew them all. "Madison went back to Earth with Kohl. Sorry to say to die. I told Kohl, to take her to Tomeka's grave bury her beside my family."

When Kohl left, he said, "Thanks for giving me this chance. I want let you down."

I told Kohl, "If I thought you would you would not be in the captains seat. I told Kohl remember do not trust anyone. Especially the Palatonian."

Kohl said, "Ject wish you were going with me."

Mornings on my world was wonderful. The morning suns were giving off their glow. I entered the lab the only people there was the the ones for training. Comp was the first.

"Greeting Ject."

"To you Comp, I said. I trust you slept well."

Comp Said, "I did, just a little excited."

"The three of you come this way," I said. Walking into the hanger, they marveled at the ships. They were beautiful all in a row. There were six big ships, three shuttles.

Comp ask. "This is what I'm learning to fly?"

I said yes, "Do you have a problem."

Comp said, "know."

I told each of them. "Flying is not all you must learn." You must also learn the art of self-defense. How to fight with a sword. Mostly how to think. It takes all this to be a captain. I give them all test., Comp mastered it.

After the last test, I excused them. I told comp to hang back. I told him he scored the highest of them. You will become my personal captain. I will train you myself. It will be hard you will see in years to come what I say is truth.

"Comp ask, of the others?"

I told him, They will be trained, just not by me. You will train on all the ships they're all different."

CHAPTER 14

Two year had past. Comp worked hard in his training. I must say he was not only a great pilot, Comp was a great warrior. I thought how time slips away. Kohl come from Earth as expected. Lon told me he transferred the DNA. Their children will be very intelligent.

Lon said, Ject my son had grown over a foot, he will be tall over six feet.

Lon said, "I want to go back. Do the same, this time to a different part of Earth. This time I will take my son. Ject I will ask, "May Tudo to come also?" It will be good for the boys. They can do their studies aboard. Lon said, "I did as you requested I buried Madison with Tomeka."

"I ask Lon, "If he transferred, Mya's DNA?"

I did not Ject. "I'm waiting for the right woman. I'm still working on a DNA test."

Lon went to the DNA bank. He took Myas DNA. A single strand, altered it at this point, took the native look away. I will look for an intelligent being here. Angies son was still here. His twin left long ago for Earth. Long time dead.

Morning come early, I went to Joey.

"I ask for a DNA sample" Joey agreed?

Taking the sample. I placed it with Myas until Lon return to Earth.

I said to Ject, "It would be a year before we left for Earth. I told him I had planned to go to the country where there was no Indians. I told Ject the difference in intelligent was greater. I told him the intelligent of Mya and the twins DNA the right woman, the child would be for greater."

I ask Joey, "If he would come to Earth with me?"

Joey ask, "If I do would he die?"

"I told him we would not be there that long. We just need to find a certain woman. You being human you could go off the ship look in the village of Earth. Joey agreed to come with me on our journey to earth.

Angies son and daughter was given Earth names. Maoke saw to that, the girl went back long ago. Joey was going with me. I told him we will leave in several months. Kohl stopped by to see if he would be my pilot. I ask him, "Have you seen Ject?"

Kohl replied, "Know."

I told him, "You must go see Ject." Kohl left the lab for the palace.

I was sitting at the stoop having a Simon. The palace sentry told me "Kohl was waiting to see me.

I went to the great hall, "Greeting Kohl."

Greeting Ject. "Lon said you wish to see me."

I wanted to ask, Are you were happy with the ship"

Kohl replied, "Yes Ject, I'm very happy."

"I told Kohl, it's yours."

"Go explores, My son with Cra, will join you on your next journey" I said. "See if you can help Lon find a human worthy of Myas DNA".

"Maybe I should not go to the ground Ject. Sometimes humans I find, well not so friendly. I am almost human. Yet I do have some native parts."

I told Kohl, I understood, Comp will be going with you.

On our world as the moons set the suns come up. Everyone was at the staging area, I watched until all were on board. I took my son embraced him. I told him, you learn from Comp, listen to Kohl. Watch what Lon does. Lon will be your guardian, while you are away."

Tudo said, "As you wish father. I will make you proud of me." For some reason my son had a look in his eyes ive never seen before.

"Gore said as much," She stood by me until the ship had gone.

Walking to the lab, Lon had left all his work here. I sure hope he knew what he was doing. I went back to the palace.

Karin said, "Ject, I will come back late."

I said to Karin, "I would be leaving for the falls, by the Marder-to-go's at day break." The suns set with the rising of the moons. I was on the stoop when a light appeared in the sky. Closer and closer a ship it was coming here. The ships landed on the staging area. It was Cam.

The ships turned, the ramp went down. Standing dressed in black, a cape blowing as he walked.

"Greeting my friend," Our hands met.

Ject Cam said, "let me look at you."

I said to Cam, "You have been gone too long." I ask Cam," Tell me of his travel?"

"Ject I've been everywhere. I will tell you this, In the Earth galley of the Milky Way." There is so many planets. Planet with humans, others also. Ject is it ok for my crew come ashore. You will know them."

"I told Cam, "Tell them to come off, tell them to come stay if you like, the hanger is available."

"Ject I need to see Bota."

I told Cam, Bota is no longer here.

Cam ask, "Who oversees the building?"

I said, "Lon is, he has gone to earth. Lon is the son of Cha."

I said to Cam, "He too has left for a more permanent place. Cha has gone to the ancient city."

Cam said, "Well then let's go there."

I told my old friend. "Sorry Cam, even I can't go. Bota can see you maybe he will come here." Cam said to me. "I stopped by my planet Cam said, no one new me. A captain asks my name? Ask about the ship.

I ask Cam, "Was his name Jung?"

"Ah Ject, "You have met him."

"Only once," I said. "He said the next time he saw me he was going to kill me." Tell me Cam, "what did you need to see Bota about."

Cam said, "I need to update my ship."

"I told Cam maybe he could do it himself."

"Ject Botas mind dont work as mine, or you're The intelligent of Bota is far beyond anyone I know. No disrespect."

I told Cam, "Bring the ship to the hanger. "Let's see what we can do." Two weeks later Cam pulled the ship from the hanger. We sat for a long time then he was gone. I never saw my friend again.

Lon's apprentice worked on construction of the ships Lon left. I must say one ship was at completion. It was as the others. I was proud to say, I was happy to live in this time. I'm sure as time come it will be even more than now. Sitting at the chambers I was thinking of Bota, how he loved to go. Well I must say I did to. Time comes and goes. It was time for Kohl to return. As I said that, a ship roared across the city. Kohl loved to fly low, still dont know why. Maybe so I would know he was back.

I walk to the staging area. Opening the hatch, the ramp went down, the first I saw was Lon.

"Greeting Ject," Lon said. Kohl was next then two young one. "My son, and Cra." My son was grown.

Tudo said to me, "Father I left you, a child, I return to you a grown being. Father strange things happen to me. I seemed to grow stronger so did Cra."

I embraced my son. "Your home now."

"Ject it was an education for both boys." Lon said.

I ask, "Of the experiment?"

Lon said, "It didn't work, I'll keep trying."

Lon told me he brought two females.

"I thought we decided not to bring more humans." I said.

"They just wanted to leave Ject

In my thought, why bring more. Things went smooth for the next several years. I would take Comp to the moon of Spores. Garf was building a large city, the works was going good. Comp landed the craft.

Greeting Ject, "Garf said how can I be of service to you."

I told Garf I just needed to get away.

I sometimes need to do that to Graf said. I reminded him of my invitation to the planet. Garf smiled as most humans do. Well Ject how would I get there.

I told Garf to build a building at the landing. "I'll place a shuttle here, with a pilot." Then you could come to the planet. I told Garf to build the building. Make it to house four people. Ah Iced where else would I go.

The ships are to go, to the planet, I said. The captains will have his orders.

"Of course, Ject."

Comp looked at me. "I do not wish to be station here."

"Comp I won't place you here." I'll send the natives. The people of the moon, was very content the way things were going. The humans thank me each time I come to the moon. I always have worked good with humans. After all, I was half human. life on our world went good for the next several years.

Tudo did have Kohl to train him. Kohl told Tudo I was the best pilot there was. Tudo or Kohl never met Bota. Bota was our first pilot. I thought Bota was the best I've seen. Bota was the best, there was no place Bota couldn't put a ship, If it would fit, Bota was you pilot.

I was on the stoop one morning. Lon come in.

"Ject he said, I've done it."

I ask him, "what have you done Lon?"

I have found a way to slow down the aging. "There's nothing I can do for the ones that's already here." I need two humans females Ject."

I said to Lon, "I wish he could find a way to mate with the humans."

"Someday we will Ject just not today."

Tomorrow Lon, "I'll send my son to a planet Bota told me of long ago." He will be going to the planet of Xon. He wants to be a pilot. I'll let him run for a while then as Maoke said to me. It's time for you to stay. When he returns, I'll send him to Earth.

Lon said, "I would like to be part of the voyage."

Lon if you go, dont bring anyone back. "The way I see it we have enough here." Tudo will also be instructed not to bring any one back. Time comes and goes. Tudo left for earth with Lon. Several years had passed. Night had come again to the planet. The city of ratio come alive with lights.

It was a beautiful morning on our world once again. The suns were showing their brilliant colors. Looking to the west a dot appeared. Flying over the city, my son was home. It had been several years since he left. It was time for him to stay home. Time for him to mate. Time to have a son of his own. The west staging area lights were on, the ship set down gracefully. I thought I could not have done better.

I watched my son stepped from the ship. Tudo walk straight to me. I took my sons hand, you have been gone awhile. Lon come from the ship took my hand also.

Lon said, "I understand Ject, I will not leave again." Lon said to me we need council. I told Lon as soon as he was settled.

The crew come from the ship. They took the pride of the planet, stored it in the hanger where it would set for several years.

Hours passed when Tudo come to me.

Father, "I know what you mean you want me to settle down." You want me have a mate, have a family.

Tudo son, "Soon you will take my place as leader, of our race."

Tell me father, "What has happened since I have been on my crusade."

I told my son there has been a boom in the human population. In the time, you have been gone over one hundered have been born. Some moved to the Moon of Spores, some went to the Moon of Corning. Some went to earth.

Tudo ask me, "Where is Kohl?"

"I sent him to Earth, My son. "He should return most any day." He has become a great pilot, better than me.

Tudo said, "I doubt that father"

Tell me son, "You left here on a five year journey, where did you're quest take you."

I said Father, "I went to the Pegasus galaxy." I stayed for a lone while. Then to Valoria. The being there are almost human. I never encountered the Palatonians. One morning my pilot woke me. We were in the earth galaxy of Alpha centauri. I told him we were going home. Father I thought of having Lon try to put communication like from ship to ship.

Tudo said, "I know nothing of this."

I told my father while I was on Valoria I saw this. "I do have some knowledge of this."

I told my son, "To go, do what you must."

Father, I did tell Cra to find a human for me to do the DNA. "I thought of a native, it just takes too long.'

I know son. That's why my father your grandfather. "that's how this whole thing got started."

Time comes it goes. "Cra found a beautiful woman for Tudo." Green eyes. she was as beautiful as the falls at the Marder-to-go's. Tudo met her in the lab. Lying on her back Tudo on his, the transfer began. It was over in minutes. The female was known more than a young girl.

The young girl asks Tudo. "Am I to be your mate as Beth was to Ject".

I said to her, "If it pleases you, you may come to the palace."

Oh, Tudo yes, "It is what I wish, after the baby is born then what."

I told her, "You may live there if you wish." This seemed to please her she smiled. Then walked away.

On the tenth day, she come to me.

Tudo she said. I have conceived, "You will be a father."

I was happy. Father called her Carrie. That's what I shall call her. We were in bed late that night.

Tudo she said. "Do you care for me."

Yes, Carrie I do very much."

"Your emotions are different than the humans," she said. "Tell me Tudo, "Why is it we can't mate with your race?"

I told her, "Our bodies were different than human."

She wanted to see. "Then she said she understood."

I said to Carrie "Someday we will."

Tudo, "A young woman has needs."

I ask her, "What do you mean Carrie."

"Sexual Tudo."

My father told me what I needed to do. "I ask Carrie to undress."

"Carrie said you can't mate with me."

"I know Carrie."

"There's other ways to please a woman. Have you ever had sex with a human?" I ask.

She looked at me with a funny look. "Know she said with a snap."

"I was young to have a child. Only two years more than Mya." My mother said, "I was only two month having my cycle."

I ask Carrie, "Are you sorry you did this, she lay down stretched her body out."

Know Tudo, it was an honor. "Think about it I'm living what my mother said on Earth," I'm called a princess. Tudo I have my palace. She smiled, now show me what your father was talking about im ready.

I said, "Are you know."

I took her, did what I had to do. Twenty minutes later she was sound asleep. Well I thought as I looked down at her lying on the bed, it was good or boring she is asleep.

The morning come with the suns showing their colors.

Carrie was calling to me. "I turned over in bed." Carrie stood over me naked again.

"Tudo it was wonderful can we do it again. "Please Tudo dont stop dont stop."

Finally, she went to sleep. "I left her that way."

Walking to the ready room. "I took a bath, got dressed." I went to the great room I cut a Simon. I took a stalk of Sweet Grass, went to the lab. Cra was lying on a table, a human female was lying beside him. Cra's apprentice was preforming a DNA transfer. She was a very beautiful woman. Something about her, then I knew. It was carries mother.

I ask Cra, "Why didn't you tell me she was carries mother." Why didn't you tell me of the transfer?"

"It was better this way," Cra said.

the woman looked at me, "my name is Nia, Carrie is my daughter. I volunteered for this I was promised a trip back to Earth, as soon as the child is born. I looked at Cra Lon come in.

Tudo Lon said. "Your father has proposed a trip to Earth." The last for many years to come. Nia did this for me. My son needs a child to carry on for me.

I went to the palace, "Father did you know Cra was doing a DNA."

Yes, my son I knew,

"You did not say words to me." My father voice was strong.

I'm still leader of our people. "Until you take my place, you will follow not lead."

I turned to my father. "As you wish, father"

I returned to my sleeping room. Carrie was sitting at the mirror, brushing her hair. Carrie ask, what has you upset Tudo? Your mother has had a DNA transfer from Cra."

My mother Carrie said, "How do you know it's my mother." She told me. "Nia is your mother." Tudo take me to her.

I did as Carrie ask?

In the lab, Nia was lying waiting.

Carrie ask, "mother why did you not tell me."

Carrie after the child is born, "I shall return to earth." I want die, I can live the rest of my life on my world. Tudo told Nia, "you may not die right away. Nia, you surely will die.

Tudo, Cra said. It's her choice I granted this to her. "I should have asked your approval? Cra said, I should have come to you if I had the time. I'm asking you now as a friend.

Mother Carrie ask, "Dont you want to see your grandchild grow?"

Nia looked as Carrie, "I'm giving Cra what he wants to get what I want."

Carrie left to go to the palace. I told her to wait, running to me oh Tudo hold me. Looking into her green eyes, take me somewhere Tudo.

I ask, her where?

She replied, "Somewhere beautiful."

We left the palace, through the city to the path to the Marder-to-go's. I stop just before the fall were visible.

"Why are you stopping?" Carrie ask.

Come here, I felt my human side coming out. "I held her in my arms."

"Are you feeling frisky?" Carrie ask?

I told her, "I did not know the word. Humans words their phrases, are different than we use.

Frisky means, well like in bed the other night. "I told her yes then I'm frisky." I had no clue what she was talking about. Walking on to the falls when Carrie saw the falls, her hands went to her face.

"Oh, Tudo the water is all different colors. How is this possible Tudo?"

I told her, "I was not sure. it's always been here. Maoke talks about it in his writing in the archives. When Maoke and the Unicorn found this, they were looking for the place where we live now. Never, before had they left the city of the ancient."

Carrie ask, "What city."

"The one my people are from, the Busies. It is forbidden even to me. I've only seen it in my dream."

Look how big the Sweet Grass grows. Let's have some, Carrie said."

I told Carrie, "This place the Sweet Grass grows, it is forbidden to eat. I ask her, If she was hungry."

Carrie replied, "Yes, a little."

Carrie had a small meal. lay on the soft grass, looked at me.

"Tudo it's so beautiful, thank you for this day"

Walking back to the palace, we met a sentry.

"Tudo, "I was sent to find you. Your father has asked for you to join him in council."

I ask, "Do you know why the council is called?"

"A ship has arrived, its hovering over the palace."

I told the sentry to take care of Carrie, I started running. Soon the palace come into sight. The ships had landed. I could tell it was Palatonian. The captain was coming from the ship. My father was walking toward them.

"Greeting from Boldlygo."

"Greeting from Plano." Captain Jung was walking behind Cot. Cot took my arm.

"Ject you remember Jung."

"Ah yes, the man said he would kill me the next time he saw me."

Jung said, "I apologize for that." I looked in to his lying eyes. He never meant a word of what he said.

"Cot it is good to see you."

"This is my son Tudo. A great pilot a warrior I'm told."

I told Cot. "let's go to the great room."

I stood by my father, never taking my eyes of Jung.

"Cot, is this a social or business call."

Cot told us about all the thing going on, then Cot ask of the Moon of Spores.

I said, "Why dont we go there."

Cot said, "That will work."

"Tudo have Kohl, ready my shuttle."

"Yes, father as you wish."

The rides to the moon went great. Cot said he has never been here. Landing he told me he was very impressed, with what Garf had done.

I told Cot Garf has done well. We send supplies almost every day. Garf met us at the landing pad.

When he saw Cot, Graf took a step back.

Ject, "Why have you brought this person here."

I ask Garf, "You know him?"

Garf said, "He is the reason were here."

Cot said, "I'm here to see this prison you have built. There is no reason you should hold grudges against me."

Garf looked at me, "Ject you know the story."

I do Garf, "Were trying to start a new relation with Plano."

Garf said, "With Palatonians, not here." They bring rotten supplies, we have yet, to use anything they have sent. It is always bad,"

Cot said, "I know nothing of this."

Garf said, "Why would you, you probably dont know much of anything that goes on. You have people to come to you. They tell you just what they want you to know. Would you show me the prison?"

I must say, "The prison was a marvelous building."

Cot ask Garf, "Anyone here?"

Garf replied, "Know we have no crime here. We have learned to live with one another. Maybe you should try that." Garf said, "Follow me, they're are twenty seven cell. We can house thirty prisoners."

Cot said, "It's kind of strange to build a prison, where there's no crime."

Graf said, "We can house prisoners from other planets. On the back of the prison it is maximum security"

Cot walk in a cell, Jung was behind him. Quickly Cot turned, Jung was in the cell as the door closed.

Cot said to Jung. "You have been found guilty of crime of Plano, the humans, the natives of Boldlygo. You are sentence to ten years in this cell." Cot walked out.

I looked at Jung, "That's justice."

On the way, back to the planet, I ask, "my father about time on our world, why is it different?"

Tudo it is not for me to say. Maoke made this world. I was a part of it long after he made the rules. I do know if you are here for a while you will surly die if you leave. The humans know this. Yet they run to their death often."

Time slowly slips away. One morning Carrie raised up in bed, Tudo it is time.

"I faced this human female I have grown fond of."

I ask her, "Time for what."

Carrie said, "Tudo I swear to be so smart the baby, help me."

Well, I didn't know what to do so i just looked at her.

"Ok Carrie, so what am I to do." Carrie said again,

"Tudo I swear to be so intelligent your stupid. Go find Cra, Lon, somebody, tell them the baby comes.

I did as Carrie ask," I told Cra.?"

Cra ran to Carrie. She gives out a scream a baby cried.

I went to the bed, she was lying looking up at me. She was smiling as humans do.

I looked at my son lying in her arms. My son had blue eyes, as his father as my father so on. Maoke would be proud.

My father asks Carrie, "What name will you give your son?"

Carrie said. "Tudo will name the child."

I told my father, His name will be Ira."

My father said, "Tudo Ira is a strong name." "Yes, it is I said."

Ject said, "He is not the keeper."

Carrie ask, "The keeper what are you talking about?"

"When you're ready I will take you, you can read for yourself."

Carrie rested the day. I entered the room Gore was there with Karin. Sitting on the bed Carrie held out her hand. "I was dreaming I think, Tudo who is Tomeka?"

Why do you ask that?

Carrie said, "I had a dream of her. She is so beautiful."

Gore looked at me, Tudo, "She left long ago buried on Earth."

A sentry come to the door. "Tudo a message. Cra's woman has had a son, come to the lab. A request from Lon."

Carrie said, "Go."

I ask Gore, "If she could stay?"

"She said of course."

Karin, "You come with me." Walking to the lab, the child was lying in a small bed.

Cra said, "A son Tudo."

I ask, "What, has happen to the females? Know females in month. A native had a child yesterday it also was a male child, they named him foo. Cra what is the name for your son."

Cra said, "He will be called Mekon. He will be great in science, as his father so on."

"I'm sure he will Cra, congratulation Cra."

"You to Tudo."

I said, "I must return to Carrie."

It was a great morning, I went to the city to find the native child. I wanted to see him. It took only minutes to locate the family. Walking to the door a voice called. enter! I told them I had come to see the child. Looking down at the child, I told the father. When the child reaches the age, bring him to the palace.

His father said to me, "as you wish Tudo. Tudo may I ask as a father to a father why, I should do this?"

"I can only say. He must take the trail of the staff, as all do at a certain age."

I looked at the child's father. "There's something that tell me he will be a great pilot. I have a captain for him."

"A captain Foo's father said."

Yes, I replied. "My son."

Tudo he said, "Foo is only two days old."

"He will be a wandering man for a while, as you wish Tudo."

I went back to the lab. Several natives, humans waiting.

Everyone ask, "Tudo may we see the baby?"

A voice behind me said, "Here is Tudo's baby." It was Carrie with my father.

I told my father of the visit to the city, to see the native child.

My father asks, "Tudo why does this child lay so heavy on your mind?"

"I'm not sure father."

Kohl, come by today. Kohl was a different kind of being. Mostly human, still has some native look about him.

Kohl ask, "May I make a trip to Earth?"

I told him, I wish I could go with him.

My father said, "Tudo you must stay here, your son, Carrie."

"Yes father I know."

Kohl said, "Lon would be coming along with me. He still looks for a female to transfer Mya's DNA."

The morning came with the suns showing their colors. It had been two month since Ira was born. Ira was with me on the pad as the supplies were being loaded. The ships were ready to leave. Kohl in the captain seat. I sent Comp with him. It would be great experience for him. Comp would be a great help to find a female for Myas DNA. Comp had been on Earth once before long ago. Tudo and I stood on the pad as the ship went to space. Our day here come to an end as the suns set. Tudo come to me with question?

Tudo ask me, Father tell me of Mya, how powerful was she.

I told my son, Go to the archives, read of the things she did, Mya at thirteen had a child. When she was eight she was teaching school. To all our people, humans as well as natives.

"Father you said she was powerful. How did she obtain the power, she was born with them? I can't explain son, go to the archives you will learn."

CHAPTER 15

Traveling through space gave me time to think. Ject had told me not to bring any one back. Tudo had already told me, I agreed. Lon told us we would go back to Russia. We would stay in orbit., take the shuttle to the floor. Lon said we would start in Russia. Comp will travel in the village, see if he can find a female. Comp would try to bring her back to the shuttle. Lon did all he could do to help us speak Russian. We had the accent down, we needed to work on the words. We had a long way to go. Days in days out Comp would study. By the time, we reach the moon of Corning Comp was speaking, Russian, very well to I must say. Lon was pleased with our progress. Two months later we landed on the Moon of Corning.

Kohl said, "Comp you go with Lon." I stood watching everyone come to the ship. Kohl introduced me to Quad.

Kohl said to Quad, "This is Comp, my second." Kohl ask me to oversee the supplies.

Quad ask, "If some of his people could go to Earth with us?"

Lon said to Quad, "It will be the young. The older one would surely die."

Quad agreed. Ten humans come aboard.

I set in my seat, as Kohl took the ship higher to the darkness of space.

I ask them, "Why would you leave a place just to die someday?"

One woman said, "Why do you leave your planet, will you not die?"

I told her no, I will return.

She said "So will I someday, or my children."

Traveling through space at the speed of the ship. Well you just didn't worry about time. Lon had found a female. I found him talking to her several times.

Lon said to me, "Comp, she is very intelligent. On the moon, she was a school teacher."

Lon sent for the woman to come to his room. Lon had to try a new way Cra had found, it would take the native look away. He tried once before, it felled now he was sure. If this did not work, the woman would have a child that would look as us. She would be put to death, the child killed. On, Earth it was what was called the dark ages. The time of witches, witch crafts. This woman would be burned at the steak. I have been to this Earth once long ago. The girls we brought back before told us all about it. It was the way with humans, if they didn't understand it they would kill or destroy it.

Lon did talk to the woman. Lon convinced her to take the DNA. Lon told her it would be the greatness thing she could ever do. We will stay for a while to see you are settle before we leave. I stood beside Lon as he spoke.

"Where will you place me?" She, ask?

Lon told her she would be placed in Russia. Before we arrive on Earth we will do the transfer, Lon said. When you have the child, it will be human. Your child, their children will always look to the stars. The child will be very intelligent, the woman said she understood.

The ships travel through space, until it was time to do the transfer. Passing the planet Saturn, the woman marveled at the rings that seemed to circle the planet.

I said to her, "It is a very deadly planet."

Comp she said, "I must say I'm afraid." Lon told me here name was Destiny. Lon said she was Quads sister.

Destiny ask, "This DNA you speak of, who did you say it comes from?"

Lon said, "It come from Mya, she was very intelligent. Mya was Maoke daughter. She was a princess, Royal Blood."

Sitting in the galley Lon said, "You will pass this DNA down through this child. You must tell the child about us. The way we look, our appearance, you must tell the humans of our world. Tell her all the thing you can, the place you're from. Tell her our names. Ject, Tudo, Comp, Kohl. Cra, Lon. Everything I have said to you the child will need to know." I have said to you, "someday we will return. You along Destiny will start our family on Earth with the DNA of Mya. A very powerful being."

Several months later when the ship come from hyperspace, then to full stop. We had arrived at the planet called Earth. Earth a big ball in front of us, Destiny's hands went to her face, so did the hands of the others from Corning.

One said, "It is real. All my life I have been told of this Earth."

Lon said to them, "Now you can stand on this Earth."

Lon called to me. "Comp we will take the shuttle to the floor." Lon said, "long ago Bota with his captain come to Earth to this very place. Bota, Cam met a family, we will look for them. This you would know only if you have read the archives. Bota and Cam found a farm in the region south of what is known as Saint Petersburg."

Lon said, "Comp we will go there first." Lon told me to ready the shuttle. We will go to several places before we leave. We will go to Mexico, that's where Myas mothers people were from.

We will place Destiny in Russian. The people are, well just say a little more advanced, than the Indians.

Destiny all the things I'm telling you, you must understand watch the child. Watch her with all your life being. Watch her as if there is nothing else to do, someday the child will take a mate. The DNA will over power the mate. Their child will be a girl. Mya's DNA will survive through many generations to come.

Flying the shuttle to the place Lon said. In a short time, I said, "We're here."

Lon said, "Comp the people will not remember the old ones. Yet it might have been passed down of Cam and Bota, something as that will not go unsaid."

Kohl set the shuttle down in a clearing behind the grove of woods.

I said to Kohl, "I will send the signal when I have found the people." It wasn't long a small frame house come in to view. The first thing I saw was an old man, he was old for a Earth human. I walked to him as the Earth sun was going down.

I said to him, "I can work for a meal. Maybe a night in the barn, the old man spoke with a heavy Russian accent. Are you running from the Russian, army?

I told him in Russian, I'm not running from anyone one.

The old man smiled as humans do. "Feed the animals the hay is in the barn." I had no clue what he was talking about. He pointed up, standing in the yard I wondered if he had saw me come into the forest.

I ask him, "Up what's up?"

"The hay, he said in the loft."

Climbing the ladder, he pointed to. I went up, the loft was packed with dead grass, I thought this must be hay. I threw several arms full down. The old man sit on a log when I came back down.

Come here he said, "You are not from here?"

I told him, "I'm was not."

In fact, "he said you're not even from Russian."

I told him I was not.

The old man said again in our words.

I watch the stars he said, "long ago someone come from the stars. I was not born, not even my father he said. Then once long ago I see again. Now you come. Tell me why you come to Russia."

I did not lie to him, there was no need. He already knew of us.

I told him, We look for a place to leave someone, a female, She is with child.

The old man said, "Bring her." I stood give the signal, less than an hour the shuttle landed. Kohl walked down the ramp with Lon and Destiny. In the house the old man said to a woman as old as him.

The old woman told Lon, The girl would be taken care of. When we pass, the house will go to her. She will be taken care of by all our friends, the ones we have.

"You, tell me the old man ask. You're not from here?"

I said to him. "We are not from here, we are from beyond the stars." I told the old ones as we said our goodbyes. Someday we will return, please tell all that is to come.

I embraced Destiny, told her she will be proud of the child. We went aboard the ship left for new Mexico.

The shuttles were prepared to leave. I walked to the edge of the desert. A small fire we saw, someone behind me said stop. Lon turned, an Indian screamed, let loose an arrow it took Lon in the chest. I reached for Lon as Kohl ran into the Indian knocking him out. I picked Lon up from the ground carried him to the shuttle. Now I didn't know much about wounds, seeing Lon the way he was. Well I know it was over for him. The rasping of breath, Lon kept saying Comp protect her. Well I knew who he was talking about. Lon died in my arm as I made my way to the sick room. It was a long empty feeling.

Kohl I said, "let's go to the big ship."

Kohl flew the ship as fast as it would fly.

I was impressed of the speed. I ask Kohl, "What do we do with the body?" I had no idea.

Kohl said, "I know where to go. I have been there before."

That night we took several humans to the planet floor.

Comp, Kohl said, "This is the place where the family is buried." The Indians saw the shuttle coming from the heavens. They knew we had returned. The tribe was waiting, when we come from the ship.

Welcome, "You come to visit the graves of the father and mother of the stars?"

Kohl said to them, "I am Kohl, this is Comp he is my friend. We must add another body to the ground."

The Indian replied, "We knows you we have seen you in the heavens, as you move across the night skies. The sprits call, we come here. They call to us in the night, they called tonight.

We dug a hole buried Lon. Kohl marked his grave. Lon a great teacher of the stars.

The Indians were a custom to our ways. Bota, Tomeka, Maoke.

I told them, Bota was a great sprint, running through the heavens. Ject you know Ject. He, give a nod.

The Indians ask for us to follow them. In the village as it was, sitting around the fire. Food was brought to us. It was simple food. There was meat, yet they did not offer it to us. A small girl brought us bread, corn. The little girl give me a sweet red fruit, she called it a berry. I found I liked very much.

The day faded into the late evening. Kohl said, "We need to go. We told the Indians goodbye. The ramps went up we were on our way to the big ship. There were twenty more humans left on board.

I told Kohl, We will place them in England, the others Spain. Then we need to go home. Everyone agreed.

Kohl said," I must take this moment to tell the crew, how great they have been."

I told Kohl, Thanks for letting me co-polit his ship. Maybe someday I'll have my own ship.

Kohl replied, "Yes you will Comp."

After placing the humans on Earth, we started our trip back home. I knew how importance this was, Lon had been killed. Flying through the night of space, planet after planet. It to me was all the same.

It was hard to believe my ancestors did this. The Indians on Boldlygo were nothing as the ones on Earth, I suppose it's different in the existence. It was hard to believe what I have become to what they still are. Humans will always kill what they don't understand. It's always been that way. This gene is in their DNA. Maybe they're just not educated enough. Maybe it's the difference in cultures, I was not sure. Before my people were brought to Boldlygo, I wondered how they ever survived riding horses and killing animals for food. Living in skin made houses, my mother and my grandmother would tell stories of the wars. How they fought with other tribes, sometimes until no one was left. They called it survival.

My thoughts went to Ject. Ject had witnessed the imprisonment of Jung, placed there by his own King. He will be an emery of ours I'm sure of that. We have no defensives as I know of. The staff I thought, how does it work. Who holds the power how can you control it? Really does it have power at all? Could it be, it's just a staff. Personally, I've never seen it work. Old Maoke found the thing stuffed away in the relic of time. Ive seen it, Ject keeps it in the palace. Maybe the staff was meant for his grandson.

I ask Kohl, "Did Tudo name his son Ira, hoping he would be the one?"

Kohl said, "He had no idea if that was true."

I stood from my captain chair. Looking through the portal. Comp, we Have a partner.

I told Kohl I'll alert the crew. I didn't call in time.

A native called out, "We have a ship." The native, ask "What do we do we have no weapons?"

Kohl said stop the ship, "let them board us."

Dropping out of hyperspace to stop, the ship come around docked to the ship. I open the hatch stepping through the hatch I could not believe my Boldlygo eyes. Walking into the ship was a woman so beautiful.

"Greeting from Bangor," she said.

I said, "Greeting from Boldlygo." I told the girl, we have no communications. We can't talk to you or anyone.

"Where are you from," she asks?

Kohl said, "Boldlygo."

She asks, "Where is this Boldlygo planet?" Then Comp messed it up.

Comp said, "You look like a Palatonian to me."

The woman turned quick, pointed a weapon of some kind, at Comp. A ringing sound so severe I could hardly stand. She dropped her weapon the others also. The ringing stopped.

"What kind of weapon, is this?" She asks. I looked at the native he just shrugged his shoulder.

I told her, It was a secret weapon.

The, woman said, "We mean you know harm. We're on our way home we still have a way to go. Maybe eighteen months.

The female, ask, "Why are you out here?"

I told her, We have been to the planet called Earth.

She replied, "They are a primitive race. The female said, My government was looking for a planet, the same as Bangor." She showed me on the map where they went on Earth.

I told her, I have been there, there's land enough, fresh water. The oceans with miles of sand.

She looked at me, "Maybe someday you will stop then."

I replied, "Yes maybe."

The woman took her escort went back to their ship. Breaking loose from the ship, then were gone.

When things got back to normal, I ask them, "What was with the ringing." "Kohl, how long you been on the planet the native asks?"

I told him, Since my birth thirty years.

Kohl ask me, I told him about the same? Why you ask?

Ject never told you Kohl.

Told me what, I said.

"Kohl, all natives have a weapon built in. Part of Maokes DNA. He told Bota and Cha that long ago. That's what was said by our family's I'm thankful for it. I told Comp, he should be captain."

I replied to Kohl, "Not me, I'm happy where I'm at."

Kohl said to me, "When I return home I'll talk to Ject of this.

After the encounter of the ship. We, begins to do our duties. Kohl and I talked of the encounter for weeks.

Kohl told me," I would like to meet her again, on different conditions."

Kohl ask, "If I had someone?"

I told him know, I'm a pilot. Ject said mates an pilot dont mix. There once was a female I was serious about. She returns to Earth long ago. I'm sure she is dead now.

Kohl, ask, "You ever think why people live, as they do on Boldlygo."

Kohl, Ject said, "It was the way Maoke was when he created our paradise."

Kohl ask me, "How old do you think Maoke was?"

Kohl, "I dont think anyone, know how old Maoke was." Ject told me all Busie were old.

I told Kohl, You think they would just give up.

I left Comp in charge of what we called the bridge. It had something to do with the levels, in the control room. I went to my sleeping room. I must say I slept very peaceful. Somewhere in my deepest thought, I drifted away to the woman that come aboard our ship. I dreamed we were together on Boldlygo, hand in hand walking the path to the Marder-to-go's. Then she was gone, faded away. I set up in bed. Well I thought, where did that come from. My first encounter, whoa! how could a woman as her hold that kind of power. A tiny voice from somewhere, "Kohl let it go."

What, What I said, "Who's there." I laid back down, fell into a peaceful sleep. I found myself again with her. She was waving come to me. She stood in front of me long dark hair flying in the breeze. She called to me saying I will give you what you seek. Her hair was the longest I've ever seen. She had the biggest eyes I've ever seen, cold, dark eyes. Eyes that would let you love her, eyes that would take charge, I sat up wide awake. Sweat beads on my face, all I could think about was her. I comb my hair dressed went to the bridge.

I relieved Comp so he could go rest. Through my duties, all I could think of was the woman I had met before. Why I'm not sure, walking around I was checking the instruments. On the screen a small blimp come on the scope. Returning to my seat, I called the crew. Everyone was running to their stations.

A native said, "It's a ship Kohl."

I ask them, "Can you tell where the ship was from?"

One natives said, "Kohl it's the same ship."

"I was to think they were going home. Come to a stop."

"Stop! I want to see why they're still there." The ships caught up fast. Coming along beside us, then docking. The hatches opened, the female come forth she was alone. The hatches closed behind her the ship departed.

She smiled then said, "I wanted to see you again."

She walked to me, grab my hair through my head back kissed me. It was good, longing for the feeling I've never had. I left the bridge I took care to show her around the ship, my room first.

The crew knew where I'd be, if there were trouble. I sure hope there was no trouble. Hours had passed, I return to the bridge.

One of the crew said, "Kohl, you know nothing of this female. How are you to explain her to Ject. You agreed not to bring anyone back."

I ask him, "Is comp still asleep?"

The native replied, "Yes I don't think we should carry her back with us, with Lon dead. Cra will want to morn is father's death."

I told them, Cra will accept it. He knows his father will ascend."

The native said, "I sure would hate to see you beside Jung, on the Moon of Spores."

I said as I went to the controls. "I would hate that to." I set thinking as Comp entered the bridge,

"What's all the chatter?" I ask.

"I explain the girl, Comp sat down."

"Kohl, what was you thinking."

I told Comp, I wasn't, its she is so beautiful.

I said to Kohl, It's done, let's make the changes carry on."

I said, "Kohl do you even know her name."

Kohl hesitated, "Yes uh its Joy."

"Where is she now?" I said.

"She is in my room." Kohl said.

Let's go Kohl, "Introduce me to her." Walking to Kohls room, opening the door. The room was empty, I turned looked at Kohl. "Dam it Kohl." I hit the alarm on the intercom I told all to look for her. I mean where could she go. We went one way she went to the bridge. Everyone was searching everywhere. "Kohl where the hell, is she." We felt the ship turn, made a dash to the bridge. Everyone was upset, this female had locked us out of the bridge. She had control of the ship.

One of the female natives come forward, "You see Kohl." She said.

I told her, I need to get in. There's no telling where we're going.

The native girl made a wave with her hand, the door open. Kohl and I ran to the control.

Joy turned, "What is this?"

I took control of the ship. Comp set the controls back on course we were headed home once again.

I told Kohl, I'll placed her in the room next to you. Since you want to be close to her.

Kohl said to me. "Comp I know what to do with her."

I looked at Kohl, "Really I said."

Koh said, "Take her to the Moon of Spores." Garf will be pleased.

I kept her in the room all night. On the morning as it was in space, Kohl brought her to me. Kohl, you you are captain. You tell us what to do with her.

I ask her, "Why did you try to steal our ship?"

She replied, "My captain said it would be easy."

I said to her, "We want be defeated so easily."

Joy ask, "What will happen to me now?"

Kohl ask her, "Are they still following us."

She said, "No."

Kohl listen as, I said to her. "You tried to steal a ship. That a death penalty on any planet."

She said to Kohl, "Was I knot good in your bed." She looked at me with those big brown eyes. Her long dark hair falling to her back, with just a stream of hair over her face. I tell you she was all woman. Of course, I have never had one before. Comp even said she was beautiful.

One of the natives said, "Kohl we cannot carry her to her planet."

Well, then I said, "I suppose we will carry her to the Moon of Spores. Then we will go talk to Tudo and Ject. We need to explain what happen. The council about Lon, then with her."

"Ject will want details." one native said.

I said to Kohl, "Ject will want to know how we brought a female on our ship. Then let her steal the ship. We'll be lucky if Ject dont place us all on the Moon, of Spores."

Kohl took her weapon. Kohl called for a council of all on the ship. We decided to let her out. She just would not leave me alone. Touching me kissing me, I loved it. It was my first time to ever be with a woman. In my mind, I could not get enough. The humans on the planet, all the humans I've been around, this just wasn't right. deprived all these years, of such a feeling. How could this have been hidden for us.

I ask, "Comp?"

He said, "I have never, I mean as old as we were."

You would think, our parents would have told us, they never told us. They would say, someday you will take a mate. They never told me of this. I wonder was it to be a secret. Did they think, it would come natural. I can't say I just wanted more.

The next day as it was in space, being dark all the time. Old Bota when he built his first ship, how did he know, to build a ship. A Busie was the most intelligent being in the universe. They had powers beyond belief.

Comp said, "Man you need to get with it." Kohl, he called. I did not hear him.

I told Kohl, That woman has gotten to you. I dont know what you were thinking.

I said to Kohl, "We have a ship following us. It's not the same one."

I said, "let me show you something Ject showed me." The ships caught us, I took the ship to stop. The other ship went flying by as if we were not there.

Comp, Kohl said, "let's go off course." Go back to hyperspace. We were gone in a flash.

"Ject taught you well." Kohl said.

Sitting in front of the controls gives a man time to think, nothing around so you just think.

Kohl spoke to me, I didn't hear him.

Touching me on the arm I jump. "What!"

Kohl ask, "Where were you."

I was thinking of old Bota. "Kohl, you ever think of them."

Kohl said, "Way before my time. I never knew them."

"Just think about it. How did Bota, know to build a ship to fly through space. How did he know, the way the outside was supposed to be? The floors the lighting, the wiring even if it is wiring. We dont know. When we arrive back home when things settle down. I will go to Cra, ask him if I can help make a ship. I need to know all this. I'm also going to ask Ject, if I can read Botas journal."

"Ject will have no problem with that," Kohl said. "Just go to the archives in the city."

"First thing first" I said to Kohl." "First the girl, to the Moon of Spores. We will make our report, then stand in front of Ject."

Days passed into month. We were only four month before home. The girl came to me, she held me close, whispered in my ear. You going to place me in a prison. As she said those words, she touched me, all at the same time. It was like I was freezing, that feeling there's nothing like it. The next thing I knew we were in bed again. She showed me thing I could never possible think of. The feeling I had when we were together, the feeling afterwards.

She asks me, lying in my arm. "Can you take me to see you King?"

I told her, We have no King. Ject was the elder, the leader.
She said, "Take me there first."
I looked into those eyes, "No" I said.

The ships come from hyperspace to impulse, then to stop.
We were at the Moon of Corning. I jump up dressed went to the
bridge. Comp had the shuttle ready.

Comp ask, "Kohl, where is the girl? Kohl looked at me with
a blank look.

He said, "She is sleeping."
I ask him, "You want to leave her asleep on the ship.".
Kohl said, "I see what you mean." I went back to my room
Joy wake up. Your coming with me.

"Where are we, she asks?" I told her were at the Moon of
Corning. Know I'm not going there. She took a swing at me I'm
not going. I thought, what have you done there. Come on Quad
will be happy to meet you. Know I'm staying, she was screaming,
kicking calling me names. Leave me alone you take me there will
tell him you made a sex slave of me. I pulled her into the shuttle.

"Quad will keep me" she said. "Quad will kill you."
Well I looked at her, "What makes you say that."
Joy said, "Quads my father." Comp was walking in circles.
"Kohl this is bad." Kohl said, "I think he will know better.
I'm sure he knows the ways of his daughter."

"If he asks, "I'll tell him the truth?"
Joy, said, "I'll kill you Kohl if you take me there."
"let's see what happens." Kohl said.

Joy said, "Take me to the Moon of Spores, I wish to go
there.

I ask Joy, "How long have you been gone?"
Joy said, "Twenty years."
"Joy, there's has been several changes thanks to Bota."
She replied, "Not that much for me."

The landing pad was as always. Quad was there to meet us.
Walking down the ramp.

Quad said, "Greeting Kohl."

Quad ask, about Ject?"

I told him I was not sure, we're coming from Earth" "Quad I have a female on the ship, I didn't know who she was. She tried to still my ship she tried not once, twice. Quad she said, "She was your daughter."

I swear Quads face turn colors.

"Take her from here. I have known reason to see her, after what she has done to the family. Kohl, we may not have much, we do have our pride."

I said to Quad, "We'll load the supplies, Ject said give you two stones, one for luck."

Quad answered, "Yes Kohl as always."

The girl stood in the hatch way, Quad looked at her. I could tell he wanted to call to her. Quad turned walked away.

I'm staying Kohl," Joy said, "I'll go to the city find a ship back to Bangor."

"Joy if that's what you want." I said, "I'm sure the crew won't mind." Joy starting walking toward the city. Quad called to her, Joy froze in her tracks she turned.

"Father, I am truly sorry for the the way I've been. I'm sorry for my mother. I have found something I want to spend my life with, he doesn't won't me."

Quad ask her, "What would that be?"

"Behind you father, the mans behind you."

Quad turned to me, "Is this true Kohl?"

I dropped my head. "I love her, I do."

"Then stay with us," Quad said. "I need my daughter Kohl."

"I didn't know you really felt this way of me Joy. I just thought you wanted to steal my ship. I do care for you, I do." Quad I said, "let me go to my world. Tell Ject of what happen to Lon. Comp will bring me back, maybe even Tudo."

Joy ran to me.

Oh Kohl! "Yes, I will wait for you."

Quad, held out his hands. Joy went to him.

Standing on the ramp, the human side showed. I feel, I have fallen in love, for the first time in my life. It was a feeling I kind of enjoyed."

Joy said before I closed the ship. "Kohl, I'm sorry I tried to take your ship. I will be here when you return."

The shuttles returned to the ship. We off loaded the supplies. Thirty minutes later I took the ship to hyper space. We were going home.

CHAPTER 15

L eaving the Moon of Cornings air space.
Kohl said to me. "Comp take control of the ship."
Two months in flight, I sent a sentry to Kohl.

Coming to the bridge Kohl ask," Are we home.?"

"I told him we were. I drop the ship out of hyperspace.

I ask Kohl, "You want to take us to the floor?"

Coming from hyperspace to impulse the planet just before
us, the Moon of Spores to the right.

Kohl took the ship to the floor passing the city of Ratio
flying low. If Ject was was on the stoop, he would be happy. I
know flying a ship was his first love. Captain, of a ship like this
would be the greatest feeling a being could have, well almost
anyway. The west staging area was lit as we descended to the pad.
Tudo was there with two small children.

Ject, Cra, come from the lab, the ramp went down. I stepped
out, then Comp, then the natives. "Greeting," Ject said.

I walk straight to him, "Ject we need council as soon as you
can call one. I told Cra to come also". Walking to the great room,
"Cra ask, of his father?"

I repeated, "What, had happen on Earth? Cra your father
is dead. He was killed by an Indian one from a tribe we knew
nothing about."

Cra said, "He was a good being, very intelligent. I own all I am to him."

Cra, never spoke of it again.

I sat with Kohl, as he told the council about Joy. I never knew she was Quads daughter. I left her on the moon, with him.

"Ject, with your permission. I would like to return to her. Quad, request I return to her also."

Ject said to me, "Kohl you're a good pilot, you will be missed. What will you do on Corning?"

I said, "Work with Quad in his business."

Tudo spoke, "Kohl you are a good pilot. I dont want to see you throw away everything. If you should want to come home, home is always here."

Tudo said, "Father I'll take him with my two sons."

"You have two sons now?" Kohl ask.

Tudo replied, "Yes Kohl, Ira you know, Ren my youngest. The journeys will be good for them.

Ject said "I suppose it will."

Ject said, "Take Comp with you, then return here take his crew.

"Tudo send Kohl to me before you leave."

Kohl went to the palace before the ship left. Entering, the palace the sentry stopped him. Kohl, told the sentry Ject, had sent for him. The sentry said, "follow him." In the council chambers Ject, was standing at the stoop cutting a Simon.

"You wish to see me Ject."

Come in Kohl, "You have been a great captain." I had planned a long life for you here. I wished for a long life there.

"I fell in love."

Ject said, "Love, I wonder about the feelings I have for the humans. Is, that love I cannot say."

"It's a powerful feeling I'm sure. As I've said Kohl, if you ever want to return come home."

I told Ject, "All I want to do is to hold her in my arms have children." Quad said, I could share in the business. Always Ject we will have trade with Boldlygo."

Ject said, "Tudo with his two sons will go with you. Kohl, I have only one request".

What would that be Ject. "Train the boys while you're in route to your new home. They can learn much in the time it will take to go to the moon.

I told Ject, I will do, as you ask?

The ships left the on the morning. Ject watched the crew go aboard. Cra let Mekon come along. He told Tudo it would be good for him. Mekon was growing, I've never seen a more intelligent being. He will find a way for the humans and natives to mate. If not him his off spring. I feel this in my body sure as the moon. The suns rise they set, Mekon will find away. Little did I know Cra had already found a way. He would keep it to himself for several years to come.

Karin, Gore came to the palace.

Ject they called. I told then I was on the stoop, come join me.

Gore ask, "Is there something I could do?"

I told them I was going to the falls. I will be gone for a while, since the boys were gone I thought I would go away for a while myself.

I took the path to the falls, there were several natives, on the trail. They would say to me. "Ject good to see you out."

"I did speak to them, I would keep walking." It was always good to get away. From the time of my birth, well until the time I could remember. The human always seemed full of energy. Even my sister Mya. Mya, was more human than me, she looks more human, I loved her. I truly miss her gone for several hundered years. When will it be my time, what keeps me here I can't say. Each time I sat alone many thought ran through my mind. Still the one thought I think of most, the Keeper of the staff. The white hair girl. When will they come.

I reached the falls took my sandals off. Placed my feet in the water, from downstream I heard a noise.

It sounds as someone walking. I placed my sandals on, walk down the stream bank, I saw nothing.

I pulled a Simon sat on the ground. Found a small bush, a soft patch of grass went to sleep. Waking up what seemed hours. I felt like I had slept for a hundered years. I looked around, I was not where I went to sleep.

Hello, a voice called, from behind me. "It was my mother and father. "Where am I?" I ask.

My father said, "You are close, to the ancient city my son."

Ject when it's time, "You will come here to live."

Father I said, "I thought the city was for the Busies."

It is my son, "It's also for a few natives, some humans always for the Royal Blood. The rests go to a different plain. The chosen watch over the city and the palace. That was our promise to the humans. "I do remember, mother I ask, "Where is mya.?"

"She in in the city Ject."

I ask, "When can I see her?"

"Soon my son, soon." I woke up to see I was where I went to sleep. A fading voice in the air as the wind, It want be long my son.

"I spoke with a whisper. I must see my son, my grandsons, I need to tell them stories. I would love to go to Earth once more. Just to look upon the miles of oceans. The mountains, to see the stuff the Indians call snow. It's very cold, I would love to smell the smell of rain".

"I will do that. I will go to Earth, one more time." Visit my family's graves. Maoke, Tomeka Mya. Where is Angie, I never thought to ask of her. I went back to the palace, took fruit set on the stoop, overlooking the Valley of the Unicorn. I thought hard on the decision I made today. Standing on the stoop I knew Maoke could see me through the portal. They have told me they watch us always. They also know when things trouble me.

The day had been very trying. I went to my sleeping room. I was making ready for the night. I laid in bed for several hours. Sleep finally caught up to me. Again, I found myself floating over my bed.

A voice called to me. "Ject come to me." Faster I went to the falls, over the Marder-to-go's.

Below, I saw a valley of mist. Looking across the valley all I could see was clouds. "Who called to me I ask?" "Where am I?"

"Your with me Ject". I turned to see, it was Mya. I ran to her, we embraced what seemed, a long time. Mya, told me of all the thing I had ask Maoke?

Sorry Ject, "I couldn't come to you before."

I ask Mya, "Where is Angie?"

Mya said, "Angie is in a different place, Holding Myas hand I didn't want to let her go."

I ask, "How did our mother come here?"

Mya said to me. "Ject mother is here because father died on Earth. Father could have lived forever. To have mother here, it was his choice. Remember Royal Blood, your time Ject is almost here. Soon you will come to the city.

Mya I ask, "Do I die?"

Mya said, "Ject it's the only way."

I told her, "I truly would like to spend time with my grandchildren. I would love to go to Earth once more.

"Go Ject." Mya said, "Tudo can control thing here him and Cra."

"Ject if you go to Earth, I have one request. Stop on the Moon of Corning. Tell Pep I miss him."

Mya I ask, "Do you think that would be a good thing?"

She thought, then looked at me. "Tell him anyway."

"As you wish Mya." I woke up in a sweat rapid breathing. I finally saw Mya".

Tudo, would be a great leader, of our people. However, I will not tell him of the encounter of Mya. Gore, and Karin, came to the palace. Sitting in the court yard Gore, said to me.

Ject, "All my children my grandchildren have left." It's time we move on.

I ask her to explain. "We're used up, we would like to return to Earth. Ject when you return to Earth please take us with you."

I ask, "What about my grandsons?"

Gore said to me. "Ject you are very intelligent. Tudo also, the boys will be even more you will see." "Even at the small age. It's as their mind never stops. i said to them,

"I know there intelligent. Answering your question."

"Where would you want to go?" I ask.

Gore said to me," Where Bota found me? Believe me I have not regretted one moment here. Take me where you placed Tomeka, Mya, Maoke."

I said to Gore, "So be it."

Tudo was on his way to the Moon of Corning. I could tell, even Tudo wanted to go back. The loves of space were in our DNA. This I believe Bota did, the thrills of space was there, my father only left the planet twice. Bota took him up in the very ship I took to Earth. Bota was a great ship right. He was the first to leave the planet. Per Bota's journal him, Cam and the Unicorn. I often think of Cam. The ships he had was Botas' first. I always hope someday he would have brought it back. Maybe for a museum, so natives, humans could see part of the the beginning.

I think some times of thing that has happen, since my birth. Things that will happen after I'm gone. It all started here in the beginning. Maoke, Bota, Cha, Tar Kia, all in the beginning. Look where it has taken us. Looking over the city, beyond the valley, to the mountains. I thought how wonderful life was here in our world.

Maoke, knew what he was doing, when he took the walk with the Unicorn. From the ancient city to the Marder-to-go's.

Maoke looked for days before he found what he was looking for. I thought how close it was. The place through the portal, the city of Ratio was built. Look what it has become, thousands of years later.

My father was never the same after the loss of Tomeka. Then losing Mya he gives up. Maoke had another plan. One, I knew nothing about, actually no one did. Maoke died on Earth, placed beside my mother, on one side, Mya on the other.

Mya, said my time was soon. Where will I die, maybe with Gore, or Karin. If I stay here I will live forever. Mya said my time was soon. What is soon, how long is that? I cannot say.

Tudo, will be gone for several months. I sat alone watching the world go by. Cra, come by to see me today. We talked for what seemed hours. Cra said to me.

"Ject you want believe the accomplishments I've made in the strand of DNA."

"I could see something was on his mind." I ask, "Something you wish to talk about Cra?"

Cra said, "Ject I miss my father? I know were not supposed to have feeling. I feel as the humans do."

I told Cra it because your half human. I told him I miss my father also.

Cra said, "You have seen you father Ject."

I replied, It was a dream Cra." Only a dream.

"I have no dreams, only memories I have."

I told Cra "I would be going to Earth soon. I'm telling you this, you will be the only one to know Gore Karin will also go."

Cra said, "Ject they surely will die. I also will not return my time is near. Tudo will be a good leader. He is my son you will see."

Cra replied. "Ject I have no problem with Tudo. He is a good being, with two sons. They will be great as my son," Cra said.

I told him there was no doubt.

"I have notice Cra, each generation the intelligent level is higher. It's always will be Maoke, said that."

Cra ask, "How did Maoke know what would be in the future?"

I ask, "You ever read the print?"

"In the archives of time, I read of humans that will come. Ject That's how I started to go more in depth with the DNA."

I told Cra, I have not read that. Ive read some of the writing of Maoke. All, of Bota's journals. Some of the writing of Tomeka, Angie.

"Ject you say your time is near. You need to go read the archives of time. Everything is there, the Keeper of the staff, the white hair girl. The great son that will be a traveling man. The daughter that will stand with the keeper. Ject, how does someone know what will happen, thousands of years before it happens?"

"They're called time keepers Cra."

I told Cra, "I will go in the morning to read this."

The next morning I went to the archives. Picking up a Simon a stalk of Sweet Grass, I left for the city.

Entering the archives, I pulled the book and opened it. There it was Maokes writing. The very first prints he ever made. Today I looked through the portal. I looked upon our world, it went on forever. I turned back one hundered pages. It must have been over two thousand years before.

My son is here with me, I call him Maoke. He will be great with our race. In years to come the Busie will be extinct. We must find, some way to save our race.

Somewhere across the great space of time, is a planet called Earth. I stopped, I'm reading my grandfather's work.

How did he know. I continued to read, In time there will be changings come to Boldlygo. Human man will come. A scientist will construct a flying machine. The humans will save us. We must build them a city so grand. We must protect them of all thing to come. In time, they will love us, we must survive. I read on for hours. How far can I go, the words we speak now, the print was on paper. The old language, has been replace by the words we speak now.

You will see my son, all sons to follow. Maoke, looked for help in area you would not think, there would be thing. The staff will help protect you from harm that is to come.

You my son, you're not the keeper. He will come as I write these words. So, all may understand in the hundered of years, thousands of years to come. There will come a white hair girl. She will be queen. By the females side part native part human. A native will be leader, my son he will be the leader. A female to come, a human. She will be strong with power. Then two then three so on. There will be a great war. The Keeper of the staff, with the daughter of a queen will stand.

I stopped reading, closing the book, never to open it again. The words were enough to let me know we will survive. The DNA Cra is working on it will work. It will not happen in my life time, to know it will work is enough for me. I'll be in the city watching through the portal at the ones I leave behind. My sons their sons will be great with our race.

I left the archives walked to the lab. Talk to Cra about his DNA.

Ject Cra said. "I will soon be able to test it. I must be sure, the only thing I'm getting old like you. Ject we're over five hundred years old."

I told Cra about my dream of Mya. She said I would soon be with her. Sometimes I wish she was still here, I miss her so much.

Your grandson, Cra said, "Ira to be ten years old, so is my son Mekon. If I took them to Earth, by the time we returned they would be fourteen."

I told Cra, "I do not wish them to be there when I ascend."

My friend, "I wish you to stay here with them."

Cra, "This will be a journey for me to complete myself."

"As you wish Ject." I said.

Cra," have Tudo take the boys to the archives." Have them study all the print, even before, Maoke? That's where I found the greatest writing. They will need it for the generations to come. For all that is written has happen, all that is written will be. They will need it to survive, in the future. Cra you could read forever, I dont think you could ever read it all. When I'm gone tell my son to lead his people. Human, natives alike."

"Let the boys talk to everyone. They need to learn, teach Mekon everything you can."

Ject I said, "He, already knows more than I did when I was his age." He will be great with our people Ject you will see."

I ask Cra, "Tell me of the DNA you're working on?"

"Cra said, "I'm not sure, not completely."

"Your DNA must be taken placed in a female. Then when you die the essence placed back into the bobby."

I just looked at Cra.

I know Ject, "It sounds complicated. It probably will be, I feel it will work. The body will lay in dormant until the essence is restored. That's why I need to go to Earth. When the essence is placed back in the body if I'm right, you can shift to human or stay as a native. You, could shift to most anything.

Cra, has finally lost it I thought. "Cra I know your still grieving your father's death. I need you to be real."

I am Ject, "Not only can you shift to human form, you can have sex with a human. Dont you see Ject it's what Maoke and Bota started, I'm almost sure."

"I told Cra, "I'd drop by later." Walking to the palace I stopped, walked back. I took one look, then asks? "If you can do that on Earth, why can't you do it here?"

Remember Ject, "You can't die here."

I felt kind of stupid. "Yes, Cra I suppose your right."

"Ject Tudo will be here with the boys soon, wait for you ascension. I need to go to Earth. I'll take Mekon with me. He will need to see this done. The experiences this trip will be very helpful for the DNA. Ject, come to Earth with me, bring the boys."

I know what he had planned. My lifelong friend wanted to ascend as I did. Die means go to another place. The ancient city I would be with Mya, my mother, my father.

I was getting on in years, not as Maoke. Of course, no one knew how old he was. I've done more with my life than most. Ive been a captain, a pilot, Ive been to eight teen galaxies. Hundered of planets. I truly would love to have a treaty with Plano, before I leave. Tomorrow I would like to go to Plano, I have no pilot.

Something about morning here on my world. I Watch the suns come over the mountains as I walk to the lab. Cra was having his Simons.

"Morning Ject," he said.

I nodded my head.

Cra ask, "Something on your mind Ject?"

I told Cra, "I needed to go to Plano, I want be gone long."

"Do you have a pilot?" Cra ask.

I replied know. "I could take the shuttle myself. Cra I need to know they will be allies to us. Cra agreed. I want be gone long."

Cra said to me, "Go Ject I'll take care of thing here."

I went to the palace, looked past the Valley of the Unicorn. Mother, father, if you see me you know what I must do. Mya said, "soon I would be with you. I'm getting old, I'm going to Plano. I must have a treaty before I leave. I dont want them to attack our world. As you know, we have known weapons. I'll take the staff of Ira with me. Just this once, let me feel the power of the staff. let me show them the power we have. My people mean more to me than all the power you could possess in a Staff. I need to protect them, natives, and humans. I wasn't sure if they were there at the portal. I just hope they were. I hope they hear me."

Inside the palace, in a place of rest, the staff laid on the stand. Sometimes it looked as if the staff glowed. The powers

I could feel it. Whoever the keeper is, he will be strong with it. Before I leave I will have the boys with Foo, come take their turn to see if they are the keeper. This is written in Maokes words in the archives.

I took the staff from its stand. Walk to the hanger, I felt a sensation rush through me. It was a feeling like nothing I have ever experienced, I knew then the power was there. I meant no one harm, just want them to know to leave Boldlygo alone. Do not come here with intent we will destroy you. This I promise you. I will tell them, when I'm gone the power will be passed on to the next leader. I will give them a small demonstration if they wish. I was dressed in white with a cape that touched the ground. I was dressed to meet a king.

CHAPTER 16

In the ancient city standing by the great wall, I stood by the portal. I watched my son, he knew what was expected of him. Once, again I gave power to the staff. Tomeka watched him, she was proud of her son.

Mya said to her mother, "I will go with Ject, I will not interfere unless needed, no one will hurt him." Mya turned to leave, bowed to her father.

"Mya Maoke said,"

Mya knew what was on Maokes mind. "Father he will not know I'm there, unless he needs me."

"Go Mya Maoke said, stay with him, stay until he returns. Beyond our boundaries, I can't watch him. Mya replied, "As you wish father."

Mya was gone with a wisp of the wind.

Tomeka looked at Maoke. "My love we need to end this."

"I can't Tomeka, it is not time. The prophecy has not been full filled."

Tomeka ask, "This prophecy you speak of, the son of our grandson?"

The white hair girl, the humans with power, all part of the prophecy.

Tomeka ask, "Do you know who she will be, you wrote of it?"

Yes Tomeka, "I do, yet I never spoke her name." Sitting on the bench Maoke said, "I need to go to the portal." I knew who the white hair girl would be, I never said. I told Tomeka as we walked to the wall. I never wrote of her, it was there before me. I dont know who wrote it. I found it with other thing in the relic of time.

Maoke, said to Tomeka, "It's time to further your knowledge of our people."

Tomeka, walked across the bridge to the ancient city. She always loves going there. Tomeka, turned to look at the portal.

"I said under my breath, I told her not to worry about her son. Tomeka, he will be fine, Mya is with him. Ject knows what he is doing.

Tomeka smiled. "I know he will be fine Maoke, he's my son."

Maoke and Tomeka walked to the archives. She sat for hours reading everything. She read from Maoke, Bota, Kia.

Tomeka told me, "Kia, is a very intelligent Busie." Tomeka said, "It was with Kia I find myself the most comfortable. Because of their emotions, Kia made me laugh, she never could understand humans humor. I sometimes believe she give me strength. Kia was very old, maybe as old as Maoke. Who know how old that is."

I read the writings of Bota. The words he wrote of me, I read of the time before Maoke. Maybe his father. I'm sure I read of the staff of Ira.

Maoke I ask, "Is the staff for the son of Tudo? Maoke shook his head know."

"He will find strength in the staff." Maoke said. "It will prove to be most useful to the ones that need it. Read my love, you will see it will be used in many ways. By several people, Ira is not the keeper. He will carry it until his ascension."

"Maoke it says, in a far way place."

"Yes, Tomeka like me."

"I have read enough today my love." Maoke, I will return until I have read it all. I must, the future depends on it." I ask Maoke, "Do you know who the keeper is. I mean do you know who he will be."

I do know, I told her no.

I simply said, "He hasn't been born yet. Even his father has not yet been born. Tomeka with each sun each moon, his time is getting closer." I walked back to the portal with Tomeka on my arm. Looking through the portal as the city of Ratio comes alive with light. How beautiful it was, the black stone towered the city. The palace overlook the city and the valley.

I told Tomeka, Each time I look at the city, the palace, marvel at the beauty. The time that went into building it. I thought what a wonderful world?"

I told Tomeka I wish she could have seen it as I did, when the unicorn and I took the walk. The journey we made across the planet. Following the rivers over the Marder-to -go's. The paths to the palace, to the city we call Ratio. It was wild country, even the Unicorn had never been there. The Unicorn had never left the valley, until the day we stood on the hill. Old Uny called to them one by one they went to the ancient city. It is where they live today, except the one that went to Earth with Bota.

Tomeka said, "I remember that, I come here with Bota. That's when I met you, when I fell in love with you.

Maoke said, "You, did didn't you."

Tomeka replied, "The Unicorn lived a good life."

Looking at the city we stood arm in arm. I let go of her hand, placed my arm around her. I looked into her blue eyes. Her hair was waist long. For the first time, I felt what she had told me so many times. "I love you Tomeka."

She looked up at me, "I love you to." Maoke will we stay here forever."

I simply said, "Until someone come with power. We will always be close Tomeka. We are the rulers of the ancient city, forever! In your reading, you will read all you need."

"When you return to the archives you will read of one to come, with his queen. Then we can go to the city."

Maoke I ask, "Does the archives really tell of one to come with a queen?"

I answered, "Yes my love just dont know who."

Tomeka said, "Look through the portal, we can see everything. The skies the city Ject at the hanger. A voice spoke from behind.

"He is dressed for a king." Mya said, "I love Ject. When we were in the palace we never spent enough time together."

"Go to him, Mya you know what you must do."

Yes, I do, "Father give him the power to use the staff." The way it has been done so many times before."

Tomeka ask, Is there power in the staff?

Maoke said, "Oh my love, there is. You will read of this, only the Keeper of the staff will have the power. The powers it has now, is what we give it, through our minds."

Mya ask, "Mother, you and father are still mates here as you were in the palace?"

Tomeka replied, "Yes sweetheart, why you ask?"

"Is it possible for Ject and I to be mates?" Mya ask.

Mya," He is your brother." Tomeka said.

Mya said, "I love him anyway. I will watch over him with my existence."

Maoke said to Mya, "That's why I let you go with him. I know you love him, Ive seen this for sometimes. I know nothing will happen to him if your with him. Now go, he is almost ready to depart. He will fill your presents,

Mya said, "Father Ject can actually see me. I called him to the Marder-to-go's. He reached out to me. He told me he loved me."

"Mya, Ject can't love you the way you want. In his body, he is not capable of loving you. Mya turned to walk away.

"Yes, father I know, Ject want always be in that ridiculous body."

Tomeka looked at me, "Maoke what are we to do of this. Even by DNA the blood is the same. Maoke on Earth this has happen. I've seen it with my eyes, I'm not sure here how that work."

Over hearing the conversation, Kia walk to Tomeka. "Dont worry Tomeka, Kia said. Even if they mate here, there can't be children. Even in their native body as you see them they can't have children. No one here can have children."

It is written, "There will be no children born in the gates of the ancient city. Even you Tomeka when the female Busie become extinct I was one of the few to survive. Only eleven of us are here today. They stay well behind the city. Some remain fertile."

When Maoke saw the future, through the portal. Maoke build the Great Wall, most of the females fled never to have contact with a male again. Maoke's word was build the wall, ill build the gate. It will hide us from the world outside. Only the Busie, ones with the royal blood can come. The natives will ascend to a different plain. Someday the Keeper of the staff will come. Then and only then, can we live with man. The walls will remain, the city open to all. You will see I'm right about this."

Maokes head went down. "I do remember, Kia that was a very long time ago. Even before you Tomeka.

Kia looked at Tomeka, "I'm glad you're here you are a treasure."

CHAPTER 17

I took the shuttle from the hanger sat for a long time. I checked everything just as Bota showed me long ago. Why he ever went to the city, I cannot say, I do miss him. I told Cra I was leaving.

Cra ask, "How long will you be gone Ject?"

I told him I would return before the two moons come. Closing the hatch a voice called to me.

"May I come along."

Looking to my right, it was Mya. She was in the seat beside me.

"I love you Ject."

Then she tried to kiss me. "Mya what are you doing?" I said.

"You love me dont you."

"Well yes Mya, I love you. Not like that, your my sister. I'll always love you, it's not right to kiss you as you have tried here."

Oh ject! "You are wrong about this."

"Kia told me, we could mate. We could not have children. Ject I know you love me."

"Mya, I do love you, just not like that.

"Oh, Ject now I'm sad."

"Mya come sit with me, you can fly the ship."

She said, "Ok Ject lets go to hyperspace."

I didn't know, what to think of the way Mya loves me. I've never had to experience that before. Tomeka told me once this happen on Earth. There is not to many that will allow it, yet there is some that will. My feeling for Mya I Amit were stronger, even as a boy Mya and I have always had a strong bond. The way she feels of me this can never be. I'm her brother that's all. I'll make her understand before she leaves.

I looked at Mya, sitting in the captains seat. "By the way little girl, do your parents know where you are."

"They sent me to be with you silly. They sent me just in case the staff of Ira needs a little push, I'm there for you big guy."

Now that scares me. I know what Mya is capable of. Ive seen Mya do some wild things.

Besides Ject, "I'm only here in your thought. If you love me with your mind. Well that would be a plus."

"Mya I love you as a sister, not a mate. I'll never have another mate."

"Mya, I have a job to do. I want to make sure my son, his sons, even their daughters, humans, natives will always be safe if they try I'll destroy them.

Mya said, "Know Ject, we will destroy them."

"Yes, Mya we will." The shuttle flew through hyperspace.

Mya said to me, "Ject you ever look at hyperspace as a hole through space."

I said, "Sometimes I do." Mya.

"Have you ever thought of the ones to come. Will we communicate with them?"

I said to her. "Mya I dont know what plan Maoke had. Tomeka, Tar, Kia what has the time keepers have us to do. I can't say."

Maoke said, "It is written, I'm sure he knows what will be. The time keeper will write, what is to come, what has happened. They will do what needs to be done." Mya, and I flew through space in silence, for several minutes.

Mya said, "Ject you really can't be my mate can you."

I told her, Know, it would be wrong.

"Mya said, I don't want to be alone."

I told her, You were never alone. When you left here went to Earth, you died. Bota, placed you in the grave. I have always been with you. Mya from your birth, even until now I've been with you. When you ran the city, when you were with Pep we were together.

"I suppose I think of him."

I told her, I'm sure you do.

"As I think of Beth. Therefore, I'll never take another mate. I want to go to Earth, I want to ascend. I want to come to the ancient city be with my family.

Mya said, "I understand Ject."

The shuttles zipped through space We was closing in Plano air space. Two ships come up beside.

I told Mya, I would take the controls, following the ships to the ground. landing on the pad the ramp went down. I walked across the yard, Mya beside me. Of course, no one could see her, but me. Looking at myself I was dressed out. I had the staff of Ira in my right hand, Cot met me.

Ject, "As his hand went out, good to see you," he said.

I said, "Good to be seen." As we walk to his chambers, Cot ask me of "Jung?"

"He is doing fine," I said

"Garf, goes every day to see him. He tells Garf, how he hates the prison you placed him in."

Cot said, "He would better himself there. Once he is released he is band from Plano he can never return."

I ask Cot, "What are we to do with him?"

Cot said, "let him live his life there. Tell me Ject, "What is you purpose, for your visit?"

"I wish to have a treaty Cot." I will ascend soon, I do not wish for someone to come to our world. I wish no harm of my people. We are a peaceful race Cot. We only have one weapon, its more powerful than you can imagine." I told Cot, "I do not wish to destroy any one, I want to know my people can live without fear."

Ject, "I have known intention of a war on your people, or any planet."

Cot told me, he enjoyed our visits."

Soon Ject, "I will come to your world, I will come to see your people. I too would like a treaty."

"Cot, and I set several hours talking, then it was time to go. Walking across the yard, Cot called to me. I turned.

"Ject you said you had only one powerful weapon." What, is it?"

I looked at Cot. "I'm surprise you ask? The weapon is in my hand. Cot ask for a small demonstration?"

Mya whispered in my ear. "I got you covered honey."

"It's what we call the staff of Ira."

Mya said, "Stretch it out, I did a small building disappeared."

Cot smiled, "I see what you mean. Your people Ject, will not have to worry, we will never have war if I'm king."

"Cot I will be going to Earth soon, it is my destiny on Earth I will ascend. Feel free to come to my world My son will be in charge. He is a fair being."

Mya as far as I knew, had never flown a ship. Until she come with me today. I was surprise the way she could maneuver the ship. Flying through space could be beautiful. Stars showed their twinkling light.

Ject, Mya said, "It will be so good when were together. Ive waited for hundred of years. It's time for you to come home Ject."

I told Mya, "There was a place I wanted to show her. I took control of the ship."

"Where, are we going?" Mya ask

I told her a small asteroid field, just outside the Moon of Xon. I spotted the asteroids field flew around looking for the right place. There, I told Mya.

"Looks like a big rock to me." Mya said.

"I sat the ship down." Mya looked through the portal window.

Oh ject! "It's beautiful, so romantic. You see Ject, if you were my mate what we could have together."

I told her, I didn't stop here for one of her games.

"I'm sorry you can't love me Ject."

"Mya I do love you your my sister."

Mya, jumped up, "Fine your just mean."

I looked around, Mya was gone.

"I left the asteroid field went to the surface of the moon." Garf met the shuttle at the pad.

"Ject, good to see you."

I told Garf, there was much to talk about. I ask of Jung?

Garf said, "He was still, doing time inside of his cell." Garf told me, "He had received two more. The chief justice brought them from the city. The chief looked over the prison, he told me the cells would hold anything, I agreed."

Ject, "I here you're going to Earth. Jung said, he would like to go. He said it would be better than here."

I had to decline the offer. Garf smiled, as all humans do.

Garf ask, "How long before you leave for Earth Ject?"

I told him, before I leave, I'll send someone here, see if anyone wants to go. Garf took my hand. It was a pleasure to serve you Ject."

"I'll send a sentry to pick up the ones that wont to go."

I told Garf he was a good human. keep true, to yourself

I left the Moon of Spores, never to return. I also knew I would never see Garf again. I wanted to ascend to the ancient city. How do you ascend? How do I do this in this body? How does one ascend, if your dead? Then how do you come back here?

Mya, Mya hear me, "Come back to me please!"

Mya appeared, She snapped at me, "what?"

Tell me Mya, "How does one ascend when you die."

Mya said, "I'm not sure, I remember when I got to Earth, I laid down over my mother's grave. When I a woke, I was in a strange place, I was in the ancient city. When I set up I saw Bota, he told me mother and father would see me soon. I was there, what seemed minutes when mother come to me. I had always been told humans dont ascend as we do."

Mother spoke to me Ject. The first thing, I ask of, "was you?" Then I ask of "father." Ject, why dont we smile? Why do we always have to be so bland? Ject, have you ever tried to smile."

I said, "no."

Mother said, "Mya he will be back." Well it was going to be too long. So, I call to you.

So, tells me Mya, "Where did you go."

"When Ject?"

"When I left the asteroid."

"I dont want to talk about it Ject."

I started to pick at her, she started to pick back. Then we were wrestling around the ship. She threw me down on the floor, jumped on me bent over kissed me.

"Mya please I'm your brother." Once again Mya said,

"Maoke said we were all as one." She jumped up threw her head back. "Ject, there's a ship in our air space. let's go see who it might be." The ships were doing, all it could do. The shuttle caught up in no time.

Mya said, "I do not know the ship. "There's markings on the ship Ject it is Xonian." Mya said. "I will be back." It was only a short minute when Mya returned.

Ject, "It is Xonian they were curious of our planet. They see the life signs there." We waited out of scanner range. Thirty minutes later they were gone.

I placed the shuttle to the left of the staging area. I Placed it back in the hanger.

Cra was there to help. Cra ask, "If I saw the ship?"

I told him, "I did."

Mya said, "It was Xonian."

Cra ask, "What did you say Ject."

I thought of what I said "I told him everything."

So just like that, "You call she comes,"

"Yes, Cra so far."

I turned to go to the palace.

Cra called to me. "Ject I need to have a council with you."

I told him to come to the palace when you're ready. I need to place the staff of Ira back. I sat for ever thinking of the thought that ran in my mind. I thought it must be something for Cra to ask for council?

CHAPTER 18

How can I tell Ject of this experiment? I would just tell him, Ject was a super intelligent being. I'm sure he will think I've gone draft. I thought if he was human, how smart would he be? Especially if he was on Earth. It was the best I could think of. Then I thought how humans did time on Earth. I thought all kind of thing.

I suppose I was getting the nerve. How long had it been since the last time I was there, I was not sure? I think of the ones we have taken back to Earth. Most are dead, others very old. What makes us live forever here on our world? Maoke planed all in his archives, yet I wonder.

Most people on earth don't live long. Thirty years in their adult hood I think. Maybe it's because they eat all the animals. The Indian can consume over a hundered pound of meat a week.

My thought turn to Ject. Does he have a problem? He said he calls to Mya. Ject, told me, she comes to him all the time. Mya has been gone over three hundred years. Why now, why does he think of her? I think of my father quite often. I'm not talking to him. Well not as what Ject is doing, I wish I could. A voice from behind said to me, as if it was on the wind. Cra, come to the fall at the Marder-to-go's. Who's there I said, now he's got me doing it?" I just let it go.

I walked back to the lab. Much work has, to be done, I was leaving soon for Earth. I still had to tell Ject, what I wanted to do? Even if I cannot convince him, I should tell Tudo. It will be his son alone with my son Mekon. I was convinced it would work. I think it will be the biggest breakthrough I'll ever make. I know it will work. I'll place to stasis pods on the ship tell him it's for me.

I placed everything I would need in the pods. My father was working on this with his father. I think old Bota may have worked on it too. I have built it to what it is now. I've said before I'm convinced it will work. I would never place my son in harm's way. That's how convinced I am. Closing the lid, I was ready to go have my council with Ject.

It was late when I entered the great room. The suns were going down over the mountains. Ject sitting on the stoop, "Cra come over." Looking out over the valley is one view I could never get enough of. Ject was having his Simon, always his Sweet Grass.

Ject said, "I had expected you earlier Cra."

I answered him, "Had several things to do Ject."

Ject said. Cra you looked a little nervous.

"A little I said." Ject just looked at me.

Look Ject, "I've made a discovery like know other. As far back as Bota, I've also made a remarkable break though in my DNA study, you want believe it. Ject looked up from his Sweet Grass.

"That would be what Cra."

I told him, "There want be a reason to carry a nanny for Mekon."

Ject said, "I know Gore and Karin would be going."

I said, "Tudo will be here with the boys soon."

"Ject said, "He knew that."

Ject "I said the breakthrough I've found. I will try it on my son Mekon." I told ject all about the DNA test.

Ject, at me with a puzzled look.

Ject replied, "Cra have you flipped out."

"Ject, I'm sure you don't approve. I'm convinced, it will work. How better to prove it, than use my own son. Think how wonderful it will be, Ject listen to me."

Ject said, "I am listening to you Cra, you're not saying anything"

"Mekon is my son. Ive already talked to him."

"Cra he is only ten years old"

Ject, "That's why it will work, he is young. I promise you he will not be in harm's way."

Ject said, "I must talk to Tudo about this."

I said to Ject, "Talk to whoever you wish, this discovery is mine. The pods are ready to go, Mekon is my son. He is willing to do this."

Mekon said to me, "Father if it works, I know it will. It will help in the future of our people. We will be able to mate with the humans."

Ject ask, "How do you see it will help him in the future Cra?"

"Ject, if he was going to Earth in his native body. He can shift into human form."

Ject ask, "Tell me how this is going to work?"

"You need a female, don't you?"

I told Ject, Many years ago, I placed a female on Earth with child." She would have past. Her decedent want be. Her name was Destiny from the Moon of Corning. The female was Quads sister. Ject, put of your ascension for a while. Kohl, told us where she was. Comp can find her. When Tudo returns from Corning we can leave.

"Cra to transfer DNA to a female is one thing. Transfer DNA to a female knowing her child will die, is another.

"Cra, do you think the humans will understand? If not how will it affect Mekon? If the, female doesn't want to do this will Mekon, survive?" Cra I said, "Think of what you do."

I told Ject, I have thought about it for several years. The child will be born, he will grow then die. When he dies, we will be there to take his essence return it back to his body, that's is in the pods. Someday it wants take so long. That will be left up to Mekon, or his child. I only know it will work.

When the child is born, first the child want remember. Then as time goes he will know. He'll have Mekons memories. His growth will be rapid until manhood, then he will die. That's all I can tell you. I wondered what we have become. We are a peaceful race. Doing this we would be no better than the Palatonias. I turned to leave.

Ject I said. "My son will do this. I will go to Earth my son will be honored. He will be remembered in the archives forever. When the transfer is complete all is well, then I will ascend also."

Ject ask, "Why do you do this?" Ject I do nothing, your father Maoke started this long ago. I'm just carrying it on." Remember Ject, "If not for what we have done, our race would have been lost long ago. Even now what I do is for the future of our people."

"Then go Cra, do what you must."

Cra left the chambers, I knew how intelligent he was. Yet what he says he can do, he was out there. I know I'm intelligent, Cra was much more than me. Mekon to, he was so intelligent I've never seen a child so intelligent. Tudo, will return from Corning soon. I will have council with him on Cra's discovery. I was deep in thought when a sentry come to the great room.

Excuse me sir, "The sentry said."

I said to him, "enter."

"Sir, the father of the child Foo is here to see you."

I said, "Show him in."

I ask, "How I can help him?"

Ject, "Tudo came to me, said when Foo was ten bring him here, today my son is ten."

"Yes, so is my grandson Ira." He will return in several days. You wish for him to take the test of the staff. Foo's father said, "I'm still not sure why."

I went to the room where the staff was cradle. Taking the staff in my right hand. I felt the power flow through me. A feeling I was not sure of, yet it was there. The keeper will be of Royal Blood this I was sure of I'll keep this to myself. I took the staff into the great room, lay it on the table.

Foo, come to me, "The boy was large for his age. Take the staff Foo, take it in your right hand. Lean it forward bust the rocks. The boy did as I ask. There was nothing happing.

Foo's father asks, "What was supposed to happen Ject." Every child born here will have the chance to see if they are the Keeper of the staff, native, or human.

Foo said, "I'm glad I'm not the keeper, I want to fly a ship someday."

"Maybe someday I can go with you Foo"

I told Foo, I think that will be a good idea, if your father will come alone you can start your training.

Foo's father said, "Training, what kind of training. Foo, will become captain of my grandsons ship. This I have written in the archives. Foo's father looked at me, as you wish his mother will be pleased."

"We will leave in one month for Earth." You may come with us if you wish. A ten year old boy well they like to be playful, this one was sincere. I guess our race takes it as it comes."

Foo bowed to me, "Sir I will make you proud."

Foo left his father, "He will make a great pilot Ject, you will see."

The ships returned ahead of time. Tudo was with a great crew, Comp was at the helm. Landing the ship as I would have done. How I miss doing that the boys ran to me, Opa-Opa. Mekon ran to his father.

Father Tudo ask, "How are you?"

I told my son, of the trip to Plano, the treaty I made with Cot. I told my son, There is a different situation here, come to the chambers. Tudo ask, should we call council?

I told my son, Tudo, this would be between me and you. I sent a sentry, to the boy Foo's home. Message to say the young will gather in the park by the falls. Tell Cra, to let Mekon, come I have stories to tell. The message was sent.

Foo's mother, ask her mate? "Why has the Royal Family taken interest in our son?"

"Foo's life has been planned by them, he will become a pilot." I, have been ask to go to Earth with them? I, was ask by Ject? He told me to bring the boy, to the hanger, his training would start the same as his grandson. I think it is a good thing.

Foo's mother said, "You will be gone for a long time. Foo's mother said, "My son will be grown when you return." He will be a good pilot. Take him she said, "I'll wait for you."

The boys crossed the bridge into the park.

The boys ask, "Opa what are we doing?"

Sitting on the stoop, waiting for all the children. I told them, "I was going to tell them a story of how we begin. I told them stories of long ago. Just as I knew they would tell their children. We set for hours telling stories." It was late afternoon when, I said "let's take a break." I told them as they left, Tomorrow we would pick up again."

Ira said, I would like to hear more of the Unicorn on Earth, all of it Opa."

"Yes, son in time, now we must go for the evening meal." The food baron had placed food on the table. After the meal, the boys were ready for bed.

Tudo said, "Father I will join you on the stoop." I was sipping my tea when a light appeared.

"Tudo a ship," I said. A ship came from space as Tudo came from the palace. The ships went back higher in to the darkness.

Tudo ask, "Could you see the marking father."

"I have no clue my son. I did not recognize it."

Tudo said, "Sometimes he thought someone will come cause us trouble."

"I would not worry about that my son, Maoke, Tomeka are watching, even Mya."

Tudo ask, "You believe in this ancient city father?"

I looked at him, "Yes Tudo, I do. Ive been t here."

"Father it was only a dream." Tudo said.

I replied to him, "Was it son."

Tudo said, "I cannot believe there's a hidden city here. I've heard of it, I've read of it, I have never seen it.

"Well, where did Bota go, Kia, Tar."

"You really have seen these being?" Father.

"Son, "I went to Earth with Bota. I've told the stories when you were young."

"I just thought they were stories."

It was real, "My sister Mya my mother, my father all real."

I got up went inside walking to my sleeping room. Lying across the bed I sleep very well.

The suns were low in the eastern sky when I open my eyes. I looked through the windows the view was beautiful. The ships sat on the pads, the smell was there, you just had to have it in your blood to enjoy it. I went to the great room, had my Simon.

Tudo come in, "Father the boys are with Karin."

"That's good Tudo,"

"We must complete the council we started, I have sent for Cra."

"There's only the three of us father."

"I have decided not to include anyone else. This will be between us, Tudo its personal."

"I'm curious father of the council."

"You should be son. It will be a long day Tudo."

Cra was crossing the court yard. Mekon went to Karin

Tudo Cra myself made the council. I stood first, everyone knew a ship was leaving for Earth."

My father told me once, that the humans saved our race. We built them a city. Protected them, loved them. We did what we said, they did what we needed. Gore was part of this. First humans, my human side will miss her.

That brings up the next subject. Cra would you speak.

Cra stood, looked at Tudo.

"Tudo, I have talked to your father of what I am to do. I have made an amazing discovery in DNA. I also have design stasis pods. I have made two of them.

"What are they for?" Tudo ask.

"I will take them to Earth. When I'm almost there, somewhere near earth moon. I'll place my only son in the pods, take his DNA. The woman Destiny I placed there long ago. I placed Myas DNA with her. She, will be long dead, her children will be the one that will take the DNA. The woman will carry the child, when the child is born he will grow fast. The child will have all Mekons memories. The child will die before manhood. I'll take his essence return it back to Mekon. Mekon will be able to shift from native to human. In human form, then we can mate with humans. Just as Maoke, ask my father, his father? It is something, I've work on, for hundreds of years. They can go to Earth, to any planet. Tudo sit looking well, in ah!

Tudo said. "You are not serious."

Cra, "I've heard you tell some stories, this one. You, believe you can do this."

Yes, Tudo I said I do. "Look I'm a scientist, my whole live has been devoted to this. Passed on by my father, if I didn't believe it I would not let my son do this. I would never let harm come to him, Tudo.

Tudo shook his head. Behind Tudo was a small figure, Ira was listening.

Ira, had become very powerful with his mind. The council broke up, I stayed had a cup of tea. A little voice called from behind the door.

"Opa"

"Come Ira. I cut him a Simon."

"Opa, I want to talk to you." Ira said.

"Come closer Ira, talk to me."

"I overheard you and father talking to Cra. I've seen the pods he built, in fact I help him make them. I was the one to volunteer for the experiment." "Cra said no, Mekon would be the one. Opa think of this what it would mean for us if it works."

Ira, "What are you saying son."

"Opa Mekon can't go alone. I want to go to."

"Tudo heard Ira talking. I will not let my son do something so stupid."

Father, "How many thought Bota, or Maoke was stupid. Thank about it, the very ship Bota made saved our race. Was he stupid?"

Ira was ten, speaking, walking around as if he was one hundred. I was proud of my grandson. I could see now, Ira someday will be a great leader.

"Tudo I've decided to wait on ascension. Go to Earth Tudo, "Take your son with you, I'll be here when you return. I'm not going to tell you what to do. Ira is right, in what he says."

"I will miss his childhood."

"Tudo if something happens to him, in this experiment, he will ascend to the ancient city. When your close to Earth if he fills the same, let him decide.

"I'll place my son, into the pod. I just hope Cra, know what he's talking about."

Ira said, "We will be fine father, you will see."

Everyone was making, preparations to leave. It would be several more day to come. Once we return to Earth the boys will be in the pods. They will be fourteen years old. The woman that takes the DNA. The boys will be grown by the time they return to Earth. This is what bothers me, both women will know at transfer the child will die. That's the way it is with humans. born to live, live to die.

The natives were loading supplies on the ship. The supplies for Corning also.

Comp ask me. "Ject will I be the pilot."

I told him he would, unless you dont think you can handle the ship.

Comp looked at me, "I was trained by you, what do you think."

I turned to leave.

Ject," Comp called what know answer?"

I simply said, "There's not an answer Comp." I kept walking. I needed to send Tudo to the home of Foo.

"My father sent me to the home of Foo." I ask, "for Foo?"

Foo's mother said, "That her son was with his father in the city."

I found then at a tea house. I told Foo's father, We will be leaving in two days. Come early on the second day. I returned to the palace my father was on the stoop. I told him of my visit to Foo.

I sat on the stoop looking across the Valley of the Unicorn. I knew Maoke, could see me. I looked straight at the portal. "Father if I'm wrong with my decision please let me no. Cra, has made a discovery with DNA. Mekon, his son will take the test, so will Ira. I'm scared of this, I know Cra, would never hurt his son. I know he would never hurt Ira. Something could go wrong, they will go to Earth. I will tell my son, this will be up to him. If all goes well I will ascend to the city. Tudo will be leader of our people."

I went to my sleeping room. lay on the bed, I went fast asleep.

Mya come to me, Jumping on my bed Ject, "Wake up."
I looked up at her. She said as she lay beside me.
"Oh, Ject we would be so good together."
"Stop it Mya. She spoke to me in a baby's voice."
"I love you so much."
"I ask, "Why are you here?"
"Father sent me. He said, "He would not let harm come to Ira. He told me great thing were to come to Ira. The tests will be the start, Mekon will survive also."

Father said, "If it works do not use it again. He said for at least one generation."

Sitting up in bed, I looked out the window the gray sky showed. The suns were coming, it would be another beautiful day as always.

"Mya said, "Ject my love, I must leave I'll come again soon."
"Bye Mya," she was gone.

I still can't understand the feeling she has for me. Same mother same father. I wondered if Cha, did something to her DNA. Even when Mya, was little she was like that. I thought at first, she was just joking around. When she tried to kiss, me I knew then it was real. However, the feeling has gotten stronger since she ascended. I went to the window mother hear me. "

Why, does Mya, feel this way of me. Tell her I can't be her mate. Make her understand behind me. A voice, I turned it was Ira.

I said, "Ira, you're getting good coming up on me."

Ira said, "I've seen you talk several times standing there. You look at the same thing. Yet there is nothing there. Are you talking to someone, or is it make believe?"

"I am talking to someone Ira. I'm talking to my mother, and my father."

"Where are they Opa?"

I told him, "Son there in the ancient city. A place you will be someday. A city so great, so beautiful.

"Where is this city Opa."

I explained, "Remember when I speak of Maoke, Bota, Tomeka Kia."

Yes Opa, "I know their names. I've read of them in the archives, I hear you talk of Mya."

"Ira, Mya was my beautiful sister."

Opa, "You were talking to her in your sleeping room the other night."

I could hear her, "She called you honey. She said father sent her."

Ira I said, "You could hear Mya."

Opa, "It sounded as if she was jumping on the bed."

My grandson, this powerful at his age.

What kind of leader would he be? I know he will be powerful. Ira will be a good father when time comes. We sat for a long while talking, Ira and me. I cut him a Simon. He would say to me, Opa this is my favorite. I told him they were mine to. I told him long ago, Maoke told of a fruit that grew here. The tastes were so great it was unbelievable.

"Where's the fruit know?" Ira ask.

I told him the trees were destroyed when the city was built. Maoke, said they never knew until it was too late. Now the only place they grow is in the ancient city.

Opa, "In two days we will go to Earth." The child Foo will come.

Ira I said, "The boy is to be trained as a captain, as you will. You must take care to help him and your brother."

"As you wish Opa."

The ships were loaded with all supplies. The Moon of Corning supplies also.

I told my son again, Tudo think of what must be done. Think hard before you make this decision. The experiment if a success will be trying. I will wait for your return. When Ira,

Mekon are placed in the pods, I hope they are peaceful. They will be there for several years.

I said, "Goodbye to Gore, and Karin." I told them Tomeka will be waiting for them. They knew as they left we would never see each other again. I've said it before, human dont want to die yet they run to death most all the time. I suppose it is their destiny. I would be alone again, with the boys and Tudo gone. Tomorrow I would walk to the falls at the Marder-to-go's.

My father watched as we departed the staging area. He would be the only one left, for the next four years he would be alone. The ships lifted off on our mission to Earth. A stop on Corning, will give the crew a chance to walk about, before the long journey to earth.

Comp said, "Tudo we have been given clearance to land. I sat the ship on the pad." Tudo was the first one off the ship. Kohl and Joy greeted everyone. Supplies were being unloaded. Pep come up to me, bowed.

Tudo, Pep said, "How are things."

I ask, "Pep may I have a word" I told Pep, it might be hard to understand. Mya said tell you she misses you.

Pep looked at me, "You know Tudo I miss her to. After all these years, she, comes to Ject all the time, it's like a bond they have."

We stayed on the moon until the sun come up. Comp stayed on the ship. Kohl was with him the night long.

Comp explained to Kohl, why Tudo was going to Earth. Comp, showed Kohl the pods.

Kohl ask, "Do you think it will work?"

"Kohl think about it, how can it work? I've seen Cra work with DNA. I know about DNA, what is this essence?" Inside the pods, the boys will still grow. The ones that take the DNA will die when born. "

I tell you Kohl, it's not right, yet it's the only way to keep their race going."

I said to Kohl, "What is wrong with the way it's going now?"

Kohl said, "Changes Comp always changes."

I told Kohl, Cra said, after the essences is restored back in the body, they can change their shape"

Kohl ask, "What do you mean?"

I said, "They can change from their native body to their human body. They can mate with humans."

Dam Kohl said, "Wish I had thought of that."

I ask Kohl, "So you agree with this?"

Kohl said, "Hell yes who wouldn't. Comp think, it's the biggest breakthrough in science of a life time."

I told Kohl, That's what Cra said. His biggest discovery. Ject told Tudo if it works, not to do it again. Something could go wrong.

Morning come to the moon, goodbyes were given. Comp took our ship higher in to the darkness of space, soon we went to hyperspace. I thought since my father and Bota made their first stop here. The moon had become a major port, A very popular place, there were several ships. Comp told me he explained to Kohl what we were doing. He agrees with the experiment.

I ask comp, "You dont agree?"

Comp said, "Tudo I dont know what to believe." I told Tudo I was not sure what essences was. I just want to be the best pilot of Boldlygo."

I said to Comp, "You are a very good pilot, captain. My father said that. My father is a good pilot. Bota will always be the best. Think Comp of what he did, where he went. How many being with help of a few Busies constructed a ship. Cross several universes even more galaxies. When Bota wasn't on a mission, well Bota was on a mission. Bota flew several hundred years."

"I get the point," Tudo.

"When we return home, Comp you will be in control of this ship. You will need to train a captain."

I said to Tudo, "If you will excuse me I have a class to teach."
Three young boys.

Tudo ask, "How are the boys learning?"

I told him Foo will be very good. Iras' mind always working.
Someday they will stand where we are standing now. Tudo ask,
of Ren?"

I said, "Ren never says much, he does listens it's as if he
absorbed all."

Time comes and goes. It was several month later, I entered
a room where Ira, had three objects floating in air.

I ask my son, "How do you do this Ira?"

"I'm not sure father. I ask them to move?"

"Ren and I do this all the time."

"Your brother can do this also."

"Yes father, Foo can do it to. Ren and I have taught him
how to control his mind."

Father, "The closer we come to Earth, the smarter we
become. Everyday something new. Yesterday I told Comp what
he was thinking, before he knew. How can I do that."

I replied to my son, "I was not sure.'

Days went to month. This morning we past the rings of
Saturn. It was not my first time, to see this. Each time I still
think of the planet. Saturn was a beautiful planet, it will never
be Boldlygo, beautiful in its own way. Saturn's atmosphere is so
deadly, it would kill any one that stepped on it.

"You would need a special suit."

"A voice from behind me said." I turned to see my son. "A
special suit Ira."

"Yes, father one with a breathing device built in. Where do
we find that?"

Ira said, "I'm sure Cra, or Mekon could make one. Father I
am getting stronger so is Mekon, the closer we get to this Earth.

I have notice Ira. "I haven't said anything. Ira, I will leave this up to you. If you feel you must do this task, I will not stand in your way."

Ira replied, "Father I have thought of this, every day in flight. I have talked to Opa about it. last evening when I was there. We talk for hours."

"Ira, what do you mean when you were there. Son we have been gone several months."

"Yes, father I know. Yet I can go anywhere I please, with my mind. The people can hear me, just before I come here with you, I was on a planet far away. People look human except for their ears are pointed. I believe it is called Galxo. Someday our people will venture there." Opa said, "He and Bota went there once. That was a very long time ago."

I spent the next few days with, both my sons and, the boy Foo.

Cra said to me, "In the next few days we will be placed in the pods." We did the thing that most children do. This I was not sure of. Mekon was doing physics I dont understand what it is. A leader to be after my father I should learn. My sons could do the simple basic. Mekon capability was beyond that. I have watch the boy grow, Mekon is what we call super intelligent. Ira said the same.

On the third day from Earth, Cra took the boys to the room, he had prepared for them. A room with an inner chamber, built with a door to enter in case of emergencies. Cra laid the boys on to a make shape bed. There was a clear globe to be placed over them. Cra started to place tubes in the boys, in the area where they were needed. Cra took the boys DNA placed it into a sterile vile, as we approached Earth.

Ira ask, "Father may I look at this place."

I told Cra. "Let my son see the blue planet called Earth." Ira looked at the planet then Ira looked at me.

"Father I will be fine, This will not be the last time I'll see this place, you will see." Cra started, fluids started through the tubs. The boys closed their eyes, went to sleep.

Foo and Ren stood beside Ira and Mekon.

Ira told Ren, "Dont worry about me. Come see me if you wish. We can hear your every word, Cra said that. We just can't answer. Come to me watch me grow, I'll watch you with my mind."

Comp, took the shuttle to the surface of the planet, he would be alone. He would have a signal stone Cha, had design it long ago. I give him three of the stones. I sat him down in a remote part of Russia. A place where Comp placed Destiny long ago. Comp walked of the ship. I took the shuttle to the darkness of space. I didn't feel right leaving him, yet it had to be done.

CHAPTER 19

I watched the ship as it left Earth.

Cra said, "Comp let us know when you find the family."

I had my stones, my coin in my pocket. It was only a short distance to the farm house. Checking around I noticed someone did live here. I hid in the barn until daylight. This planet was to cool for me. I cuddle in the hay waiting on the Earths sun, that had not come up yet. Watching the house as a light went on inside. Well I thought, someone is up. Moments later a young girl come from the house. She was carrying a bucket in hand. She went to a stall where a big animal was. Sitting on a small stool she did something under the animal. What was she doing I thought? I stood up fell right through the floor. As I was falling I thought, hell I just blew it. It was several hours later when I woke up. I had a cut on my face. I also had a broken arm, I was lying in a bed when I woke up. I closed my eyes went back to sleep.

The Earths sun was warm on my face. I eased out of bed, looked out the window. The same little girl was coming from the barn. She had a bucket in her hand, something in the bucket. I opened the door a woman I took to be thirty Earth years was at the table. She was cutting what look to me as bread. I spoke to her in Russian. The little girl came through the door, she placed the bucket on the table. There appeared to be a white liquid in the bucket. The little girl got a container dipped into the bucket, took a long drink. They both were looking at me, as if I was an alien. Well I suppose I was to them.

The older one ask, are you hungry?"

I told her I was.

She placed on a plate slices of bread, fruit.

She said, "It was apples." The woman cut a slice of what she said was cheese,

I found I like a lot. I told her so.

She took a small container dipped it into the bucket, handed it to me. It was warm, it was very good.

I ask, "What is this called?" They looked at me as if I was crazy.

Its milk she said, "You never had milk before?"

I said, "I never seen milk before. We dont have this where I'm from." Then I remembered I was on Earth, I need to watch what I say, I thought.

My arm hurt, I had no idea what was wrong. I had a wooden splint on it.

The woman said, "It's broke."

I was afraid I never had a broken bone. I ask her, "Will I die?"

She looked at me funny again.

Let me guess she said, "You dont have broken bones where you're from."

I told her know, then I remember the coin in my pocket. I placed my fingers in my pocket. I took out the coin. The little girl was watching every moved I was making. I laid the coin on the table.

The woman stepped back. "Nancy come here now." The woman said.

"Please I want hurt you." I said.

She was holding the little girl close, "Who are you?"

"My name is Comp, why did you jump." She went to the mantle above the fire. She removed a brick, took a small box.

Opening the box as she walks back to the table. The woman showed me the coin, it was the same. The woman said her name was, "Lola."

Lola said, "I have had it for so many years. We have waited for you so long. My great grandmother told my grandmother my mother, now my daughter." She asks, "Are you here to take them back."

"I ask, "Do you want to go?"

"I dont know" she said. "I'm not sure."

"You said your great grandmother, told you about us."

"Her name was Destiny," I said.

She said yes. "I need to talk to you, maybe not in front of the girl."

Lola said, "It would be ok, Nancy is very intelligent. She just acts this way around people."

Lola said, "We were told you were not human. Some of us aren't, they do have human features."

"We would never hurt anyone," I said.

Lola said to me, "We have been told of our family of the stars. Why after all these years you come back."

I told her, "The stories of the people, We have a way to repopulate the city."

The little girl said, "I've never seen a city, I've been here my whole life."

Lola ask, "What kind of way do you to repopulate."

Sitting with her, I tried to explain about the boys. I could see she didn't understand a thing. Lola walked to the water pumped, a couple of pumps water came out flowed into a pan. I thought at home we just turn a nob, water comes out.

"Comp, is that why you brought my great grandmother here."

I told Lola, Destiny was given a transfer of DNA of a very intelligent being. This was done to bring forth intelligent life here. Someday as now we would have a place to stay, do our research. Lola, we need two women, two grown women. We need them to have two children. The women would carry the children raise them. The child would grow very fast, the child would die by their eighteenth birthday. We would carry their essence back to the ship transfer it into the boys. The boys would wake up. I left out the part of them shifting. I just told her they were sick. She did not need to know anything more.

"Then what becomes of the women?" Lola ask.

I said, "Give them a choice, go home or stay here. We would take care of them, We would give t hem stones, worth a lot here.

Lola said, "I do not know anyone, there's just me, my daughter. No one ever comes here. My mother told me before she died, If you come I must help you. She, told me Destiny was of Royal Blood."

I told her, all about Mya, the women sat at the table with tears in her eyes.

"Sound to me your world is no different than here."

"Lola, it very different," I said.

Comp," Children having children," that's bad."

"Lola, the age is not the same."

"These children, you say are sick. What is wrong with them?" Lola ask.

Nancy said, "You know I can read your thought. If you want my mother's help, you must be honest. "Comp you said, "The two boys in the pods that is true, the reason is a lie."

I told Nancy, You are powerful like Mya. I've read in our archives of her.

"Yes, Nancy it is a lie only the reason. The child will grow very fast, them die.

"It dont make sense," Lola said.

I agreed. "I stood up started to the door."

Lola said wait, "I never said I would not help. You're right Nancy is strong, she is ten years old. She is very intelligent. I've tried to hide her, I will do it, I will help. I'll find you two women for this then what?"

"We will take them to the ship."

"Lola talked of thing of the farm."

Lola told me of her family, ones she remembered. She told me there's several people. Most of them had left Russia. Mostly because of the Russian government. The Russian army comes here often. I water their horses, sometimes feed then what I can.

Sitting on the porch sipping a cup of tea. I watched the Earths sun go down.

Lola said, "Comp you can stay in the house. Since you are family."

"I will stay in the barn," I said. That didn't work out, I went to seep, her talking to me. It was morning when I woke up.

Lola had the fire going. She poured a cup of tea for me. It was different than home. Taking the tea, then the question started.

"Comp tell me, what will happen on the ship?" she asks. I must tell you," It scares me to death just to think of it."

I told Lola its very safe. I come two years on the ship. It's not my first time on a ship. I'm a captain, as to your question. We will take the women to the ship, do the transfer, we will stay here for a while. Just to see how the transfer goes, then we will leave.

"What then?" Lola said.

Well Lola, "When the babies are born, they will be males."

Lola ask, "How do you know this?"

Lola, "We are so advance trust me it will be as I say."

"Then why can't you do this on your world?"

I told her you can't die there.

"Not ever, she asks?"

I told her not ever. This transfer will let us live on Earth. It will let us mate with humans. We can't do that in our native body.

Lola said, "I dont understand."

"Nancy, Comp if you can't die there, how old are you."

220

The Staff of Ira

I replied, "One hundred thirty six years." Yet our time is different than Earth.

Lola said, "It has been passed down through time, we must help you when you come." Some of my people wish you had come in their life time. They said if you come in someone's life, find them.

What you asked? "I'm not sure."

I have an older sister that lives in Saint Petersburg. She has two daughters. We must go there.

Nancy looked at her mother, "Mother am I old enough?"

Lola said, "No Nancy you are not." Nancy ask, "Comp can I go back to your world?"

"Without your mother." I said.

She looked at her mother, "I think it would be good for me."

Nancy, I said, "You would be a blessing there."

"If your mother gives you permission you could come with us, then return later."

Nancy looked at her mother.

Lola said, "She would think about it."

"In the barn, I was trying to harness the horses." Lola came in and saw what I was doing, she laughed so hard.

"I suppose you don't have horses on your world, "she said.

"You're right," I said. Everything is there for us. How it gets there I can't say. You can go into the city, take what you want, go home and come back tomorrow. Bring it back as if you never took it, like magic."

Comp, she said, "Move! Let me show you."

The way she moved, you could tell she had done this for a while. I gave her and Nancy a hand in to the wagon, we were gone in minutes.

"I'm a pilot Lola, not a farm boy."

Lola said, "Where did you get those muscles?" They are nice.

Lola, let the horses lead them self. It was as they knew where they were going.

I said, "as much."

Lola said," My horses are smart, they just follow the trail."

Lola ask, "Are you going to tell me where you got those muscles?"

I told her it takes hard training.

"What kind of training?" She wondered.

"Lola I'm not only a pilot, I'm also a warrior."

I ask her, "How long it would take to go to Saint Petersburg?"

She said, "One day maybe."

I told her it would take ten minutes in the ship.

She said, "We would go with the horses. If someone came to the house and finds the horses, they would ask too many questions."

We rode several miles in the dark.

Nancy said, "Mother I want to go to sleep."

Lola stopped the wagon. It was a beautiful place, used by several passerby's. There is a stream that ran by the road. I took the horses to the stream watered them. Lola made a fire made tea. Now I was not sure of things on Earth. One thing I did know, horses were great animals. I tied the horses to a tree. I told Lola this place has been used before. Wood was stacked high.

"Nancy was lying in the wagon," she screamed! I jumped up and grabbed a stick.

"Mommy someone's there!"

"Come out!" I said in Russian.

An old man came from the bush.

Lola shouted, "You should be ashamed of scaring a little girl!"

The old man said, "I'm sorry, I meant no harm. When I heard, you coming I hid, I thought you were the Russian army."

I ask, "Have you done something to hide from the army?"

"No," The old man said, "Nothing to hide, just dont want to be found."

I said, "Well we won't bother you, you stay over there." We'll stay here, we will be gone at first light.

The old man said, "I see you have a horse, I could use a horse."

I looked at Nancy, she knew what I was thinking. The old man started walking towards the horse.

A big rock hit him in the head, so I tied him up. When he awoke, he yelled all night

I yelled at him, "If you don't be quite I'll take you to the Russian army myself." He never said another word. With the gray of morning, Lola harnesses the horses.

The old man said, "You're not going to leave me here, are you?"

"Surely not taking you alone."

I checked his ropes, still tight. I got in the wagon, as we started off I threw his knife out. I told him it's only seventy five yards. You can make it by dark. If the Russian army don't come by.

"I'll see you again mister."

"It won't be nice what I do to you. Then I'll do what I want to your family." I told Lola I like it.

She said," What do you mean?"

My family. I told her to stop the wagon. I walk back, took a leather strap from the wagon. I ran the strap through the ropes, I threw the strap over a limb. I pulled him high off the ground, we left him screaming.

Arriving in Saint Petersburg as the sun was setting.

"Comp?" Lola ask, "How many times have you been on Earth?"

I told he several times. I told her there was a mast of land east of Russia it is Hugh. The people that live there, some are friendly, some not so much. In fact, they killed Lon, Cras father. He was our head scientist. That happen on our last voyage.

Lola ask, "Were you born here?"

I told her no, I was born on my world.

"Lola, you would not believe it when you see it, it is so beautiful. Every day is the same. The rivers, the lakes, it's like looking at a rainbow. The mountains of the Marder-to-go's, I can't explain it. You would need to see it, we have a simple life there."

"Lola, I've noticed at your house you severed no meat."

Lola said, "We don't eat meat. It has been passed down, all the way from Destiny. It has been said do not eat meat.

Someday you would come. If we went back, your world will only eat fruit, vegetables, and bread.

The bread is made from breadroot. Our bread is not the same as your grain bread. Ours well, it's better. I mean nothing against your bread. You would have to try it to understand, I told her.

Lola pulled the horses outside to a small building. I jumped off the wagon, took her hand to help her down. Then I helped Nancy down. Lola took a scarf from her apron pocket, tying it around her hair. She walked inside. Comp, will you stay with Nancy? Lola asked. Moments later she walked from the small building. Out of nowhere a man grab her arm, "Where is your old man now?"

I had no clue what was happing. I reached for the back of his shirt, sent him sailing across the cobble stone street.

The man jumped up, and said, "Who the hell are you?" In Russian.

I'm her old man. I startled toward him, he turns to run. Nancy threw a bucket between his feet just to fall at my feet. I grabbed him again.

"Mr. I have no idea who you are. If you ever come close to her or the child again I will end you!"

"Yea yea," The man said no more. I walk back to Lola.

"Comp he is a very bad man. He will run to his brothers, he will be back."

"Really?" I replied.

Lola said, "Let's find my sister."

I thought she might be here. Her husband owns the place.

Boris said, "She was at home." Leading the horses around back, I tied them outside on the rail. Lola walked through the door, the woman jumped up from the table. Lola gave her an embrace, then looked at me.

She asks Lola, "Why are you here?"

There was no need for introduction.

She then said, "It took you long enough to get here."

I replied, "For that I truly am sorry. Looks as if you have done well. I'm so glad someone was at the farm."

She asks, "Are you alone?"

"I told her no, the big ship is in space."

"I remember my grandmother before she passed, telling of things that happened." Things to her, her mother.

I told her she was from the Moon of Morning. We brought her here to the farm. We knew the old man. We helped them in bad times. Of course, Cha, come long ago before Destiny. That's how we knew to come here. "Have you told your husband of your past?" I ask.

She told me no.

"Your children?" I asked.

Lola said to me, "Comp this is Sandy, my sister."

Sandy said, "I have two children. Two cousin, their father is in the Russian army. Their mother dead."

"Are they educated of the planet."

Sandy said, "know they are my husband's family." Sandy took my hand.

"I have so many questions for you."

I said to her, "I'm sure you do, I'll try to answer all your questions."

Sandy said, "I'm not sure how I knew who you were, somehow I just knew."

Tudo Cra, "Are some names you will know."

"I have heard of them, also Ject."

I told her he was at home. Tudo is here, we must do an experiment. We need to do this. This can only be done on earth. Sandy looked at Lola. Sandy, we need two women. Old enough to have a child, must be at least seventeen years old. We need to carry them to the ship, do a DNA transfer. Like we did with Destiny your great grandmother. This time the woman would have the child as on Earth. The child will grow fast, then the child will die.

Sandy jumped up are you mad. I tried to explain, she could not comprehend what I was saying.

Lola said, "Comp let me talk to her my way."

I left the room, walked outside checked on the horses. Humans were odd people, then I thought I was human. Yet, nothing as Earth humans. I've often wondered, humans dont like to be enslaved. They do this to their animals. I really did not understand.

I caught a shadow cross the back of the building. I thought to myself, I'm having company. I reached for the roof. I pulled myself up lying flat on the roof. Three men come around the corner at the same time. Whispering in Russian, I could hear every word said.

"They must be inside," one said. "This is their horses. We will wait until he comes out. Then we will have him."

Little did they know I was already outside. I did something, I saw a native do on board a ship. I started screaming so loud they were covering their ears. When they put their hands to their head, I kicked one in the growing. Slap one across the face, poked one in the stomach. Then I ran around the corner. I found a piece of wood it was perfect for a club. The leader come around the corner I smacked the him in the mouth, I ran to the other corner. Drawing the club back, one hit me from behind. I went down going into a full roll, came up hit one over the head. I started for number three. The man was running, I was running after him. The man tried to turn, fell on his way up. I smacked him on the head he laid on the ground, I took two strips of leather tied them together. Then I made them walk around to the third. I picked him up, tied them together. I took them to the eatery, opening the door pushed them inside.

The other two were sitting at the bar. "These your brothers?" I ask.

"They are brothers one said." They were bleeding from the head and the nose.

One said, "You do this all by yourself."

I told them I was not finished.

"What does that mean." he said.

"I'm ready for you," I said. The men looked at the other.

He said, "You will have no more trouble from us."

"I thought somehow, I don't think it was over."

"Mister, next time I'll go to the Russian army."

"I'm passing through."

One with the mouth wound said, "You need to keep on going."

I jumped at him, he went to his knees. I looked at the man behind the bar, he smiled. I went outside back to the house.

In less than thirty minutes, I had met people taken care of animals got in a fight. Only on this planet could this happen. I tell you I ready for sleep.

Walking in the house, Lola ask, "What has happened to you?"

"Why do you think something happen?" I ask.

"I had a funny feeling Comp." Looking into those blue eyes, I knew I was done for. I know now what Kohl felt.

"Comp, your shirt is ripped."

Lola ask, "Did they come back?"

I said to her, "I tied them up took them to the eatery. The other two brothers gave me no problem. I ask Sandy, "Would it be ok for me to stay in the barn? It's a warm night I prefer to be outside." She said "It would be ok." I took the horses around the house. Leading them to the barn I took the harness off. Rubbed them down as instructed by Lola. Lola came to the barn to check on me. Mostly to check my work.

Smiling at me, "You did good Comp. You will make a good farm boy."

"Oh, no not me."

"Lola said, "Comp do not talk around Sandy's husband?"

Lola, I said, "She needed to tell him a long ago. This is something you can't hide, their coming soon."

Lola dropped her head. "Then you will leave."

Yes Lola, "It's my ship. I must return to my world."

"You have a woman there?" she asks.

I told her there was no one. I also told her I've never had no one.

I sat down on the hay.

Lola sat beside me. She was looking at me kind of, well a look I've never seen.

Lola said to me, "Will you take me."

I said, "If you want to go, sure."

"No Comp take me. I've not had a man since Nancy was born."

I told he again, Lola I've never been with a woman. I'm not sure what to do." Lola turned to me. She kiss me, pulled up her long dress. I've never experienced such pleasure. The years I've been on Boldlygo I could have done this, what a waste of life. I made love had sex or whatever you call it. I look at Lola. I think I would make a good farm boy. It was wonderful, it was a feeling I wanted all the time. I see why Kohl went to the moon to be with joy. Lola was lying beside me.

She said, "You bring the woman out in me, so many times. My husband hardly ever."

Well I still didn't understand. We just kept on going, Lola whispered in my ear.

"Please stay with me." I'll take this DNA if you stay, be my husband."

I thought I was tired after the fight. Now I was weak.

The next morning I woke up, Lola was gone. I called for her several times. Coming from the hay. I started to the house. Lola met me with a cup of tea.

"Ah, tea just what I need."

"It's not tea Comp," she said. "It's a new drink, that people started buying in Russia. It's called coffee." She said.

I took the cup placed it to my lips, took a sip. I smiled, "Yes I like this coffee." She gives me a peace of sweet bread.

"I've never had this either," I said. Lola kissed me on the cheek.

Comp, "You make me very happy." Lola said. I told you last night I will take this DNA if you will stay with me. Sandy's oldest child said she would take the other. If she can go back to your world. Of course after the child is born. She is to marry a Russian guard, she doesn't want to do this. If you transfer this DNA you talk about. She will move to the farm with me. Comp, "I will need a man to do the work. I can't do this If I'm having a baby, Mary either. Nancy can show you how to do some things."

"Then we need to go back to the farm Lola." "Lola I must ask Tudo about this. I cannot do this without council approval. If council give their ok, I will stay with you, love you."

"Someday when they return, maybe you can go to my world for a while."

Lola ask, "Can Nancy go to."

I replied, "Yes Nancy to."

We went to Sandy.

Sandy said, "Comp my daughter will take the DNA transfer. She only wants to go back. Through the years, I have told them of you, your world. Your people, how you look. The things you can do, the thing you will do."

I ask Sandy, "Where is the girl, I would meet her."

Sandy called the girl, "Entering the room, a very beautiful young girl come in."

Dam I thought, She was beautiful her hair long, black, with the bluest eyes ever. Lola's eyes were blue not like this.

I told Sandy. "She has blue eyes, that is Royal Blood, as Lola, Nancy. Mary is the oldest. Tudo will be honored." I said

Sandy, "You must tell your husband, He must know of our existence."

She started to cry, "How can I?" Sandy said. "He will think I'm crazy, send me away."

There is an alternative, "If he does not believe you, you can come with us. I promise you we will welcome you. A woman of a princess you are. All of you, from Myas DNA. Jects sister at eight taught school, at a young age had a child. Mya come to Earth to ascend. That we will always be sorry for. It was planned long before me. Therefore, women on Boldlygo must be seventeen years old to have a child.

Comp Sandy said, "I must know more about this DNA. Will it hurt my daughter?"

I told her no, It will be painless. You will see the children, when we reach the ship. They will not look as you, they have a native body. Let me assure you the child you will have, will be human. The woman may have a problem having the child, loving the child. I'm sure the part of the child dying will hurt. You must remember all the memories of the child, will be passed to the boys when they are awakened. You lose one, yet gain another.

"I promise you this will be the greatest thing our family on Earth will accomplish. You see you will still have a son, the boys will still have a mother." I ask Mary, "What do you think of this?"

Mary ask, "What will become of the bodies?"

"We will place them in a container take them to a place here on Earth, bury them."

Mary ask, "How long will it take to do this?"

"The child will grow fast." I said. To you the child will be twelve year old. In reality the boys will be grown."

Mother, Mary ask, "How are you going to hide this from father?"

"This will disgrace him." Georgia said.

"We have waited on this day our whole life," Mary said. "I have been taught about you in secret. Now you stand before me. I remember my grandmother, before she died. How she would tell her stories. I was a very little girl, yet I remember. The stories of Ject, Lon, Tudo. I remember the coin aunt Lola hides in the mantel. This is what we have been told all our lives."

Georgia had tears in her eyes. "Comp, we have books of writing of Destiny, that she wrote. When she was left at the farm. My children will be taught the same, if I'm alive I will write of this. I see things in the sky, others dont see. Last night I saw a great light in the sky. I took a book from my pocket, showed Comp."

Comp said, "She wrote of this."

I ask Georgia, "Could I see the book?" She handed me the book. I read for what seemed an hour. I said, "She was right in her writing." I told Georgia, You should tell all the children that's to come. As long as there's life, someday we will return.

Lola has asked, "To do the DNA?"

"I will stay here with her."

Georgia said, "Then I will co me to. There's so much I want to know. Comp can I go with you to your ship when you do this DNA."

I said to her "Yes, you will be scared at first, believe me it is safe."

I told Sandy we will leave at first light.

Georgia said, "There's so much I want to know of my people, the world they come from."

I told her it will all come in time. I excused myself went outside, Sandy followed me out. "Sandy, you must tell your husband. Weather he believes you or not you must tell him. There's one more thing."

Sandy ask, "What is that?"

I told her we leave tonight.

Later I lead the horses around the house. Loaded it with the thing Lola had bought. I told Lola to make ready. Take the back streets, no one will expect us to leave at night. By mid-morning we should be almost to the farm.

"I looked at Sandy, "You must tell him, I can't stress this enough. In two days if he don't believe you. Have him, bring you to the farm. I'll give him all the proof he will need, this I promise."

The day went easy, I saw the brothers twice watching the house. I knew they were up to something, I just didn't know what it was. I had a feeling I was going to find out if we stayed here. It was middle afternoon when they came. I open the door the to the Russian army.

The man said, "I am a lieutenant in the Russian army." I replied, "Well sir, how can I help the Russian army?"

The lieutenant said, "You whipped up on some of my citizen."

"They're not citizen." I said.

"Sir, whatever they are, they are protected by the Russian army."

"Sir, am I not protected by those same laws. Beside it is like a coward to attack a man, in the dark when he is outnumbered three to one. I whipped them, sent them into the street so the public could feast on them."

He said, "I could use a man like yourself."

I told him I have a farm to run, with my woman and child.

"Lieutenant my woman's sister lives here. We, leave at first light, her two daughters will be with us. I do not want to have any trouble with the brothers. I wish to be left alone to run my farm. If they come looking, I promise the outcome will be different. Now sir we were sitting down to dinner."

I left the brother alone with the lieutenant walked inside closed the door.

Sandys husband said, "That took guts, to stand up to the Russian army."

I looked at sandy, "Yes it takes guts."

Lola made cheese and bread.

Boris ask, "Do you wanted beef?"

I told him, I do not eat meat.

He, look at Sandy, "It's not natural, it ant human."

Sir, you have been married for what, eighteen years to your wife? Two beautiful daughter, neither one eat meat. Yet you trust them."

Of course, he said laughing, "It's just I've never met a man, that dont eat meat."

"Well, now you have." He got up walk to the door. He placed his hat on.

"I got to go," he said."

I ask him, "If I might come alone?"

He just mumbled, "Come on yes, it will be good". Leaving the house down the cobble stone street to the eatery.

The brothers were waiting, a I thought.

"Boys you now I dont open until sun down." Boris said. "Why are you here."

"We, wanted to talk to you," One said.

Well talk, "I got thing to do."

"We're not talking in front of him."

Well I'll leave." I just wanted to see what it looks like in here. I've never been in an eatery. Where I'm from we have tea houses." They all laughed.

"Well I'm going I need to sleep. We're leaving at first light." I went to the barn I called Lola and the girls. Helping them in the wagon. I told Lola to go to the end of the street. Wait for me there, I watch them turn into the street. I told Sandy I hope to see her again. Remember Sandy, Myas' blood runs through your veins. Mya was a princess of our world. Dont disgrace her, tell him or your daughter will, maybe even Lola. Tell him, then bring him to the farm.

Sandy I said, "Two days we leave for the ship. The DNA will take place. Then we leave this planet."

I walk back to the eatery. Looking through the window, the brothers were their all five of them. Running down the back street, I caught up with Lola. The girls had made a bed behind the wagon. Georgia said, "It was nice under the stars."

I took the rings of the horses.

Lola said, "They would stay on the road."

She laid her head on my shoulder, really I dont know how she slept. About one hour later she woke up, looking around.

"I was tired," she whispered.

I told her I can't sleep like this. I said, "I can move through space at thousands of miles an hour, never miss a wink."

Riding In the wagon, the short time I have known Lola, she has fell in love with me. I think I love her too. I do feel different when she is close.

We pulled up by a stream to let the horses drink. I also got water for the girls. Behind me I heard something. The horses jumped, Lola grab the rings.

"Whoa" she said.

I placed the water on the wagon. "Who is out there," I said.

There was no reply, a faint wind picked up, the night was warm. It felt good on my sweaty skin, then I caught a faint smell of whiskey. A man appeared, I stood ready. I had placed a long stick I had used in town in the wagon. In a fight with the brother, I took the stick, from the wagon.

Nancy sat up. "Oh, know not again." "Comp, everywhere we go you're in a fight. You sure like to fight."

Little one I said, "Maybe that won't happen."

Nancy said, "Sure it will, that's the man you hung in a tree."

"Well Nancy there's going to be a fight." He came closer.

The old man said, "I'm going to teach you about hanging a man in a tree. Then I'm going to take your woman."

Georgia and Mary, had raised up. The man had no idea what was about to happen to him. Hell, I didn't even no. The girls gathered in a huddle in the wagon.

Lola said, "Now girls."

"I jumped out of the way when a strong wave of air hit him." It sent him flying across the road. I went to check on him he was dead.

Lola ask, "Is he ok."

I told her just knock the breath out of him. Later I told her the truth.

Lola said, "Will teach him to mess with my farm boy."

I said to Comp, "I never knew they could do that."

Nancy looked at me, "See I told you."

I climb back on the wagon, we were on our way again. I'll be glad to get there I was very tired.

I watched Lola build a fire in the make shift stove. Lola believe this. "We have lights, cooking surfaces on Boldlygo. It works on electricity."

"What is that Lola ask."

"Well, say you are in the cooking room, you go to the bed room. You touch a button on the wall, a light comes on. If you go to the cooking room, you turn a nob the surface heats up, were so advance. So much more than Earth, someday Earth will be there. That's a long way off."

I told Lola in six hundered years, Earth may go to your moon. I've already been to your moon. The very one we looked at each night. You can't live there, On one of our moons you can. I've been there there is a large city, Garf oversees the moon. The girl listen as I talk. Georgia had so many question, I could hardly keep up.

Georgia ask, "Is there humans there."

I said, "On the moon, or Boldlygo."

Both girls said, "Either."

"There's hundreds, on the moon. I'm not sure how many is on our world. At one time, there was humans everywhere."

"What happen to them." Mary ask.

Mary, I said, "Humans are a strange species. Always moving fast, some come to Earth, some to other places."

"Well if it's as wonderful as you say, why leave." Lola ask.

"That I cannot answer."

"On Earth, we dont know about thing like that." Mary said.

"Georgia before I was as old as you I had my own ship, had went to several planets."

She ask, "How old are you?"

I told her I was old.

Georgia, replied, "Know you're not."

"Georgia, on my world you would stay the same forever."

Mary ask, "How is that even possible? What of the other girls?"

I said, "They would continue to grow until the reach their female age. Then it stops, You can never die if you stay on the planet. Cra can answer you better. You will meet him soon."

"Humans don't want to die," I said. "Yet they run to death every day. I suppose humans just get bored, take your powers. The child you have, will help the boys in Stacie's. Ira someday will be leader of our planet. I had started the boys training. For several years, we trained, as your child, Lola's child. I will stay as a protector, plus help here. I just a short time have fell in love, on my world I never knew love. On a mission to Earth. Kohl, met this woman from the Moon of Corning. It was a place Destiny was from. He stayed with her, he fell in love."

"Tell us of Mya, "They said.

"I really can't tell you much of her. Mya, ascended long before me. There's writing of her in the archives. I know she was a princess. Ject, says she comes to him all the time. He calls to her she shows up."

"A ghost." Nancy said.

I told her I'm not sure of that.

Nancy ask me, "Comp how far is it to your world."

I told he it takes about two years.

She said, "That's a long time."

"It is, by the time we got there you would be all growed up. The traveling there would be worth the trip."

Lola said, "It was time for dinner."

I ask, "What are we having?"

"Lola said, "Bread, with cooked apples with milk and cheese."

The girls took care of the cleanup.

Lola ask, "Comp, will you walk outside with me? She said she wanted to show me the farm." We walk to a small hill. She kept looking back.

"I ask her, "What are you looking for."

She said, "To see if we were out of sight of the house." Then she grabs me, kissed me all over my face.

Then we were having sex as they say. I promise I did not try to stop her. Afterwards I looked at her.

I was going to ask "When we could do it again?" I know I was ready anytime. It wasn't long before the woman come out in her as she says. This time was different, She let out a moan, something she did not do the first time. She kept on moaning, almost a scream. Well at the end I did a little moaning myself. Lola was shaking as if she was cold. I didn't know what was happening, she kept saying "oh God." She said this, the faster I went. Then Lola fell of me, lay helpless on the ground. Seconds later she turned to me, laughing.

Oh, my Lola said, "That was wonderful, I've never had such a feeling as that before."

I ask, "Lola who was God?" She hit me on the arm. In less than thirty minutes we had dinner made love went to the orchard. Only here on this strange planet can this happen.

The morning come to quick, It come with rain. I was drinking coffee Lola had brought from Sandy's. I tell you of all the places I've been, this drink was the best I've ever had, I loved it.

Lola ask, "You want to see the rest of the farm?"

I told her sure. It's raining something I've never seen on our world, or the snow that falls.

Nancy ask, "You don't have snow?"

I told her not in my life time, it was always the same each day. Maoke created the planet as far as I know. He made us a paradise. Maoke is Jects father, that's what I read in the archives.

"How old is he? Lola asK.

I said to the girls, "Maoke past long before me. He is in the ancient city, a city hidden from all. It a place where the Unicorn, the Pegasus live with the Busie."

The rain had stopped, I said to Lola, "You ready"

Lola showed me the peaches, I tried them, I love them. The apples the grapes. I told her I wish we had these on my world. She told me to take cutting of them.

We do have fruit, all kinds just not like this. We have Simons.

"What is a Simon," she asks?"

I told her it is long, round fruit, you peel it then eat."

She showed me the goats, "this is where the cheese come from."

"I wish we had this on my world to." We walk back to the house. Mary had made coffee. It was my third time to have it.

Walking to the table, I pushed Lola against the wall. I was kissing her on the face, the girl started laughing.

Lola said, "We dont do this in public."

I said, "What about the barn the field."

Mary said, "Aunt Lola you didn't."

I said, "Oh yes she did."

Georgia said, "Walking around the room. You may not need the DNA transfer."

I ask her, "What that meant."

Georgia said, "She could already be with your child."

That not true. "I have not given her DNA."

Georgia said, "You are silly man, How do you think you get with child on Earth."

I'm not sure, "She was my first."

Mary said, "Comp, to come from a planet so advance, you really dont no much."

Well I said, "I do know one thing."

Mary ask, "What would that be?"

"I wanted more of it."

Mary said, "Yeah men do."

We talk late into the evening. I stepped out while the girls got ready for bed. I saw the light, they were waiting for the signal. The light was still there when Lola come out.

Lola said, "It's cool for this time of year."

I told her, It stays the same year round at home. I told Lola to look up. Considering the the heavens Lola saw light.

Lola said, "Comp, that's the brightness star I've ever seen."

"It's not a star Lola. It's Tudo they're coming. They're waiting on my signal, I will send the signal tomorrow night. I will show you how to use the stone." I took it from my pocket and showed Lola. "Take the stone hold it to your chest, the warmth of the body causes the stone to open. A pulse of light will shoot up. The ships will come."

"Comp what if you're on your planet?" Lola asked.

I tried to thank of an easier way. "Lola the truth, it would take two months for the signal to arrive. Two years for us to get here. I know it's a long time, it's the only way."

Lola asked me again, "Will you stay?"

I told her, "If Tudo gives his ok I will stay."

"What if I ask him?" Lola said.

"I'll tell him I'll do his son's, I'll take Ira's DNA." "I want you stay with me, Comp I love you. Nancy will have a father. Something she has never had."

239

I ask, "Where is he, your husband?"

"I dont know Comp, he left long ago. After I realized I was going to have a baby. He left one day and never returned."

I took her in my arms and kissed her. Let's go in I said, turning I caught a shadow from the vineyard.

I told her to close the door, go to the girls. I went to the fire and picked up a small ax she called a hatchet.

"What is wrong?" she asks.

I said, "Someone's in the vineyard, blow out the light." Out the back door I placed my back to the wall. Many, many years ago, the old man that Destiny came to live with built the house in a hill. Access to the roof was easy. Dirt was brought dumped on top, with sod planted. Crawling on top I slide on my stomach. I could see the vineyard and the orchard. Whoever it was, he was sitting on the ground waiting. Like a thief in the night. I thought, what was he waiting for. I watched him several minutes, timing is everything. If you wait long enough someone will move. Ject always said patients is your friend. Wait the enemy will move.

When the shadow moved, I waited several minutes. It was a man, he walks to the barn. I moved from the roof. Where I could see the barn. The moons had broken out from behind the clouds. I could see the farm from every angle. I lay waiting for whatever it was or whoever it was. I thought in my mind, what will I do. The words just kept going through my mind. Wait the emery will move, wait for your moment. From where I was I could see the barn the yard. He was holding a weapon in his hand.

Whoever it was walk humped over trying to hide. Creeping closer to the house, he never saw me, it was too late for him. The man was looking through a window. I made my move, I hit him hard, he was down out like a light. I jumped up on the porch, Lola was waiting. I told her I need a light, Lola handed me a candle.

I placed it to his face. I ask, "Do you know him?"

"Yes, Comp it's my husband."

I said to her, "Well now he is your dead husband." I'm sorry Lola.

"Comp lets drag him to the barn" she said.

I told her, I would dig a hole, in the barn yard. Lola fell into my arms.

Oh Comp, Lola said. "I'm so glad you were here. The Russian army made him leave, for the thing he did to me and Nancy. He was a very mean man. I suppose he come back to help himself again," Lola said.

I really was not sure what she meant, so I left it alone. Behind the barn, I dug a hole in the sandy soil. Five foot deep. Rolled him in covered him up. I took her in my arms, "you'll never have to worry about him again.

Morning come early, after digging a hole all night.

Mary ask, "What was out there last night?"

"Someone wanted to sleep in the barn." I said.

Lola said, "He has already gone."

Mary give me a quick look." I'm sure he is cold to I'll bet."

I give her a quick look. She just smiled. Lola give me coffee again. This I would miss if I left. I must insist on Tudo to try the coffee. There was a noise outside, then a wow. I looked at Lola, it was Sandy and her husband.

I said to Lola, "Well I guess he needs more proof."

Sandy enter the house, her husband behind her. I could see she was scared to death.

Sandy I said, "Something bothering you." Her husband with a strong voice, "How dare you put crazy thought in my family's head."

I told him, When we were in town we were never introduce. He said, "I am Boris."

"I am called Comp." I'm from a planet two hundred fifty light years away. It takes two years, to travel here."

In a heavy Russian accent, "Boris said bull shit. I will break you into. I should have let the brothers kill you, as they wanted to. The lieutenant wanted to place you in jail. I should let him do that."

Boris, I said. "Are you scared of me."

"Ha!" He said with a laugh.

I reached for my coffee cup, Boris took a punch at me. I ducked he missed, I didn't. I dont no, where that come from. I hated this planet, humans always fighting. Boris hit the floor I took a chair placed over his chest. I sat looking down on him.

"Now Boris, will you sit and talk like a man. We could keep fighting. Sir, I assure you I'm a warrior on my world. Your too confident in your size. That's what got you through life." Boris was six foot four, at two hundered seventy pounds. No doubt if he had hit me it would have cause damage.

"I will let you up, if you will talk to me as a man. Boris, I was trained good."

Boris said, "Let me up. I want know more trouble." I moved the stool from his chest give him my hand. Sure enough, he did what I thought he would do. I pulled him up, he took another swing. I decked him he went to his knees.

"No one does this to Boris," he said.

Sandy jumped up. "Enough Boris, in front of the children. We, believes him Boris, why can't you."

"There is no such thing as space people." he said.

Boris still on his knees, I told him for over one hundred years, it has been passed to the girls, of us what we look as our race, their DNA.

"Boris, ever notice its only girls we have." Lola said.

I said, "Come my friend sit," Sandy poured coffee.

"Why did you do this," Boris said?

I told him," Boris I was not going to let you beat me."

"No, you tell them you are from space."

"I am Boris."

"You can't prove this."

I told him I can, I will tonight.

My daughter, "My wife said she is having a baby."

"She will Boris." I said.

Boris said, "She is to marry a Russian guard."

"She will not marry him, she will have the child. Boris, haven't you see how they look in to the night sky. Always looking to the stars."

Yes, I have, "Sometimes I have, almost every night, that it is clear."

"Boris, did you wonder what they were looking for?" I ask. Boris, had that look of thought.

"Maybe they were just looking into the heaven, at the stars." Boris said.

I told him, Boris they were looking for home. They dont belong here anymore.

What you say, "My wife cheated on me, with a space man."

I told him, look you fertilized the egg. The DNA was already there, they have the human look inside of them. She is part native of our world. Can't you see how intelligent they are.

"Mary, Georgia, Nancy, Your wife Sandy, Lola without turning around they all walk to me." The girls stood in a circle. I walked to the fire place, took a piece of wood. I laid it on the table, Boris watched with concern.

"What is to happen know?" He said.

The girls went into deep thought.

Boris said, "See Sandy this is bull shit."

Boris didn't even get the words out, when the wood flew into pieces.

"You need more proof Boris." I said.

Lying on the floor Boris said, "Oh God, what is this."

Boris, I said, "They can do this with humans also."

I ask, "You need more proof?" The ships will be here soon Boris, want to go to space. You can never tell anyone about it. If you do, they will lock you in a prison so fast. Your family will be with me on a ship to our world."

Boris dropped his head. "I dont know my own family."

Boris pulled himself to his feet. Started to the door.

Sandy, went to him, took his arm.

"Boris I do love you." Sandy said. "I should have told you many years, ago. For that I'm truly sorry."

Boris said, "I need to be alone, Sandy."

Sandy replied, "Yes I suppose you do."

Boris walked outside. I saw him go toward the orchard. Several hours passed when Lola ask, "You think he is alright?"

I told her I need to go to the barn. I was cleaning a stall, I didn't know much about. I found a small wheel, took some lumber made a plat form. I was wheeling the manure to the place Lola showed me to pile it.

Lola said, "We can use it on the garden."

Boris came into the barn. "I want to think you for what you did for Lola in town. The brothers are bad people, Lola deserves better."

"I answered," she does. "Boris where I'm from you dont treat women as that."

"Comp no one has ever done that and live. Not against the brothers."

I told Boris, Always the first time.

The day went on Boris sit drank vodka."

Boris ask, "Comp have a drank with me."

I took the bottle turned it up. I spit it out, "know I do not like it. I'll drank coffee Boris."

Boris ask, "Where is this ship from space you talk about?"

I told him, Come out side. I took the stone held it to my chest. A beam of light shot out.

"Well where is it" Lola said.

Boris said yeah, Space man where is it."

The ships appeared, Boris went to his knees, Mary did also. Lola stood by me holding to me so tight it hurt my arm. Nancy, Georgia looked in ah.

The Staff of Ira

Boris was speaking in Russian. "Oh God, Please help me." The ships landed, the ramp went down. Tudo appeared, "Come quickly," he said. The Russian army is coming. So far, we haven't been seen." Everyone was running, I took hold of Boris, arm he like the others were scared, except for the girls.

I ask, Lola, "When they come they want find you."

"Dont worry," she said. "We'll make an excuse. It's worked before, Lola said. There is a small room under the house. We hid there from the raiders. Trust me I know what to do."

The pilot took off, we still haven't been seen. From the dark they could not see how Tudo looked. The ship went higher, Inside the ship, the lights come on. I turned to look at Lola, she stood staring out the portal as Earth was left behind. Boris well, he looked as if he needed a bottle. Mary stood by her mother. Georgia, Nancy was talking to Ren, Foo as if they were children which they were. Lola took a small book from her pocket, on the parchment was drawn a likeness of them. Cra walked over to Lola.

"I was a very small boy when we brought Destiny to Earth, It was my father, I was alone for the ride. I see she did well."

"Foo, Ren, Nancy stared to leave."

Lola, reached for Nancy.

"Lola let her go," I said.

Tudo said, "I feel that you are uncomfortable."

"Scared," Lola said.

Tudo walked to her, "Trust me we would never hurt you."

"I'm not afraid of you," Lola said. "This is something you dont see every day. I'm not sure what we are doing."

Boris said, "I need a drink." Turning his bottle of vodka up, the bottles went half way down. Tudo watch this, looked at me. Mary still looking at Tudo. Tudo started to speak to her.

Mary spoke. "The stories that has been passed down to us, will live in our heart, our children forever. Mary, bowed to Tudo."

Georgia said, "We have waited our life for you, our family's before us. My family the ones I know, always said, they hope you would come in their life time. As we did the same, each night we say tomorrow could be the day, here you are." Tears fell down her face.

"I am Georgia, fifth generation of Destiny. A descendant of Mya, a most intelligent being of the planet of Boldlygo. If family is the same there, she would be your aunt, your fathers sister."

Tudo said, "That would be correct."

"That sir would make us Royal Blood."

"You are correct." Tudo said.

Georgia said, "I can only say, there's others. We dont know them, in the years that has passed the family's left to others places. The ones that are here are the ones I know. The coins aunt Lola has, is our only connection to you. We have honored it throughout the years. Passed down from Destiny."

Georgia said, "Now it's time for us to go home."

Cra looked at Tudo.

Tudo replied, "It will be an honor to have you."

Tudo said, "Mary I've been told you will do the DNA transfer. If you do this Tudo said, you must stay here on Earth until the child reaches manhood."

Lola spoke. "I will take this DNA for you. Under one condition."

"Only one," Tudo said. "What would that be."

"You must leave Comp here as a watcher. We will need a man to take care of things. Things we can't do."

Cra said, "Having a baby here on Earth, I've been told is quite different than on Boldlygo."

Tudo said to Sandy. "Tell me you have said nothing."

"The two girls are my daughters." "Mary ask to do this?" Then ask, "If she could go back with you?"

Tudo looked at Lola, then Sandy, Tudo said, "The two young girls, could come with us now. I promise you they will be respected through the years they will be gone. There's fine schools they could attend. The boys can help the girls alone the way."

I said, "Tudo they have powers."

Tudo ask, "What powers Comp."

I placed a pillow on the floor. The girls destroyed it. Tudo said, "I see what you mean."

Boris said to the girls. "All your life I knew you were different, smarter. I want stand in your way. Georgia, I love you. Mary, I love you to. My girls you always have been. Go if you ever want to come home I'll be here for you. Maybe I want pass before I see you again. If I do always remember I love you."

Foo, Ren took Nancy by the hand. They become friends instantly, they would stay that way for many years to come. The boys took the girls to the bridge.

Lola ask, "Should we leave them alone Comp."

I told Lola, Hard as it is to believe, the boys could fly the ship at six year old, they will be fine.

Comp Tudo said, "Bring them to the pods. I will show them the boys, In the chambers that had been prepared for them." Tudo said, "Mekon is to your left, Ira to the right."

Mary ask. "When the babies are born, will they look as they do now?"

Cra said, "Your child, when born will look as human as you, I promise you."

Mary said, The reason I ask, "If they look as they do now the army will kill them."

Boris still could not comprehend what was happening.

I told him to stop drinking the vodka, enjoy the ride. Everyone was relaxing soon the transfer would take place. It wasn't long before we were heading back to the farm.

Mary ask Tudo, "Will you leave after, or stay for a while? There so much I would like to know. So much I want to ask?"

Tudo said. "Mary, we will stay several days, you will see us again. I will send the shuttle for you, maybe come myself."

"Comp tell me of the fruit you have in your orchard.

Tudo talked to me of the Lola's request.

Tudo I said, "I think it would be a good idea to stay. Mary and Lola will need help. The pilot will take the bridge on the way back home."

Tudo said, "I see a great woman in Lola. Even her off springs." Tudo also told Mary when we return. If you still want to go you will be welcome

Almost as it started, it was over. We were going to the floor. Tudo scanned the farm there were only animals. landing behind the hill where Lola and I was before.

Tudo told then, "Tomorrow we will come for a talk. I know there is a lot of unanswered question. We walked to the house, as the ship went higher in to the darkness.

CHAPTER 20

Lola and I spent the next several months together. Her and Mary had gotten so big they waddle. Sandy and Boris come often. He, as always has question. I had built a room on the house. Showed her how to cure the apples. We were having a simple life.

Every now and then the army would come by. The lieutenant as always would try to get me to come along. Today was no exception, I was milking the goats, when they arrived.

He took a bottle of vodka. "Comp, lets drink a toast to mother Russia."

I replied. "Lieutenant you know I only drink coffee. I have too much to do.

"Comp, you must drink with me."

The vodka I dont care for. I told him, "Tell your men to water the horses, hay in the barn."

Tell me Comp, "Where is the little girl, I've been asking."

"Oh, you mean Nancy. She went to school, somewhere to the west. Georgia went also. They will be gone for a while."

Looking around he said, "You have been busy since I was here last."

"Boris, from town, comes here often. Boris brings his wife here, Lola is her sister."

"Yes, I know, tell me Comp;" "Boris said he was selling his business in Saint Petersburg. He tells me is daughter is having a baby, also Lola."

"She is," I said.

Tell me Comp, "Mary is having a baby from a Russian guard."

I told him, I've never met him, I can't say.

The men had their meal. The lieutenant said goodbye. Comp the lieutenant said. "I will see you after the winter snow." I went to Lola I ask her about the snow?

Comp she said. "You dont have snow on your planet."

"No I replied,"

Lola said, "You dont have a coat."

Boris said, "I have a coat, I'll bring it from Saint Petersburg, on the next visit."

I ask Lola, "How do you stay warm."

Lola said, "Wood for the fire keeps us warm. You take an ax and a saw, you go to the woods with a wagon. Cut down trees, bring the wood to the house."

I ask, "How long before the snow comes."

Lola thought august, September, October, November "four month."

Boris left I told him I had to cut wood. I'll see you when you return.

Boris said. "I need to talk to you. Much I need to know."

I ask Boris, "Did Lola give him the supply list."

"Yes, he said."

I told him, If he saw someone in town, that needed a job cutting wood, I could use them.

Comp, "How can you pay them."

"In your business, you meet people with monies."

Boris said, "Yes I meet people."

"Well maybe you could sell something for me."

You Comp, "What would you have to sell. I cannot sell a space ship."

I reached in my pocket took out my little pouch. I open the pouch, four stones fell out, I showed him the red one.

"Ah my friend let me look." Boris said. "This will pay for two men, pay for the supplies. It will give you some extra monies. Comp what of the other."

"I will leave them for you, when I leave for my home."

Boris left, I finished my chores, went into the house. Lola was on the sofa, looking kind of sick.

I ask, "You feeling alright?"

She said, "I'm tired." Mary was lying on a cot.

Mary ask, "You want to talk a while." Believe me after seven months I was talked out. I was ready for them to have the babies.

I ask her, "What she would like to talk about?"

Walking over, I sat down with Lola.

Mary said, "Tell me more about Mya. I told you all I know of her. As 'I've told you before, Mya died long before I was born. All I know is what I've read he archives. Of course, Ject talks about her all the time. When Tudo arrives home, you will be placed in the archives also."

"You, will be known as Mekon, and Ira Earth mothers." I've told you before, when the child is born he will grow fast. It will be ok to attach yourself to the child. When the balance is restored with the essence. You will not only loose them, you will gain them back. Mekon and Ira will have all the memory of the child you have. The bodies will be carried to a place of choice buried. Dont let it upset you, Ira never knew his mother. Carrie left on a ship so did her mother, after Ren was born. I took my pouch from my pocket, showed them the stones. All the girls looked at them.

I told Sandy, I give Boris one to hire me two wood cutters. Pay for my supplies, he could have the rest.

Mary ask, "where did you find them"

I told her they're everywhere on my world. in the streams, the forest the Marder-to-go's. On the side of the paths. People have them all in their homes. You can just pick them up.

Comp, "Is everyone rich," Mary ask.

"I'm not sure of the word." I said.

Sandy said," Does everyone have money."

I looked at Sandy, "Only on Earth do you need money." On the planets, we trade with stones.

"So, when you go to the store, say to buy a dress you, use a stone," Sandy said.

"Know there is no dresses."

"So, what do you wear, "She ask.

I said, "Robes some do wear other attire. You go to a store as you say, take what you want go home. "No payment required."

Lola, said with a smirk, "I do not believe you."

"It has always been that way Lola. Back to the beginning, Maoke and the others. What you take today it will be back tomorrow. Ject said you can have them. The only way to leave the planet with the stones is by permission by him or Tudo. if you are caught leaving with stones. You cannot return you could be sent to the Moon of Spores."

Mary said, "The stones are just lying everywhere."

Yes, "Mary everywhere, sometimes I think it's the stones that make the water turn color. The falls at the Marder-to-go's is as a rainbow. I told them it's my belief that the sun shines on the stones that reflect that changes color.

Sandy said," I'm not that smart."

I took a glass of water held it to the sun. I Placed it so you can see through it. Sure, enough look I said "see the colors." It's the glass, water sun. After all glass is from sand; sand is a stone. It's been crushed, heated to a liquid. I spent several days talking to Mary, Lola, Sandy. I found they're wonderful humans."

CHAPTER 21

Our ship was several months in flight to our world. Cra, has spent most of time at the pods. I truly hope my son will not hold bad ties for me. The boys lay in stasis, Yet they continue to grow.

Cra said, "Tudo, Ira can hear your every word. He just can't answer you."

I ask Cra, "What have we become?"

I told Cra. Maoke could see everything. Do you think he could see this? Why did he not stop us?

Cra said, "Maybe Maoke, wanted to see how we did this."

Tudo, "Ject did say Maoke said, not to do this again. To go this long without him, I'll miss his childhood. Someday Tudo, I hope we can go further. I believe my son will or their children. We can't have the city all natives. We need the humans help. I have a feeling they'll always will be a few to help us. Look what they have accomplished, from well from Kesha to where we are now. Gore, Madison, Tomeka the other females."

I ask your father, about coming here? He told me humans were easier to deal with. Especially the Indians. They believed we were the great sprits that lived in the stars. When Tomeka her sisters were taken back we wrote in the archives, so did the

Indians. They told their stories around their fires as they will do forever.

Cra I said, "It was still hard for me to see my son lying in those pods. Regardless of him being half human half native." I walked to the portal, staring out. A sentry came to me, "Tudo, there a ship on the scope." I went to the bridge, "captain."

Tudo, "Something is here."

I looked, "It is a ship bring us out of hyperspace, then to impulse."

"As you wish," The pilot said.

The other ship came along side of us. It was a ship I've never seen, I watched them go off to the right. I told the captain, take us back to hyperspace. I went back to the boys. I sat talked to them for hours before I retired for the night. I told Cra, I would be in my room.

"Have a goodnight Tudo."

I slept very well this night in space. I woke up early went to the galley for fruit. I wish for the drink comp give to me. I find it was very tasteful. Especially with the stuff he called honey. I thought, why we dont have thing like that. Maybe we do, we just haven't looked. I'll ask my father, on my return?

For the next several months in flight, we never saw another ship. The ends of the fourteenth month we landed on the Moon of Corning. I must say I needed to feel ground under me. I did like space travel, not as my father. My father could have gone forever, me not so much. Landing on the pad, the hatch opened.

"Everyone, ask if they could exit the ship."

I told them to come with me, I walked down the ramp Quad meet us. Georgia stumbled I caught her. I could read every thought that went through her mind. "We can't mate Georgia. You are a beautiful woman."

Georgia said, "I know Tudo, I just wanted to be close. Tudo I'm coming into woman hood. I will take a mate someday somewhere."

I said to her, "First your schooling. Nancy also.

"I do wont to learn all I can." Georgia said.

"I could contact Cot on Plano. The schools they're the best."

Pep was there to greet us also, Pep was older than me. He was three hundred years older. He would be the same age as Mya. I never knew her, not that I can remember. Greeting were given.

"told them I had passengers.

Quad said, "Tudo please bring them forward. Nancy come first, then Georgia."

Pep fell to the ground. It's not possible," Pep said.

Pep I ask, "You ok?"

"She's dead, I was there."

"Pep who do you think she is," I ask.

"It's Mya" he replied.

"Pep this is Georgia, from Earth."

"She is Mya," Then walked away.

Georgia ask, "May I go for him."

I told her if, she wishes.

Quad said to me, "It insane Tudo she is a picture of Mya. I knew who Mya was."

Cra said, "Tudo she is of Mya's DNA its possible."

Quad said, "I only know Mya was beautiful."

I said to Quad, "Georgia was a descendant of his sister Destiny."

Quad replied, "Then she is family to me as to you."

Georgia caught up with Pep. they spent most of the day talking.

Pep ask, "Are you afraid of us?"

Pep, Georgia said, "I have from the beginning of Destiny lived for this moment. We grew up knowing you were different."

Pep ask," Georgia what was her planes."

I told Pep all about them. The experiments of the boys in stasis. What the experiment was supposed to do. I told him I wanted to learn all I could of my people.

"Georgia, we only met, if I do this will you mate with me?"
Georgia said to Pep, "You were Mya's mate".

Pep said," Yes I was."

"That would kind a of make you my grandfather."

"Yes, I suppose It would," Pep said. Pep took Georgia in his arms, I suppose you are right, in some ways. You dont have my DNA, so it would be permitted. Ject is going through that with Mya."

"Pep, "You said she is dead."

Yes, she is, "Only Ject, can see her." Mya wants him to ascend so they can be together in the ancient city."

I was told, Maoke want allow it to happen.

Pep said, "It doesn't matter, Royal Blood should stay in the family. I knew when you stepped off that ship you were of Mya's blood. I remember the trip to Earth, when Lon did the transfer. The woman was from here. She was a teacher."

Pep brought Georgia back to the house of Quad. Everyone was busy loading supplies. I sat long in the night with Pep, Quad, Kohl, Joy stayed for a while.

Joy ask, "Tudo may I speak to the girls."

Tudo said, "Yes I'm sure they would like that."

"Joy told them Destiny come from here, she was my aunt."

Nancy said, "So you are our people."

Joy said, "Yes I suppose I am." You are our family also family of Boldlygo."

The girls returned, said they were going to the ship to retire for the evening.

I told them of all the thing that was going on. Kohl ask of Comp. I told him he wanted to stay with Lola to help on the farm. I told them Nancy was Lola's child.

I ask Quad of Destiny? He was eager to talk.

It was late when I returned to the ship. I sat on the side of my bed thinking of my son, and Mekon. My thought went to Earth, the children will be doing well by now. I'm sure Comp, is treating then very well. Comp will be a great inspiration, teaching them all the thing that was to come. He will lead them through the journey that has begun for them. Comp is a very loyal person. I think of him often, for some reason I dont see him coming back to stay. Lola will want him to stay, I can't say I would put blame. Lola is a very beautiful woman. Comp is his own man, he will teach the boys on Earth everything they will need to know. I hope someday this DNA will prove to be beneficial.

For some reason my my thought went to Carrie. It had been years since I've thought of her. The things I thought of her, Carrie was a beautiful woman. Carrie give me two sons, Ira and Ren from DNA. They will never know the differences.

The morning came early, we said our goodbyes to all, on the Moon of Corning.

Pep ask, "Tudo I wish to come alone?"

Quad granted him his wish. He only wanted to be close to Georgia. The voyages to our home was quite the trip. Ren, Foo, Nancy spent hours in the stasis room. Cra was preparing, for the boys to come off the ship when we arrived. From the time, we left home, until know, I could not believe how much they have grown. Ira takes DNA from my father. I myself did not grow so tall. Maoke was six foot two inches. Ject six foot three. Ira will go over six foot, Ren will also. I try to picture them in their world. I see Ira six hundered years old with long white hair, long beard. I look at my father, he already looks as this. My father would ascend now if he could. He tells me he must wait until he can leave the world in my hands. That would be hard for me. I was ready to step in, If he was to ascend, I feel he wants to see Earth just once more.

In my thought, I find, why does this blue planet called Earth. Why does it have such a strong pull on us? Maybe old Bota placed something in our DNA long ago. A place if need, we could go live among the humans. Maybe therefore we experiment on them so we can live with them. I feel some day that will happen. Humans with DNA from us, Destiny did, see what the return was. Georgia, Nancy, Mary, Lola. Everyone that took part there on Earth.

I myself would never think of leaving my planet to live on another. Through the years many people have come and gone, even back to Earth. If a being knows what to look for they can spot the alien blood. There's just a little different in them. Beside were not the only being on Earth or races, or colors. The best I can tell there were at least seven different planets living there. My father told me there was throughout the galaxies there's over one hundered fourteen planets that have humans living on them.

Earth has Palatonian, Centurian, Valorian just to name a few, In the Earths galaxy of the Milky Way. How can they not know this, yet they're not that advanced? I think sometimes we should conquer the planet, claim it for our self. I myself would not live there To much water. There is danger in the water, very mean animals. Beast that would harm you. On our world, we all live as one. This is what I dont understand of the humans. Why they want to leave our world. We have given them a paradise in space. I think after my son returns from this ordeal I've put him in, I'll never leave the planet again. I want even go to the Moon of Spores.

Several months later we enter the galaxy of our world. In minutes, we were flying over the planet. Making our descent to the surface. The captains roared across the city. Ive seen this done many times. My father's friend Cam, started this with old Bota thousand years ago, the tradition continues today.

The west staging area lights came on as we sat down. My father was there to greet us. My father embraced me.

My son he said, "Good to see you home."

"Father it was a long journey. "I said.

He looked up as Georgia walked of the ship. Falling to the ground. "He whispered Mya."

"Father, it's not Mya. Her name is Georgia."

My father said, "She is of Myas blood." Standing up my father took her hand.

Come child, "Much to talk about. Georgia told my father of Nancy. They turned to see Ren, Foo, Nancy enter the palace."

Georgia said, "Well I see she is home."

I walked to the lab. Sentrys were helping Cra take the boys from the ship. Cra placed them in a room built before we left. How long will they be here before there? Placed back on the ship for their return to Earth? I thought, the Earth children would be two years old by now.

I left Cra with his work. I went to the palace to visit with my father. Watching him talk to Georgia, I thought this would have been the way he talks to Mya. Since everyone said she looked as Mya. Walking in to the great room my father said to me.

"Tudo come son, Georgia was telling me of the descendants of Myas DNA." My father said he remember when Destiny went to Earth. That's how it started, our family of Earth,

"Georgia said all females." Georgia ask, "I would love to see the city? When we flew over its the largest city in the world, 've never seen a city. Saint Petersburg was more of a village. Looking up I ask, How do you put oil in the light so high?"

"I looked at Tudo oil!"

"Oh, father it's a liquid they place in a reservoir with a flame." I walked over to the wall, Georgia look, I made a motion with my hand, a light went off. I did it again the light come on.

She smiled, "I've never seen anything like it." This world is my world."

I told her if you will stay.

I told my father to go to the city. Show Georgia the city, let her see the greatest city on the planet.

"Is there other," Georgia a

"Only one, know, one knows where its located. It's the city of the ancients."

"Comp, told me of a water fall" Georgia said. "He said the water was as a rainbow." May I see it also?"

I replied, "Soon." My father took to Georgia as I knew he would. I went back to the lab. Cra said he had placed the boys in the room. Walking back to the palace Ren was sitting with Nancy, having fruit with bread.

"I ask, "Nancy if it's good?"

Nancy said, It is. "I miss my mother badly. Ren is a good friend. He tells me he wants to be a pilot." The greatest pilot of all."

Well maybe he will. I looked at my son. Ren I said, "You think you can stand in your grandfathers shoes."

"I'm not sure father, I was thinking I want t to be more like Bota. The words I've read in the archives."

Nancy ask, "What is the archives?"

I t old her it was a place of history. "Ren must take you there."

"Mother taught me to read words." she said. Really, I think I already knew. You know, I am f rom Mya. I am Royal Blood.

I told her I did no. "Mya would be pleased with you."

Everyone was at the great room when I entered from the sleeping room. I took a Simon, bread. My father called to me.

"Tudo join us."

Nancy said, "She would share her bread with me."

"I ask, What was going on?"

Georgia said, "They were talking of the archives." Georgia, Nancy brought laughter to the palace. Carrie laugh at most everything. A human expression. I dont know why we dont do that.

I ask Cra once, "He said it wasn't in our DNA?"

I ask Georgia, How was your, trip to the city?"

"It is a magnificent city, I've never seen a city so big. Moscow was the biggest city I have ever seen. Compared to Ratio it was small, very small. I was amazed of the lights, No one on Earth has lights. No one."

I told her in the years to come, Earth would be heavily populated, they will have flying machines. She just looked at me with a strange look.

The night went on. My father said he was going to his sleeping room.

Nancy ask, "Where are we to sleep?"

"Ren, didn't you show her?"

"Know Opa, I was not sure."

"Place them in the room where Angies children were."

Father turned went to his room. "Girls we'll go to the falls at the Marder-to-go's tomorrow." See you for the morning meal.

"I love you," Nancy said."

Walking to my room, sit on on the bed. I was looking through the window across the staging area. The ships were sitting there calling to me. Oh, how I wanted to go. I wanted it so bad, leave it all behind I thought. Then I remembered, where would I find a captain. Comp, was on Earth, Kohl was on the Moon of Corning. I just did not have the time to train another.

I took my robe off, sat on the bed. A voice spoke.

I've waited all night for you to do that. It was Mya.

"Where have you been, I've called you several times?"

"Mother, would not let me come Ject." Then father would not let me go. Then Bota then so on, I tell you Ject its getting a girl, can't have time for herself. So, honey what's up.

I said, "Your jumping on my bed, stop calling me honey."

"Oh, Ject your no fun."

"Dont start Mya, I called you for a reason."

"I know, mother saw the children. The one that looks as me."

"Ject, do you really think she looks like me."

Yes Mya, "You have more human look than I do. The DNA passed down, you do look as she does. I was stunned when I first saw her. So was Pep, he is here."

"I want to see her Mya said."

"Go I said to her. They're in the twins room."

I went to the twins room. I mean I knew where it was. After all I, did live here once. Looking down on Georgia and Nancy I thought, yes, she does look as I do.

I starter to leave someone spoke. Turning to see the small child.

"Who are you." she asks? Georgia ask, Nancy who are you talking to?"

"I pointed, to her silly. Never mind she is gone." I went back to Jects room, looking a little different. "Ject when are you coming to the city, I'm so tired of being alone."

I broke up the conversation. Tudo said, "Pep took to Georgia right away, that's why he is here. He wanted to be close."

I said to Ject, "Guess he never got over me I do think of him sometimes." Ject why is it, "You, and the little one are the only ones that can see me."

"I jump from my bed."

"What did you say?"

The little girl Nancy, "She can see me."

"Mya, she must be stronger than we thought."

"Like you when you were here." Georgia, Mary her sister, with Nancy their very strong together."

You know Ject, "It is written in the archives three will come with powers and ability's."

I know Mya, "It's not then, as my grandson is not the Keeper of the staff."

The night went on, Mya left, I finally went to sleep. Next morning I was on the stoop having my Simon. Looking across the Valley of the Unicorn. Taking in the view, I felt a pull on my robe, it was Nancy. "Well, good morning little one." She took my hand pulled me down. Whispered in my ear.

"I got to pee."

Oh dear, "Ren did not show you," I ask.

"No, he just wanted to show me off to everyone. I think he likes me. He, would say to everyone, this is Nancy. She is from Earth"

I showed her the room.

Nancy said, "Ive never peed in a house before, how does it work."

I said to her, "You sit do what you must, then push the button." She did what she needed to do. Come from the room, where you going.

Looking at me, "I forgot to push the button."

Ive found a daughter I've never had. We sat had bread root, with a Simon. The world around us come alive. Nancy told me the valley in front of us was called the Valley of the Unicorn. I told her that was right.

She said, "I know about Unicorns, I've never seen one," she said. My great great grandmother wrote about a Unicorn that flew to Earth from a place far away. I listen at Nancy talked on. The gray streak of day had come to the morning sky. It sure looked as if another day would come to our world.

The sun come up as Nancy talked. How many times did I here that story. The stories she wrote was true. The Unicorn come from here.

Nancy ask, "Will you tell me the story sometimes?"

I told her I would be delighted. Ren, Foo some of the others will be in the park today. When we return from the falls I will tell the story to all you. You know, after all its my favorite.

The trips to the falls went very well. Georgia's hands went to her face, tears filled her eyes. "It's just the way Comp, said it would be." Nancy saw little furry animals. She told me, "on Earth there called rabbits. Some people eat them."

Nancy I ask, "Do you eat them."

No sir, "Know meat on my plate. Only fruits vegetables."

I said to her. "Good girl." Georgia said the same.

Ject Georgia said, "For seventeen years of my life it was a daily thing. We were taught of you coming. We had to be prepared, now I'm here. The ones that come before me. From Destiny to Nancy whatever happens we're here now. Ive waited my whole life for you, as the women before me. They knew someday you would return. Now if I go back to Earth I will be some much stronger, more intelligent. The Russians will look up to me."

"You can't let them know that you come here. Their government will not allow you to live in public. They will keep you locked up." I told both girls, take time to adjust to our world. If you wish you can start your studies. I may suggest the archives a place to start.

The girls did start their schooling. We would spend hours at night talking, it was always the same. A story as we eat, It had become a custom. Cra, Tudo, myself would tell stories. A young female native joined us, her name was Soy. She was as eager to learn as the others. She would listen as Georgia and Nancy would talk of Earth. Soy and the girls became very good friend. We were a big happy family.

Time slips away, I could not believe how long it had been since the girls had arrived here. It had been twelve years. Georgia has grown into a very beautiful woman, Nancy also. She still in my eyes look as Mya.

Mya would come to me, we would talk for hours. Nancy could no longer see her, that troubled Mya. When Nancy was, small I could hear, them talk. I could see her, even now. I could tell it bothered her to.

One night we sat by the great room. Nancy came wearing a red gown. It was bordered with black lace, why she called me father, I'll never know. She looked at me with tears in her eyes. Father,

I stood, "Nancy what is wrong child?" She looked at all of us. "It's time to go home."

Georgia ask, "Why do you say that Nancy?"

"Comp, has sent the signal."

"Tudo had started to the stoop when Cra come in."

"Tudo its time."

"Tudo said, We will leave tomorrow."

Georgia, Nancy was crying so hard. Georgia stood as I embraced her.

"I want you to know, I have loved you my whole life. I know we can stay here, yet I feel our place is on Earth. I believe we will strive to keep a place for our people to come, believe me there will be others.

I stood went to them. Standing on the stoop looking over the Valley of the Unicorn, we said our goodbyes.

I told them to always tell your children of us. The way we look, the way we think. Careful to let the humans no that your very intelligent. I told Nancy, I never had a daughter.

Nancy said, "Well now you do. I will always love you father. I will let our children know of you.

Nancy turned to Cra, "Take me to the lab. Give me the DNA."

"Georgia said me to."

I told them it would not be so good now. Cra went to the lad, took the boys form the room, where they were placed long ago. I looked at them every day. The boys had grown to manhood before my eyes. The pods locked in place, as Cra prepared them for the trip to Earth. I knew I would never see the girls again on our world. In the light of the morning sun, the ship went higher into the sky. I was alone again."

CHAPTER 22

Watching the snow fall, the morning was cold. I walked from the barn to the house, after the milking. Walking into the house, Lola mixed the flour for bread. I thought how I loved it. She would serve it with apples, pears sometimes I would have eggs. I loved the bread, hot from the oven. I would pour honey on it, with butter from the churn. The boys were growing, they looked as Mekon, and Ira in human form. I thought as I poured my coffee, two years to travel here that would be October. It was a trying time on this planet. The lieutenant, would make his last run this week. I went back to the barn. The snows would come faster and deeper. Boris, would make his last run with supplies, for the winter. I give him another stone. He smiled.

"Comp, I know what to do with it." Comp you said, "You would give them to me when you leave."

"I'll have more when they come back. I promise you four stones, you will receive four stones."

"Mary come to the barn," she calls to me. I was in a stall rubbing down one of the horses. Horses are amazing, wonderful animals in every way. Mary began talking, when Mekon jumped from the loft.

"Mother you look radiant today."

My son, "you are so sweet."

"Where is Ira," I ask Mekon?"

"He is with aunt Lola." Mekon said.

They were smart both. We started to the house when I heard the horses. The Russian army was coming, I told Mary, we need to set the table.

It was about five minutes when the lieutenant stop in the yard. Lola met him in the yard with fried pies made the day before. Lola carried them out to the troops. We stood around talking with the men.

Each said, "Thanks for the pies."

The lieutenant said, "Comp I will be leaving the Russian army. This will be my last run."

I ask him, "What will you do with yourself. He smiled as humans do."

"I'm not sure."

He asks, "Comp, can we stay in the barn tonight."

I told him it would be fine. I also told him no fires. The lieutenant was drinking coffee, He had another pie. He told Lola the pies were the best he has ever had.

I replied. "She can sure cook good."

The lieutenant said. "Funny how you to had babies at same time. How they both were boys. They're different these boys. It is my belief, that they are very intelligent."

Lola, and I sat looking at him.

Come on Comp, "They're too smart for their time. It's as if they're from somewhere else."

"Lieutenant you have seen these boys grow up, you know they're not from somewhere else."

"I know Comp, I can't put my finger on it, they are different."

In my thought, if you only knew.

Comp, "Come walk with me before dark?"

We took a walk to the orchard. The western sky was on fire, it appeared that way. The sun was setting, left a red glow on the horizon, it was a beautiful evening. Stopping by a pear tree the lieutenant reached up pull one off, a shooting star flew through the sky.

"That was beautiful," he said.

A thought went through my mind. You should see it from my world.

The lieutenant said, As the stares showed in the sky. "Ever wondered what is out there?"

I answered him by saying." Rabbits, wolfs, other animals".

No Comp, "Out there."

"Out where sir."

"Waving his hand, the lieutenant said." Don't you ever think about it comp."

I thought every day. I ask him, "How would you get there?"

My friend, "I've seen thing things in the night skies, I've never said anything to you about it." One night long ago, we were on our way here. I saw something that night, my men were tired, I never said anything to them. We stopped at the springs for the night. Whatever it was it come here, before sun rise it come back. Then Mary come here, she was to be my wife. Shortly after Mary come here she was with child. The child is not your, the one Lola had been not yours. My friend I'm not stupid."

"Sir, I never said you were. Let's go have coffee," I said.

The gray morning sky showed to the east. The lieutenant had his men up. Lola and Mary fed them cheese, with bread. The men all thanked us them left. The lieutenant shook my hand.

"Comp I will be back in the spring." I want be in the Russian army, maybe we can continue our conservation." Leaving the yard past the orchard, the lieutenant turned, waved then was gone.

I was working in the barn thinking of home. The morning was cool, from the wind that blew from the mountains in the distance. I stood up as I heard voices. It was Boris, from the look of the wagon, he had done good with supplies.

Comp, Boris said, "I brought everything you ask? I also brought you a new ax."

I told him I sure need it, from the years on Earth I had built up quite the muscles. My arms, chest was hard as a rock. Lola said she liked it.

I found myself thinking of her often. What will I do, when Tudo comes. Will I stay, or will I go. I have fell in love with her. Yet my love for home is more. Lola was getting on in age. She was not as old as me, Earth age was different. She was forty six Earth years old. From the time, I've been on Earth I was one hundred fifty years old. I was still stronger than the humans.

The boys were always trying me. I was feeding the horses when they jump me. Coming from the hay they thought they were hid. Landing on my back, I slung them to the ground. Ira said to Mekon.

I told you we couldn't do that. The boys knew why they had been given life, they also had started showing signs. I hope Tudo want be late.

We unloaded Boris's wagon. We sat talked most the night, he still did not know what to think of the way we were doing things. Sometimes I didn't know myself. Cra new, he was a very intelligent being. His son Mekon will be more. Mekon was always doing thing with the trees. Mekon grafted a plum with a peach. The fruits it produces taste as a peach and a plum, it was unbelievable. It went over fast. Farmers come from surrounding farms to see this done. Mekon would tell them go home do this to your trees. Prune the trees in the fall. Graft them in the spring when the sap comes from the roots. We did so much while we were on Earth, questions were being ask.

Sometimes we feared someone would come. We feared someone would try to take them from us. This was the reason I trained the boy to fence with a sword. Believe me I was good with a blade. Ject trained me. Ira, I swear it was like a blade was part of him. I've never seen a man that could handle a sword as Ira. Ira's sword was always tied to his back when he went to the woods. Ira was a cunning warrior. All the memory's will stay when the essence is restored to his natural body. Both will remember everything. I have stress through their training, that we were a peaceful race. The defense is in case we are provoked. Even then we strive not to engage in battle.

I took the boys to the woods one last time before the winter set in. Boris came alone with his vodka. We cut wood all day stacked on the wagon, carried it back to the house. I had also picked up quite amount of quartzite rock. Mekon said it would burn with a very hot flame. It would leave cinders in the fire. Mekons mind was always working. The food as crude as it was cooked on an open flame. Mekon would show Lola, and his mother how to process the milk to cheese. Boil the milk first, skim the cruds. Then let the milk sour it was used for making bread. The tastes it gives the bread was the best.

On this planet as any, time comes it goes it waits on no one. The first snow of winter fell, before long the ground was covered then a foot. Three weeks later three feet, It was still falling Lola told me it would be a bad winter. I wanted to go home I wanted the warm weather we have. I want to see the suns come up. I wanted Lola by my side, I had fell in love with her. I still wondered if I would go home, when Tudo comes I could not say. Looking from the big window I had placed in the house Lola loved it. We were completely snowed in, nothing moved. Mekon, and Ira would shovel a path to the barn today, tomorrow it would be covered over. I took one of the old quilts to the barn covered the horses. The goats would stay with the cows. It looked as if we would survive another winter.

In the next nine month until Tudo arrives I must make sure the boys were watched every minute. They must be careful of the thing they do. Mekon constantly doing, Ira always studying.

Well me I was getting older, even Lola could see. I sipped my coffee with my apple pie. Lola come to the table, sat with me.

"My love," she said. I see time catching up with you. If you dont leave soon, I know you will die." Lola said, "I have decided to stay here on Earth when Tudo returns. As much as it hurts, I must stay. Nancy will be coming back, she will need her mother. Georgia will come back also."

"They will not be the little girls that left. They will be grown."

She said she knew. Lola said she feel they will open a place for our people.

"Our people," I said."

She answered. "Our people that will come, way into the future." They will come here to live with us. We will look for them Comp. Just as you look for this Keeper of the staff. This person you speak of will be great with the staff. I feel my son will have control of the staff of Ira as you call it. My son will not be the keeper he is yet to come."

"I had a dream of a woman coming here from your world." She will be very intelligent. Even more than Mekon. I looked at her.

"Lola I said, No one is that intelligent." She smiled as humans do.

"You will see my love."

I told her before that happens I will pass. It will be something I would see. Yet I knew that will never happen. I knew Lola was right. It appeared that each generation they would be smarter. Ren was intelligent more than Ira. The thing with Ren, he wanted to be like old Bota. Ren just wanted to be a captain, fly a ship. Always standing in the shadows never saying much, answer if ask. That was Ren.

It had been a long winter. Gives a man time to think. Outside the snows had started to melt. Only what was called spring snow fell now. Looking across the orchards, a few grass patches showed. As time drifts, away the trees give away to their leaf's, the plants brought their flowers. I was in the barn early one morning when the lieutenant showed up. Finishing the milking, I turned, "ah lieutenant I was just thinking of you."

"Hello my friend he called." Comp, the lieutenant said, "Tell me what is your last name."

I told him I only needed one name

"Comp, "My name is Arman Polanski."

"Lieutenant with a name like that, you only need one name."

"Where are the boys," he asks? He reaches, for a shovel, I told him the boys were at their studies. For another hour.

"Yes, studies are good. I might give you a lesson Comp."

"I ask him, "what would that be?" Just as I thought he took a swing at me, I ducked he found himself on the ground.

"I can see you still have the fight in you. Therefore, I say you're not from here."

"Lieutenant you want me to place you in a hole, cover you up."

"Is that what you did to Lola's husband."

My thought went to that night. I looked at him, what's that supposed to mean.

Comp, "I was sent here to investigate his disappearance."

"I can't tell you anything of the man. I never met him."

Arman said, "Well I must talk to Lola."

"Talk to her if you wish." Ira come from the house with his sword. He was on his way to the woods.

"Ira call to your mother." Ira went to his mother, then come to the barn.

Ira, stood with his sword in his hand. The lieutenant saw this.

Arman, said, "That is a nice blade. Come here let me show you how to use it,"

Ira said, "Ok sir, show me." He flips tipped the blade. I could have already taken the sword. The lieutenant went to his horse, took his blade.

"Come young one, he said to Ira. Let me show you." The lieutenant was about to get a lesson in Boldlygo magic.

Walking to Ira, touching blades with Ira, that's all he got to do. Ten times they touched blades. Ten times Ira took it from him. The lieutenant, was mad to the bone, he thought he was good.

"Ira, he said with a snarl. Who taught you the blade."

Ira pointed to me.

"You," he said."

Lieutenant, I said "I'm highly trained in the art of self-defense. That's with any weapon, even my mind. Mekon, was coming from the house. The lieutenant grad him, well again the lieutenant had to learn another lesson. I smiled at him. Just think the Russian army is supposed to be the best. He come from the ground. He went into a fight stand.

"Come on, I'll show you how good I am." I sat the shovel down, placed one hand in my pocket. I walked to him he took a punch at me. I put his ass on the ground, I looked at him on the ground. You want to try me with two hands.

No Comp, "Ive had enough."

I offered him my hand. "Let's go have coffee Lieutenant." Lola had started from the house.

"You boys played enough."

"Just goofing off," I said.

I told Lola the lieutenant wanted to ask her some questions.

Lola ask, "What kind of questions?"

I told her I think it's about your husband.

Lola never looked at me. "What you want to know of him?"

Arman ask, "Where, is he?"

Lola said, "I have no idea, my husband, left long ago. Went to Saint Petersburg, never come back. I hope he got drunk, fell in a hole. Maybe he's dead I haven't seen him since."

"Good enough," the lieutenant said.

"Well I must get to work. "He said.

I looked at him. "Work."

He said, "Yes work. I will work for a place to live and eat, my choice. I cut wood, do farm work. He looked at me. Then talk to you about something, the lieutenant walked outside.

I whispered to Lola. "I'll try to get rid of him Tudo, will be here soon. This was may, only five more months."

The lieutenant stayed on, we become good friends. Mekon showed, him things he just could not believe. Mekon showed him the star patterns, the clusters in the heavens. Ira told the lieutenant about the planet.

He asks Mekon, "How do you know about things son. Ive been to several of them. Then Mekon laughed out loud." Something I've never seen him do in his native body. Ira was looking at the stars on a clear summer night. Arman and Ira was away from the house,

Arman ask," What are you looking at son?"

Ira turned to the lieutenant. "look, see it moving."

"Just a star," Arman said.

"No, lieutenant, a star does not move unless it has lost its will to live. Then the star falls to Earth. Have you seen one on Earth Arman replied, "no."

Ira, told him it could be a ship. Arman, I come here on a ship so did Mekon and Comp. The girls left on one.

"The girls," the lieutenant said."

Yes, the girls. "My sister Nancy, aunt Sandy daughter Georgia. Comp came here to be our protector." "Lola, is not really my mother. Lola, only give me birth on Earth so I could be born.

"I dont understand," the lieutenant, said.

I told him in a few months. Mekon and I will die, our essence placed back in our native body. Our native bodies are on the ship, that will be here soon. The lieutenant looked sick what's wrong lieutenant. Look there it is again, Ira and Arman returned to the house. I must say he did look just a little green.

The lieutenant said to me, "I saw something moving. Comp tell me the truth, I'm not going to say anything. Besides they think I'm crazy, you no. What did I see, did I see a ship?"

I looked at Ira. "How far was it Ira." The lieutenant you could see was getting antsy.

"Ira said, maybe around Saturn. Three month away."

I said, "It was a ship lieutenant. They're coming here for us, I lied when I told him November the end of the month."

Arman ask Lola. "Where did you daughter go, Georgia to?"

Lola said to him. "They went home Arman, they went home."

"Comp, told me long ago they went to school. Now you say they went home. They're not in Saint Petersburg."

I sat listening to all of it, I stood, walked to the fire. In my thoughts, I was going to kill him.

Mekon looked in to my eyes. "Let me do it."

Ira said "Let's just wait a while." Ira said to the lieutenant. "Arman if you want to live, dont mess this up. If you do, I'll take you to the Moon of Spores. I'll leave you with Garf. You will not like it there."

"I'm not going to say anything."

"I hope we have answered all your question," I said.

Comp the lieutenant asks, "Can I go with you, it's got to be better than here."

"Prove yourself lieutenant we'll see."

"Arman said he needed to go to town tomorrow."

"Then we'll go with you,"

I said, "All of us." "Mary will need to be with her son, as much as she can, Lola to"

The lieutenant said, "Then its settled we leave at first light."

Lola had mad fresh bread. I took a whoop, of cheese, slicing the cheese with the bread apples with fresh berries.

Arman said, "I've been here for a while, I've never seen you eat meat."

Lola said, "We never eat meat."

Arman smiled. "Is that a space thing looking at me."

That's right Arman, "We have no meat on our world."

Mekon and Ira come back to the house, they had gone back the orchard. It was an every night thing for them. Mekon loved watching the stars. He told me once the galaxy of Earth was so full of mysteries.

Mekon said, "Comp we walked to the top of the ridge, there's a fire to the east. Maybe several riders maybe the Russian army. We dont need to leave if their coming here. They could mess things up."

Arman said, "How could they."

Mekon said, they could find some of my work."

Arman said, "Hide it."

Mekon said, "I cant. You would not understand."

Arman said, "Try me."

Mekon told him someday, the only thing I can think about is leaving this body I want to go home. I miss home.

Arman, said to the boys. "How can you miss a place you have never been."

Mekon said, "lieutenant I have memories of home, the city the lab. Comp tell him so he will understand."

I sat by the fire, sipping a cup of coffee. Everyone had gone to sleep. I was feeling a feeling I've haven't felt in quite sometimes, an insecure feeling.

Arman sat dozing then said to me. "Comp you look a little worried."

I looked at him. "I'm here as a protector, you might say a body guard." I'm entrusted by their father to watch over then."

That's why I told you I was a warrior on my world. I'm also a captain in the Royal guard. When you were in the army I did not fear the army. "Arman the Russian army is one thing, not knowing who is out there is another. Ive tried to have Boris to bring all we need. Going to town, well it would have caused trouble with the brothers. It's been a long time, yet they hold a grudge. I need you to stay here with Lola. I pushed out my hand, he took it, then said."

"Comp what this about."

"I need you to promise me you will take care of then, promise me you will with your life." You want my trust then you earn it.

Arman ask, "Comp what are you going to do."

I just looked at him. "Ive got to see who is out there, they whoever it is knows the house is here. If it was the army, they would have come here, you know that."

Arman said to me. "Yes, Comp if it was the army, they would have come here."

"Arman if I'm not back by first light. Send the boys after me, they are the strongest together.

"What do you mean comp?"

I told him I would explain later. I went out the door crossed the porch, walked to the top of the ridge. There it was whoever it was, sure had a big fire. I was certain it wasn't the Russian army.

I could still move very fast even as old as I was. I thought maybe two miles, the fires at this distance was huge. It must have been a monster there. I took off running I was there in about twelve minutes. That was kind of slow with the hills, I thought it was good timing. I stopped just outside the camp. Sitting around the fire, I counted ten of them that i could see. I settled down in the grass thinking of what must be done.

Ject trained me well. I remember at a young age, we were a peaceful race.

Ject said, Comp we always need to be ready. He was right. I sat in the tall grass just waiting. I had time after thirty minutes I started to move when a sound to my right. Two more men come to the fire. Whoever it was spoke in Russian, damn it was the brothers. Looks as if they brought the whole damn family. One of them at the fire said."

"They're all at the house even the lieutenant. They plan to go to Saint Petersburg at first light. I left a man at the barn, he'll wait until we're there. Then we need to move soon one said."

I ran back to the farm. I came from the back of the barn. The man had gone to sleep. First it was very bad to sleep on guard duty. Second it was deadly, third I found a shovel. I pulled back, spoke to him. It was the last thing the man will ever here. I dug a hole beside Lola's husband buried him. I had a feeling he would not be the only one I planted there.

I walk back to the house. I told the lieutenant it was the brothers they're coming here.

Arman ask, "Comp what you want to do."

I told him, wake every one up. I spoke to Lola.

Mary ask. "Comp what is wrong?"

I told them to come to the front room. Arman had called to the boys.

"Comp, what is going on?" Ira ask.

"The fires you saw last evening it's the brothers."

Ira shook his head. "The one you told us about long ago."

"They're not only coming for me, they're coming for you to lieutenant." I heard them speak your name. Arman something you want to say."

"I know why they're coming Comp. You were not supposed to see them. They're coming for Mary.

"How do you know this," I ask." he sat considering the fire. "lieutenant, why did you not tell us."

"Comp I have been here for a long time. Then you told me of the things with the boys. We become close friends. You ask me to protect them with my life. I thought with all that has happened since I've been here. I thought I was one of you."

Ira, said as he wiped his blade. "I thought you were lieutenant."

Lola was with the girls at the fire. "I buried one out behind the barn. There will be others buried there when they come. In fact, I'll bury them all.

Arman looked. "Comp there's ten of them."

"No, there's twelve of them. There was thirteen, he did not know, you never sleep on guard duty.

Mekon said, "Comp I'm not a warrior as you. I don't compare to Ira. There is no one as good with a sword as him, we should carry it to them.

Arman said, "You never take a fight to know one."

"Arman think about it Ira said." The surprise, catch them off guard it would be the last thing they would expect.

I told Ira and Mekon, gather your things. I cleared the table, showed them where they were.

Mekon said, "There by the springs."

Ira said, "That's a good place for a fight. They can't move around comp I'll take at least three. Mekon at least one."

Comp said, "We'll hit then on three sides strick hard fast then move. Just like I trained you, remember hard fast then moved back here.

Mary, had tears in her eyes. Mekon went to his mother.

"Dont cry for me mother I will return."

Ira looked at his mother, Lola went to him. "This is part of you heritage, my son. This is what you were born to do, lead your people."

I said to my mother. "We will be back for breakfast." We started for the door. I told Arman take care of them.

"I'm coming to, he said."

"Arman, we can move much faster than you." I embraced Lola kissed her lightly on the lips. Tears were streaming from her eyes. She never said a word, Lola knew what we had to do. We went out the door at a hard run. It took several minutes to go, to the place I had been before. Stopping short of the springs. Mekon went to his place, Ira to his. There was no need to have a battle plan. The boys knew what we were here for. That's what we did, when the boys were ready. We went into the camp screaming. Everyone was drunk or asleep. The boys were stabbing, slashing, damn it was over fast.

Gathering our self, we ran back to the farm in minutes. Arman open the door as we walked in.

"It's over," I said, "Most of them dead."

"Unbelievable," Arman said, "Three people took on twelve and won."

"The element of surprise," Mekon said."

Lola, gave her son an embrace, so did Mary.

"You have reach your manhood my son," Lola said. "I will lose you soon."

Mary said the same. "The boys said at the same time."

"Mother if you are alive you will never loose me. I may leave this planet, yet I will always live in your heart. Both women had tears in their eyes. I know mother I will always love you.

"Mekon said the same."

We made the trip to town. Boris came to us.

Comp, out by the farm did you hear of the the massacre at Rock Springs.

lieutenant was quick to answer. "Tell me over a cup of ale." We sat waiting for something to happen. Boris, only said the brothers were out with his family hunting. When they were attacked by at least twenty men.

Boris ask, "Did you see anyone coming in to town?"

I told him know, yet we did not look for anyone. We stayed the night and day with Boris. Arman and I stayed in the barn. Mary did tell her mother, she was going back with Tudo when he come for the boys.

"I understand Sandy said."

Boris come to the barn early.

"Ah Comp, I see you have done the milking."

I told him it was a good night.

Boris whispered, "Tell me Comp, "How you take out the brothers."

"I didn't Boris." How were they taken out?

"Boren, the oldest brother, the only one alive said they were killed by blades."

"That's is awful Boris."

Boris said eleven people dead. How many people do you think it would take.

"Yes, Boris"

"Never mind comp." Boris walked back to the house.

The boys were loading the wagon with the supplies.

Boris said, "He and Sandy, would be out in a couple of days."

The fight with the brothers was the talk of the town. Everyone was talking about it one man said he saw a light come from the sky. It was people from the space let them talk. I really didn't care just leave us alone.

I ask Mary "You see Arman."

He went into a shop comp, the one on the corner.

I walk to the shop she pointed to. Arman was looking at dresses. I walked up behind him well this is your color. He was embarrassed

"I do not wear dresses, I look for Mary, it's her birthday a gift."

Well Arman, "she loves red."

"Yes, Comp you help me."

"I pointed to one that looks her size."

"You buy for Lola yes."

I told him Lola had enough dresses.

"Then I buy for Mary this one."

I told him he made a good choice.

Mary could see the smile on his face. She knew the package was for her so did Lola. I had no idea what was happing. Everyone looked at us as we left Saint Petersburg's. We just smiled at them as we passed. Several hours later we stopped by a wide spot. Long ago an old man tried to rob us. The girls killed him.

Mary and Lola made a crude dinner.

The lieutenant said, "I wish I had a rabbit. Sorry Mary forgive me, Rabbit is good meat. It's just for so many years I eat meat, sometimes I miss it."

"Lieutenant you want have meat on our world."

"I know Comp. I've heard you say. Through all the years I come to the farm. I always notice Lola never offered us meat. The pies always were enough."

I had hooked the horses to the wagon. When the race of hoofs surrounded us. It was the Russian army. It was the same group of men that served with the lieutenant.

The one in charged ask. "Why are you here?"

I told him we were having dinner. We're on our way home.

Sir one of the men said. That's Comp, "Him and his woman has an farm not far from here. We stayed there several times."

I told them they were welcome anytime.

Arman came from the woods with sword in hand.

One said, "lieutenant Arman, the men dismounted their horses, gathered around, talk went on forever.

I told the lieutenant we need to go. I told their new leader to stop any time.

He replied, "On their last run they would stop." Well I thought that would be close. It will be almost the time Tudo will be here. I let my mind drift to home, my old teacher Ject. Ject would be around six hundered years old, he was there lone before me. I was not sure how long he had been in the city.

Over one thousand y ears to build. The great wall took many hundred of years to build. I dont think there was anyone alive there, could tell how old Maoke was. I come back to myself. Arman calling me. I jumped, what?

Lola ask, "Where, were you?"

I told her I was just thinking of things on my world.

Lola dropped her head. "It want be long before your back there." "Comp, I had you for all these years Tudo made my dream come true. He left you with me, you gave me a son."

I know Lola, "When Tudo returns, he will bring back the child he left with. Lola Nancy will be a young woman. She will be twenty eight, Georgia thirty four. I told Lola as we rode on the bumpy road. They will be with child when they return.

Lola looked at me, "I sure hope so." She was still looking at me, it will give me something to hold on to."

Pulling into the barn yard, Arman and I unloaded the wagon. The boys started their chores.

Arman said, "I give Mary the dress tonight. This is ok Comp."

"Yes, I said, "That will be fine Arman." Walking in the house, Lola was by the fire. turning I could see she had been crying. "I ask, "What is wrong?"

Oh Comp, "I will miss you so, my son will leave me also." I will have nothing to hold on to.

I'm sorry Lola. "I've tried to give you a child, I dont know why I could not." Maybe when Cra returns, I'll ask him? Lola if I had given you a child. The child would have gone back, this I'm sure of. If you wish you could always have another DNA transfer. You could have one even from me.

Lola said, "I love you Comp. So many time, I've fell in love with you. If I do this again, I must have a girl. The child must be a girl."

"Lola I wish I could stay with you forever, If I remain much longer I will die, here you can tell my hair is turning colors. My face has wrinkles."

Lola said Comp, "It is Destiny for humans to die, I told her not on my world Maoke saw to this.

I told her, if I could I would stay, you could come with me. "I can't," she said. "My daughter will return soon. I must be here for her I feel she will lead our people to have a home for them that will come into the future. We have waited for you since destiny. That's the way it will be. We will always be waiting until we are all are dead or taken home."

I told Lola. Then let's go, we dont have to come back. We can live there forever.

Days turned to weeks then to months. The boys were losing their strength. The lieutenant could see the difference in them also.

"Comp, he has said to me several times. Why is this happing to them."

I told him they were dying. That's, why they were born Arman. We will not lose them, when they die they will become more powerful than you can image.

"I dont understand Comp."

I told him it will be ok, if Tudo gets here in time. It was the end of September the boys were in bed. Ira would say, mother please help me. It was horrible to watch, I know I never want to see this again. I never knew it would be as this. I sat long into the night thinking. Maoke, did say not to do this again. I'm sure he saw this, maybe therefore he told Ject not to do it again.

The morning came way to early. Mary was outside with Arman.

I heard Mary call," Comp, Comp." Mary ran into the house. "They're here Comp. "There's a large light in the sky."

Mary I said go quick. "Tell Arman to come now." Arman ran into the house.

"Yes, Comp what am I to do."

"Take Mekon I said, I'll take Ira." We ran to the back of the ridge. I give the signal the ship come in seconds. Cra had two sentrys to take the boys to the lab. I met with Tudo. Lola, Mary was standing beside me.

Lola ask," "Where is Nancy."

"I'm here mother," Lola turned to see a most lovely young woman, Georgia also. Mary looked upon her sister.

"You truly are a princess my sister." Mary said. Both girls were with child.

Lola said, I have missed your child hood."

"You may have missed ours mother, you want miss your grandchild, Nancy said. She will be great with our people. She is the DNA of Tomeka, Jects and Myas' mother."

Lola looked at Georgia. "Your is from who?"

"Mine aunt Lola, is from Angies DNA. Angie took Tomeka place, alone side of Maoke. There was no man aunt Lola. It was all done in the lab."

Mother, Nancy said, "The father is not important."

Tudo come from the place where Cra was working on the boys. Lola come lets join the family. Arman was introduced to Tudo.

"Arman said, "I wish to come with you if possible."

Tudo looked at me. I told him he was a good one. Tudo talked to Mary, then to Lola. There was so much laughter. Really it wasn't funny what Tudo was saying. Yet they just kept on laughing. Mary Georgia all were joining in. There was so much to talk about so little time. The family stayed two days on the ship."

A sentry come to Tudo, "Sir there's people coming to the farm." Tudo told him to watch.

"The sentry replied, as you wish."

Lola ask, "When, the boys were to wake up."

"Tudo, answered, soon Lola soon."

Mary told Tudo, she had decided to stay on Earth.

"My family, the girls will need me." Tudo placed his hand inside his robe took out a coin. It was the same coin Lola had hidden behind her mantle. He gave Nancy, and Georgia one also. Girls keep them always you are family. Pass them on to your children, someday someone will come again. Tudo went to the cabinet, open a door took out a pouch, walked to the girls.

Make a wish Tudo said, "place your hand in side. Take a hand full, Mary did the same. The pouch was full of stones."

Nancy said, "Father may I also."

"Yes, "You and Georgia." Comp told Lola to give the ones to Boris, the ones in the hiding place. These stones you can live a good life. Never tell where you got them.

I told them to let Boris take care of it, they agreed.

Georgia said, "Aunt Lola I wish you could see the Marder-go's."

Lola said, "I wish I could also."

Tudo saw the look. "He knew the look, Lola why don't you come with us for a while?"

"I can't leave them, Lola said."

"Nancy spoke to her mother, took her hands."

Nancy's said, "I'm not a little girl any more mother go, go with Comp." Let him show you the world of our world.

"Aunt Lola we will be fine Mary said."

"Who will take care of the farm the orchard the animals." Lola ask.

I will, "I will take care of them." Lola turned looked straight into the eyes of Arman.

Arman turned to Mary, "If Mary will marry me I will stay. I do love her."

Mary stood up to face him. "You are a good man Arman I saw this from long ago." When you were in the Russian army. You sent the brother after me. Them stood to defend me, they come anyway. You still stood to protect us. I must tell you, I come here this time, same as before of my own free will. Arman I will take another DNA transfer, the child will not be yours. Can you love and raise the child as yours, without regrets? The child want die as the boys did."

"Yes, Arman said, yes Mary I can do this."

"Mary said, "Aunt Lola go to Boldlygo, we will live on the farm with the family."

"You need not worry Nancy said, to her mother. When you reach Saturn dont be a sleep. That's when you make a hard left turn. It will be something you will carry in your mind forever. Something you can tell your grandchildren."

An hour later Tudo come in. Ira was followed by Mekon, both boys were still weak from the many years laying in the stasis pods. Ira looked at Mary, then to Lola.

"Ira said, Mother! Lola went into tears." The boys were still in their native bodies. Mekon looked at Mary. Mary stood waiting for him to say.

"Mother I'm not the son you raised in this body. I have the memories of him that give me life. My heart is full of love for you. Mekon looked at his father. "It took long enough."

Cra said, I'm sorry my son I'm close. It will be up to you to carry on. It's close to my time of ascension."

"Tudo said to Ira." it was a long time I have missed all your childhood. Your grandfather said not to go this far again.

Ira told his father. "You dont know the love the humans have in their hearts. Father if you could fill their love.

Cra told Ira and Mekon to stand."

Cra, said, "I give you the boys you have come to know. Boys the way it works, you must concentrate on changing into human form. Mekon had known problem, Ira had a few tries then before their eyes, their were to natives boys that had change into to humans."

Tudo had the captain to take the family back to the farm.

Tudo said, "Lola it's just a precaution someone my come. You and Mary can stay we will be here for several more days.

"Tonight, I will come to the farm. I would like to try some of the fruit the girl talked about."

Lola said, "It was a good year."

Mekon, and Ira stood beside each other. Tudo said, "Your grandfather will be proud."

Ira said, "We must have human clothes as before."

"Mekon said to Ira you remember."

Ira told Mekon, "I remember, I remember everything." Ira ask, "Where is my mother."

Lola come in to the room. "I'm here my son." Ira looked at Lola, she had tears in her eyes again. Lola took both boys embraced them. The boys that grew up on Earth, to give your life. Please do not let them die in vain. Remember their life's always.

Two days later Tudo said, "It was time to go to the surface."

Standing in the late afternoon sun, standing in the orchard Tudo taste several different kinds of fruit.

Tudo said to Lola, "I love them all."

Tudo walked with Lola across the farm. He was so concern of different things. Coming to the house we had coffee. Tudo had several cups.

Comp Tudo said, "I really like this new drink, I told him it was a man's drink."

Several hours later it was time to leave. It would be Tudo last time on Earth for a very long time. Tudo would return home to stay.

Georgia told Tudo to tell father I love him. I'll never forget him. I will tell my family the tales of Boldlygo if there's life in me.

Nancy embraced Tudo. "Whispered in his ear, I will always love my father of the stars."

We walked to the hill stepping onto the ship. Lola told the girls to take care. The door closed, we went higher into the darkness of space.

Lola could not believe the stars. Holding onto my hand, she said "They still looked far away."

I told her if she was ten million miles closer, they would still be as far. We had travel several months. Comp said to Lola, "look out the portal. This is what Nancy was talking about."

Lola's hands went to her face. "Oh, my words would you look at that. In my life, I've never seen anything so beautiful."

I told her, Wait till you see my world.

We flew through space so easily, living a simple life, we lived. I ask, "Lola at different time if there were any regrets?"

She said, "No, no way." "The only regrets I would have had if you had not taken me with you."

Running to my arms Comp she said. "I love you." "I never want to be without you."

We were lying in bed when the ship come from hyper space.

"Lola raised up, what was that."

"We have come the atmosphere of the Moon of Corning. You need to dress I told her. I want to introduce you to Kohl. Kohl was the one that placed Destiny's on Earth. He has been to the farm before. Cra, Lon even Bota, had been there before."

Lola said, "She really did want to meet him, Lola smiled."

I ask, "What's on your mind."

Lola said, "You remember you told me the story of his mate stealing the ship. I thought I would ask of it?"

I told Lola do it." Joy will laugh about it." The captains took the ship to the surface placing the ship on the pad, he was good. I do not think he was as good as me, well I was good. Quad, was the first to meet us. Kohl, was beside him. Tudo walked down the ramp, the boys were beside him. Kohl, saw me, then Lola. Kohl, greeted Tudo looking at the boys."

"Who are the humans," Kohl ask.

"Tudo said, "Kohl, I'm surprise you dont know then."

Kohl said, "I dont Tudo."

"It's Ira, and Mekon." Tudo said. Kohl ask, "What happen to them?"

Remember the experiment I told you about well this is what happen. The boys can shift from one body to another. Mekon, went to Kohl took his hand, moments later he looks as Kohl.

Kohl said. "Well that was something."

"Joy said, "Yes it was."

Joy took Lola to the house of Quad. Joy told Lola, she had spent time on Earth. In a small village near Moscow. Lola told Joy she was from a farm south of Saint Petersburg. Joy told Lola, she loved the snow as it's called.

Joy ask. "How did you meet the natives of the planet?"

Lola told the story of Destiny.

"Joy said she remembers that, she was from here." Joy said, "That was a long time ago."

Lola ask, "May I ask you a question?"

"Joy said sure anything."

Lola ask, On your world do you live forever?"

Joy said, "She was not sure. If not, you live for a very long time. I'm over four hundred, Kohl is the same. My father is ancient, I'm not sure how old he is."

"Lola ask Joy of her mother?"

Joy said, "I'm not sure she left one day never returned."

Comp said, "On Boldlygo you could live forever, only if you stay on the planet. Comp has aged so since is stay on Earth. If he returns I'm afraid he will die."

Joy ask, "Tell me about the boys from DNA to death."

I told her all about it.

"Lola wasn't that hard on you," She ask.

"Yes, Joy it was yet I got them back, for a while anyway."

Joy ask, "What do you mean?"

Lola said. "I will be going back to Earth. "I come here to see the Moon of Corning. The places where Destiny was from. I want to go to see the planet where Comp lives, where Tudo lives. I also want to meet Ject. I can't stay my Destiny is on earth. My daughter, granddaughter. I will stay for a while, then I must return to earth. The people of earth I must teach them of the world of these people. Tudo told me I could learn more from the archives. He said, there was more than I'll ever read.

Comp come to the door. Joy and I had finished our talk.

Lola Comp said, "We need to go to the ship, we will be living soon."

Lola told Joy she would see her again.

Joy replied, "Yes I feel it to." Lola started to leave, Joy said, "she was my aunt you know."

Lola ask, "Who was your aunt."

Joy said, "Destiny." "She was my father's sister, that's what I was told. Kohl knows the story."

"Comp said, "In some ways you are part of the house of Quad." Comp Lola said, "I wish I could spend more time here." Maybe I could find more to tell the children of Earth."

I told Lola, "Maybe we could stop again.

CHAPTER 23

The ship roared across the city of Ratio, as we always. Our captain set us down on the west staging area. Lola was in ah, looking across the city. Her hands went to her face when she saw the palace.

"Oh Comp, She said."

The boys went down the ramp to Ject.

Ira kneeled before Ject, "grandfather," He said.

Mekon took Jects hand. "Rise, let me look at you." Standing in their human body Ject, looked at Tudo then to Cra. "You did good Cra."

"It took to long for this Ject." Ject, looked at is old captain then to Lola calling her by name.

Lola said, "How did you know?"

"If you had known Mya, you would see. Georgia look more as Mya, than anyone I've ever seen. Come Lola lets go to the palace."

Tudo Ject said, "Take care of things I'm going to show Lola around."

Lola gasped as she walked into the great room. Lola's hands were on her face. "Comp told us about the palace, I never thought it would look as this."

Ject ask, "How did you think it would look?"

"Well, this is more," Lola said." It's beyond my thought."

Walking through the room, Ject stopped at stoop. The palace stood high above the city of Ratio, from the stoop you could see forever. Lola froze as she stood looking to the mountains.

"This is the Valley of the Unicorn."

"Very good," Ject said."

Lola said, "The mountains to the west is the Marder-to-go's. The falls are as a rainbow the water is green, red, blue, yellow,"

"Ject said, "You have been taught well."

Lola told Ject, "I have been taught this my whole life. We wrote of all that has been passed down. Sorry to say, we hide it from the Russian army. They would take it if they knew."

I showed Lola everything I could about the palace. I told her everything she would need to know while she was here. I took Lola to the great room. Looking around Lola saw a basket of fruit. Taking the fruit from the basket I cut the fruit handed it to Lola. I told her it was called a Simon.

"I have been waiting for this. Comp has told us all how wonderful it was." Lola told me of the fruit in the orchards. Biting into the fruit the juice was so great it ran down Lola's face. "It would have been nice if I could have brought apples," Lola said. They would not have lasted for long. "I did bring Tudo coffee. I never told him. I hope it kept I wanted him to share with his father."

Ject said, "Georgia, and Nancy ask for a DNA before they left? I told them at the time it would not be good to do this.

Lola said "Ject, Cra did transfer the DNA of Tomeka, Angie."

"Angie, I said that was so long ago."

I told Ject as we stood eating the Simon. The girls said tell father they would love him and miss him forever.

Ject sat in a chair lean back. "My loving children what words can I say, the daughters I never had, ones I wish that would stay."

"Excuse me Lola, my sister is here."

"Your sister."

Ject replied, "Yes my sister Mya." Nancy and Mya become close when she was young as children on Earth, they can see thing, adults cant."

Lola ask. "You can see her?"

Ject replied, "When she wants me to, sometimes she likes to play games with me."

Lola ask again. "You actually can see her?"

"Once again," I said yes. "She knows you are part of her DNA."

"Is she pleased at what she sees?" I ask.

"She said Georgia, is the only one that will be close to looking as she."

Lola said, "I have heard the stories."

"I wish I could meet her."

"Mya showed herself to Ject." Lola's hands went to her face She give a loud gasp.

Ject said to me. "Are you ok?" he ask.

"She is here."

"Ject said, "Who is here."

Mya. "She is there."

"Ject ask, "You can see her?" Lola stood with tears in her eyes.

"Yes Ject, I see her she is so beautiful."

"Ject ask, "You dont really see her."

Lola said, "She is dressed in a yellow robe with white lace, her hair is very dark very long. The bluest eyes I've ever seen. I thought Georgia and Nancy's eyes were blue. Their nothing as this, she is sitting on a chair beside you."

Mya looked at ject, "Just a little something I've learned. I missed talking to Nancy so I learned to come to you. Mother and father said not to do it all the time." Mya said to Ject, "I'm going to take her from you now. I'll bring her back soon."

Lola fell on the floor, fell into a deep sleep. I picked her up, placed her on a table. I called a sentry, go find Comp. Tell him Lola has fell.

It was a short moments later Comp, ran to the palace.

"Ject where is she, what happen."

Ject said, "She saw Mya, Mya said she was going to take her for a while. Then she went to sleep."

I was sitting with Comp, talking of thing on Earth. Lola moved on the table.

"Comp," she said."

"I'm here Lola."

She said to Comp. "My what a dream."

Ject ask Lola. "Do you remember talking to Mya?"

"I dont know, I'm not sure. It was as a deep dream I was in. I was flying across a valley with clouds. A Huge water fall with colors. A Hugh mountain with black rocks. I saw strange animals, I was talking to someone." Then she told me to wake up, I did I was here. "Comp it was beautiful, only in my dreams could I picture such beauty. I was talking to a woman, she said she would come again. I hope she does."

I took Lola to a sleeping room, where we stayed while we were here. Lola laid down went to sleep. Lola was sleeping very well, when a sentry come to call.

Comp, "Tudo wishes you to come to the chambers." Tudo, Cra was talking waiting for the boys.

Ject said, "My son it is time for you to stay home, watch your sons grow. Mekon will soon take his father's place in the lad. Tudo you will take my place in the palace. Just a few more years it will be my time of ascension."

The boys enter the room Opa you still have stories to tell.

I told my grandson. Not many Ira, "you have heard then all. I was bound here when Maoke left. You will be limited to how far you can go. Always try to stay friends with our neighboring planets. Someone will always look out for you, pass that on to your children.

Ject ask Comp, "What do you plan?"

Comp said, "What do you mean Ject?"

"What is your plans with Lola. Will you stay here or will you go back to Earth."

I told Ject I was not sure. I told him I believe she will return to Earth.

"Ject said, "I believe that also."

"Lola is still young Ject, she wants to make a safe house for the ones to come."

Ject, "There's no need hiding it, I do love her. Ject she wants to have a child. For some reason, I can't have one with her. If I go back to Earth I will die. I mean look at me now, my hair has changed my skin wrinkle. I want to be with her."

Ject said, "It was Destiny for humans to die."

"I ask Ject, "What makes us different."

Ira said, "It's got to be the Simons."

"I think your right Ira, Mekon said."

Ject replied, "I'm not sure why we are the way we are. I only know if we are on the planet we can't die, Maoke said that." I told Comp tomorrow when Lola wakes, carry her to the archives.

The next morning I woke early. I turned in bed, "wake up Lola. I want you to see the suns come up as you saw the moons go down." Lola was speechless as she laid her head on my shoulder.

"Comp, when I go back to Earth. I will write a book to be passed down to our people."

I ask her, "What would you called this book?"

Lola smiled, "I would call it, my life with a space man."

I told her it would start at the beginning to whenever.

"Comp, Lola ask may I go to the archives today?"

I told Lola, I would take her. I have work to do you will be alone. Lola and I were having our morning meal. Soy and Foo come in we told them the plan of the day.

Soy said. "Let me take her. I'll stay with her you can do whatever you need to do." Foo also has work to do." Leaving the girls at the archives Foo and I returned to the hanger for a class. The boys were studying class, with Mekon.

Lola stayed at the archives all day. Soy come to the palace with her.

Lola ask, "Comp how do you stay here at the palace. How can I stay here? The palace is for Royal Blood.

"That right Lola it is, I'm here because of you. If you like I can leave."

"Why am I here, I'm not Royal Blood."

"You are part of Mya, Lola actually you are a princess. I have a place in the city, I will take you there tomorrow." I showed Lola my place in the city, where lived.

She said Comp, "After all this time, it was still here,"

"I loved it," She said, The view of the city was breath taking.

Lola study hard for several weeks between the palace the archives and others thing. I could see she was home sick. I ask her, "You want to go back to earth?" She turned to me, she was looking across the Valley of the Unicorn.

Comp she said, "I wish I could stay forever. Then why dont you," I said.

"I need to be with my children. I've have longed for another child. I have Nancy's memories."

I told her Ira will always love you.

"I know my love," She said."

Lola laid her head on my chest tears flowing.

With a choked voice, she said, "I know you will not stay on Earth. In my heart, you will always be on Earth with me, my spaceman." Sobbing so hard, "Comp what will I do without you."

I placed my hand behind her head. "Lola I do love you." Pulling her head back I told her, the only woman in my life. I will go back to Earth, I will stay with you until my death. Lola it's time for us to go home."

I went to Tudo. I told him it was time to go.

"Comp, I feel you you will stay on Earth. If you ever want to come home come." Tudo give me a bag of stones. There were several stones. In the stones were three signal stones.

Tudo said to me, "Ira was getting antsy. He will take Foo as his captain, Ren will also go. You can leave mid-week."

I went to Lola, "She said she would be ready." There would be something I didn't know. I would find out later. Lola went to see Cra before we left.

On the Moon of Corning we landed on the north pad. Everyone was there to meet us. I stood looking all around. As I did when I left my world. I knew in my heart I would never see this place again. Quad took his supplies as we took on supplies. Ira paid him in stones he had a bag of stones. Tudo must know, the rules were no one was to leave with stones. I would speak to Ira of this later. Everyone said their goodbyes. Foo took us higher into the darkness of space., then to hyper space. It would be a long twenty month to earth.

Lola and I spent all the time we could together. She told me one morning.

"Comp I'm having a baby." I wanted to have a baby with you. I went to see Cra before we left. I told him to do the DNA from you. Lola looked at me, I hope you didn't mind.

I told her not at all.

"Comp you're going to be a father," She said."

For the first time in my life I felt like a human. Time goes on, Lola had the child. The child had dark hair, the bluest eyes. She had the Royal Blood, by the time we reach Earth the child would be walking. Lola tried to spend time with Ira. She tried to tell Mekon of Mary when she was a child. I spent time with Ren and Foo. Something I never got to do, when they were very young.

He was full grown know. Even in his native body, Ren was a handsome being. Both boys talked to me when they could. Ren was busy with the ship, Foo was doing whatever he needed. Lola and I went to our room.

A sentry come to us. "Comp Ira ask, for you on the bridge."

I ask, "You know why he sent for me."

"A ship has been spotted," He said."

"I jumped into my clothes ran to the bridge."

Ira saw me enter. "Comp a ship on the screen it's to our left.

Looking at the scope I said, they're following us. I told Ren to bring us out of hyperspace then to stop. The ship scanned us as before, looked us over I suppose they seen we had no weapons then veered off. This has happened before. I looked at Ira, you really like your human side.

"I do Comp, why you ask?"

"Since you shifted you have not shifted back."

"Just trying to get used to the change."

"Ren said, he bothers me. He looks funny."

"Ira said to Ren, I'm still your brother. I do feel different, it's a good feeling, I do like it," Ira said.

Foo took the ship back to hype space as we continued our way to Earth.

We were sailing through space. I told Lola we were entering the Earths universe tomorrow we would be in Earth galaxy."

Comp Lola said. "Please can we stop the ship from afar."

I told Lola I would ask Foo?"

The next day we come to the planet on a hard run to Earth. Lola and I were lying in bed. I felt the ship come from hyperspace.

Lola ask, "Are we home."

I told her know. You ask to stop?

I told Lola to come see. She took the baby, We named Zada. She was so beautiful she would reach for me when I came close. I guess she felt secure. Lola looked as the planet of Saturn. Later, the bridge Lola thank Foo for the time, stopping by the planet.

Lola said to Ren, "I know I'll never see this again, thank all of you." "Lola said, "Ren I love you."

I told her Lola we will be home within, the next three month. She looked at me with tears in her eyes.

"Yes, Lola I'm staying with you. I'm staying with my daughter." Lola ran to me held me so tight I hardly could breath. The day had come to an end. I took my daughter with her mother, back to our sleeping room.

We were sleeping in one morning before we reached Earth. Zada woke up, I did not here the door open neither did Lola. turning over in bead. "Lola where is Zada?"

Lola jumped up. I scramble to my cloths, I went into the corridor I was looking everywhere. "I don't see her," I said to Lola. I ran to the bridge, there she was, sitting on Foo's knee. She was looking at all the lights. Zada starting laughing when she saw me. She reached out for me, I thank Foo.

Foo said, "Comp she enjoyed the lights."

Lola took Zada to the galley, we were having breakfast when the ship come from hyperspace.

I looked at Lola, "Were home." We will stay here in space until night fall. Foo showed our self, a beam of light shot up. We took the shuttle to the surface, Arman, Mary greeted us. Walking to the house.

Arman said, "The orchard did good Comp." I take monies build room to house, this pleased Lola. Nancy come in with two little girls, they were eight years old.

Lola said. "I've been gone a long time."

Nancy said, "Mother you grandchild, I named her Sara this is Mary's, She named her Alice.

Lola said, "When Comp came in, there something I want to show you".

Comp had a little girl.

"Nancy your sister, her name is Zada."

Sandy said, "Well one big family." Ira came in dressed in his human clothes. He was always carrying his sword.

Boris said, "He was happy to see all.

Arman said, "Since we had been gone, the orchards has done well. I take monies give to Nancy. Mary help to. I still love her very much.

Arman said, "The Russian army don't come here anymore. There is a war up north, the war keeps them busy. It dont make me mad always asking questions."

"I ask him, "Reminds you of anyone Arman. He just looked at me."

Ira stayed for a long time, then it was time to leave. Outside Ira told me.

"Comp from the time I was born, until now. Even in my earth body, you were a great teacher live long if you can my friend. In my heart as a human, now I can feel the pain. Pain of goodbye I know I'll never see you again.

Comp said to me. "Tell your mother goodbye, tell her you love her." Lola and I stood on the ridge as "hold me Comp"

"Lola said, "In my heart I know I'll never seen him again."

CHAPTER 24

L ooking down on my family as the ship went higher into the darkness of space. I knew I would never see them alive again. In years to come I did return to Russia. It was long after Lola and Comp had passed. From time to time I would watch our Earth family. Foo, Ren, myself traveled to several places on Earth. We travel to different planets in the earths solar system. We had been gone several years. Ren told me one morning,

Ira lets go home, "Foo wants see Soy, I would like a break."

I told Ren, Take me back to Earth." I wanted to go to a place I've never been. I wanted to go to Spain. I had Ren to set me down on the surface. I told my brother to leave me. I was going to live amongst the humans. I wanted to study them. I told them to go home, father will be wondering of us. I have a stone I'll send a signal when I want to return. I stood on the hill just beyond a small clearing watching the ship go higher into the dark. Moments later a voice spoke. I saw no one then again, I turned to see a human. My first thought was, hey did you see that, what was it.

The man answered, "It's not the first time I've seen one."

"One what" I said.

"A visitor from mars," he replied."

I told him I know nothing of this Mars, is it close I shall visit this Mars.

"The man said to me, son it's out there."

I ask, "So how do you go there?"

The man said "You don't, there's only one way. They have to take you, I've sat at night watch the light in the sky move."

I said to him, "Perhaps the stars are moving."

"I doubt that son," he said"

"Where you bound young man," the man asks? I could tell he was a Spaniard.

I told him I was not sure. I'm traveling here, there, I have been to several villages, towns. I've been across the sea. I've seen the lands, they're strange people. They living in skin houses, they eat the animals. They use their skin for houses cloths."

"He asks me, "Do you eat animals?"

I told him I surely dont. I eat fruits, vegetables, bread, cheese you know good stuff." My new found friend and I walked along the road, we talked about several things. I told him my name was Ira."

"What is your last name," he asks?

"I only have one name, my mother said, Ira is fine."

I see the man said. "Pushing out his hand, my name is Reyes."

I took the man's hand.

"Reyes ask, "Where I was from?"

I told him I was born somewhere, I dont remember.

"When I was very little my mother come to Russia. I lived there until I left. I left several years ago, I'm not sure if she is still alive. I do not wish to live there again, so I set out traveling."

Reyes ask me. "How do you survive?"

"I work here and there, I have had several jobs. I'm very intelligent, my last job was on a farm. I worked in orchards work with animals. I also was trained by a very intelligent teacher. I know my way around if you know what I mean."

Reyes said, "I see you wear a sword, are you good with it."

I told Reyes, My teacher said, I was the best he had ever seen. I always thought he was the best, one day I took his sword. Ira, he said to me I cannot teach you any further. He said there was nothing more I could learn. He told me to walk proud, never take a life unless there's no other way."

Reyes said, "Sounds like a smart man."

"Yes, he was," I said, I told him the sword was not the only thing he taught me. He taught me to use my head. Think before you do something you will regret, never rush in. Wait, someone will move first, that's when you move.

"Reyes said, I have a Traven in Madrid. It was on a back street, You no Ira, I could use a man like you."

I told him I shall think of this. There's other places I would like to see.

I tell you Reyes, "I will work for you until spring. Then I must leave to other places."

"Good enough," Reyes said. Madrid is a long way off we must stop for water."

I ask Reyes, "Do you not have a horse to carry you?"

Reyes said, "I had one someone took it last evening. They're ahead of me somewhere, the tracks are fresher than before."

I stopped him. "Wait smell," I said, "What do you smell?"

"The air I suppose," Reyes said.

I told him I smell smoke from a fire. Its close lets be quite I said in a whisper. We went off the road eased our way through the forest.

Reyes said, "Ira, there is no finer animal than a Spanish horse, you will see what I mean."

I stopped him again. "Let's wait here."

Reyes said there. "Ira my horse is tied to the tree."

The horses were watched by to men. I told Reyes there's three horses. That means there is three men two anyway. Remember what I told you about Comp. Wait, someone will move. I heard something. Look two more men, if we had charged we would not have survived.

Reyes look. "Two on the ground, two on horses. The other one behind the tree."

Reyes said, "Now that's using your head."

Let's see what happens. For over an hour we watched from the trees.

I whispered to Reyes. "See what I mean, three of the men left on their horses, now we can go".

Reyes walked over to one side of the camp, I the other. The men jump up, "who are you?"

"I come for my horse," Reyes said. "You took her from me last evening."

One guy drew his sword. I smiled as I walked in this will be very easy. Sir they both turned to face me. my sword still in sheet.

One man asked, "Who are you?"

I am Ira, "I'm here to see you give Reyes, back his horse."

They both laughed you are a baby.

I thought, I'm 30 years old. How old are babies where you come from.? "Well, yes I am, the fact remains, you will give Reyes his horse back, and a token just for fun I'll take the other one. You can pick him up in Madrid."

They were laughing so hard.

The one with the sword came at me. I parried right caught him with my knee, knocked the air from him. the other one dashed at me with his sword he thrust, I parried cut him across the arm.

"He screamed."

"Well you want more?" I ask.

Reyes looked with awe. "You are a superb swordsman, you let them live yes."

Yes, I said, "I tied them up saddled the horses and went to Madrid."

The thing about Spain, it was a beautiful country. The ocean, the mountains, nothing as ours, but beautiful. All the beauty in the world could not be as great as the beauty I was about to look upon. I walked into the tavern behind Reyes. I looked into the eyes of the most magnificent human, I've ever laid eyes on. This human female was even more beautiful than Georgia. I could not move, it was as if she could see right through me. She could read my ever thought as I stood here. I could not believe how beautiful she was. I couldn't speak, or move.

Reyes said, "Come here Ira."

I could not move, I really wanted to, I wanted to run to her. I felt her wanting to do the same.

Reyes said, "Ira are you okay?"

It was her who brought the first words.

In a Spanish language, she said to Reyes. "I think the cat has his tounge father."

In my thoughts, I said father. This was this his daughter. I dont think April will ever come, at least I hope it stays winter forever.

This woman spoked to me.

"Would you like to come and sit down," she asks?"

I came to my senses, "uh… umm, what?" What was it you said?"

Reyes said, "Come here Ira."

My hands were sweaty my legs were heavy.

"Father, maybe he wants to stand."

"No, I'll sit." I said. She poured me a drink. I asked, "What it was."

"She replied, "Apple juice, my father makes it."

I drank it down in one drink.

My she said, You were thirsty."

"It's really hot in here," placing my finger in my collar moving it around."

"I said to Reyes, not taking my eyes from her." "I'll take care of the horses, the one we borrowed I'll leave tied up to the rail."

Reyes told her the story of the horses. Walking out of house to the barn, I stabled the horses and rubbed them down. Comp said it was good to do that, they would go roll then the horses would be fine. I threw hay into the trough for them. I started for the tavern when I saw the other horses tied outside I looked through the window and saw Reyes laying on the floor his head bleeding. One of the men had, then I thought. I dont even know her name. They had her up against the bar trying to have their way with her. I went through the door sword in hand, one man pulled a weapon that made some loud noise. Later I found out it was called a gun. I sliced his hand the other one I sliced across his stomach, another I thrusted the blade into his leg. That left the one trying to have his way with her.

My sword in hand, "I called Mr. I swear let her go or I will kill you here, now."

"Kid," The man said, "You need to run home to your mommy."

I told him it would be too far you would be dead before I returned. Sir that would be a waste.

"Why is that kid."

I smiled, "I'm going to kill you here, now." The thoughts of what Comp taught me came rushing back in. Kill only if there's no other way, believe me there was not. This man came at me swinging. In three steps, I had his blade in my left hand. My blade through his stomach. "See what I mean," as I whispered in his dying ear. "You thought you were good." I retrieved my sword looked at the girl I'm sorry you had to see that. She was crying as she ran to me. This female held on to me so tight. I looked into those blue eyes, and I knew I was done for.

"Please dont ever leave me," she said? When you walked through the door I looked into your eyes, I knew you were the man for me, always and forever."

I told her let's see about your father. Kneeling by her father I asked, what is your name?

"Kayla." "My name is Kayla."

"What a beautiful name, for a beautiful woman."

Kayla smiled, "We picked Reyes up, as he was coming to.

"What the hell happened," Reyes asks?"

"I think one hit you on the head." I said.

Looking at me, Reyes said, "Ira did you do all this?"

"I did sir, they asked for it so I gave it?" I told the others if they wanted the horse, take them and go never come to me again. I told them the man that is dead, I'd take his belongs for myself.

That's fair enough, "The man looked at me and said, that's alright by him I'm not sure about his brother."

I told them, send him to me. Tell them Ira, would be waiting.

Reyes took to me very quick.

Ira, he said, "I see there is no none since about you. I do see all you have showed me, well it works." Kayla is my daughter as you know. "She loves you I know you care for her."

I told Reyes I love her with my heart. I would die for Kayla.

Reyes said, "Yes Ira, I believe you would. I've never seen her act around other men, the way she does you. Kayla has had several callers, turned them all down.

She would say Papa, I will know when he comes. I want no others.

Reyes said Ira. "The others will come for you, you must leave here. Ira I know these people, they will kill you."

I just looked at Reyes, smiled at him, "You must trust me Reyes."

Reyes said. "I do trust you Ira, other than my daughter you're the only one I do trust." Reyes said, "I must go to the tavern. I'll see you later."

Kayla come to the barn after her father left. She watches me moved in every way.

"Ira, she said for month you have been here with us. I love you Ira."

I told Kayla the same.

"Come here Ira, sit with me on the hay."

I was not sure about want was to happen. Kayla kiss me, I kissed her back.

Kayla said, "Take me Ira."

I ask her, "Where am I, to take you."

Kayla said, "Take me to bed silly."

I looked at her. "It is not dark yet Kayla."

"Ira for someone who is so smart. You're really dumb."

I jumped up, "What did I do." I took Kayla by the arm. She melted in my arms, looking at me with those eyes.

She whispered, "Make love to me."

I looked at her, as I held my love. "Kayla I've never had a woman." I felt this feeling in my pants, a feeling I've never had, I didn't understand. Kayla placed her hand in my pants took my private in her hand. She started pushing in a stroking motion. I've never had such a feeling. It all come back to me what Comp said the humans called sex. The humans way to transfer their DNA.

I picked Kayla up, laid her on the hay.

She pulled me down, "raise up Ira." Kayla took my private guided it in hers. She told me to move up and down. I did as she instructed, a wonderful feeling. It was a sensation I'll never forget. She started moaning, moving, she let out a little scream. I let out a moan myself, then it was over. What a feeling, such pleasure. I see now what Opa was wanting to do, even Maoke. I read, his words in our archives, he knew the feeling. It had been told to him by the humans. Kayla and I laid on the hay for several minutes. Kayla looked at me.

"Ira, You want to do it again?"

I said, "Yes my love." This time it was longer, Kayla let out that little scream. Seven times, each time Kayla would shiver as if she was cold.

"Ira hold me," she said. "I love you so much, then she started to cry."

"Kayla, You ok?" I ask. Did I do something wrong? Kayla, did I hurt you?" She was crying so hard. Through a choked voice, Kayla said.

"I always knew it would be as this. If I had the man in my arms that I truly love, I truly love you Ira."

"I love you Kayla."

Life was wonderful. Kayla and I would walk down the street, of the small village of Madrid. Stop, Kiss then laugh then walk on. There's always someone to mess everything up. We were stopped outside a shop, two men come around the corner, almost knocking Kayla down. The two kept walking, I called you two,

They stopped looked at me. "You talking to us."

"Yes, that's right. You need to watch where you walking. You almost knocked the lady down."

"She's know lady," one said.

I started toward them. Kayla grabbed my arm. "Ira its ok, I'm ok."

"Listen to your girl, little boy." He said.

I stepped closer.

Kayla said, "Ira please I'm fine."

I spoke without taking my eyes from them. "Someone needs to teach these rouges a lesson."

"Is that right one said. It wants be a lesson by you boy."

Well you know me. I smacked one so hard he went to the street. The other come at me with a stick. Comp, taught me to defend myself in different ways. He made a swing at me missed I didn't. I knocked him out, his friend was up. I stood waiting.

"Look I'm sorry about the lady."

"Then you tell her your sorry." I said.

The man looked at Kayla, "Madam I'm sorry, for my friend also."

I told him to take his friend leave. Never cause me trouble again. If you do the outcome want be nice.

Kayla and I went back to the tavern. She told Reyes what happen.

Reyes said, "I'm afraid that will happen a lot son. Every man in this village envies you."

I ask, "Why?"

Reyes said, "Because of Kayla, every single man wanted to call. She turned them down. I suppose she waited for you. She always said you would come, not your name, The way you look when you came into the tavern. The way you looked at her, the way she looked at you.

Reyes said. "Ira I think you should take her away."

"Take her where Reyes."

Reyes just looked at me.

Did he know about me? I wondered if he saw me come off the ship. This I was not sure of.

Kayla and I was working in the tavern one night. There was a large crowd, I was serving ale to the people. A much younger male stood at the bar, watching every move I made. Holding the tin cup, he would slam the bar shout out something.

"You he shouted, you!" I looked at him, there was talk from the crowd, then silence.

One man shouted. "He's drunk Ira pay him no mind." He slammed the bar again.

I ask him, "Please don't do that?"

"I challenge you to a duel."

A costumer came to the bar. "Come on Doug, let's go back to the table."

The young man hit the man, knocking him down. The young man took a swing at me, knocking Kayla down. There was a hush upon the crowd. A man ran to Kayla helping her up. Kayla looked at me. Walking over to her, never taking my eyes from him. I've never wanted to kill a human as bad as I wanted to at this moment. I took Kayla by the hand. I ask, "Are you ok Kayla."

She replied yes, 'Ira please don't," she said.

I was so mad I was trembling.

"Ira please?"

A voice from the crowd. "He has been challenged."

I looked at the young man. "Do you have a family?" I ask.

"A wife a child." He said, "So what."

I ask, "Anyone here know this man?"

The voice said "Yes."

I told him to come forward. Ira, he has a family.

"Take him home to them."

Ira the man said. "He has challenged you."

I know, "Take him home, let him say goodbye. When he returns, I'll take his life."

"Ira this is Doug. he has served on the guard. He is the finest swordsman alive."

I told him, He want be for long, if I take his life.

The man said, "Ira I do like your modesty sir."

The man looked at Doug, "Do you accept these terms."

Doug replied, 'know.'

Kayla said to me, "Ira please dont kill him."

"I whispered to Kayla."

"I'll embraces him my love. That will be worse."

"Doug said "Here now."

He made a slice with his blade. That was it, I said to him, let me retrieve my blade. The greatness swordsman stepped back. I stepped out with my blade.

He said, "This will be good, I'll give you a lesson in pain before I kill you. Then I'll take your woman."

Thought ran through my mind. I will give Doug a little Boldlygo magic. We crossed swords, he went down my blade. I moved to the left took a slice from the leg. Across his back, the man had blood running down his body.

He took his blade bent it double. Doug said, "Now I will kill you."

I took his blade threw it in to the ceiling. Doug was standing helpless, run me through.

I looked at Kayla. She had tears in her eyes, I smiled at her.

"I do not wish, to run you through." However, I said, "If you're supposed to be the best swordsman, you need to go to your teacher, tell him he failed." He stood in bloody clothes. The crowd looked on in ah. They could not believe what just happen. I told Doug, Go home, let your woman take care of you. Doug dropped his head walked out the door I never saw him again. I stood before the crowd. I said to them,

"Any one wish to retrieve his blade." no one moved. "If one want to draw steal on me, come now or never draw. That man is alive because my lady asks me not to kill him. I have no reason to hurt anyone, to protect my love I will kill. Kayla is my life, without her I am nothing. I'm just a man as you, where I'm from I'm a prince. I wish to make my own way."

Someone ask. "Where are you from Ira?"

I told him, a long way from here.

The night ended. The sun broke the darkness of the dawn. I walked in the house from the barn. I fed the animals, done the milking.

Kayla ask, "Ira you some eggs."

I told her I preferred fruits cheese, and bread.

Kayla said to me, "I'm going to cook you an egg." She took a small kettle, poured water placed the eggs in the kettle. It took several minutes to cook. She called them boiled, well they were good.

I told her I never had them this way. We have no eggs where I'm from.

Kayla walked around the table. I watched her as she walks to me. I knew in my heart she would make a wonderful queen. I could not believe how beautiful she was.

Ira, "Where are you from. You said last night you were a prince."

"I am Kayla"

Please Ira, "Tell me where you're from."

I looked into those topaz eyes. "Tell me, where did you get those eyes?"

Kayla said with a snap. "Ira your changing the subject."

"No, I'm not. I was looking at her the way she says I do."

"Don't look at me like that Ira. Oh, Ira I can't resist you when you look at me as that."

Kayla fell into my arms. "I hate you when you do that."

I said, "Well if you hate me I'll leave. I started to the door.

She embraced me, started kissing me all over my face. "Promise me you will never leave me."

"Tell me where you got those eyes."

"The Spanish people have brown eyes. Your father has brown eyes."

"My mother is dead. She was a very beautiful woman. Father said I got her eyes."

"Kayla where I'm from only Royal Blood has blue eyes." The natives have brown, or green. The Indians have black eyes."

"What is an Indian."

I told her they were like a Spanish person. Dark hair, dark eyes. she kissed me again.

"Tell me where you're from."

"Kayla, the time is not right, I will tell you before they find me, before they come."

"Before who comes Ira"

It had been four years since I had left the ship that night. I feel my brother Ren would be at home. My brother was a traveler. Many thoughts had run through my mind of my fathers, his thought of me staying on Earth. If only he could see Kayla. My Opa wanted to ascend, if he could have met a human as Kayla, he would live forever. Before I came to Earth I heard him talk to my father of staying on our world. It was his time to take his place. Tudo never got to do much, he did go to other places. He has never done what I've done, I believe there will be others. Opa told Cra, not to do again what he did to me and Mekon. I think Opa was wrong telling Cra that. If I was the leader I would let Mekon do the experiment on any one that was willing. Cra is always looking and trying to find to make each child look more human. I remember my father telling stories by the pod where I grew up.

My brother grew up on Boldlygo. Opa missed my childhood, I believe that's why he told Cra what he did. I sat alone with my thought. Kayla had heated water for a bath.

"Ira, come help me."

Going to the room where she was, pour the water in the tub please. Two big pots I tilted them in the tub. Kayla looked at me with that smile.

"Ira take off your clothes, I'm going to give you a bath."

"Kayla no one has given me a bath, since I was six."

"I'm going to give you a bath, Ira take off your clothes, "She said.

I just stood there.

"Ira I've seen your body before now undress."

I wondered if she could see my native body what would she think. How would she react, I was terrified to think of this? When they come for me I would leave in the night, never to see her again.

The water was hot. Sitting down Kayla poured the water over my head. She told me she would be right back. I lay back in the tub, let the water come to my neck. I must admit it felt good. I closed my eyes, somewhere in thought I went home. The water was so relaxing, for a moment in time I forgot everything.

In my thoughts, I was looking across the valley of the Unicorn. To the Marder-to-go's. How I do miss it, the city of Ratio. What would I miss the most, Kayla or the planet I'm from if I stayed? I sometimes wonder if I'll ever go back. Lying in the water coming to my neck. "Father I said, I love Kayla. I must tell her of my world, father."

Kayla was beside the tub, "Ira who are you talking to."

"I was thinking out loud."

"No Ira you were speaking, as if someone was here. You said, I love Kayla, father." Ira, it as if you were talking to him."

I never notice she stood above me naked. I realized it when she stepped in to the tub. "I think it's time we took a bath together," she said.

Sitting between my legs. Kayla had her head laying on my chest. I had my arms around her. She took my hands placed them on her breast. She was a beautiful woman, her breast was full, her body slender. There was nothing of Kayla that wasn't real. Kayla was a perfect woman, a Divine human. A queen in every way. I mean after all I was a prince on my planet. We laid in the water until it turned cold.

From nowhere Reyes came in. I think I drink ten gallons of water. I was choking on the water when he said.

"He looked, "Ah a bath very nice," he said. Then walked on by.

I said to Kayla, "That was really embarrassing."

"Don't worry Ira, Kayla laid back again. Ira is there a woman where you're from? I mean do you have a woman there?"

Know Kayla, "Theres know woman, if there was I would be there. I promise, you are my first and only. I want know other."

"Ira, will you marry me?" she asks.

"Marry you, what is marry you? I dont know the phrase."

"You know Ira, a man and woman together maybe have a baby."

"My thought went to my world, my people, then to my Earth family. Oh, I said. "You mean you would like to be my mate, do a mating ritual."

"Ira if that is how you do it, then yes," she said. "I need to no more about you."

"My love, there is one thing about me you may not like. In fact, it would scare you, I'm afraid to let you in." We had dried off, changed into our cloths. Kayla was sitting by the fire her long black hair was drying.

"Ira, there is nothing about you that would scare me." She turned to kiss me.

I ask, "Even if this wasn't my body you were looking at."

"What do you look like Ira?" A voice from the dark spoke. Reyes stepped from the dark.

Reyes said, "Still not ready to talk."

"I'm not sure what you're saying."

"I've never told her son. Ive waited for you to make the move."

I knew what he was saying. "How can I tell her, I dont want to lose her."

Reyes said, "Show her Ira. If you dont you will regret it." Reyes said, "Come here Ira."

We changed places.

Kayla said, "Ira now your scaring me. Ira please tell me, what is happing?"

Reyes said wait. "He walks to the window closed the curtains." Reyes said to her, "Kayla there's a reason Ira so intelligent. Why he knows more than others. Hell, more than anyone I no. Can't you see he is different."

"I know all of this father so he's smart."

"Honey, Ira is not from here."

"Father I know he's not from here. Ira has said he live far away."

Reyes said, "You wouldn't believe how far."

I knew, "Reyes saw me that night long ago, come from the ship." It had been years, he has never said a word to anyone. I know now, I could trust him. I knew I always did.

"Ira what is going on, "Kayla asks?

"I went to her, down on one knee. I love you Kayla."

She said the same.

"I would never hurt you."

Kayla said the same.

I looked at Reyes.

"Tell her son."

"I'm not from here, I do live a long way off. Kayla there is nothing on this planet that can take me home." Well let's just say the blue in her eyes could not believe what she was hearing.

"Kayla I'm not what you see. The body you see my love is a fake body. I'm afraid to show you my true self. I'm afraid I will lose you. Remember when you ran to me told me never to leave you. I want leave you now." Kayla stood looking at me not believing in what she was hearing. "The truth needs to be told. The night your father and I met. Reyes help me please."

Reyes said, "Kayla Ira is from the stars. A place we can't imagine being from. I saw him come from a bright light. It was a flying machine." Remember long ago when you were a little girl. Lying with your mother in the field. You looked up in the sky, you thought it was a shooting star. I knew it wasn't, stars dont move then stop.

I looked at Reyes, "You never told me of that."

"There was no need to son. How could I tell you of something you live?" We both looked at Kayla, she had turned a shade of white, tears filled her eyes.

I started toward her, She held up her hands to stop. "Kayla please dont do this, dont push me away."

"Ira, I need to be alone for a while," she said."

"I slipped on my booths. I walk to the barn, Reyes come out."

"Dont l let it get to you son. She will be fine by morning."

The night give away to morning. Kayla wasn't fine, I called from outside her door.

"Kayla, please open the door."

"Go away" she said."

"Kayla if that's is what you want. Goodbye my love." I felt then what I've heard of humans. I was hurting so bad, my stomach hurt. My head ache I wasn't sure when it happens. I had become human.

I went out to the barn again.

Reyes said, 'Son I got to open the tavern.

"Kayla, has asked me to leave? Reyes at her request I must go."

Reyes ask, "Ira where will you go?" I thought for a moment. "home Reyes." "It will take them two years to come here. I've been here several years. My father may have a ship somewhere close."

Reyes ask, "You can call them?"

I showed him the stone that let a beam of light shoot from it.

"Then what," he said?"

"Wait for a light to appear in the sky, I'll signal them again, they'll come.

"So, Ira, "What do you do until then. Travel I suppose."

Reyes said, "Your giving up to easy Ira, I think you need to wait."

"I dont want to leave Reyes, she told me to go away."

"I just wanted you to leave my door Ira. I didn't want you to leave the house. I can't believe you would through it all away."

"I was doing what you ask?"

Kayla started running to me.

Oh Ira, "I never want you to leave me. Father I'm ready to see."

I looked at Kayla, "You sure."

Reyes said to me, "Ira show her son, show her your real self."

I looked around to see if there was someone watching. I saw no one, I shifted to my native body.

Oh my, She was startled, not so much at my body, just the fact I could do it. She come close, "it's not so bad. I've seen others that wish they could do that."

I changed back quickly as Kayla took me by the hand.

"I'm hungry Ira. let's go make breakfast."

I looked at Reyes as we walk by, he just shrugged his shoulder.

The day ended, with the rising of the Earth moon. Behind the barn, I sat looking to the what the humans called heaven. Stars sparkled as a Dimond, my thought went home. I miss home, I suppose I should send the signal. Walking back to the house, I took a breath of the air before going in. Sitting around the table, Kayla massaging my shoulders.

Ira, "You are trouble?"

"I pushed her against the wall, I love you."

"I love you Ira," she said. "Tell me my love, what is wrong."

"I think it is time to go home," She looked hard.

"Come with me Kayla, have my children."

"I can't leave my father Ira."

"Reyes, can come to. Dont you understand on Boldygo you can't die. Tudo my father is over four hundred, better yet I think he I s five hundred".

"How old are you, Ira?"

"Well let me think, almost t thirty four."

"Bullshit," Kayla said.

Kayla please, "I dont lie about this, I promise you." Kayla turned to look at me. "You see me now, the way you saw me in the barn. Your father saw me come off the ship. I can't understand why you find it hard to believe."

"Ira, I just dont want to think of you leaving me. I dont want you to go."

I threw my hands up, I went to bed. Kayla had to finish what she was doing. Coming to bed she lay in my arms. I felt something on my arm, she had started to cry.

Kayla I ask you again, "Please come with me?" I set up on the side of the bed.

"Ira, where are you going," she asks?"

I kissed her on the face. "I'm going to the field behind the barn. I'm going to send a signal, if there is a ship, they will come for me. If not it will take two years before they come, Kayla they will come."

Standing in the fields, Kayla stood beside me. I took the stone from my pocket, held it close to my body, for the warmth it takes to open it. A beam of light shot straight up.

"That was beautiful," Kayla said.

I said, "It will take two month to reach our world. I hope there is a ship close. I really want to go home."

Kayla ask me, "When they come ira, how will you know?"

I told her a bright light will appear in the sky.

She just looked at me.

I knew she really didn't understand. I told her a light will appeared as like the Earths northern star, or Venus. It will be as the sun reflection against it." "Kayla, haven't you looked into the night sky."

"I did when I was a child, not so much now. Ira how far are the stars."

I told her if she was there, where the stars are, they would still be as far. I told her most have there on system.

She asks, "What was that?"

I told her galaxies and universe. There are so many of them, I think old Bota was the only one of our people to go to several of them. Maybe my grandfather traveled far, he come to Earth several times.

My Opa's and my father's mates were from Earth. Carrie, Beth. I didn't tell her about Mya, wanting to be his mate."

We set on the ground talking for hours. I pointed into the night sky. See Kayla. "The cluster I described, this is what your Earth people calls the Orion system. The big dipper, the little dipper. I pointed out all I could see. I have showed you are star charts, it is what a pilot navigates their ships to Earth, they're many others, they're not visible from here."

I told Kayla, my Earth mother was from Russia. She is there now, I think we should go there. They all would love you. Nancy, Georgia, Mary, Lola, Sandy.

Kayla ask, "Are they from your world."

I said to her, "Know they're our Earth family, they are descendants of Mya. Mya was a princess, sister to my Opa. She died on Earth several hundered years ago," She ascended."

"What is that ira?"

I told Kayla when you die you go to a different place. She is in the ancient city on Boldlygo.

"Oh, I understand," Kayla said. "Like heaven."

"I dont know Kayla, all I know the ancient city is for the Royal Blood."

"Sound a lot like heaven, Ira does God live there."

"I looked at her, I know nothing of this. I'm not sure Kayla, I'm just not sure."

"Ive heard you speak of Ject, and Tudo."

"Tudo is my father." "We did an experiment my father was against it. I wanted to do it because of Mekon, I couldn't let him do it alone. Cra and Tudo placed us in stasis pods. This was to let us become human, so we could mate with humans."

"Well, I think it worked Ira." Kayla said.

"Come with me Kayla. Let me show you around my world, take you to the Moon of Spores. The falls at the Marder-to-go's. Taste of our Sweet Grass."

Kayla said, "I forgot you dont eat meat."

I told her it was forbidden to eat meat.

"The animals on my world are not afraid of us. The natives, humans animals, Kayla we are as one. We all live in harmony with each other. The Pegasus the Unicorn, all live in the ancient city."

"Ira, there is no such thing as a Unicorn."

"You know of this Kayla."

"I've seen pictures Ira."

I told her if there was a picture it was real. Bota brought one to Earth several thousand years ago, It was Bota, Cam and the Unicorn.

"Ira tell me more about your mother."

"I never knew my mother on Boldlygo. Lola my Earth mother, was very beautiful. My mother on my world had me, that's all I know. I was raised by my aunts, or whoever. That's the way it is there. When I was six, I could already fly the ships my brother also."

"Ira, the city you talk about, the city of Ratio what of it?"

"The city of Ratio was overseen by Maoke. The Pegasus, the Unicorn with their magical powers, the natives the Busies played an important part. After the Great Wall was built Maoke walk several days with the Unicorn to find the the place where the city is today. Kayla, it is so beautiful there, please come with me. Ive seen your world, please come see mine."

"Ira my father said he would not go. I have talked to him of this he has ask me to go with you? I will go with you; this I promise you."

Kayla and I made love in the field. The Earth sun was coming up Kayla and I were still making love.

Kayla said, "Ira know more, Ira please know more. I can't do it anymore, this is how I know you're not from Earth. Ira, know Earth man could ever make a woman do that. You have brought the woman out in me so many times. I love you so, I suppose we went to sleep, laying in the field. I woke her up.

Kayla said, "Look the sun is so beautiful."

"My love, wait till you see it on my world."

We were on our way back to the house. I caught a movement I stopped her.

"Wait Kayla," Someone is in the barn wait here, I told her. I eased my way around the barn door. I looked up twenty feet. That was no problem I kneeled. Jumping up I caught the rope sung into the loft. I found what I was looking for. The person was hiding in the stall, with sword in hand. I looked to see if Kayla was where I told her to stay. She was gone, I scanned the yard. Kayla was hiding behind a bush, I thought good girl. I eased closer to the stall, over head of him I picked up a bale of hay through it down on top of him. He had started to rise as I was on him. The man dropped the sword, we fought around.

Picking up his sword, I reached for the pitch fork.

I said to him, "I'm highly trained in this weapon, as well as several others. I see you are a coward, a yellow coward. Oh, I touched a spot, calling him a coward."

"I'm know coward," He said.

"What else could you be? You hide in a barn with a sword. You were waiting for me to come by. That's a coward to me. If it's a fight you want, sheath your sword like a Spanish gentleman. Go to the street, wait for me."

He said as he departed, "Please dont keep me waiting Ira." He stopped said with a snarl. "Dont make me come for you." The gent walked to the street, standing in the middle swinging his sword. You could hear people talking.

Someone ask, "Who is that?"

"People started gathering around. "One said what does he want."

"One man said, he's waiting on Ira."

"Ira one said, How do you know this. A young man, in the middle of the street with a sword. What do you think he is waiting on winter?"

One man said. "I hope he has his affairs in order if he's waiting on Ira."

One said. "Ira will do as always, he want kill him. Unless there's no other way."

I heard this as I come from the tavern, Kayla by my side. I kissed her on the cheek. "Kayla stay on the walk you understand." She had tears in her eyes.

"I understood Ira."

I stepped in the street. The young man said, "Today you die."

I said to him, "I must know who you are. What I have done to you."

He replied, "Nothing personal, it's just you. There's only room for one swordsman in Spain."

Ira looked at the sword. That's it, people were standing waiting.

"That's it."

I was smiling. "Then my friend you win. I have no reason to fight you." I turned to walk away.

The young man shouted. "When I'm through with you I'll take your woman."

"I froze, looked into the blue eyes of Kayla."

"Ira, I love you," Kayla said.

Everyone knew how I felt about Kayla. Kayla was my world. More than once I have defended her.:

Kayla said, "Ira, do what you need to do my love."

I turned drew my sword. Walk to the young man. "Up with your sword, "I said. I swish, and swank until the man's cloths fell to the ground. People were saying, "I've never seen that before." The young man was on the ground. I said to him. "Now you must live with this, the greatest swords man in Spain."

Someone shouted. "Now Ira you are."

"I've never said that, I never will. I just had a good teacher." Looking over my shoulder Kayla was walking toward me,

Someone screamed.

I turned, blocked his thrust he missed I didn't. I said to him, "I should have killed you." I withdrew my sword, that went through his right shoulder.

"Kill me he shouted, dam you kill me. I'm no good like this."

I looked at him. "You should have thought of that, before you come for me." I left him on the street shouting at everyone to help him. I never saw him again.

CHAPTER 25

Foo, and I were on the Moon of Corning, doing a supply run. We had been to Plano and Xon.

I said, "We should ask my father to let us go to Earth to look for my brother?" "Foo, I will ask him when we return?" Pep was helping Foo load the last of the supplies. We said our goodbyes then we went to the darkness of space. It took four month to go to our world, it seemed faster.

"Foo said the same."

We roared across the city, landed on the pad. A sentry was waiting,

"Ren your father is waiting. He said come quick." I told the sentry to see the supplies were unloaded.

"As you wish," he replied."

I told Foo father has sent for me.

"Foo said for me to go ahead, he would come later." Foo wanted to go home to Soy, they have taken the mating ritual. He told me he wanted a child, Foo had been with me for a long time. We started together with my brother Ira.

Father was waiting for me as I entered the chambers. Father was talking to Opa.

I spoke, "Father you wish to see me."

"Your brother has sent his signal, it is time to go to Earth." Ren decide to leave mid-week. "There's humans that wish to go also."

I told him, I'll take Foo and my regular crew. I met Foo on the way in. I told him Ira had sent a signal. We leave in two days.

"I must go home to Soy." Foo said.

I told Foo I would overlook the unloading.

I stayed on the pad watched the supplies being loaded for the trip to Earth. I walk back to the palace Opa was eating a Simon.

Come here son, sit with me. "I will be going with you," he said. "This will be my last run, Ren I long to be out there. It was a love I never got over." Maoke said, I had to stay home, as I told your father. He will tell Ira the same. Your father wanted to be a pilot. It was his time to stay, time to take my place. "Just as he will ask you someday."

Know Opa. "I'm not a leader, Ira yes, not me. I want no part of this, when it's time for Ira, to take his place beside my father. I will stand beside him. I'll listen to what he has to say, I'm not a leader Opa."

Ren sit talking to me, for a while longer.

Opa Ren said, "Why do you say this is your last run."

My grandson, "It is time for me to leave you. I wish to ascend."

"Opa you dont need to ascend, if you want to leave. Just walk to the city."

"It is written Ren even Maoke, had to die."

"Opa in Botas writing I've read it, he just walks to the city, Kia too. It is true, they were pure blood Busies I'm not, Maoke wanted to be with Tomeka, that's why he left."

"Who do you wish to be with Opa?"

"I'm going to Mya, she has loved me al ways"

I told Opa we would leave at first light.

"I'll be ready grandson," he said.

The night come slowly, as the suns set over the Marder-to-go's, Mya come to me, Mya sat beside me. Ject, "You really coming this time," Mya ask.

Mya, "This time I will let it be done. Across your grave I will take my last breath. Then to the ancient city I will come to stay."

Mother, and father waits for you Ject, so do I. Then we will be together always."

"Mya, please I'm your brother."

"Ject you dont understand. I'm not looking for a mate. I need someone to talk to, mother and father is always busy. I want you there for my own reasons. No one has time for me, Bota is in his lad, mother and father at the portal. I help them sometimes. Tudo will be a good leader. Ira, well on Earth he has met a beautiful woman. She is coming here, just to let you know. You should go see her before you ascend. You leave tomorrow, so I should go let you rest."

Sleep over took me, when I woke up Mya was gone. Walking to the window, looking across the sky, morning was coming. I looked toward the Marder-to-go's, soon mother soon. Looking at the place I slept for so many hundred of years, I knew I would never sleep here again.

I walk to the great room, took a Simon cut it. I thought, this was my favorite fruit on the planet. Tudo was sitting on the stoop. "My son your up early." Tudo was looking out across the Valley of the Unicorn. The suns were up enough to see the outline of the mountains.

I spoke to my son. "I shall never see you again. On the very Earth, you long to be, I shall ascend. I shall see you in the ancient city when you arrive. My son you will be a good leader of our people. Lead our people well. your son Ira, he will be great with our people. Let him run a while, then bring him home. "Tudo let him learn from you." Mya said, He has taken a human, she will come here with him. I wish to go to the ground where my family is buried. I will ascend also, the Indians know us there, the ground is sacred. Tudo looked at me. Father, is that what you wish. It is my son. Remember Tudo I will be with you always. Sometimes I will come to you, I want be far away.

My son walked with me to the pad, everything was loaded. Cra, Mekon, stood by. Foo said his goodbye to Soy. Soy was growing, she had become very intelligent. Soy will be great in the city for all that is to come. Cra ask, if he should come alone? I knew what he wanted, I looked at my long life friend. "If you wish Cra."

"Cra told Mekon, "Son the lab is yours until I return. If I dont return take my notes, work hard on the task of the experiment." The ship lifted off we were on our way to the blue planet called Earth. One stop on the Moon of Corning.

Flying by the Moon of Spores, I thought I should stop see my old friend Garf. Sadly, to say I will miss him. Garf had done well by his people. He took a moon, built an empire. Our trade will be carried on with them. The ship flew on to The Moon of Corning. It will be good to see Quad. It had been over two hundered years since Bota, and I first landed there. Bota, and Cam would stop by when in their area. Cam, I thought of him. Cam was very old when he left the planet the last time.

My thought went to Mya.

She said, "Ject I will take you to the Valley to see the Unicorn, when you arrive. Ject, I will show you everything, the city last."

I ask her, "Why the city last?"

Mya said, "Ject when you enter the city you can't leave."

I ask Mya, "How do you comes and go the way you do?"

Ject, "Mother, and father can leave the city. When their replacement comes, they will go to the city.

I ask Mya, "Who is there?" Mya never answered.

We had been four month in the flight. Ren come to me.

"Opa we are coming up to the Moon of Corning.

Ren ask, "Opa you ok?"

I told grandson I was fine. Sitting down on the pad, Quad was there to greet us. Coming down the ramp Quad took my hand.

Ject he said, "Tell your crew to take liberty."

I told Quad, They're not my crew, They're with Ren and Foo. I'm alone for the ride.

Pep come in. "Ject my old friend, how are you."

I ask, "Quad may Pep could join us." Quad, said Pep, has been a big help us. He has shown us several ways to better thing. He is quite intelligent."

How long has it been? Pep, Mya would run through the street of Ratio? Mya, would stay gone for days. II remember it very well. I sat listening to Quad, Kohl, Joy talk. After several hours, I excused myself went back to the ship. The morning came early. Foo took the ship to the darkness of space.

Flying through space as a leaf on the wind, passing clusters, asteroids. What a beautiful thing. Foo made his turn at Saturn gradually to the right. We were holding a steady course to Earth.

We stopped just outside Earth atmosphere. What a beautiful site, a big ball hanging in space. Knowing the people there were so uneducated. I'm sure in time they will grow in to a great nation. A knock on my the door brought me back to myself.

Ren ask, "Opa why did you want to stop?" Opa you dont look right," he said"

"Dont worry of me. I must see Georgia before we go further." I told Ren to ready the shuttle, scan the farm. If all is clear, we will go to the surface."

"Ren did as I ask?" One hour later we landed. I could see three children run for the house. Comp, was the first to reach the ship. We cloaked the ship on the ridge.

"Comp said, "The the Russian army don't come here anymore." Arman came to meet us.

"Ah Ren, How are you."

Ren told Arman, "This is my Opa, Tudo father"

Arman said, "Yes I see, come in the house."

I walked in the house, the children stood by the wall.

Georgia came into the room, "What is all the noise," She asks? Looking around until she saw me. "Father, oh father."

Georgia ran to me. My heart was aching as I held her. So many years I have longed to hold you child. She was beginning to age, Comp also. He had turned gray, wrinkles in his face. Nancy was a beautiful woman. Lola was sick I could see this. I feel she will die soon as the humans say. The children stood in line against the wall. They had been told of us their life long. I waited to meet them as the girls could not stop asking questions of home.

Comp ask, "Ject would you like coffee?"

I told him, With the sweet stuff maybe a bread cake. The children laughed. Come children let me talk to you. I must know your names.

Georgia said father, Tye is Mary's and Arman's. This one is Nancy, youngest.

I said, "Georgia Your child."

Katie, "She is from Tomeka's DNA.

"I ask the girls if they had seen Ira?"

Georgia said, "No father not since he left long ago."

"Ira, has been gone a long time, we have come for him. He has sent the signal, he is not far. Ira, is in a country called Spain."

Tye said, "We have been told of you our whole life, I'm only seven. I hoped you would come in my life time.

Tye showed me a picture, it was of the city of Ratio. The palace, it was if Maoke had drawn it himself.

I ask, "Child how did you do this?"

Tye replied, "From Comp, Georgia, Nancy, they told me. I drew this twenty time before I got it right."

I ask him, "You know what this is?"

"Yes, silly it's the Marder-to-go's. Its where the rainbow fall is. This is the Valley of the Unicorn." Tye ask, "Opa, you ever seen a Unicorn?"

I have not I said, "You must believe me, there in the hidden city with the Busies the Pegasus. We have been told, as you have been told of us."

Most of the day everyone was talking of things. Georgia never leaving my side. Georgia took my hand as we walked in the orchard with the children. I tasted the fruit from all the trees and vines. The apples, plums, grapes. I loved them all. I tried the peach as they were called. It reminded me of Simons.

Comp said, "Ira and Mekon planted them long ago."

Everyone walked from the orchard to the barn. I thought how awful it was to house the animals. They need to run free I thought. "I said as much."

Georgia said, "The animals is how we take the fruit to market."

We walked back to the house.

Ren said to me. "Opa it is time for us to leave."

The girls gathered around, started to cry.

Tye looked up at me. "See you later big guy."

I told him, "See you little man.

I told the girls not to cry.

Georgia said father, "I shall never see you again."

I held all the girls at once. "I'll always live in your heart. Georgia, Nancy, Mary always tell them of us. Let them know someday someone will return." everyone walked to the ship.

Ren, Nancy, Foo embraced.

Ren told Lola, "Mother it was good to see you."

Lola told Ren "Tell your brother I love him."

Ren said, "He would pass it on.

I ask for my bag, Ren brought it to me. Inside the bags were stones. "When the children are older, give them one each." Mary open one of the bags, inside the bag were fourteen stones. They didn't notice at first. There were coins in each bag. I said, "Goodbye to all Ren closed the hatch."

We left the surface of the planet. Everyone knew I would never see them again.

Georgia said, "In my life time I spent time with the father of the stars. I will never forget him."

little Tye said, "I will never let him die in vain."

Comp said. "He was my teacher, my long life friend."

Ren flew over the country of Spain. The ship come from impulse, we sat for a long while.

Ren was scanning the surface.

"Opa we found him."

I told Ren to send the signal." A great light was seen in the sky.

On the surface a young man come in the tavern. "Did you see the size of that star. It was the biggest star ive ever seen."

Reyes knew that my people had arrived. He knew it was time for me to take his beloved Kayla away. This would be good Reyes thought. Anything would be better than her wasting her life away here in a tavern, he thought. Kayla was destin for bigger things. I never realized she would become queen of a plant, until later in life. Ira returned just before my passing, told me everything.

I saw the light running to the house, "Kayla I called they're here."

"Who is here?" Kayla ask.

"Ren, my brother come out side hurry. look!" A huge light was in the sky.

Oh, "Ira is it really them."

"It is my love, "You ready to go home?"

"Yes, Ira I am."

"I've seen your world Kayla, now come see mine. I promise you, if you are not happy I'll bring you back."

"Then let's go."

"I must leave the village to send then the signal." Kayla, "Go to your father spend time with him. We leave before dawn tomorrow."

Kayla went back to the house to be with her father. I had already scouted the area. I had done this so many times. I scouted four places, then I decided this place was the best. It was a small clearing surrounded by big oaks. It would be an easy walk from the house. Kayla and I would leave in the night. No one to see us except Reyes. Kayla stayed with her father through the day.

The day passed slowly as night approached. I thought it would never come. Kayla had tears in her eyes as she prepared her father his supper, as he called it. It would be Kayla's last meal ever on Earth. The sun went slowly down as the stars appeared in the sky.

Reyes said, "Ira can you see your world from here."

I told him yes, I lied to him. I pick out the north star. See the one far to the right, that's it. I just wanted him to have something to hold on to. "That's where we will be Reyes, two hundred fifty light years away."

I sent the signal a beam of light shot from my chest. I saw the ship as the stone burned out. "Look Kayla!" The ship landed, the ramp went down. Opa was the first one I saw. Kayla was holding on tight. She was scared to death. Opa reached out his hand."

"Come child dont be afraid."

Kayla said, "I'm not afraid." She went to Ject, "embraced him."

I been told of you for years. This must be Ren."

"Ren, took Kayla in his arms, then bowed to her. My lady, welcome to our world."

My lady, "I am Foo, you are most welcome."

Opa said to Ira, "Son I see you have done well." I told Ira of the visit to the farm. The family is growing, several additions has been added. Lola is very sick, Comp is very old, Arman said hello. "Comp was like a father to me Opa," I said.

Kayla said, "I don't know him I have heard Ira speak of him."

Ject said, "He was the one to train Ira in his skills."

Kayla said, "Well he taught him very well. His training has come in handy more than once."

"We must hear of this Ira," Opa said.

"Yes, Ira" Ren said, "We must."

Opa, you said, "Lola was sick."

I thought before I answered Ira, "She will pass Ira before you reach home." Comp will shortly go after.

Leaving the Earth's atmosphere reaching the big ship. "I ask, Foo to circle the ship I wanted Kayla to see it. Kayla was completely in ah."

Oh, my she said, "Its bigger than my village."

Docking with the big ship, we went aboard.

Ren ask, "You shifted for her?"

Kayla said, "He has Ren.

"I know about the experiment, Ira has kept nothing from me. I admit it was a shock at first. My father knew the night they met. He knew he was not from Earth. Ira was to smart, to intelligent. The humans we knew were not like him." Kayla said, "Your ship is not the first ive seen. When I was a little girl, my mother and father would lay on the ground watch them go for a longtime. I would watch until I would fall asleep. "Kayla said., "I dont think your alone out here."

I told Kayla I would show her to the sleeping room.

Kayla noticed one of the crew was a female, she was very young. The young female stood looking waiting. "That's ok Ira, let her show me."

"You sure Kayla."

Yes Ira, "I want to talk to her, I'm glad she's here. it would be a very long trip without a female to talk with."

I kissed Ira on the face, "I'm sure you have some catching up to do. I spoke to the female you ready?" She bowed to me took me to my quarters.

Wait I said, "What is your name."

She answered, "I am called Jen."

I ask her, "Well since you are the first native female I've met, could we be friends?"

Jen said, "Well it is a long way home." Jen said, "We would be stopping in a place called Mexico. Ject will leave the ship."

Why I ask, "It is his time to ascend?"

I said, "Ira has spoken of that."

Jen told me, The place was a burial place where the Indians spent time with them. I hear they're savage people, eat meat make houses from the skins. I myself have read of them in our archives. I have never seen them. I know they killed our head scientist Lon, Cra's father. Lon was a good being, that was one hundered seventy five years ago.

I said what, "How old are you?"

Jen said, "I'm not that old, I'm only one fifty of your Earth years."

I said to her, "That's old on Earth." "You look twenty five." I said.

Jen said, "We don't age as humans do, no offense."

I told her none taken.

Jen ask, "Do you love Ira?"

I replied, "Yes with all my heart."

"Why, have you not had his child."

Then it hit me. The years on Earth, the many time we made love, I had not become pregnant. I looked at Jen.

"I dont know why."

Jen said, "Maybe you will need to have a DNA transfer. If you like we can go see Cra, he will be in the lab."

Jen took me by the hand. "You want me to be your friend Kayla, you must trust me."

I hesitated, "I feel doing this without Ira knowing well, I feel it would be wrong."

"Tell him later if you wish. Cra will say nothing." Leaving my room Jen took me to see Cra. He was a true native, a very strong will being. Jen whispered, "He too will be leaving the ship. Jen called to Cra. "Cra, this is Kayla, Iras' woman. They will have the mating ritual when we return home.

Ah Kayla, "You are most beautiful."

Jen said, "Kayla has a question?"

Cra said, "Yes Kayla, how may I help you."

I told him Ira and I have been together for several years. I haven't become pregnant, I never thought about it until Jen ask?"

Cra ask, "Would you like for me to examine you."

"I suppose"

"lay down" Cra said. "Jen find her a robe. She needs to lose the Earth cloths."

Jen went to the storage, came back with a robe. "Cra told me to undress, lay on the table." I covered up with the cover. jen standing by me as Cra brought the machine close to the bed. Cra took a probe with a cord, placed it to my stomach.

I ask him, "What is this?"

Cra said, "Look this is your insides Kayla."

I ask, "How is this possible, I've never seen anything as this."

Cra said to me, "Kayla we are so advance from the people of Earth." After several minutes Cra looked at the machine.

"You can raise up now Cra said."

Jen give me the robe.

Cra said to me. "Kayla I'm not sure why you have not had a child. You appear to be very healthy."

Cra said, "I'll tell Ira."

I said to Cra, "Let me tell him first."

"Then you must wait until you go home." Cra said. "You will see my son Mekon."

I thanked him, "Jen and I walked back to my room."

On the way, I told Jen, I was hungry.

Jen said, "Let me show you where we eat. It is called the galley."

Inside the galley, I took tea with bread. I said, "I wish for cheese."

Jen said, "I've had never heard of it."

"I think you would like it jen. It's made from milk."

Jen ask, "Kayla, what is milk?"

Leaving the galley, Jen took me to my room. Jen sat talked to me for over an hour.

I looked at Jen, "Did we stop."

Jen said, "Were over the place where Iras' Opa will leave the ship. Ira knocked on the door.

"Kayla, we are over the place where my Opa, and Cra, will leave the ship. A place where they will ascend. You want to be there."

"I do not wish to be Ira. Is it ok if I stay?"

Ira said, "It will be fine."

Ira and the others left the ship on the shuttle.

Jen said, "Come with me."

I ask her, "Jen are we the only ones on the ship?"

Jen said, "Yes."

"Who is flying the ship." I was scared to death.

"No one is flying it, we are sitting still Jen said."

I ask, "How is that possible?"

"Jen it's so big. Why does it not fall?"

Jen said, "Kayla you going to get your first lesson in physics."

Jen, explained to me the laws of gravity and physics. I didn't understand.

Jen said, "Why would you, on Earth you had no reason to learn this."

I ask, "Ira that night if Jen could spend time with me."

Ira said, "She can spend as much time as you wish Kayla."

We did spend a time together, after starting my schooling Jen said to me, "You are intelligent, even if you are a human."

Jen would come to me every day, report everything Kayla would learn. In the twenty month, we were in the air before reaching the Moon of Corning. Kayla had evolved into a very intelligent person. it was unreal.

Kayla ask, "Before we reach the moon if I was pleased."

I told her I was pleased. "You didn't have to this for me Kayla."

I no Ira, "I never knew of things as I've learned. The things Jen has taught me, Ira she is very intelligent."

I said to Kayla. "Some of our people are even more intelligent than others. Mekon is the most intelligent one on the planet." I told her I wish I was that smart.

She said, "You are Ira. You're the smartness of all."

"I love you Kayla." We kissed made love late into the night. Lying in bed Kayla told me of her visit to Cra. I will have Mekon look at me also when we reach home. Somehow, we will have a child. I need a son".

"Ira, are you mad with me for not going to Earth with your grandfather?"

"Know my love, "I understand."

I ask "Would you talk to me of this?"

"There's a place where my family is buried. I've told you of this."

"Why do you come to Earth to die? "I ask.

"I've told you of this Kayla."

"You can't die there. We have no sickness nothing, if you stay on the planet you can live forever. If you leave you age quick. When we reach home, after all is done, Jen will take you to the archives. She will stay with you."

"Ira, did you know Jen wanted to have a child.

"Jen said, "She needed to have a mate."

I ask Ira, "What happens to the natives there. There must be several that was as old as Ject.

"They just live their lives as always Kayla. I think the reason they ascend is they have nothing to hold on to."

"Could Ject have lived on."

I told her he could have lived on, Maoke was, well he was ancient. Some say when Maoke ascend he was over five thousand year old, I think he was much older. It was my Opa's choice Kayla, he was ready to go to the city."

I ask Ira, "Is the name of your planet called heaven?"

I told her know, "It's called Boldlygo."

Kayla told me, "On Earth if your good when you die you go to heaven."

I told her, "I know nothing of this." The ship flew through the darkness of space. I lay in bed holding her in my arms. I watched her sleep, Kayla was a beautiful woman. I was one lucky man.

lying in bed, Kayla lying beside me. I tried to slide from bed.

Kayla ask, "Ira can I sleep just a while longer."

I told her to sleep if she please. Kayla turned over, she was fast asleep. It was always dark in space. You never can tell when it supposed to be daytime. Your body just seem to tires out. Some time you just can't tell the difference.

I strapped my blade on, then decided to leave it, I really had become parcel to it. I went out the door, walked to the bridge. Foo was at the controls, Ren came from his quarters.

I ask my brother, "How was your sleep?"

Ira Ren said, "Why dont you shift to your native body? I dont think you should be in your human body around us."

"Do you have a problem with humans?" I ask. He just looked at me, turned to the controls. Ren I shouted, "I ask you a question?"

Ren replied, "I have no problem with anyone. The problem is you."

"Well little brother if it's with me, let's talk."

Ren said, "Ira it would be to your best interest to leave the bridge. I'm not a violet being, you keep pushing I could be."

"Well let me push little brother."

Ren jumped at me, I decked him he never saw it coming.

"Ren I had a good teacher. Now give me your hand." I pulled him from the floor. I told him I was sorry for hitting him.

"Forget it, Ren said, I pushed it."

"Ren, it would seem you are jealous of me. Did you want to take the experiment?"

"Yes, Ira I did, there was only to pods."

"Would you like to do this Ren, I can arrange it. There are women that will do this for us." If not from our Earth family of Destiny. We will find others."

Ren said no, "In his heart he really wanted to say yes."

Kayla over heard the task between Ren and myself.

Ira, she called, "Is there a problem with me being here."

I told her no, "Ren and I were having a discussion Kayla. Kayla looked at Ren, he never looked up from the controls.

Foo called out, "We're entering the orbit of the moon."

I looked at Kayla, she had turn two shades of white.

I ask, "You ok?"

Kayla was shaking," Scared," she said."

Jen spoke up," Scared of what."

"I just hope people will like me."

Jen said, "I dont see the problem."

I told Kayla to look out the port side of the ship. We were passing the Moon of Spores.

Oh, my Kayla said, "Ira it is so beautiful." She asks, Can you live there?"

I told her the one were passing, the other one with the purple haze no.

Ren called to Kayla, "Come look from this portal."

We dropped through the atmosphere to the planet below. Kayla's hands went to her face. The mountain of the Marder-to-go's was the first thing she saw. Then the Valley of the Unicorn, then the city of Ratio. It stood in the foot hills of the mountains to the cliff of the palace. Kayla turned to me walk slowly to me as the ship touch down.

Kayla said," Ira I'm home."

Kayla had her long dark hair down. Her and jen had been in her room all morning preparing herself to meet the family of Boldlygo. The blue in her eyes sparkled like the stars in the sky. Foo sat the ship down in the palace staging area.

Kayla said to me, "Ira how many ships do you have."

I replied, "Well Kayla I've been gone for a while, I'm not sure."

She gazed at the palace. "Is this where we live."

I told her, It's for the Royal Blood.

She asks, "Then where shall I live." I'm not royalty.

I told her you will be as soon as we have the mating ritual. Kayla looked at all the people waiting.

"Who are they waiting for Ira?"

I said, "They are waiting for you."

"Ira that's impossible, "How could they know I was coming.

Ren said, "It was Mya, She told Opa before we left."

"Mya," I said. A cool breeze passed, Kayla's hair blew.

"Ira I caught a chill."

"You will be fine Kayla, it was Mya."

"Bull shit." Kayla said.

Ren open the hatch. Kayla looked up on the creation of Maoke. Something I had told her of, for so many years. She was greeted with a cheer, as she stood in the hatchway. Everyone knew I was coming home. They knew I was bringing home a human. Mekon, Soy, Jens family, Ira's father. Tudo was standing tall, as a king on the throne.

I ask Ira, as I pointed to Tudo? "Is that your father?"

"Yes, Kayla that's him."

Kayla and I were the last to walk down the ramp. Kayla in the long yellow robe, me in my white paints red shirt. My sword strapped on my side. Kayla took my hand as people cheered, as if we were a king and queen. I walked to my father kneeled to one knee.

"My son, "It has been too long."

"Father this is Kayla, she is to be my mate." Kayla bowed to Tudo, Tudo took Kayla by the hand. "You are very beautiful Kayla."

Kayla answered, "Think you sir."

I told father, She has waited for this moment, for many years.

Tudo said, "I never believed Ira would bring someone as you home. I am very pleased." Kayla bowed again. Tudo said, "Bowing to me is not necessary. I'm just a being, a leader of my people of the planet." "I'm just showing respect sir."

Jen and Foo went to their families. I swear I was treated as a queen. Most of the natives were very friendly. Some just looked at me. In time, I will learn all their names, after all this was Boldlygo. I can live forever. I look at Ira I will be his mate. Someday I will have his child. I'll never tame him, but that's was ok, I have him now. I looked upon what this Maoke started thousands of years ago. On Earth I thought, what would people in my village think. I mean I was here I still think I was in shock. Ira tried to show me all he could. Yet time waits for no one. My first night on this wonderful place was coming, I looked into the evening sky, I got another shock. It was as Ira told me all those years. The moons come up as the suns went down. A tear of happiness fell down my face.

I stayed close to the palace, for the first few days. Standing one morning looking across the Valley of the Unicorn a voice spoke to me. Looking over my shoulder Tudo spoke.

I said to him, "This is the Valley of the Unicorn, beyond is the Marder-to-go's. The falls of the rainbow waters. Further still is the city of the ancients."

Tudo said to me, "Well Kayla I see you have been taught well."

"I've tried to learn everything I could. Most of all I wanted to please you."

"You already have Kayla. I see, you will be very strong with our people. Humans and natives".

Tudo cut me a Simon. It was so juicy, the juice ran down my face, dripped on my cloths. We both laughed out loud.

Ira came in, Well he said. "I see you two, had your Simon.

Tudo told Ira, "Kayla has learned well from you and Jen."

I told my father, Kayla did not want to disappoint you."

"Father ask me of the trial I had with Ren?"

I told him Ren wanted to do the experiment also. There were only two pods.

Tudo said, "I never knew, Ren never said a word of it. I was against it from the beginning. I missed all your child hood."

Father, "You had me several years before."

"I know son, it wasn't enough."

Kayla had excused herself earlier. Coming from the sleeping room I must say, she looked radiant. "Where are you off to?" I ask.

My love Kayla said, "I've been in the palace long enough. I want to see the rest, all of it."

"I must help Mekon today."

"That's ok Ira, Jen will escort me, to where I must go."

I walked out with Kayla, waiting in the courtyard for Jen. Moments later Jen come to the courtyard.

Jen said, "This is the closest I've been to the palace. I've past it before never come this close."

I kissed Ira on the cheek. Jen and I walk down the path, past a beautiful waterfall.

I told Jen, Ira was right.

"Jen ask, about what?"

The stones, "There everywhere."

Jen said, "Yes Kayla they are, there know value to us, only on other worlds. If the outside world knew they were here, they would come destroy our world." I heard Ject say that many times. That's why we stay away from planet with ships.

I said, "look Jen there's a huge one." I picked it from the water. I was right it was as big as my head.

Jen said, "I believe this one Kayla is called a emerald. Come on Kayla I want you to meet my father and mother."

Jen introduced me. "They ask me if I would like tea?"

Jens father sat looking at me, turning to me.

"Tell me, "What is Earth like? The humans that have come here, there has been several, we've never ask? Tomeka, Angie, the others that live in the city. We have always tried to stay away from humans. No disrespect."

I told him none taken, I told them they should always work with the humans. They've played an important part of the survival of your race. If not for humans your race would have been extinct by now.

"That is true, "He said.

I told them there is so much I want to do. I dont nowhere to start.

Jen mothers name, was Edith. "The best place to start is at the beginning."

I smiled, "I can't start there, I wasn't there in the beginning."

Edith said, "Kayla start at the archives, read all you can. You will never read it all, you must also write, place your writing there also. There so much you can learn."

Jen, walked with me to the archives. She talked to me of having a child.

I told her she needed a mate. Yet one is no necessary.

Kayla," I cannot have a child without a mate."

"Then Jen we must find you a mate, I said. Then the mating ritual. You can do this with Ira and me."

Jen said, "It is not permitted, Ira, is Royal, you soon will be. Kayla I'm just a native."

A voice called from behind us.

"Soy ask, may she could join us?"

I said to her "please." We stopped for a cup of tea, went to the falls at the edge of the city."

I told them, in my dreams have I seen such beauty.

Soy said, "You must have Ira, take you to the fall at the Marder-to-go's."

Kayla, you must, "We can take you, Yet it would not be the same."

Jen and I, told Soy of the child Jen wanted to have.

Soy said, "She could have the DNA transfer.

Jen said, "I want a mate before I have a child."

"You will give up your place on the ship. You know it takes a long time to have a child. "Soy said. Soy said," Humans are lucky, your children come fast."

I ask, "How long."

Soy said, "Years, some never do. Some have more than one. There is a native female in the city that has had two. The waiting is what almost cause my race to be extinct."

"If you want to have a child Jen, see Mekon, a mate is good. Yet as Kayla, told you, one is not necessary." Jen told Soy, "Kayla wanted me to take the ritual with her and Ira. Soy looked at Kayla."

"Your joking right Soy said."

I jumped up. "look I dont see the problem, are you afraid."

Soy said. "Royal blood sharing space with a common native."

"Well this made me mad. I sit down, tears filled my eyes."

Soy and jen looked at each other.

"If I ask you, will you come?"

Soy said, "Yes"

I told them I need to go to the palace. I'm going to put a stop to all this.

Soy said, "What you're going to do, is open a Sweet Grass basket."

I said, "I dont know what that is."

The day was ending. I sat at the table I was the only female here. I placed my hand on Iras' hand. "I love you."

"Ira, said the same."

Ira I ask? "Can females speak in here?"

Tudo put his hand up. "Kayla I assure you if you have something to say," "Please speak!"

I stood weary like not knowing what to expect. "Well, why do you not talk or share time with the natives as you call them. Just my short time here I have made so many friends. They tell me the Royal Blood never come to the city." "Why I ask?" They're wonderful being. Some try to stay hid, You told me everyone here was as one."

Tudo ask, "Kayla what is your question?"

"I want to have my friend Jen to share the moment of my mating ritual with me. I will find her a mate. She will be married beside Ira and me. They think the Royal Blood does not want to share space with common natives. Is this true?"

Tudo said, "Ira, she is learning quick. Kayla there is no difference between us and the natives. We make choices every day to keep them safe."

I said, "Well you should let them know."

"Tell me Tudo, "How long has it been since you were in the city." "Ira, you haven't been since you were a small boy. You will go with me to the city tomorrow. You will meet your people, someday you will take your father place. How can you lead your people if you dont know your people?"

I excused myself went to my room. I looked as I turned the Corner. I heard Tudo say, "Well I suppose you will have your day full tomorrow. I smiled, went to my room.

Ira, and I went to the city the next day. He met several families of the city of Ratio. Each family said to him, we never seen the Royal Blood.

Ira said to them," I will try to come more often."

Soy and Jen was there. I heard Soy said to Jen a "Sweet Grass basket."

"Well Jen said," We will see more of them now." Ren walked up with Foo.

Foo's father said, "He only met Ren when he was a small child. Foo has been in service with the Royal Blood for, well for years."

Several days passed. Things had come down as Soy said.

We started to look for Jen a mate. "That's just what we did, Soy and I found Jen a mate. In the afternoon of Mekon lab. There he was a true native, sitting in the back waiting. Mekon had started his training.

Walking toward us, "Good morning Mekon is at the palace."

"I ask his name?"

"Kevin." looking at Jen all the time.

I told him it was him we come to see.

Kevin ask, "For what may I ask?"

I ask, "Are you looking for a mate?"

Kevin said, "Well I am available."

I said, "Thank you then walked away."

Kevin thought as we walked away, Well why haven't I not seen her before.

Soy told us outside what he said.

Jen ask, "How did she know that."

Soy said, "Sometimes I could read peoples thoughts. I've never told anyone." "We told soy, it would be our secret."

Time passed into weeks, Ira got restless.

"Ren and Foo said as much." After tea, I took leave to my room. Sitting brushing my hair Ira came in. Ira I said, I can see your getting restless Ira kissed me. He still makes me feel so wonderful inside. The way he loves me was not human. I loved that, no human could ever bring out the woman in me like Ira could. That's what made me love him so. Tonight, was no different. I fell into his arms when it was over. "I love you Ira."

Ira said, "The same."

Lying in his arms I said to him. "I know you want to go, I have a suggestion."

Ira said you do. "Well my love lets here your suggestion."

"Tomorrow you take me to the fall for the day. I have been here for month I've not seen it yet."

"Then Kayla, we shall go." Ira said.

I laid my head on his chest sleep very well.

I woke up found myself floating above my bed. "Ira, please my love help me."

A voice called. "Do not fear Kayla,"

"Who is there? I ask, "Where am I?" Somewhere high on the top of a mountain of the Marder-to-go's I stood. The wind blowing my long hair, my silk robe was flying in the wind. "Where am I?" A man, know wait a being stood before me. "Who are you?" I ask?"

"I am Maoke." "I am the great Busie of the ancient city. Once leader, and creator of our people of the city of Ratio."

I fell to my knees.

"Please, child stand. You do not need to kneel before me. Kayla, you and Ira are to mate before he leaves for Earth.

I ask, "How do you know this?"

"I see all Kayla."

"May I ask something of you?"

Maoke said, "If you wish."

"Will I ever have a child."

Maoke said to me. "A child you will have, a son."

Maoke, talk to me for what seem several hours.

Kayla, "You must read the archives, you must. Walk the streets of the city, you and Ira. Walk side by side."

I told him we have.

Maoke said, "Talk to the people, most of all read the archives."

"I did start to read," I said. "I got to the place where you found the Staff of Ira. Sir does that mean it is his.'

"The staff was named that lone before me Kayla." Maoke. said. "Tudo, will be a good leader, work with him. Mekon always working, he too will have a child. A female."

I ask, "Maoke have you been to them."

Maoke said "I have not Kayla there is no need. Kayla, you are a smart one."

"I thought when Ject, you met him on Earth. I thought when he come here, he and Mya would keep the portal. They choose to go to the city. So, my precious Tomeka and I, will hold the portal. Someday you and Ira, will take your place here at the portal. Then Tomeka and I will go to the city there we will stay, well until."

I ask, "Sir, I thought the city was for the Royal Blood."

"Kayla, you are Royal Blood. Time to take you back."

Ira woke me up.

"Kayla, Kayla."

I open my eyes to see him. I jumped into his arms, my God Ira.

Ira ask, "What?" "You were dreaming. "No, no I wasn't I was there."

Kayla, "Where were you?"

"Ira I was on top of the Marder- to- go's."

Ira replied, "You were dreaming."

"Ira look at my feet, I said. I remember, the ground was moist."

"Ira pulled my feet to him, there was dirt on both." Ira looked at me with a puzzled look.

Ira said, "There's dirt so where were you."

"I was with Maoke. He came to me in my sleep." Ira Maoke said, "We must have the mating ritual before you go to Earth." Ira looked at me again, this time with a different look. Ira Maoke said, "I would have a son, Mekon a daughter. It would happen in time. He told me to read the archives, work with Tudo and Mekon while you were gone."

One week later Ira, and I did take the mating ritual. Jen, Kevin stood beside us. There were people and beings come from all over the city. It was a beautiful thing.

Jen said, "Kayla I cannot believe what you have done." The natives of this planet never cry, yet the human in her come out. there was tears In their eyes, well they did water.

Ira made his trip to Earth, one of many. Each time he would return, he would tell me of our Earth family. He said they had the biggest farm in Russia. He told me of my father's passing. I was truly sad of that. Yet I gave it know thought. I had been here on Boldlygo for over fifty years. I still look the same. It was truly great to see my husband each time he would return from his quest. Ira left today on a crusade. Before he left Tudo told him it was time for him to stay home.

Ira answered Tudo, "As you wish father when I return."

Ren said, "I will stay a lso, I have had enough."

"Ren, "If that is what you wish. You can continue to fly with Foo if you wish, Tudo said.

Jen had a child over the years, her child had a child. Mekon told her she was almost human. He said, with each generation they will become more human. I wondered what my child would be, native or human.

"I ask, "Mekon one day at the lab."

Mekon said, "Kayla your child will be native." I didn't care I wanted a child, of course there was several children here. I loved this place, I was treated as a queen. In the city, everywhere I went. Sometimes I would hear someone say when I was in the city. "That's Kayla, Iras' queen" I was so happy even more if my husband was here with me. I told Ira this before he left.

Kayla," Ira said, "Mekon did a test. He said I was healthy. I told Mekon, of the dream of long ago. He said several people have those dreams.

I spent all this time in the archives when Ira was away. Sometimes I would spend time with jen.

Sometimes her child would come with me. Most of the time Soy was with me. Soy and I had become very close. Soy would teach me all the thing I needed to know of our people.

One day Jen and I, were walking in the city. I was taking all in, Ira had been gone several years. I tried as hard as I could to learn everything I could. I mean after all I would be here a long time to come. I thought, Maoke did say Ira, and I would come to the portal.

Jen touched my arm. "Kayla where were you."

I was lost in thoughts, I told her.

Looking up, "Jen what does this say."

"I'm not sure she said." We could ask Soy?"

"Jen I want to go to the archives." I read all day, I could find nothing. "I ask Mekon? Then Tudo. Tudo ask, Kayla show me?" I took Tudo to the street where I saw the writing.

Tudo read out loud, "only the Keeper of the staff can move us. A child to come with a female by his side with great power."

Tudo what does it mean?" I ask.

Tudo said too me, "Kayla I'm not sure. Keep this between us for now."

I told him several knew of it.

Ira was still out in space somewhere, It had been several years now. I wonder if he is safe, I truly miss him. Day after day I would watch the sky. Day after Day I would spend in the archives. One day I was reading I froze. There it was, a native would spend time on Earth. The native would take a human wife. The human female would become first queen of all Boldlygo. Why not Tomeka, Angie?" Why not one of them?" I will go to Tudo, I will ask him of this? I will not tell him of what I have read, See what he tells me.

I went to the great room for the evening meal. Tudo do you know of Tomeka, Angie.

Tudo said, "They had left long ago, before me." Mekon, said the same. I read in the archives almost every day. "Maoke speaks of them. He never said they were mates."

Tudo said, "I believe that's right, Angie, lived with Maoke, after Tomeka left.

I said, "It is my belief that Maoke, loved Tomeka very much." "Being a Busie, Maoke could not show his love as humans do."

Tudo said, "He remembers reading that."

"So, neither of them were queen? I ask. Mekon, and Tudo, both looked at me.

"Kayla, in my learning Tudo said. There has been no queen, even before us." Kayla Tudo ask, "Why are you asking this?"

"The writing on the wall Tudo. I found it in the archives."

Tudo, looked at Mekon. "How did you find something that we did not."

"I can't answer that, yet I found it. A native will spend time on Earth. He will take a human wife. They will have a son, that will be great with his people. He will take a human wife with native DNA. They will have a son."

Tudo ask, "This is writing in the archives?"

"It is I tell you. There will be a child born from DNA with white hair, a female to be queen. It reads of Kia, Destiny, Tomeka, Angie. I've read for months, it all there.

"Kayla, now that you know all our secrets of Boldlygo."

They both stood at the same time. I was afraid. "What are you doing?" I ask.

"Kayla, if any one deserved to be a queen, it would be you." They both bowed to me.

I went to my sleeping room. lay across my bed how I long for my husband. I think I sobbed several minutes before I fell asleep.

I woke up this morning, as the suns were coming up. I walked to the west garden to see the Moons of Spores. How beautiful it was. I walked to the open window, overlooking the Valley of the Unicorn. I called out loud to Tudo.

"Kayla what is it."

A ship I said, "Coming to port. It's not Ira."

Tudo ran for the lab, Mekon met him, it was a huge ship. A ship they had never seen before. It was a ship that carried the Boldlygo crown. Tudo and Mekon had never seen this ship, yet they had been told of it in stories, that Ject would talk of. It was the ship of Botas, It was his first ship. The ship landed landed the ramp went down. A figure of a man come down Dressed in black pants, white shirt a red cape blowing as he walked. "Greetings my friend." I stood close to Tudo. I never saw this man before. I was not certain of him.

Tudo said, "Greetings back."

"My ship, give to me by Maoke and your father Ject."

Tudo ask, "How do you know I'm Jects son."

"You are the son of Ject, the son of Maoke." He looked at Mekon. "You are the son of Cra, the son of Lon.

"You would know this how?" Mekon ask.

"Trust me son."

Tudo said, "You are not Cam. Ah you have heard of him."

Tudo said, I have, Cam and my father was mates on the ship."

Yes, I know, "I have been taught this in my learning.

Tudo ask, "Who you are?"

"I am the son of Cam. I have return from Earth. I met your ship with your crew Jects grandson Ira and Foo, Ren."

Tudo said, "I am the father of Ira and Ren."

"Tudo you were a very young child when my father come for repairs.

"Come son of Cam, let go to the chambers, the woman is Kayla, Iras' mate."

"Ah he has done well. He looks good as human."

Mekon said, "I will tell you all about it over tea."

"So, you finally did it. Lon was working on that for years. My father told me all about it. "Where is Ject I ask?"

Tudo told me, "Ject had ascended. My father give me a message to tell Ject."

Tudo ask, "What is it your father called you."

"My name is Ozo. I am very young, yet I was taught and learned from one of the best. My father was human my mother was from the Pegasus system of Valoria."

"You said you had a message, Tudo said.

Trouble is brewing on Plano. The king has died there is a power struggle."

Tudo said, "I was afraid that would happen."

Ozo turned to Kayla. "Your husband lived on Earth for several years.

I looked at Tudo he gives me a nod. I told Ozo, if you go to Earth you can never go off your ship. You take from your mother. Hu man will not accept you."

Ozo said, "I wish I had taken from my father."

"My husband could shift from his native body. He can go anywhere."

Ozo said "Well I gave you the message, I must go."

Mekon ask, "Before you leave could I see Botas, ship."

It was wonderful to see what Bota did all those years ago, It was hard to believe, wish I had been there. Mekon said.

Kayla stood watching Ozo leave. It would be the last time Ozo would be on the planet for several hundered year.

Days went to month to years, where was my husband. Ira has been long time gone.

Jen said, "Her daughter had a son, as mekon said. He was almost human, It was hard to believe, she had another child.

Mekon said, "When this child grows up he can mate with a human.

I ask, "Mekon if the child could shift as Ira does. "

Mekon said, "Kayla I'm not sure."

In the months to come Jen had a daughter, it was hard to believe. Kiven could not believe he fathered an almost human child. Jen named her Ninda, she was a beautiful child. We spent the next few years watching the child grow.

One morning I was standing by window. I watching the bright light. It reminded me of long ago in the field behind my father's barn, just before I come here. As the light fell over the Valley of the Unicorn, a mighty roar. The big ship zoomed by the city, my heart beat so fast. My husband had come home. I past Tudo in a hard run. I ran to the staging area, Soy was already there. The ramp went down Ren was the first off. Ira come down the ramp wearing his long cloake. It had been twelve years. I ran to him, crying kissing him. "How I have missed you my love." We stood there with the rest of the crew. I looked at Ira. He was holding to my hand.

I'm truly sorry Soy, "He was taken by a Palatonian, or that's what they said."

I reached for her. She looked at Ira.

"I did avenge his death. I took the life of three, Ren took two. We were on a small moon beyond their system. I bowed to Soy," He died brave."

Soy said, "Thank you ira," then turned walked away.

I let her grieve for a week, before I went to her.

I kissed Ira on the cheek, early morning.

"Where are you off to this day."

I said, "I'm going to the city." "

"Ira ask, "Want some company."

As we walked the streets some would say, "Good to see you Ira and Kayla."

"Ira stop here tea is best here. The tea was the same at all the houses, so was the bread cakes. I never told anyone. Yet Jen, Soy myself had our favorite place. A few native as humans ask, Ira would be going back to Earth?

Ira replied know. "I'm through with the stars. I will stay home with my wife. We are trying to have a child. Several people ask if they may go? I told them to ask my father? There was a hush upon the group. Ira and I stood to leave.

One ask Ira, "Could you ask for us?"

"I said to them "We'll see."

Ira went with me to the home of Soy. She told me, "Kayla I've had my moment of morning."

I told my friend to joined us for tea. Setting at the table I told Ira Soy would be joining us at the palace. She would become my first hand maiden. She will become nanny to our child, if we ever have one. I kissed Ira bye, Soy and I walked off to the archives.

CHAPTER 26

Several years went by, Ira and I were inseparable. We were all over the city. Ira, took me to the Moon of Spores. I met Garf, and his family. He had done well here, Garf, had built the first prison system in the universe. Tudo, was with us, he was happy to go off world. Another year had gone by. I went to Mekon. Mekon has a child from DNA four year earlier. A female child, just as Maoke told me so many years ago, I felt I had failed Ira as a woman. I failed him as a mate. In bed, tonight, I told him. Ira, I do not deserve to live here in the palace. Ira I have failed you as a woman.

Ira, took me in his arms kissed me as he has done a million time. I swear it felt the same as it did the first time. He kissed me again said he had a suggestion. "I said, I have one to."

Ira said, "Let me here yours."

"You need to find you another woman Ira. Take me back to Earth. I guess Maoke was wrong."

Kayla, "Maoke, don't make mistakes. Tomorrow you will go see mekon, he will give you a DNA transfer."

Mekon told us, there was no reason why we could not have children. On the morning, we went to the lab. Mekons daughter was there, she was four now. I have since the day she was born played with her, always coming to me. Sometimes she has called me mother. Mea was so intelligent, she would go to the park city alone. We would have spent time with Jen and Soy. Mea, was so smart she would do work Mekon could not do. Mea at four had enhanced the DNA transfer. Natives could have DNA now. When Soy, heard this she also wanted a child. She took the very first DNA transfer to be given to a native. It worked, Soy was going to have a child from Foo's DNA. I was still without a child.

Mea come with me to the archives one day. Just to see what I did there. She started reading in two weeks Mea had read the entire archives. It was something I could not believe. Two week later Mekon greeted me at the lab, he took me to a room Mea was with us. From the DNA bank Mekon took Iras' DNA transferred it to me. Them made me lay in place for several hours.

The following moon cycle I missed. I knew then I was pregnant. I wanted one more cycle to make sure. That night I lay in bed with Ira. I told him I loved him, Ira walked to the window. I jumped from the bed, ran to him. "Hold me Ira please.

Ira ask, "Kayla what is wrong with you?"

"Oh Ira, the greatest thing has happened."

"Tell me my love what has happen"

"I'm pregnant Ira, I'm going to have a baby. The look on his face was unreal. Ira stood in front of me with is mouth open. Then muttered a few unsound words.

You, you, you, oh, oh, oh, "You're going to have a baby. I got to tell father, have you told anyone."

I told you.

"I love you Kayla."

In the time, it took for the baby to arrive we had done so much. I got to the point where it was hard to walk. I stayed close to the palace. One night sitting in the great room, I felt a strange feeling.

I said to Ira "I was going to bed. Ira helped me to our room". My water broke as to say. I fell Ira picked me up took me to the lab, with Ira by my side, Soy took the child. Soy washed him as

Mekon turn his full attention to me. Someone called from the front. You could have waited for me. It was Jen. Soy laid Iras' son by my side. You could tell the child was Iras' child. There was no doubt as he made his way to my full breast. His soft baby lips knew what they were for.

As time went on I began to feel strange. I tried to fight whatever it was. I talked to Mekon, Tudo, Jen, Soy, nothing help." I watched my son grow. On his first birthday Ira give him his first ride in a space ship. I stayed with Soy, Tudo, Mekon, Mea lifted off. Higher and higher, when the ship had lifted out of sight I fell to the floor of the staging area. Soy and Jen picking me up.

Soy said, "Child what is wrong with you." I was crying so hard, sobbing.

"Oh Soy, I must leave I must go back to Earth."

Jen ask, "Why would you want to go back to that planet?"

Kayla Soy said "You are loved here." Ira, Tudo, Mea. Mekon, your son Dorn tell me why?"

"I'm not well, something is wrong with me, I must leave."

That night I told Ira. Setting on the bed Ira, just stared at me. Several hours later Ira spoke.

"Kayla, do you not love me. What have I done to lose the greatest treasure there is?"

I just cried harder, "I do love you Ira, I do. There is something inside of me, calling. I must leave Ira please, take me back to Earth."

"As you wish Kayla." Arrangement were made. Ren and I with several others, Jen come with us, I think she just wanted to be with Kayla. Jen had been with Kayla since the beginning. I knew the trip would be fast. Soy stayed with Dorn and Mea.

Mea walked to the front of the lab. Took Kayla by the hand., pulled her down. I'll never forget you, I'll never let him forget you. Everyone was standing on the pad, Kayla kissed Dorn goodbye. Dorn watched his mother go aboard the ship bound for Earth.

It was a warm evening as I took Kayla, from the shuttle. Her hair had turned white, her skin was wrinkled. Kayla, had aged so, she was so weak she could not walk. I picked her up carried her to the woods. She died in my arms, of all the pain I have suffered as a human. There was no pain as bad as it was in the wood that night. I dug the grave for my beloved wife, the queen of all Boldlygo. I did not mark the grave. I walked back to the ship

Ren ask, "If I would go somewhere else?"

I stood, shifted into my native body. I looked at him. "There is one place I need to go"

Ren ask, "Where Ira."

"Home to my son."

The trip home was the longest I've ever taken. Through the galaxies, universes, planets, until my home come into site, there my son waited. Just as he was when I left. He had grown so much, talking as an adult. I went to Dorn picked him up, went to the palace. Dorn and I stayed for weeks. My father would come to the door. "Ira come outside son." You need to come be with family. Mea tried to have him open the door.

Tudo said, "Ira let Soy take the child.'

Ira replied, "know." "Soy I have another job for you. Take everything of Kayla's. Place it in containers."

Soy, said "Everything Ira."

Yes, "Dont leave one thing out."

I did as Ira requested. I picked up a small locket, there was an image of Kayla inside. I handed it to Ira.

Even in my native body I felt the pain. It was a feeling I never wanted to feel again.

Soy worked for several hours. Coming from my room, I took Dorn, for a walk. We walked to the house of bread cakes. I tried to have tea, my father come alone. He tried to talk to me I never here his words.

"Ira I dont know Kayla feeling. From the first time coming here until she left. Losing her was as if losing my own child. I was never so close to a human before. Son Kayla was my child."

"When you were in those pods, I felt pain I've never felt before. I hope I never do again. I never knew if you were coming back to me. Our bodies are not design to have emotions. Maoke said that long ago. Trust me as we sat here in our native bodies. We are going through some thing that is not supposed to happen.

I ask my father, "How can I ever tell Dorn of his mother. Some day he will ask? I hear him speak of her. Mea Ive heard her call Kayla mother. More than once, Kayla loved it. Kayla, wanted a child so. She had one, then father she went absence. It was as if she cared of nothing, no one. I can't believe she went back to that planet."

Father ask, "If I went to the farm?"

I told him no. All I wanted to do, was come home to my son.

"Father I need to go away for a while."

My father said, "I understand, take Ren and his crew. Go to Plano check out the schools."

"You mean see if Ozo was right about the war."

Tudo said, "Well it has been awhile. You could mix business with pleasure. If you know what I mean."

I looked at my son. Sitting eating the bread cake. He looked at me," I love this bread cake father."

Soy, and Mea, never left Dorn. Mea, would sleep in bed with him, she would have it no other way.

Mekon, would tell her to come home.

"Father, Dorn needs me."

Mekon told Mea, "Dorn could sleep at their home."

"Father, he is just a baby."

Soy came to me as I was walking into the palace.

Ira, "I have done as you have asked?" All Kayla's thing, "Her belonging is together in the lab." Soy past a small book to me.

Ira, "She wanted you to have this."

"I do not wish to see it Soy, place it with her other thing. I'll be there soon, wait for me at the lab. I ask my father to join me." My father, Mekon, Mea, soy, Jen. Everyone was in a room in the back of the lab. My beloved thing was placed there. They were keepsakes I thought were long time gone. I took the chain with the coin locket placed it around my neck. Someday Dorn might ask? I sealed the door. "It will be forbidden to speak of this again. Dorn knows nothing of his mother. He will forget that I am his father. He calls me Ira. It is also forbidden to tell him of this. I turned walked away. I never thought of it again."

I stepped on the ship the next day, Dorn was waving bye to me. "I told my father to take care."

Ira, he said. "My time of ascension is near. Son dont be gone long."

Ren took the ship into orbit. Our first stop was the Moon of Spores. I wanted to see Garf. "I explained my lost." I ask him, "Garf come go on a journey with me. Your son Alex can take care of thing here.

"I should go," Garf said.

Alex told his father "Go."

Ren took the ship into space.

Garf ask, "Ira where to."

I said, "The Moon of Corning. We zipped through space at a speed Garf could not believe.

Garf said, "I have not been of the moon since the Palatonians placed me there long ago. It was a long time before your father was born. Your grandfather Ject was a young man, I called to him. I ask him to come to the moon, he did." Comp, Kohl they all come. "Ject help with supplies I built a great city." We talked about things in our pass. The good and the bad. Garf told me of the prisoner he had for ten years. The king of Plano placed him there. Ject, and the Plano king when he was placed there. The look on his face.

I ask Graf, "Whatever happen to him."

"He become the model citizen Ira. He's now the mayor of the Moon, does a great job."

Weeks passed, until we come into the Moon of Corning atmosphere. Ren received clearance to land. Pep, Quad, Kohl was there to greet us as we walk down the ramp.

Quad said, "Greeting, come it is so good to see you." Pep greeted me, I never had the pleasure to meet him. I did know who he was. Pep dated back to Mya. That was long ago I read of him in the archives. I told Quad, what we were doing.

Pep ask, "Ira, if its ok I will come along also."

I told Pep, We will leave soon be ready." When Ren took the ship into orbit, well no one had any idea where to go.

Pep said. "Earth."

Ren looked at me.

I said, "Sure."

Entering the Earths Milky Way, I remembered a small planet I read of in the archives. I give Ren the go ahead. Moments later Ren took an empty pad. I went to my room, took my sword strapped it on. It was the first time in years I have had it on. Later I found I was glad I did. Going into the city, We found, it was a huge city. Ships were coming and going from everywhere. We stopped in an eatery, I ordered tea for us. We sat at the table, talking of thing.

I told Ren, I was surprised of the different species that was here. There were several planets here. Some of then we never heard of. Some were drinking a drink as the lieutenant drink long ago in Russia. Kind of like vodka. I suppose this place, is like the place on earth. You hang around long enough someone will challenge you.

Ren, Garf, Pep, myself were minding our own business. A Palatonian stood.

"You there at the table."

Ren said, "Are you addressing me."

In a drunken voice, he said. "Know I'm not addressing you."

"The other one, the one with the sword. It belongs to me. You soled it, I want it back."

I ignored him. He threw a glass at me. I stood up took the sword from the sheath. A hush come over the crowd.

I ask him, "You said, the sword belong to you?"

He answered, "Yes it does."

"You ever been to Earth?" I ask. The sword was given to me by a close friend of Spain."

"You are a liar."

"Palatonian, you have called me a thief, a lair. If the sword is yours, come get it." Ren, Garf, Pep backed up.

"I said to Ren, in our language, "Ready the ship." Pep stayed with me.

One person asks, "What are you doing."

I took the sword held it up, "Come and get it." He drew his sword made a thrust. I went down his blade in a spiral. Took the blade slammed it into the ceiling. Everyone stood as they did in Spain long ago inside Reyes, tavern, everyone stood in ah. Pep walked out, I told them not to follow me if you do your mine. Now as always, there's someone that is no one, they will come out, in fact there's was three of them.

This still was no match for me. Comp taught me long ago never run, I didn't. The three come on, a slash a thrust a parry it was over. I sheath the sword went aboard the ship as Ren took us higher into space.

Ren, knew when we reached Earth he could not go to the ground because of his native look. He told me again he wishes he had taken the experiment. I told my brother, I to wish he had. Pep will keep you company while we're gone."

Ren took us to the surface in the shuttle. I told him as I left the ship, I would signal him, when I need you to come back,"

Ren "agreed."

Passing the moon Ren ask, "Where do I set you down."

I told Ren, Take us to Russia. I shifted to my human side. Ren dropped us to the north of the farm. I knew in my heart everyone I knew would be gone. I was surprised when we topped the ridge. The farm had been sized by the Russian government. I told Garf, see what I mean. They took it away from the family.

Garf and I made our way to the road. I told Garf, wait here until I come back. I went to the house Russian troops were everywhere. It reminded me of the times when Arman would come by. I realized this was different. I knocked on the door, a young girl come to the door. Opening the door door, I looked into the bluest eyes. I knew she was family, her eyes were more blue than Kayla's. She spoke to me in Russian. It had been many years since I had spoken the language. I said to her, "My Russian was rusty." I think that's what I said.

She asks, "May I help you"

I said, "Long ago I passed here it was a farm. What has happened."

The young girl walked on to the porch. Closing the door behind her. "Sir the Russian government has seized the land from everyone. All people."

I ask, "Of the orchard to the back?"

She said, "They took it to."

"The family that lived here, what has happened to them."

"Sir, I am not to say."

"Well I want to know."

"Sir please!"

I ask, "Are you part of the family that lived here."

"I am sir." She said.

I ask her, "Then you are a descendant of Lola."

"She looked at me fast. Is the coin still in the fire place?"

She spoke to me in English.

"Who are you. I am Ira, son of Lola."

367

Tears filled her eyes. "Why have you waited so long to come back. I know who you are. My family, all are dead, in prison scattered."

I walked past her into the house. I ask, In Russian "Who is in charge here."

A man stood smiling the man said, "I am in charge, general Pronoski of the Russian army.

"This land you have seized, I made a gesture with my hand. It belongs to my family. The Russian government took it. You must give it back, take your men leave here now."

He laughed out loud. I cut him across the face with my sword, he went for a weapon in his waist band. I cut him on the hand slapped him on the face. I thrust my blade into two more men. "This will happen again if you do not leave. You have until tomorrow to move all your men from this farm." I ask the girl, "What is your name."

The girl replied, "My name is Linda"

"I ask her, "Come with me? Where is your mother, I asks." Come with me I'll show you."

In the back of the farm in a grave yard of twenty five grave stones.

"There" she said."

I saw the graves of Lola, Comp, Georgia. I stood in silence for a moment. There was an alarm going off. Linda and I ran into the woods. Garf came to me.

Ira, he said, "What have you done. We have no weapons to fight these people."

"I said to him, "We want need them." I told Garf to stay with Linda, stay in the woods. I ask Linda, Do you have family in town."

"Replying, "There is a few, I know them."

I told Garf, to take her to the town, stay off the road.

Linda ask, "What are you going to do."

"I'm going to make them leave. Linda, this land belongs to the family."

Linda said, "They're all dead, or in a lab. Somehow they knew we were different."

I told her I'd take care of it. I ask, "You know where they are held?

Linda said, "Outside Saint Petersburg."

I told her, I know the place. I left Garf with Linda watched them go into the woods. I shifted to my native body. I let them see me.

"What is that thing." one said, "shoot it."

I had them all running after me. Three on my right, I took them out. Two of to the left got rid of them. That leaves twenty that I took out also. I wasn't even breathing hard, I stacked them in a pile outside the door.

Daylight come the general was screaming, screaming at the top of his voice.

"Who are you."

Still in my native body I come from the side of the house real fast. Before he had the chance to move I placed my sword to his throat. Leave here general, think about it, I did all this with a sword.

"What are you," he said."

"I'm not of this world," I said. There are others like me, all I need to do is call them. We will take over this world. Now you leave here, never to return. Go tell them to let my family go. If they do not do as I say, will call the others, do you understand."

The general did leave, took all his men. I was standing on the porch. "General you have three suns, counting this one, to have my family here, back on the farm."

"The Russian government will not go for this. "He said.

"General if they don't, I'll come for you." On the second day coming into Saint Petersburg. Garf told me later, it had been a long trip, we were tired, hungry. Making their way to one of the family that didn't agree with the government. Knocking on the door Linda waited. Moments later a man appeared. Linda come in bring your friend. Sitting around the table the man told Linda it is not safe to come here. Graf watched out the window. A woman come into the room Linda stood, aunt Betty. The two took hands.

Linda said. "He's here aunt Betty."

Betty ask, "Who is here Linda."

Ira, "This is Graf from the Moon of Spores. She looked at me."

I told her it was true, I am Garf. What has happened here. Ira said, "this was a beautiful place."

The man spoke, "Betty, who are these people, what is the Moon of Spores. I've never heard of this." Betty put her hands up, "I've never told him."

I stood, "Sir we are not of this world, we are from space. It's hard for you to believe, yet it's true.

Oly, Betty said, "These are my people, all are from another world Oly.

Garf said, "Oh yes I remember. Destiny from the Moon of Corning."

Linda said, "That's right."

Betty went to the chest took an old coin. Bringing it to us Betty showed it to me. I told them that is a token of Boldlygo. Lola, Georgia, Nancy.

Betty said, "In Lola's writing she wrote, she went there. Stayed several years. Betty ask, "Linda you say Ira is here,

Aunt Betty, "He is making the army leave we will have our home back."

Oly said. "If you do the army will make it hard on the rest."

I told them not to worry. Ira will take care of that.

Oly said, "He's only one man."

Yes Oly, "He is very smart."

Oly looked at me. "You human Graf."

I replied, "Yes, in fact there's one hundered and fourteen planets with humans on them. Take the planet of Plano, it's all human, like most planets they let outsider come in."

This Ira Oly said, "He cannot fight the Russian government, they will kill him. They will come here and kill us. You will see Betty", Oly said.

I said to Oly, "Dont underestimate Ira sir. On his world, he is a warrior. He spent many years on Earth he was in human form."

Oly said, "In human form."

Oly, "Ira can shift from native body to human."

"Get out of my house," Oly said, "How stupid do you think I am?"

Oly looked at his wife. "I can't believe you. Defining the Russian government. Leave never come back."

Betty took a scarf, placed around her head. "Come with me, I know a place we can go." Betty looked at her husband, it would be for the last time, she would never come back. Betty took us to a house outside of town. A family she knew well. Arman and Mary's granddaughter. Betty knocked on the door. The blue in the eyes give them away. Betty told her who I was.

She looked at me, "My whole life I have waited for you to come," she said. "Times here are not the same as they were then. I'm truly sorry, we once were free, then the government took over. There are some that would fight."

I listen to them talk. I walk to the window, turning I said to them, "You could fight." I told them I was not sure how long it would take.

Betty said, "Something to a man at the edge of the yard. "The man said, "We wait on Ira."

CHAPTER 27

Sitting in the kitchen, that Lola loved so, waiting on the third sun, as I told the general I would. I strapped on my blade, had a cup of tea, stepped out the door. I sent the signal to the ship, Ren sat the ship down behind the orchard. I told Ren "go to the ship. When I give you the signal, bring the ship into the Earth's atmosphere. Bring the ship to the city, stay about four thousand feet above the city. Then come here" Ren said, "Your enjoying this aren't you."

I said to him, "Oh yeah."

Ren I said, "Tell your crew come of the ship." When ask.

"As you wish Ira."

Ren placed me back on the ground. I was walking toward the house, One hour later I heard the wagons and horses. I ran to the edge of the orchard. The apples were good this time of year. Just before daylight the signal was sent. Ren took the ship to the city. I could see the ship, thirty miles away. The ship was huge, circling around the city several times. Watching the ship suddenly, the ship dropped to the roof top. Oly, in his mind it was true, the suspense was so intense, Oly hung himself.

Garf saw the ship "He yelled come we go to the farm." Over three thousand people in wagons, horses, walking, running. Everyone headed out of Saint Petersburg. It was as if something was after them. Russian soldiers were trying to control the people. The soldiers were killing, cutting everyone they came to. On the edge of Saint Petersburg, Garf said to Linda. "You see some died to make it so others could live."

Linda ask, "Do you think they will follow?"

Yes, Linda the general will be at the farm."

Linda ask, "How do you know this."

I said to her, "Because Linda, he is not here. Dont worry of him Ira will take care of him." I told the people to pass the word back. We will not stop until we reach the farm." Several hours into my journey I realized we needed to stop. Reaching the spring Ira, told me of. We stop for a while, I let them rest for an hour. I sent word to the rear. "We are moving."

I was waiting when the general come into the yard. Ren had come over the house. The men were running from the barn through the yard. Some were screaming, some were shouting God help me. Ren circled the farm. Then went backward to the clearing then stop. Sitting five hundred feet above the farm.

The general said, in a strong Russian accent," What are they waiting for?"

"General I said, "They are waiting for me. Where is the family of the farm? I give you three suns. You come back with your army. You want more dead soldiers."

The general said, "You cannot defy the government."

General if you want an army I'll give you an army. The afternoon was coming to an end. Soon a rider come in spoke in Russian. I listen to every word, He told the general over three thousand people had left Saint Petersburg.

I said to the general, "You want a war, I'll give you a war you want forget." I sent the signal to Ren, he took the ship up. The general left with his men. Late afternoon the people come into view.

I said to most that could hear me. "I gave him three days to bring the family here that lived here. I told him three suns or I will destroy them."

The evening of the third day sun, the general showed up with some of the family of Lola. They all come to me.

"Ira, we know who you are, we have been told of you our whole life." We thank you.

I told them it's not over yet. The general an I rode for over a week. Even shared talk at times. I found the week I was with him, marking boundaries. I found I did not like him. I should have taken his head. We marked streams rivers trails, until we come to the Ukraine border. Then we returned to the farm. The day we returned to the farm the general said.

"We will leave guards, if they cross I will leave orders to kill."

"General remember this, we have the farm, orchards the cows. We dont need anything from you. I told everyone, go bring your belonging. The general has given three days. I told Betty and Linda to build them a city twenty miles to the south. You have everything you will need to do this. I showed them on parchment. This is your country, rule it well."

One ask, "What will we called this country?"

The only thing I could think of was Georgia. I said, "name it Georgia. I will stay until all is back. Then we must leave," I said to them, "At first it will be hard, you will manage." I told them to find the family.

We stayed for several days. There were several hundered Russian soldiers at the marker. There were people everywhere. They were not family, they just wanted to be free. Ren would come close some time just to scare them. The Russian army was building a fence to mark the border. It had signs that read "Cross you die." I saw the general, jumping the fence the general call kill him, kill him.

General I said, "You need to make a treaty with the new country."

The general said to me. "When you leave, we will take it all back."

"General if you cross that fence you will be killed. I will leave word, this i promise you, Sign a treaty with them."

"The government don't want a treaty," he said."

"Then leave the people of Georgia alone. If I'm called back, I will kill you. I will kill any one that stands in my way." I said as I left the general. "If anyone wants to leave come now." Three hundred people ran for the fence. Ren took the ship into orbit. I stayed for a week.

Garf said, "Ira, I've never had so much fun, It has been a wild trip."

I said to Garf, "Tomorrow we would go to the boundary to check them.

Betty told me all the family members said how good it was to meet us." Some wanted to go to our world. Walking to the barn I was talking to Garf. A very beautiful little girl come to me. The girl pulled my arm. I bent over, "What is your name little one."

"She answered, in Russian. "My name is Amy."

"Where is your mother and father", I ask,

"I don't know", she said.

I called for Linda. "I have a job for you. This girl is family." Linda ask, "How do you know."

I said, "Look at the locket. the locket carried an image of Lola and comp."

Linda said, "Ira if I can't find her mother and father I'll take care of her." I gathered everyone around. I told them, someday we will be back. Take care of each other. Most of all take care of you home your country, take care of Georgia. I told the two boys to take care of Amy and Linda. Protect them always. Be there protector as Comp was to me. I took Otis by the hand, I told him and his brother Millard, some day we will come again.

Garf and I went aboard the ship. Ren went into orbit, I told Ren to take me to Spain. I stayed in my room that night. I knew I would never be back Russia. Maybe someday someone would, I went to the bridge. Garf was telling Ren of the fun he has had.

Garf said, I have never seen anything like it. I had tea went to my room I slept. lying in bed I could see everyone wanted to go home. We had been gone for several years. When I wake, I'll tell Ren to go home?

CHAPTER 28

Coming into the atmosphere of our world, Ren sent the ship down. Walking down the ramp my father was the first I met.

I ask, "Father where is Dorn?"

Tudo said, "Ira I sent him to Plano, to study. Plano has one of the best school in all the galaxies. Dorn was here not long ago. He asks of you?"

"Did he ask of, "Ira or father?"

He asks of "Ira."

Father, "How did he leave?"

"He left in a shuttle, he has become a very good pilot. He soon will be back; how long will you be this time Ira?

Father I said. "It keeps my mind off Kayla."

"Ira, Kayla has been gone twenty years." Mekons daughter is a full grown female. She has raised Dorn, she has always been there for him."

I said, "I must think her." I walked to the palace, standing looking across the Valley of the Unicorn to the Marder-to-go's. I felt a feeling I haven't felt in a long while. "Grandfather I'm home, I want to stay I just dont know."

That night in a very peaceful sleep, a voice called to me. Ira come to me, rise Ira come with me. On the very mountain top where Kayla stood, a voice kept calling to me. I saw a shadow of a being, "Who are you." The shadow appeared as my grandfather." Opa," I fell to my knees.

Ira, he said, "Rise son." "Ira this I must tell you. "Kayla will see you in the city of the ancient."

Opa I said, "I wish I could see her know. Opa I thought the city was for Royal Blood the Busies, some natives." "Yes, Ira it is, yet Kayla was Royal Blood. Then she will be there for me. Ira, you and Kayla will take Maoke and Tomeka's place at the portal."

I ask, "Opa why not you?"

My grandson, "I have gone to the city with Mya."

"Then Kayla, and I will be together."

Yes son, "There is much to do, tell your father you must return to Earth. Take your own son, tell Mekon to place him in the Stacie. The experiment he will need in years to come. You will see I am right. When he has finished school on Plano, he will travel for a while. Dorn will return home, take him to Earth. Let him do this one of the family of Earth has fled to Spain, go find her. She will know who you are. You met her on Earth several years ago, She is in the town of your Kayla's home. Ira what she will do for our people, she will be great. Ira does Dorn know he is your son."

I said, "Opa I dont think so, someday he will know."

Well, "We'll think of that later, as you wish Opa."

I woke up all sweaty, heart pounding. I walked to the window for fresh air. What was happing to me, did I had a dream. I didn't think so. My feet were wet, leaves still cling to them. Kayla had a dream as this once, my thought went to her. I still can't understand why, she went back to that place.

The morning sun was high as I walked to the stoop. Cutting my morning Simon, my father come to me.

"Morning Ira."

I greeted him the same. I told my father about the dream.

"Ira, Mekon must go along. Did my father tell you, not to tell Dorn you were his father?"

Yes father. "That was the message." I give my all and all for the next several months. Late in the evening a ship appeared from the west. It was a shuttle low over the city. Then all at once, the shuttle went straight up."

"My father said, "You son is home."

Tudo and I met him at the hanger. Coming from the shuttle Dorn, ran to Mea, first. I thought to myself how much he was as I when I was a young man. Dorn called to Mea.

Mea, "I have so much to tell you."

Dorn turned to me, "Opa, Ira, good to see you back.

"I'm content Dorn."

"Mea, where is Mekon, I have much to tell him."

"Dorn, Mekon would join us later," Mea said. "You know how he is when he is working on something."

I did not expect a warm welcome from Dorn, why should I. Mea told me he has no memories of his child hood.

Mea said, "Dorn, also thinks he was created in the lab."

Mea and I talked for a while. I told Mea of the dream, I told her what I must do.

Mea just looked at me. Mea do you think he will go alone with it.

We must ask Mea, said. I would do it myself, If my father would give his permission. Ira let me talk to him first.

"We need to leave soon."

Mea said, "She would come to me in two days."

Mea told her father.

I said "Yes." I was waiting for Me a to give me his answer. We will be ready to go when Mea come to the ship.

On the morning, I went to the ship I told Ira.

"Dorn has given his answer Ira. He agrees to do this."

I was talking to Mea when Dorn come in.

Ira," Why didn't you ask me?"

"I was going to Dorn, Mea suggested she would talk to you."

Tell me Ira, "What is it about me you do not like."

I was shocked. "Dorn I assure you everything about you I care for deeply. Dont ever say that again. you are very smart, very intelligent. Son, dont ever think I dont care."

"Then tell me Ira, why was you not there for me growing up." Dorn turned walked away. I wondered does he know I'm his father. Then I decided there's no way. Unless!

I tried to talk to him several times. He just didn't want to have anything to do with me. In the galley, I was having tea, Mekon came in. Sitting at my table, I said "I should have stayed for him."

Mekon said, "Ira you did what you had to do. Ira, Kayla was a beautiful woman, she died on Earth. Dorn lived on boldly go. You were torn between two worlds."

"Mekon, "If I had not gone back, the family would fail to exist today."

The ship went through space at a healthy pace. I said to Mekon, "When we get close to Earth let me know I'll bring out the pod myself. We past the Moon of Corning. I ask, "Are we not going to stop?" Mekon said, "Not this time."

"Mekon, I must find this girl Opa told me of." He said, "I would know her when I saw her. Yet I have no clue." Sitting at a table having tea, I looked up as Dorn enter the galley.

Ira, he said. "Tell me of this experiment, I must do."

Mekon said, "Dorn you dont have to do this."

Dorn replied, "Oh yes, yes I do if it pleases Ira."

I ask, "Dorn why all the anger for me. I was a pilot, I had a crew. I went to help our people."

"For twenty five years Ira." I remember you when I was a child. You cut Simons for me, told me stories bathe me. Then one day you were gone, I thought you were my father. Growing up in a lab, I realized I was created in a lab. Mea my mother, Mekon my father."

"I'm sorry you feel this way of me." Dorn.

Tell me Ira, "Ren and you are Tudo sons. How is it he is my Opa. I dont even know my mother. I will be honored to do this experiment. Maybe I want be as lucky as you. Maybe I want wake up."

I slapped the table, let out a roar from my throat. It sounded as a ship taking off. Even Mekon jump when I slapped the table. I've heard enough, tell Ren to turn us around were going home. Dorn jump up from the table.

"I'm sorry Ira, I apologize. I said, "Ira let's just do this. Tell me what I need to do."

I told him, When we reach Earth I must find the woman Opa was telling me about. He said, she will know me, she will do the DNA transfer. The woman is part of our Earth family. Opa said, she left Russia, she now lives in Spain.

Thought of my beloved Kayla, come crashing through. Mekon could tell I was troubled.

"The girl will take your DNA," Mekon said, "When time comes, we will come for you. You will see the light, there we will be also. Dorn, you want remember at first, when your born."

Dorn looked at Ira, as he walked off. "Mekon what is wrong with him."

"Memories of the town, that we must go to. It was a long time ago Dorn. Ira was in love with a human."

"A human Mekon"

Mekon said yes, "Dorn a human, she lived on Boldlygo for over three hundred years. One day she went wayward went back to Earth. Ira buried her there. You will see Dorn, as you grow older, you will become wiser.

I said, "Mekon I've never heard that story. It's not in the archives.

I said, "Dorn some things are not what they seem. This planet you're going to, the people are so far behind, there is a few that are very intelligent. The off spring of Mya, over one thousand years ago, Very intelligent. We have been coming here for many years. Bota, was the first of our people. Ira has fought combat there; more mental than physical he was the best I've ever seen with a sword. To my knowledge, he still is.

"I would take him on." I said.

Mekon, looked at me. "You would lose son, I've seen him take the sword from over a hundered people."

I ask Mekon, "Did he take their lives also?"

"Dorn as far as I no. Ira has only took fifteen lives. There was no other way."

Dorn ask," Mekon what do you think I'll look as when this is over?"

"You will look as you are now Dorn, in your native body. It will be up to you to determine what you look when you change."

"I dont understand," I said.

"Ira never wanted to look as anything except what he was. Myself I have changed into several different being. All you need to do is touch someone you can shift to anything."

Dorn ask, "How long will I be down."

"Ira and I it was seventeen years. You will have all the memories of what your life will be as you grow up on Earth. When we come replace the essence to your native body. You will still have that, so everything you learn on earth you will keep."

Moving through space, the ship took a right turn at Saturn. Two more months we would be at Earth. I looked out the portal. It was a sight I'll never forget. I looked upon this blue ball in space, I feel it would not be my last time I'd see this. Next time maybe we will go slower. Hard to look at thing in hyper space. It was all there, just as I study in my teaching of the universe.

Entering the bridge to talk to Ren, when the ship come from hyper space.

Ira said. "Dorn I will take Mekon go to the surface, see if we can find this girl."

"I'll come to Ira"

I said to Dorn, "The humans will not accept you. In fact, they will try to kill you. Dorn, as time goes on you will see what I mean.

"Ira, I've been before humans."

I said to him, "Dorn not like these humans. They would burn you at the steak or Hang you. it's because they dont understand. The humans on Earth kill or destroy what they dont understand.

I said, "As you wish Ira."

Mekon said to me. "Dorn he's not lying there really that way, some are intelligent.

"This is what your placing me in. You can shuttle us to the surface. Then come back pick us up. When we find the girl, we will bring her here. "

"As you wish Mekon."

Mekon, and I walked of the shuttle in the dense forest. Moss all over everything, my thoughts went to another time. Kayla and I were here before. I swear I felt her presence, as if she was here beside me. It took two days to find the woman that would know me. I swear I had no idea who she was. Mekon search one side of the street I the other. We dared not ask, to many questions? The year on Earth was fourteen sixty. It was a trying time on Earth, when people thought of witches. I did hear of this, yet I never saw one. It was as if you did something unnatural well you were a witch. That's the way it was.

At a small fruit market, I went in off the street. I had a feeling I was been followed. I was right, two men come in behind me. I could tell they were not from Spain. One of the men, spoke to the girl. it was clear they were from Russia. I understood every word they said, they were talking of thing that happen this day. I knew them it had been a long time. It had to be Otis and Millard. When they left, I came from behind the pole, The girl looked at me, placing her hands to her face. Tears filled her eyes.

"Ira, she whispered."

I said, "Yes, yes I am, You remember me."

She said, "I was a little girl I remember you."

"Why did you leave Russia, I ask."

"Ira, the army came back took everything we had, killed so many. That was ten years ago, I took what I could. The two men come here, I dont know why Ira they think I'm a queen." They said, "They must protect me until you come back."

"I ask them to take care of you Amy."

I ask Amy, "Where is Linda."

"The Russian army, killed her in the city one day. I have missed her so much. When they came, they came at night? We never had a chance."

I looked at Amy, "Do you know why we're here."

"Ira I know why you're here," Amy said. I've had this dream of you for years. I am to have a child raise him, he will be great with our people. I just dont know how we are to do this. Everyone is watching everyone."

I told her we must go to the ship.

We talked for over an hour. I ask, "Amy did the Russian take everything." Amy said, "They burnt the house the barn, they cut the orchards. The general had them to stacked the trees, set them afire."

I ask, "Is the general was still alive, he was when she left.

Ira, "We went to Ukraine, then here. I dont think the general would be alive now."

I told Amy, to walk with me, up and down the street. Let's let everyone see us tomorrow I will rent a buggy well take a ride.

"They already know Ira."

"Why do you say that." Amy said look, coming through the door was the boys, followed by Mekon.

Amy said, "The boys protected me, trying to get her out of Russia. They killed twenty five people.

"They knew I was here once Amy. They knew this is where I met Kayla."

Amy told them they must bring her to Spain.

Walking through the small village, I could not believe how it had grown. Yet the stores were still here. Reyes place was still here I had to go in. Stepping in it had not changed at all. I looked up the swords were still in the ceiling. I ask, "Bar keep said, sir stories go Ira was the best man anyone ever seen with a sword. All Ira wanted to do, was to be with Reyes daughter, Kayla. In others stories they left together one night, they were never seen again. My family bought it from Reyes. Handed down through the years."

I told him, I was here to call on Amy.""

The man said, "She is a beautiful woman. Those two men really protect her."

I went back to Amy, I told her I will come early, Mekon, and I went back to the ship.

The afternoon came quick. Ren set us down on the back side of the village. Mekon and I walk to the livery. I rented a buggy told Mekon I would meet him by the sea. I picked up Amy coached her on what to do. Walking to the street, she laughed so did I. We laughed all the way out of town. For over an hour we rode down the road. Then took a trail to the sea. One of the boy were there, The other one at the shop. Ren picked us up, took us to the ship. The DNA took place. Mekon had placed Dorn in Stacie's, he was as dead, as I was long ago.

Amy stood by the portal looking out.

Turning to me she said, "Ira I can see why you love this. It is strange I suppose, some would be afraid. I'm not afraid, I wish I could go with you."

Amy walked to me. "Hold me Ira."

I placed my arms around her.

"Amy said, "Ira you are so warm,"

I could feel his strength flow through me, as he stood holding me. I could really feel it. I looked at him told him what I felt.

Going back to Earth, Amy kissed me on the face.

"I am honored to do this. He will grow to manhood in my presence. Before he leaves me, I will tell him of his family of the stars."

I said to Ira, "I'll never see you again, just remember I do this for our people."

On the beach, I left her with Otis. I gave her a bag of stones. I told Otis, See she is taken care of.

Otis said to me in Russian, "I always have."

"Ira, you do good here with Amy, Otis take care of my son. We will come for him when the time is right"

THE END

This ends the story of the beginning The Staff of Ira. There will be others. Let's see what happens.